CLOVER MOON

HAVE YOU READ THEM ALL?

WHERE TO START
THE DINOSAUR'S
PACKED LUNCH
THE MONSTER
STORY-TELLER

FOR YOUNGER READERS
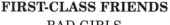
BURIED ALIVE!
THE CAT MUMMY
CLIFFHANGER
GLUBBSLYME
LIZZIE ZIPMOUTH
THE MUM-MINDER
SLEEPOVERS
THE WORRY WEBSITE

FIRST-CLASS FRIENDS
BAD GIRLS
BEST FRIENDS
RENT A BRIDESMAID
SECRETS
VICKY ANGEL

STORIES ABOUT SISTERS
THE BUTTERFLY CLUB
THE DIAMOND GIRLS
DOUBLE ACT
THE WORST THING
ABOUT MY SISTER

FAMILY DRAMAS
THE BED AND
BREAKFAST STAR
CANDYFLOSS
CLEAN BREAK
COOKIE
THE ILLUSTRATED MUM
LILY ALONE
LITTLE DARLINGS
LOLA ROSE
THE LONGEST WHALE SONG
MIDNIGHT
THE SUITCASE KID

ALL ABOUT JACQUELINE WILSON
JACKY DAYDREAM
MY SECRET DIARY

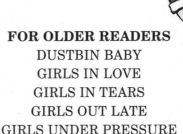

HISTORICAL ADVENTURES
CLOVER MOON
THE LOTTIE PROJECT
OPAL PLUMSTEAD
QUEENIE

HETTY FEATHER SERIES
HETTY FEATHER
SAPPHIRE BATTERSEA
EMERALD STAR
DIAMOND
LITTLE STARS

TRACY BEAKER SERIES
THE STORY OF
TRACY BEAKER
THE DARE GAME
STARRING TRACY BEAKER

CLASSIC RETELLINGS
FOUR CHILDREN AND IT
KATY

FOR OLDER READERS
DUSTBIN BABY
GIRLS IN LOVE
GIRLS IN TEARS
GIRLS OUT LATE
GIRLS UNDER PRESSURE
KISS
LOVE LESSONS
MY SISTER JODIE

STORY COLLECTIONS
PAWS AND WHISKERS
THE JACQUELINE WILSON
CHRISTMAS CRACKER
THE JACQUELINE
WILSON TREASURY
JACQUELINE WILSON'S
HAPPY HOLIDAYS

LOOK OUT
FOR FABULOUS
**JACQUELINE
WILSON**
STATIONERY!

✩ ABOUT THE AUTHOR ✩

Jacqueline Wilson is one of Britain's bestselling and most-loved children's authors, and the creator of such memorable characters as Tracy Beaker and Hetty Feather. She has written more than 100 books, which have sold almost 40 million copies in the UK alone. Jacqueline has been honoured with numerous awards, including the Guardian Children's Fiction Award and the Children's Book of the Year. She is a former Children's Laureate, a professor of children's literature and the Chancellor of Roehampton University. In 2008 she was appointed a Dame in recognition of her services to children's literature.

Visit her fabulous website for more information and fun at www.jacquelinewilson.co.uk

Jacqueline Wilson

Illustrated by Nick Sharratt

CLOVER MOON

MOON

DOUBLEDAY

DOUBLEDAY

UK | USA | Canada | Ireland | Australia
India | New Zealand | South Africa

Doubleday is part of the Penguin Random House group of companies
whose addresses can be found at global.penguinrandomhouse.com.

www.penguin.co.uk
www.puffin.co.uk
www.ladybird.co.uk

First published 2016

001

Text copyright © Jacqueline Wilson, 2016
Illustrations copyright © Nick Sharratt, 2016

The moral right of the author and illustrator has been asserted

Set in 12/17pt New Century Schoolbook by Falcon Oast Graphic Art Ltd
Printed and bound in Great Britain by Clays Ltd, St Ives plc

A CIP catalogue record for this book is available from the British Library

Hardback ISBN: 978–0–857–53273–2
Trade Paperback ISBN: 978–0–857–53274–9

All correspondence to:
Doubleday
Penguin Random House Children's
80 Strand, London WC2R 0RL

For Alex Antscherl
Thank you so much for the last twenty years!

1

'**W**HO'S COMING TO PLAY** then?' I yelled, running out of our house.

'Me!' said Megs, jumping up from the front step, where she'd been waiting for me patiently.

'Me!' shouted Jenny, Richie, Pete and Mary. Bert can't talk properly yet but he crowed.

'Me!' shouted Daft Mo from two doors down. He's a great gawky lad now, but he isn't right in the head and can't start work at the factory, so I let him play with us.

'Me!' shouted Jimmy Wheels, bowling up on his wooden trolley, the cobbles making it rattle violently.

Jimmy's my special friend. Some of the alley folk think he's as daft as Mo because he talks funny, but he's sharp as a tack.

'Now don't you encourage them kids, Clover Moon,' said Old Ma Robinson, leaning against the crumbling brick wall of her house and lighting her pipe. She puffs herself silly, Old Ma. Her face is turning as yellow as a smoked haddock. 'They're wild enough left to their own devices, but with you stirring them up they get up to all sorts.'

'Quit nagging her,' said Peg-leg Jack, stumping his way down the alley for his lunch-time pint of ale, his scrappy terrier trotting beside him. 'Clover's like a little mother to all the kids.'

'Better than a mother,' Megs muttered indistinctly, sucking her thumb.

Our own mother died when Megs was born. She can't remember her, naturally. I'm sure *I* can. Her name was Margaret. Megs is called after her. I wish I was, but my name is special too because Mother chose it.

She must have been thinking of a lucky four-leaved clover. I'm sure Mother wanted me to be lucky. And though I started off with blue eyes like all babies, they're now clover-green. Mother was sweet and soft and beautiful, with manners like a true lady, and she sat me on her lap every day and played with me. She still does so, in my dreams. Fat chance of Mildred ever doing that. She's Pa's second wife. She doesn't even cuddle her own children, never mind Megs and me. She shouts and she slaps and we try our best to keep out of her way.

Jenny and Richie and Pete and Mary and Bert are Mildred's children, our half-brothers and -sisters. Bert is the baby. I carry him even when I'm doing my chores. He howls whenever I set him down. He's fourteen months old so he should be toddling around, but his legs buckle whenever I put his funny fat feet on the floor. Pa's worried that there's something wrong with his legs and he'll end up like Jimmy Wheels, but I think Bert's just lazy.

Jimmy Wheels gets around all right on his trolley, even though he can't walk. Megs used to be frightened of him, especially when he came up close. She squealed like he was a mad dog about to bite her ankles. I had to give her a talking to – Jimmy Wheels is sensitive and I didn't want his feelings hurt. His dad makes it plain he's ashamed of having a crippled son, but Jimmy's got a lovely ma. He's lucky he doesn't have a stepmother like Mildred. Sometimes I think I'd sooner have spider's legs like Jimmy's so long as I didn't have Mildred.

She'd been nagging at me since six in the morning, when we'd lit the copper for the big wash. I hate

Mondays – all that soaking and scrubbing and boiling and rinsing and wringing until my hands are crimson and my arms ache and my dress is soaked right through and even little Bert tied on my back looks as if I've dropped him in a puddle.

But now the sheets and underwear and aprons were flapping on the line across the cobbles, and there were a dozen other lines all down the alley. Only half the folk bother to do a weekly wash. I don't think Old Ma Robinson ever washes her bedding, her clothes or herself. You can smell her coming before you see her.

'What do you want to play then?' I asked.

'Families!' cried little Mary, rolling up her pinafore to make a cloth baby.

'Murderers!' shouted Richie and Pete, pulling manic faces and curving their hands as if about to strangle someone.

'Grand ladies! And I'll be the grandest lady of them all,' said Jenny.

'Races!' said Daft Mo, who had the longest legs.

'Yes, races!' Jimmy Wheels pleaded, because he was the fastest of all, thumping his hands down on the cobbles and rattling along like a cannon ball. He could speed freely under the sheets, and didn't mind being dripped on either, but the rest of us would be slapped in the face by wet cotton as soon as we took a few strides. But the white sheets had given me an idea.

'We'll play sailing ships,' I said, seizing the bottom of a sheet and making it billow in the wind.

We'd never seen the sea and hadn't seen any sailing ships when we walked all the way to see the filthy Thames – just barges and tugs and rowing boats – but every child had peered at the tattered pages of the nursery-rhyme book I'd stolen off the second-hand stall in the market.

I was the only one who could read. Mr Dolly had taught me when I was six or so. I was already in charge of Megs and Jenny and Richie, who bawled non-stop when he was a baby. Mr Dolly was shocked that Mildred wouldn't let me go to school, but I was much more use at home being her skivvy and minding the little ones. Mr Dolly said it was a shame because I was a bright little thing, so he showed me all my letters and made me figure out a story about P-a-t the d-o-g and J-e-t the c-a-t, and before I knew it I could read any column in his newspaper, though I didn't have a clue what all the politics were about.

I loved my stolen nursery-rhyme book though. I learned the rhymes by heart and could see every detail of the coloured illustrations even when I closed my eyes. *I Saw Three Ships* was one of my favourites, especially the comic duck in Navy uniform peering through his tele-scope. Mr Dolly let me peer through his old telescope to see how it worked. He didn't need to explain the Navy to me though, because you can see Peg-leg Jack any day of the week down the Admiral's Arms public house.

So we played sailing ships. We each seized a sheet and shook it hard and jumped up and down, pretending we were sailing on a choppy sea. I let Jimmy Wheels have Mrs Watson's longest double sheet that nearly trailed on the ground when she hung it on the line. He seized hold of it, rearing his head up and singing his version of a sea shanty. His hard, calloused hands were filthy from propelling himself along the ground, so the bottom of the sheet suddenly had a new black palm-print pattern. I hoped Mrs Watson wouldn't notice when she came to take in her washing.

We shook our sheets, pretending to race each other, and then I seized hold of the big black apron Daft Mo's ma uses when she's out with the coal cart.

'Watch out, sailors, here's an enemy ship approaching!' I yelled, waving the apron.

'That's just a piddly little ship! *My* ship's much, much bigger,' said Richie scornfully.

'Yes, we're not scared of teeny tiny enemies,' said Pete. 'We'll push them overboard!'

'They're small all right, but they're deadly,' I said, waving the black sail. 'Can't you see the flag they're flying? It's a skull and crossbones. Oh Lordy, pirates!'

'Pirates!' the girls shrieked.

'Yes, pirates, and I can see their captain at the helm. He's small but he's burly, with a big black beard and bloodstains all down his pirate cloak and a peg leg,' I said.

'I'll bet it's just Peg-leg Jack that you can see and I ain't afraid of him,' said Pete.

'No, this is a real pirate captain, I'm telling you, and he's got a hook for a hand that'll rip the innards out of you, and a cutlass in his teeth that will take your head off at one blow,' I said, to make him squeal. He picks on my Megs sometimes, so he needs to be put in his place.

'He's not really there, is he?' little Mary quavered, hiding behind her own sheet.

I shook my head quickly to reassure her, but then shouted for everyone else's benefit, 'He's coming, he's coming, his ship is getting nearer! Any minute now he'll swing over on his special rope with all his pirate army and he'll have your guts for garters. Watch out, Pete – he always goes after boys like you first, to stop them telling tales.'

Pete waved his sheet violently. 'He's not going to get me. I'm sailing away, faster, faster. I'm leaving that silly, smelly old pirate far behind, see!' he yelled. He tugged his sheet so hard there was a sudden snap as the frayed washing line broke. All the sheets sailed to the ground and lay in a sodden heap.

'Oh Lord, better run for it!' I shouted – but we weren't quick enough.

Mrs Watson came charging out of her house, her blouse wide open because she'd been in the middle of feeding her baby when she heard our shouts.

'You wicked, pesky little varmints!' she bellowed. 'I spent all blimming morning washing them sheets. Who did it? Was it you, Clover Moon? You're always the ringleader in any mischief. You wait till I tell your mother!'

Pete stared at me, red in the face with fear and guilt, terrified that I'd say it was him. But I wasn't a pathetic little tell-tale.

'See if I care,' I said. 'And that woman's not my real mother anyway.'

I hitched Bert higher up my back and marched off. Megs ran after me, thumb in her mouth like a stopper.

'Oh, Clover,' she said indistinctly. 'Oh, Clover, now you're for it! She'll wallop you.'

'Then I'll turn round and wallop *her*,' I said, though we both knew that Mildred was much bigger than me, and far stronger too. Her arms were like great hams from heaving huge trays of bottles at the sauce factory before she married our pa. She walloped seriously, with all her strength, until her face was as pink and moist as ham too. 'Yes, I'll wallop Mildred – *whack-whack-whack* – and then I'll tip her in the coal hole and lock the door on her, and then you and me will run away together,' I declared. 'Perhaps Bert can come too. If he's good.'

'Will we really?' Megs asked, her eyes round.

'Of course we will!'

'But where will we go? And where will we live?'

'We'll run away to the seaside and we'll go sailing, just like we played. And we'll make a house in an old boat on the sands. We'll make it so cosy. We'll have one bed with lots of blankets and soft pillows, and we can squash up into one chair. It'll be such fun playing there.'

'What will we eat?' asked Megs.

'We'll eat fish of course. I'll go fishing every day and catch lots of fishes, and then we'll make a fire on the beach and cook them in a frying pan for our dinner, and we'll buy day-old bread and a pot of jam for our tea,' I said.

Behind me, Bert heard the word *jam* and started crowing and clapping, thinking he was about to get a spoonful. His cries became urgent.

'In a minute, Bert. Megs is going to take you home,' I told him.

'No! We're running away, the three of us,' said Megs.

'I wish we could. We will soon. But we need to save some pennies first,' I said. 'Now go back home, Megs. Don't worry about Mildred. You know she hardly ever wallops you. You can say you were looking for me but couldn't find me. And then say Bert started crying so you took him home. Go on now.'

'But what will you do?'

'I'll sneak off by myself for a few hours until I know Pa's home. She won't be so fierce with me then,' I said.

'Oh, Clover, I don't like to think of you by yourself. And I'm not good with Bert the way you are,' said Megs. 'I don't think he likes me much.'

'He absolutely loves you, Megs.' I loosened the ragged blanket tying Bert to me and eased him round to my front. 'There, Bertie – give your sister a big toothy grin. You love your Megs, don't you, darling? Pull a funny face at him, Megs, and tickle his tummy. That's it – make a big fuss of him.'

Megs tickled Bert and he hunched up, chuckling.

'There now! He's laughing at you. Look, he's holding out his hands. You want a cuddle with Megs, don't you, Bert?' I unravelled him and thrust him into Megs's arms.

'I can't suck my thumb now,' said Megs, struggling.

'Well, you can't in front of Mildred anyway, because she'll rub bitter aloes on it and then you won't be able to suck it for ages. Here, I'd better tie Bert to you, just in case he wriggles too much and you drop him. We don't want him ending up like poor Daft Mo, do we?' I said, busily binding him tightly to Megs's narrow chest. 'Don't wriggle so, Bert! Tuck your little arms in, there's a good boy.'

I got them sorted and then gave Megs a little pat on the shoulder. 'Off you go, lovey. I'll see you later.'

'You'll miss your tea.'

'Never mind. Maybe I'll go down the market and scrounge something. I'll be all right. Bye now.' I ran off quickly, knowing Megs couldn't run fast enough to catch me up, especially lugging Bert. I ran to the end of Cripps Alley, down Winding Lane, and then ducked into Jerrard's Buildings and hid halfway up their stairwell. It was pitch dark there, and you could hear if anyone was coming.

I hunched up, my head on my knees, and had a little private weep.

'Hard as nails,' Mildred always said, because no matter how hard she walloped I'd never cry in front of her. I'd clench my teeth and ball my fists and glare right back at her. One time she hit me so hard I fell over and whacked my head against the fender, but even then I didn't cry. Afterwards my shoulder bled so much I couldn't peel my frock off, and my forehead came up in a lump as big as a hen's egg, and I was so groggy I nearly fell down again when I was pulled up – but I *still* didn't cry because that would mean Mildred had won and I was never, ever going to let her.

I didn't cry doing the chores, not even when I burned my hand on the iron. I didn't cry when the big lads from the Buildings seized hold of me one Saturday night when Pa sent me out for a jug of ale. I didn't cry in front of anyone. Of course I cried in bed when the pinky-purple burn throbbed, of course I cried as I tried to scratch the feel of the lads' hands away when I was alone in the privy, of course I cried privately for my own mother when I saw Jimmy Wheels' ma watching out for him tenderly.

I wished Mother was with me now as I huddled on the stairs and wept. I imagined her putting her arm around me, rocking me gently, murmuring words of comfort. I tried smoothing my own hair, hugging my own shoulders, whispering softly to myself.

'*There now, Clover. Don't cry so. I know you were only trying to look after all the kids. You weren't making deliberate mischief. You just wanted to get them all playing so they could have a bit of fun. Don't fret – if Pa's home Mildred won't whack you too hard. And even if she does, you're strong, you can bear it, you're used to it,*' I mumbled. I slipped my hand down the back of my dress and felt the long raised scars on my shoulders. '*It won't hurt for long,*' I lied. '*Come on, you've had your weep. Dry your eyes and get cracking before someone stumbles over you in the dark.*'

I scrubbed at my face with the hem of my dress and then took a deep breath. It was a mistake because half the lads mistook the stairway for a urinal. I ran down the stairs for a gulp of fresher air and then set off down the road, head up, arms swinging, trying to look as if I didn't have a care in the world.

I got to the market and eyed up the fruit on the stalls, wondering if I dared snatch an apple or an orange and then run for it. Most of the stallholders knew all us kids from the alley and yelled at us to clear off if we came too near. I'd do better later, when they were packing up for the night. Old Jeff the Veg saw me sighing and offered me a carrot.

'Thanks, Jeff!' I said gratefully, taking a large bite. The carrot was old and woody, but it was better than a raw potato, which I'd sometimes eaten in desperation.

I wandered off and stood outside the bread shop, breathing in the warm smell of newly baked loaves, pretending the carrot in my mouth was delicious crust. Inside, Mrs Hugget saw me staring but turned away to serve a lady. She was good to Jimmy Wheels and Daft Mo and gave them free currant buns, but she'd never weaken when it came to the rest of us.

I so loved Mrs Hugget's buns. Once a gentleman gave me a shilling for handing him the wallet that had just fallen out of his pocket. I spent it all on a huge bag of buns, some with currants, some with icing, some with extra lard and spice. I shared them with all the children in our alley and we had a lovely feast, though I suffered for it when Mildred got wind of my sudden good fortune.

'You should have handed that money over to me, you useless spendthrift. I'm your mother!' she'd said, shaking me.

'You are *not* my mother, thank the Lord,' I'd said, so she shook me harder, flapping me like a dusty doormat. For two pins I think she'd have used a carpet beater on me.

Still, I was the winner that day. I'd bought the buns and shared them immediately because I knew that once she saw the money she'd want to get her hands on it. We all had our buns safely in our stomachs. In fact Megs had two because there'd been one left over and I insisted she have it because she's the skinniest.

I looked hopefully at passing gentlemen now, and any ladies with dangling reticules, but couldn't spot any fallen wallets or purses today. I walked on, chewing the last of my carrot, dodging in and out of the stalls, then skipping quickly down the length of the road to warm myself up. I didn't have a shawl, let alone a coat, and my feet were always cold because the soles of my boots were patched with newspaper.

I saw myself reflected in the shop windows and turned my head abruptly. That ragamuffin girl with tangled black hair and ugly rags wasn't *me*. I wasn't Clover Moon from Cripps Alley. I was little Miss Clover-Flower Moonshine from one of the big villas opposite the park, and I was on my way with my mama to choose a new doll for my birthday present.

I slowed down and walked more decorously because my imaginary mama told me it wasn't ladylike to skip in the street.

'*Watch your conduct, Clover-Flower,*' she said. '*You need to set an example to all the poor ragged children who play in the gutters.*'

14

Oh, I was good at mimicking her swanky voice and stiff manners!

'*We're nearly there, child! Can you see the sign over the road? There, under the candy-stripe awnings. Dolls Aplenty! G. A. Fisher Esq., doll-maker to the gentry.*'

That was Mr Dolly's real name, Godfrey Arthur Fisher. I never used his proper name, though he was well-christened, because he was a true godfather to me, and though his hands were old and gnarled with rheumatism, each doll he created was a work of art.

I peered in his shop window eagerly. He had a new display for the coming autumn season. There were small brown and gold and green leaves scattered all over the bottom of the window, and a couple of cardboard trees spread almost bare branches at the top. Two jointed dolls were having a leaf fight in the middle of the window, caps on their heads, little mufflers and knitted mittens keeping their wooden necks and clenched fists warm. Little girl dolls with fur-trimmed bonnets and velvet coats were sharing secrets in a corner, pink painted smiles on their pale wooden faces. A larger nurse doll wheeled twin wooden babies in a miniature perambulator while a small black wooden dog with a red tongue ran behind. I sniggered when I saw another dog lifting its leg against one of the trees.

'You're a naughty rude man, Mr Dolly!' I said, bursting into his shop.

Mr Dolly came out of his workshop and beamed at me. His chin barely cleared his counter top. He was bent over sideways because he had a crooked back, but he kept himself as upright as possible by leaning on his carved cane.

'Hello there, Clover! And just why am I a naughty man?' he asked, peering at me over his spectacles. His brown work apron was streaked with red and pink and white paint. It looked as if someone had been randomly embroidering berlin woolwork roses all over him. He even had pink streaks in his wild white hair.

'You've got a little wooden dog weeing in your window!' I giggled.

'Nonsense! He's just stretching one leg, that's all,' said Mr Dolly. 'It's a treat to see you, my dear. You haven't paid me a visit for a little while. You've not been ill?'

'No, just busy. You know what Mildred's like. She lolls on our sofa while I have to do all the work,' I sighed.

'She's in a delicate way at the moment, isn't she?' said Mr Dolly.

'Delicate? Mildred? She's as delicate as a warthog!'

'I meant there's going to be a stork visiting soon with a new little baby.'

'A stork!' I scoffed. 'I'm too old to be fobbed off with stork stories. I had to help Mildred when Bert was born and I was only just ten then.'

'So you're an old lady of eleven now,' he said, pulling a lock of my hair. 'And you know all about babies being born.'

'I bet I know more than you, Mr Dolly,' I said, 'seeing as you've never been married.'

'I've certainly never experienced wedded bliss, but I give birth to babies every week of my life,' said Mr Dolly, glancing through the door at his workbench. 'My dolls are my babies.'

There were bits of dolls not yet born – bald heads, and pieces of arms and legs, and woolly wigs, and a velvet case of beady glass eyes set neatly along the bench. Then there were assembled dolls, big and medium sized and very little, all with jointed arms so they could wave and kick their legs, but their heads were eerily blank, needing to be painted. The dolls who had happy smiles and rosy cheeks and shiny varnish were hanging from the ceiling to dry, but they were still naked. Yet more dolls were clustered together in their underwear – tiny bodices and petticoats and white muslin drawers – all patiently waiting for their frocks to be cut and fitted.

'So many babies!' I agreed. 'Imagine if they all started crying at once, Mr Dolly! And how happy you must be that their napkins never need to be changed! Do you know something? I am never, ever getting married and having babies.'

'But you're so good with all those children.'

'Yes, but I'd like to do something else with the rest of my life.'

I ducked under the counter and wandered into the workshop. I picked up a half-finished doll and twirled her in my hands. 'Maybe I could come and be a doll-maker too?' I suggested. I said it playfully enough, but I was suddenly serious. 'Oh please, Mr Dolly, do consider it! I could be your apprentice and learn all your doll-making tricks and then you wouldn't have to work so hard.'

'I'd love that, Clover, but how could I ever pay you? I don't make enough to pay myself more than a few florins a week,' said Mr Dolly.

'You wouldn't have to pay me at all! Just give me a midday meal. I'm not a big eater. If necessary I can go foraging in the market. And I'd stay up late every evening, sewing by candlelight. I don't need much sleep either. I could just curl up on the floor with a blanket,' I said earnestly.

'And what might your pa say, hmm?'

'Pa wouldn't mind too much. Jenny's his favourite now. Jenny and Mary. He favours the girls.' I said it lightly but my heart thumped hard in my chest. I'd been Pa's favourite once. He'd sit me on his lap and run his fingers through my dark hair and kiss the tip of my nose and say I was his little lucky four-leaved Clover, then pop a sweet from his pocket into my mouth.

He tried to make a fuss of Megs too, but she was always a sad little thing, wailing miserably most of the day and half the night, and she also had itchy rashes, so her little mouth had big red sores and her elbows and knees were covered in crusts.

But then Pa foolishly courted Mildred at the factory, wanting a warm wife to look after him and comfort his two poor motherless daughters. I'm sure she didn't love him and she didn't like the look of Megs and me, but she was already thirty and no other man had shown any interest in her, so she promised to love, honour and obey him when they wed. She didn't do any of those things, but she did provide him with more children – too many: Jenny, Richie, Pete, Mary, Bert, and another due in a couple of months.

Jenny was fair and rosy with curly hair, tall and strong like her mother – much taller than Megs, the same size as me – and she had a winning smile. Pa gave her so many sweets she often needed the toothache rag tied round her head.

There were only eleven months between Richie and Pete so most folk took them for twins. They were very alike in nature as well as looks, rowdy fidgety boys, forever up to mischief. They tried tormenting little Mary when she was a baby, but she was born shrieking and stood up for herself. She had a mop of curls too, and a smile that could melt even Mildred's hard heart.

'What about your stepmother?' Mr Dolly asked. 'Wouldn't she mind if you left home?'

'You have to be teasing! You know the way folk put out flags to welcome someone home? Well, she'd have banners and bunting announcing my departure. She'd give anything to see the back of me,' I said.

'She'd miss all the skivvying you do for her,' said Mr Dolly.

'Yes, you're right there, but Jenny would take over. I don't think she'd mind too much,' I said.

'What about Megs?' asked Mr Dolly, his eyebrows waggling up and down.

'Megs . . .' I said softly. Oh dear, perhaps I couldn't leave Megs just yet. She might not be able to cope without me.

'And Bert. You're like a little mother to that baby. Where is he now?'

'Megs took him home for me.'

'And I take it you're wandering about because you're in trouble again, you pickle,' said Mr Dolly. 'What have you done this time?'

'Nothing! Well, I suggested a game of sailing ships and all the children loved it, but then someone got too excited and pulled Mrs Watson's washing line down, and she'll tell Mildred, so I daren't go home yet or I'll get what for.'

'Say no more. I understand. Well, you're more than

welcome to spend an hour or so with me, Clover. I doubt I'll get any more customers this late, so I'll shut up shop and we'll settle ourselves in the workshop. We'll see if those little hands of yours are any good at painting rosy cheeks,' said Mr Dolly.

'You're going to take me on as your apprentice!' I gasped.

'No, dearie. You're too little to shut yourself indoors twelve hours a day, and your eyes too bright to strain just yet. You never know, your luck might change: your pa might come up with some scheme to get rich and then you could have the education you deserve. I'd give anything to have the wherewithal to send you to a good school. You were born for better things, Clover Moon.'

'What things, Mr Dolly?' I asked.

'You wait and see! But meanwhile let's see if you can make my little babies blush prettily.'

Mr Dolly pulled down his blind and locked the shop door. We went into the workshop and he selected a small wooden doll, a palette of deep pink paint and a dainty brush. But before I could get started there was an urgent jangle of the bell.

2

'**ALL RIGHT, I'M COMING,** I'm coming,' said Mr Dolly, sighing. 'It's always the way, Clover. Nobody knocks all day long, yet the moment I shut up shop that bell starts up.'

He seized his cane and shuffled through to the shop in his carpet slippers. They were worn down at the back, showing his socks, each with a gaping hole at the heel. I heard him opening the door and then talking to someone. It seemed to be an exacting customer because Mr Dolly started taking dolls out of the window, and then opening up further drawers and cabinets to show off his wares.

I thought of the pale ovals of skin showing through his old socks, the rips in the worn muffler round his neck. It seemed sad that he should stitch such exquisite little outfits for every doll while he didn't bother to darn his own clothes.

I picked up the wooden doll he'd selected for me. I painted her two pink cheeks and a pert pink nose. I loved the slight bounce of the brush on the smooth wood and the gleam of the paint. I itched to see what the rest of her face would look like. I rinsed my brush carefully and found the red paint and the black laid out neatly at the side of Mr Dolly's workbench. I gave her a mouth next, a little Cupid's bow. I wobbled just a little but the slight slant to her lips gave her a saucy expression. Then I rinsed again and tried to make the brush as pointy as possible. Breathing hard, I painted her two alert eyebrows with two beady pupils underneath.

'Now I'll paint your eyes properly,' I said. 'Would you like blue eyes or brown?'

The doll seemed to be holding her breath. I waited, blinking.

'Would you like green eyes like mine?' I asked.

She smiled with her new red lips.

'Your wish is my command!' I said, quoting Mr Dolly's book of fairy tales.

I selected a palette of clover-coloured paint and with great care circled both black pupils in green. She looked beautiful with her unusual eyes, a perfect little doll.

'There!' I said, with a shiver of delight.

She smiled back at me, clearly happy that I'd created her.

'What's your name then, little doll?' I asked.

I made her tilt her head up at me and whisper in a tiny voice. 'My name is Anne Boleyn.'

Over the years, while he cut and polished and glued and painted and sewed, Mr Dolly had talked me through the kings and queens of history.

'Anne Boleyn, my dear? A very pretty name, but you'd better make sure your little round head stays firmly glued to your neck,' I said, walking her over to the line of dresses hanging at the end of the workbench. 'Shall we find you a lovely dress to wear now?'

We inspected them together and chose a bold silk party frock, deep purple with a thin black stripe, with a wisp of black lace at the bodice. Anne Boleyn was so excited that she danced up and down on her tiny wooden feet.

Someone burst out laughing and I jumped, hiding Anne Boleyn behind my back. Mr Dolly had left the workshop door open. A strange man was peering through at me, shaking his head.

I stuck my chin out. I didn't like him laughing at me.

'Hello, dear,' he said. I could tell by his voice that he thought me much younger than I was. 'Are you perhaps Mr Fisher's little granddaughter?'

'No, sir, I am Mr Fisher's apprentice,' I said with dignity. Well, perhaps I would be one day.

'Are you indeed? And yet you still like to play with all the dollies?'

'I don't *play*,' I said. 'I was testing this doll to make sure her legs could move.'

'Well, I don't think there's any doubt about that. She was practically dancing a jig. Or perhaps she was simply trying to get warm because she doesn't have any clothes on yet,' said the gentleman.

I couldn't help giggling then. He was a strange man, clearly a proper gentleman with a fruity voice and fancy manners, yet here he was chatting away to me as if we were equals. He wore good quality clothes – any fool could tell that by the cut of his suit – but he was no city dandy: his jacket pockets were bulging with notebooks and pencils, he sported a floppy scarf instead of a tie and his brocade waistcoat was buttoned wrongly.

'Can I have a closer look at Miss Anne Boleyn?' he asked.

'Yes, but be careful, sir, for I've only just this minute painted her face,' I said.

'My, my,' said the gentleman, peering at her in the lamplight. 'You've done a very good job too. I love her expression.'

'Really, sir?' I said. 'Or are you teasing?'

'No, you're very skilled.' He sounded as if he actually meant it. 'What's your name, little apprentice?' he asked.

'I'm Clover Moon, sir.'

'Clover Moon! Now there's a distinctive name,' he said. 'Almost as memorable as Anne Boleyn.'

'I'm glad you like it, sir. I do too. My mother chose Clover because she wanted me to have a lucky name. Four-leaved clovers are considered very lucky, I believe. And Moon is my pa's name, and I'm very happy to have inherited it because the moon is so beautiful. My sister Megs and I often look out at the moon at night and wonder if there really *is* a man in the moon. It doesn't seem likely, but we wave goodnight to him all the same,' I said. 'I am pretty certain he isn't made of blue cheese though, like it says in the nursery-rhyme book.'

'I dare say you're right, Miss Moon. How do you do?' he said politely. 'I am Mr Rivers. I've been looking for a special doll for my little girl, Beth. I went to the biggest toy shop in London but could find none that took my fancy. Then someone there recommended this curious little shop in Hoxton – and it seems delightful. I am absolutely spoiled for choice and simply can't decide which doll will delight my Beth. Poor Mr Fisher has shown me so many beauties that I've got confused. Could you come and give me your opinion?' he asked.

I hesitated, not sure how Mr Dolly would react. But he limped up behind Mr Rivers and nodded his head.

'Yes, come and advise the gentleman, Clover,' he said, lugging three large boxes in his arms. 'You might like to have a look at these dolls too, sir. They're very fine, made of china, with several sets of clothes each: coats and bonnets and muffs, a change of dress with a pinafore, and a little nightgown. I stick to wooden dolls nowadays, as there's no call for these beauties round here. I keep them to show very special customers.'

I was certainly keen to see these dolls that had lain silent in their boxes without my ever being aware of them. I ran out into the shop, wiping my hands on my dress to clean them up a bit, and then helped Mr Dolly unpack the boxes and prop up each doll with her clothes displayed around her.

'Oh yes, these are very fine,' said Mr Rivers. 'What do you think, Miss Moon? Would you like your father to give you one of these dolls for your birthday?'

I gave him a look. Was he simple? Pa couldn't afford even the smallest wooden doll, and Mildred would explode at the thought of him wasting so much as a sixpence on me.

'I'm sure your little girl would be utterly thrilled if you bought her any of these,' I said.

I imagined Megs's face if I put one of the special dolls in her arms. I tried to decide which she'd like best. She might choose the blonde doll with bright blue glass eyes and a silk dress exactly the same shade. Or would she prefer the brunette in pale violet with her own parasol? Or the auburn-haired doll with dimples in a sea-green costume and little kid boots with heels?

'It's hard to select just one, sir,' I said.

'Do they have names, like your little Anne Boleyn?' asked Mr Rivers. 'How about giving them botanical names, as you're Clover?'

'Botanical?'

'Mr Rivers is suggesting you give my girls plant names,' said Mr Dolly. 'Flowery names.'

'What a good idea!' I said. 'Well, this one's Hyacinth because of her eyes, and this one's definitely Violet, and *this* one's Marigold.'

'Excellent!' said Mr Rivers. 'You've got a fine little protégée, Mr Fisher. You must be very proud of her.'

'I am indeed, sir,' said Mr Dolly, putting his arm round my shoulders.

I could feel him trembling. I knew he was terribly excited at the thought of selling one of these expensive dolls. I desperately hoped Mr Rivers wasn't going to disappoint him. Very occasionally rich folk wandered into the shop and made Mr Dolly display every single doll, but then they shook their heads and said they needed to go away and think about it. They never came back.

However, Mr Rivers was taking the task seriously. At first he seemed smitten with Hyacinth, and then he tried out Violet's parasol to see if it worked properly, but he was eventually overwhelmed by Marigold's dimples.

'I think I shall choose Miss Marigold as she has such a charming expression,' he said. 'How much is she?'

Mr Dolly took a deep breath. 'She's five guineas, sir.'

I stared. I'd seen the price pencilled on the cardboard box. Mr Dolly had more than doubled it. Surely he'd made Marigold much too expensive! Mr Rivers was probably rich, but he wasn't daft.

He smiled. 'She's very costly, but she *is* a work of art,' he said. 'I'll take her. Parcel her up, please.'

'Certainly, sir.' Mr Dolly was blinking with emotion, his eyebrows working overtime. His hands shook as he laid the doll back in her box and smeared the price with a wet thumb. I went to the rag bag and started tucking old scraps of material round the doll's head and outstretched fingers – the parts that might get chipped or damaged in transit. It was standard procedure, but it charmed Mr Rivers.

'Oh, look at little Clover Moon! She's tucking Marigold up in her bed just like a nursemaid, bless her,' he said.

'She's a very caring child,' said Mr Dolly.

'She is indeed,' agreed Mr Rivers. 'And talented too. Very skilled with her paintbrush.'

Mr Dolly raised his eyebrows at me enquiringly but didn't comment.

When I'd finished protecting Marigold I put the lid on the box, and Mr Dolly tied it tight with string. Mr Rivers had his wallet ready and handed over five pounds and five shillings, then shook Mr Dolly's hand solemnly. He insisted on shaking my hand too, and thanked me profusely for my help.

It was the very first time anyone had shaken my hand and I felt honoured. Then Mr Rivers strode out of the shop, holding the large cardboard box out in front of him, like a Wise Man with a precious gift for baby Jesus. (Mr Dolly didn't give me religious instruction, because he said he wasn't a Christian, but he'd shown me a book of reproductions of great paintings and the Nativity scenes had taken my fancy.)

When the shop door was shut and locked Mr Dolly put his arms round me and we did a lurching dance around the room.

'Five guineas for a doll I'd given up on selling!' said Mr Dolly. 'Oh, Clover, you're definitely a plant of the four-leaved variety! You've brought me such luck, my little one! Here, my dear. Take the five shillings. You've more than earned it.'

Five shillings! I'd never had so much money in my

life. But I knew what would happen if I took it home. Mildred would find it, no matter where I hid it.

'Thank you so much, Mr Dolly. But could you possibly keep the five shillings safe for me?' I suggested.

He nodded understandingly. He put the five pounds in his cash box, and the five shillings in a little embroidered purse in his waistcoat pocket.

'Here it is, safe about my person. I shall act as your personal banker. Come to me whenever you need to withdraw a few pennies! Now, let us have a celebration supper! You can stay a little while, can't you?'

'Of course I can stay, Mr Dolly!' I said eagerly. 'I don't have to leave until eight, and then I'll walk Pa home from the factory.'

I played with Anne Boleyn while Mr Dolly cooked our supper on his spirit stove. He admired her newly painted features extravagantly.

'I'm so impressed by your artistic skills, my dear, especially as it's a first attempt. That little doll has such a pretty face!' he said.

'So are you quite sure you don't want me as your apprentice, Mr Dolly?' I asked artfully.

'I wish I could take you on, my dear, but even if I did, I'm sure your family would object,' he said, turning the lamb chop.

I didn't try to argue further. I knew he was right. Mildred hated me spending so much time with Mr Dolly.

She didn't like him teaching me and said he gave her the creeps. Even Pa wrinkled his nose at the very sound of his name and claimed he didn't trust him.

They were both fools. Mr Dolly was the sweetest, kindest, cleverest man in all the world. The smell of his chop was making my mouth water, but he only had one, though he was frying a good pound of sliced potatoes and onions in his pan. When he dished up he took a couple of plates, cut the chop lengthwise and distributed all the vegetables equally.

'Here you are, child. Get it down you,' he said, offering me the plate.

'I can't eat your supper, Mr Dolly! Especially half your chop!' I protested.

'I'll be buying a big steak tomorrow! Now eat, dear. You deserve it. Heaven knows, you look as if you could do with a good meal. What does that Mildred feed you, bread and scrape?' he asked.

'Pretty much,' I said.

She gave Pa meat for supper every day because he'd done a hard day's work at the factory, while she had a kidney or a slice of liver because she said it was good for the growing baby, but us children mostly made do with hunks of bread and the dripping from the Sunday roast. She'd sometimes give her own kids a rasher of bacon, even little Bert, but never Megs or me.

If I did the cooking I always tried to slip a slice to

Megs, and I frequently stole currants and sultanas and sugar and dabs of butter from the pantry, squashing them all together like a patty – a treat we called Clover Cake. Megs stayed skin and bones though, her cheekbones sharp in her little face.

Halfway through my supper I pretended to be full, hoping to take a portion home for Megs in a paper poke, though smuggling it past Mildred would be difficult, but Mr Dolly insisted I ate up every mouthful or he'd take offence.

When I sat back at last, my stomach tight as a drum, Mr Dolly gave me a tiny glass of ginger cordial for my digestion. He sat back in his easy chair, having a little smoke of his pipe. I downed my drink, pretending it was gin. Mr Dolly soon nodded off, snoring softly. I carefully knocked out his pipe and washed up the dishes. Then I played a game with Anne Boleyn, making her a little house out of an old box, and a bed and quilt and pillow with scraps from the rag bag.

Mr Dolly was still fast asleep when I heard the sound of the factory hooter. I took off his old slippers, covered him with a plaid rug, tucked him up carefully and then slipped away.

The streets were full of men and women trudging homewards from the sauce factory, reeking of onions and pickle and vinegar. I shivered to think I'd be one of them in the future. I slipped in and out of the crowds, searching for Pa. It seemed an impossible task. He had a slouching walk, his head bent, hands in his pockets, thinning hair lank, his face sallow, his work clothes shabby, his boots down at heel. This description fitted almost every man in the street. Every time I called 'Pa' at least twenty heads turned in my direction.

I searched until the crowd had thinned to a few stragglers shuffling along. I was sure I must have missed Pa. He'd be home now and Mildred would have told tales, trying to work him up into a rage against me. But then I spotted a familiar slight figure turning into Cripps Alley. I ran wildly to catch up with him before he got home.

'Pa!'

He turned and waited for me under the gas light. He gave me a tired smile, his mouth barely moving. 'Is that you, Clover?' he muttered.

'Of course it's me, Pa,' I said, running up to him.

'What are you doing out this late, girly?'

'Looking for you! I wanted to walk you all the way home but I couldn't find you. Did you have a hard day? Is your back bad? Would you like to lean on me to walk down the alley?'

'Oh, that's very kind of you, sweetheart,' said Pa, grasping my shoulder. 'My little walking cane,' he added fondly.

We walked up the cobbled lane together. All the

washing had been taken in, apart from Mrs Watson's. It dripped on us as we ducked underneath. She must have washed it all over again. My own reddened hands itched in sympathy. I felt really bad for her now.

Pa sighed to himself as we neared our house. I remembered Mr Dolly's words.

'Do you ever try to figure out how to get rich and lead a different kind of life, Pa?' I asked.

'What?' He bent nearer, as if he hadn't heard me properly. I smelled ale on his breath. He must have downed a swift pint on his way home. 'How am I going to get rich? You tell me, girl. I can't see any way off this treadmill, unless I get myself a gun and rob a bank. Then I'd rot in prison, and Mildred and you and all your brothers and sisters would end up in the workhouse.'

'But when you were younger, Pa? When you first fell in love with my mother, say? Did you not have schemes and ambitions?' I persisted.

'I dare say I did,' he admitted. 'I thought we'd perhaps settle in the country, somewhere fresh and clean, and I'd find some kind of farm work. I was stronger in those days, and took a fancy to working on the land. We said we'd rent a little cottage, get a few sticks of furniture and work for a farmer until we could start up a smallholding ourselves. We wanted to grow vegetables to sell at market, and keep some animals – a few cows and some hens.' Pa laughed. 'Your mother fancied having a little donkey! What use would a donkey be? I ask you. You can't milk a donkey or sell it for meat. But she stuck to her guns. She wanted that donkey. She even had a name for it – David Donkey! She was always naming things, your ma. You take after her, Clover.'

'Do I really, Pa?' I said. 'And did she ever get David Donkey?'

'No, of course she didn't. We both worked in the factory to save up for a year or so, but then you came along and your ma was too poorly to work for a while, and then she had Megs and . . .' His voice trailed away.

'I so wish we could all have gone to the country, Pa,' I said.

'It was all a pipe dream. And it's too late now, anyway. Mildred would never budge. When we were courting I tried taking her out for a day in the country and she was bored silly – said there was nothing there but a lot of trees and hills. She couldn't see the point of it.'

'Yes, well, what else would you expect from *her*?' I muttered.

'Hey, hey, I heard that! Don't you be so disrespectful of your mother!'

'*Step*mother. And she disrespects me all the time!'

'Well, you need to be put in your place, miss. You've got a sharp tongue on you, and sometimes you don't even need to say anything. You just look with those great green eyes of yours, making it plain enough what you think,' said Pa.

'I can't help my thoughts, Pa,' I said.

'You can hide them! Do yourself a favour. You're permanently in the doghouse with our Mildred.' Pa peered down at me in the dark. 'Is that why you're not home, getting the little ones tucked up in bed? Have you had another set-to with her?'

'No, Pa,' I said – because I hadn't had a set-to with Mildred *yet*.

The moment Pa and I were in the door I made a rush for the stairs. Mildred had to get Pa's dinner on the table, so I hurried Richie and Pete up to their narrow mattress. The girls were already in bed and the baby in his cot, though he was wailing fitfully.

I picked him up and gave him a cuddle. 'It's all right, little Bert, Clover's here. There now. My, you've got yourself worked up into a state. You're all of a quiver.'

'He kept fretting for you,' Megs whispered. 'And I did too. Oh, Clover, Mildred's in a right lather about you. She had to set to and help Mrs Watson do her sheets all over again and now she's furious. I'm so scared!'

'Don't be, Megsie. Pa's home now, and she'll never risk giving me a beating in front of him.'

I laid Bert down in his cot and he curled up with a sigh and was almost instantly asleep. I pulled my ragged frock over my head, kicked off my broken boots and climbed into bed.

'Budge up, girls, make room for me,' I said. Jenny and Mary turned over sleepily and I squeezed in, nestling against Megs.

I was nearly asleep when the door burst open, and I heard the harsh rustle of Mildred's skirt and apron as she strode across the room. She felt in the dark for the edge of the bed and then seized hold of my arm.

She didn't say a word. She just jerked me upwards, took aim and whacked me hard about the head, five or six times. She was wearing her brass thimble. I felt blood trickling from my temple. I pressed my lips tight together to stop myself crying out.

She threw me down on the bed again so hard that I bounced, and all my sisters along with me. Then she stalked silently out of the room.

'Oh, Clover!' said Megs, in tears. She patted at me in the dark. 'You're wet!'

'It's just a smear of blood. I'm all right really,' I said thickly, though my head was still ringing and I was half stunned.

Jenny and Mary sat up too, murmuring sympathetically. Then Pete climbed on to our bed, starting to cry.

'It was all my fault! You should have told on me, Clover. I should have got the whacking,' he sobbed.

'Oh, give over, little man,' I said, sitting up to give him a cuddle. The room suddenly tilted sideways, as if Mildred had seized the whole house now. I felt my stomach lurch too. I scrambled out of bed and fumbled for the pot beneath it. I was horribly sick, losing all my chop and potato.

'Oh, Clover,' Megs said, over and over, holding my hair out of the way.

'It smells,' Mary complained.

'And I need to wee now,' said Pete.

'Oh, for goodness' sake, hold your tongues,' I said weakly, leaning against the bed. The room was still whirling and I wasn't sure I could see straight, though it was difficult to tell in the half-light. 'Jenny, take the pot and tip it out in the privy,' I said.

'Why can't Megs do it? She's second eldest,' she said.

'You know Megs won't ever go to the privy after dark,' I said. 'Take it, Jenny.'

'I can't. It'll make *me* sick.' Jenny started to grizzle.

Pete was still crying. Bert woke up again and started a steady dreary wail.

My head felt as if it was bursting. 'I'll do it then,' I said, trying to pull myself up.

'You mustn't, Clover!' Megs protested. 'If Mildred sees you she'll start hitting you again.'

'If Mildred sees me I'll throw the pot of sick all over her,' I said.

That made them all start giggling feebly. I felt a little better, as if I'd really done it. I stood up, took hold of the pot and walked purposefully out of the room, pretending I wasn't afraid.

Out in the hallway I could see the flicker of candlelight through Pa and Mildred's half-closed door, and hear the sound of Mildred's footsteps as she walked backwards and forwards, muttering to herself angrily.

'Only crazy people talk to themselves,' I whispered into the dark, though I suppose that meant I was crazy too.

It was an effort to think straight because my head was hurting so. Maybe Mildred's blows had truly damaged me. Perhaps I was like Daft Mo, who'd been dropped on his head when he was a baby. Who would look after me if I couldn't talk straight or do any chores? Maybe I could live with Mr Dolly. I could sit on a chair in the shop, not saying a word, just like one of the dolls. Mr Dolly would paint my cheeks pink and my lips red and keep my hair well brushed.

I walked stealthily down the stairs, holding the pot at arm's length. I could hear Pa snoring in the living room. I slipped into the kitchen, opened the back door and crept out to the privy.

Megs wasn't the only one frightened of going there at night. It was too dark to see if there were any spiders or rats lurking. The not knowing was somehow worse than seeing them.

I stood shivering in the back yard, my legs suddenly locked.

Pull yourself together, Clover Moon!

I stumbled over to the privy, darted inside, emptied the pot and then ran out again. Done! I let myself back into the house, swilled out the pot at the sink, and then tiptoed towards the stairs. I didn't make a sound, but Pa's snores stopped. He peered at me blearily, holding up a candle.

'Is that you, Clover?'

'Yes, Pa.'

'What are you up to now?'

'Just emptying the pot, Pa.'

'What's that mark on your head?'

'Nothing.'

He walked unsteadily towards me, holding an empty glass. Perhaps he'd had another drink or two with his supper. He held out his hand and felt my forehead. Then he looked at the blood on his fingers. 'How did it happen?' he asked.

I didn't answer, just looked upwards, where the floorboards were creaking as Mildred paced.

I wanted Pa to go storming up the stairs and yell at her, even though I knew she'd hate me more than ever and batter me senseless when Pa was at work.

But he didn't do it. He just shook his head sorrowfully and took a swig from his glass, even though it was empty.

Mildred stopped pacing. 'What you doing, Arthur? Come up to bed!' she yelled.

He walked past me and left me there. I hunched up on the floor, clutching my head, waiting until the room upstairs was still and silent. Then I crept up myself. Megs was still awake. She put her arm round me and I lay against her, my head burning hot.

I went to sleep and dreamed of Pa and our mother in a cottage in the country, cows and hens and a donkey in the garden, and Megs and me picking flowers. We were so happy, just like a family in Mr Dolly's story books.

3

WHEN I WOKE IN the morning I found my hair had stuck to the pillow. I had to douse myself under the cold tap and rub hard to get rid of the dried blood. It hurt terribly. The children said I looked scary. When I sidled into Pa and Mildred's room and looked in her precious mirror I saw what they meant.

I had several gashes on my temple, which had swelled horribly at one side, giving me an odd lopsided appearance, and I had a black eye into the bargain. Even Mildred looked concerned when she caught sight of me. She made me stand in the daylight with her hand under my chin, having a good peer.

'What have you done to yourself now?' she said, as if I'd whacked my own head with a thimble.

I stared at her.

'Don't look at me like that with those witch's eyes. And don't go telling tales on me to no one. It was all your own fault anyway,' she said gruffly.

Mrs Watson came calling, her baby in her arms, her little girl hanging on her skirts. She came to give me a scolding, but she was shocked when she saw the state I was in.

'Merciful heaven, Mildred, what have you done to the child? You've bashed her about good and proper!' she said.

'Well, there's a cheek,' said Mildred. 'You were the one who said she deserved a good hiding!'

'Yes, but I didn't mean mark her like that. I was annoyed at the time because washing day's such a trial – I was so tired with the baby not sleeping that I couldn't bear the thought of having to do it twice. But it was only a piece of childish mischief all the same. I'm not even sure your Clover pulled the sheets down herself, though she was certainly the ringleader,' said Mrs Watson. She peered at my face. 'You nearly took her eye out, Mildred! What were you thinking?'

'Don't exaggerate! I just gave a her a smacking,' Mildred told her. 'And it was well deserved because she ran off and stayed out all hours, probably hanging round that weird old doll-maker, and then she started sweet-talking her pa to get him on her side. She's the craftiest little baggage. She needs sorting out or she'll really go to the bad. I'm only doing my Christian duty as her stepmother.'

'There's nothing Christian about marking a child for life, and that's what you've done, Mildred.' Mrs Watson took my hand and squeezed it hard. 'I'm sorry, pet. I shouldn't have lost my temper.'

'I'm sorry too, Mrs Watson,' I said, enjoying the situation. Mildred was starting to look really worried.

After Mrs Watson had gone she didn't say anything more, but when she heard the street doctor calling for customers at the top of Cripps Alley she went hurrying out, purse in hand. She came back with a small blue jar.

'Come here, you,' she said to me. 'Look what I've got you. A pennyworth of Arabian Family Ointment. Doctor says it's the best for inflammation of the eyes. And it's good for chapped hands too, which I blooming well need, seeing as I did two full washes yesterday.'

She hooked my hair behind my ears and dabbed on the ointment.

'Ouch! You're hurting!' I protested.

'Well, keep still, you ungrateful little miss. I'm trying to make it better for you, aren't I?'

'It smells!'

'Oh, Miss Hoity-Toity! I'll shove it right up your nose in a minute if you keep up this nonsense.' She slathered it on as if spreading dripping. 'There, that should clear it up,' she said. 'Now, take the baby and get out from under my feet. I can't stand to look at you. And don't you dare go running to that creeping crookback or I'll have your guts for garters.'

Mr Dolly said the pills and potions the street doctor sold were all useless rubbish, likely to do you more harm than good, but the ointment did stop the throbbing just a little. I longed to go and see him but didn't quite dare, not so soon. I wound a blanket about my shoulders and sat out on the doorstep instead, with Bert on my lap. Megs came and sat beside me. She kept giving my sore head worried glances.

'It doesn't really hurt,' I said reassuringly.

'It still looks funny,' she said. She huddled against me. I could feel her shivering.

'Here, it's chilly today. Have my blanket.' I eased Bert forward so I could shrug it off.

'But then you'll be cold, Clover,' said Megs.

'I'm warm as toast, truly,' I said. I was actually burning. Perhaps I had a fever. I still felt addled inside my head, unable to think straight.

Megs had been given the burnt porridge pot to scrape clean with a scrubber. The other girls were making the beds and sweeping the floors. Richie and Pete staggered outside with the mats to shake. I'd usually be inside, helping Mildred with the ironing, but she didn't want me anywhere near her today.

'So lucky me,' I said to Bert. 'No chores at all. We're free as birds, aren't we, Bertie? You're a little bird. My little duck.'

'Duck!' said Bert. 'Duck!'

'Oh my! Did you hear that, Megs? Bert said *duck*. He really did. Say it again, Bertie! *Duck!* Say *duck*!'

'Duck!' said Bert.

'Oh, you clever little boy. Listen to your brother, Richie, Pete. He can say *duck*!' I said.

'We can say *duck* too, silly. Anyone can say it,' said Richie. 'Duck, duck, duck!'

'Duck, duck, duck!' Bert repeated, and made us all laugh.

'Let's play a game so that Bert can join in too,' I said. 'It's a bird game. We'll each choose a bird, and then, when I point, you have to say your name and flap your wings. We'll do it ever so quick, but we'll slow down for Bertie because he's little. You play too, Megs. You can be a little sparrow.'

'I don't want to be a little sparrow,' said Pete. 'I want to be a big, big, big bird.'

'Then you can be an eagle,' I said. 'They're the biggest of all.'

'*I* want to be an eagle,' said Richie, predictably enough.

'You can be a hawk. Oh, how all the little mice and rabbits tremble if they sense you flying overhead.'

So we started the game, and then Jenny and Mary came running out and joined in too. Jenny was a beautiful white swan preening herself, and Mary was a speckled hen clucking at the top of her voice. Soon Jimmy Wheels came bowling along and I declared he was a kingfisher, the most beautiful and brightly coloured of all the birds.

I'd turned the pages of Mr Dolly's *Book of British Birds* but it was a struggle thinking up new birds when half the children in the alley joined in. The twins five doors down were two cuckoos, and pretty blonde Angel was a yellowhammer who said, 'Little bit of bread and no cheese.' Angel's baby sister was too little to say anything at all, so she was just a fledgling who cheeped whenever she wanted. I added a parrot and a hummingbird, though I knew they weren't British, and Sukey down the alley and Daft Mo were very loud in their interpretations. Sukey squawked alarmingly and Daft Mo hummed furiously even when it wasn't his turn.

The rules of my game fell by the wayside but it didn't seem to matter. Little Bert cried, 'Duck!' every time I pointed at him, extremely pleased with himself. I lifted him up and down, making his stubby legs dance on the cobbles, and after a minute or so he was trying to do it himself, practically performing a polka, though he tipped forward if I let him go.

Halfway through our noisy game I became aware that a strange man was leaning against the wall at the top of the alley. He kept looking at us and then seemed to be writing rapidly in a notebook. He was in the shadows so I couldn't see him properly. I wondered if he was the police, making notes of our whereabouts.

The police hated all us alley folk. They'd arrested all three of Old Ma Robinson's boys for thieving, they'd kept Peg-leg Jack in the cells many a night for drunkenness, and they were forever harassing Daft Mo's big sister because she liked to go off with gentlemen.

Then the stranger edged a few paces nearer. He wasn't the police. I recognized his floppy scarf and his fancy waistcoat and crumpled suit. It was Mr Rivers, the gentleman who'd bought Marigold for his daughter!

I sat Bert on his bottom, still 'ducking' merrily, and ran up the alley towards him.

'Mr Rivers! Hey, Mr Rivers!' I called.

He looked up from his page and then did a double take. 'My word, it's the little apprentice. Miss Clover Moon!' Then he gasped as I crossed the alley into a patch of sunlight. 'Dear goodness, what's happened to your face, child?'

I'd completely forgotten. My right hand went to my head, hiding the gash and my black eye. 'Nothing, sir,' I said stupidly.

'That's the worst case of nothing I've ever seen.' He took hold of my hand and gently prised it away from my face. 'Who did that to you?' he asked. 'By God, I'll report them and have them thrown in prison.'

I shook my head. 'No one did it,' I said quickly. 'I just fell. My bootlace was dangling and I tripped. I'm an awful clumsy girl.'

I wasn't lying to save Mildred. I'd have loved her to be marched off to prison. I'd have been happy if they locked her up and threw away the key. But it wouldn't be Mildred who got taken away, it would be me. There used to be a man in the alley who beat his children every night, so badly that they sometimes bled right through their clothes, and his wife told on him, and the police came, but they didn't arrest the man. They took the wife and children away instead and put them in the workhouse.

I didn't want to end up in the workhouse. I'd heard such tales about it. I'd sooner deal with five Mildreds than one workhouse matron.

'You tripped?' said Mr Rivers.

'Yes, sir. Definitely, sir,' I told him. 'Did your little girl like her doll Marigold?'

'She absolutely loves her! I'm very grateful to you, Miss Moon.'

'So why are you here in our alley? You don't live near here!'

'That's right. I'm taken with the area though,' he said.

'You must be daft, sir! It's rough round here. Look!'

'It's very . . . picturesque,' said Mr Rivers.

'Are you taking notes about us?' I asked, pointing to his notebook. 'You're not going to report us, are you?'

'Of course not, Clover. I've not been taking any notes. I've been sketching,' he said.

'Sketching?' I didn't believe him. Why would anyone want to draw anything round here? Especially Cripps Alley! It was dark and dank, the terraced houses tumble-down, the cobbles greasy, the air full of smuts from the chimneys. The gutters were choked with rubbish and worse, and the rats were so bold they darted right over our bare legs.

'I've been sketching you and all the other children,' said Mr Rivers. 'They can't all be your brothers and sisters, Clover . . .'

'Half of them are. And the rest are like family too,' I said. 'I keep them all in order and make up things for them to play.'

'Do you let the other girls play with Anne Boleyn?'

'She's not my doll, sir. Children like us don't have proper dolls,' I said. 'I made rag babies for Megs and Jenny and Mary once, but Mildred gave them to the rag-and-bone man because she said they'd been bad.'

'Mildred?'

'My stepmother.' I pulled a terrible face.

'Oh dear,' said Mr Rivers. 'Is she a bit of an ogre?'

I glanced over my shoulder. Our front door was open and Mildred had big ears that poked through her hair. She could sometimes hear us all the way down the alley. 'She's ever so kind,' I said loudly, but I shook my head vigorously at the same time.

Mr Rivers was quicker on the uptake than I'd thought. He pointed to my sore head and mouthed, 'Did she do that?'

This time I shook my head seriously because I couldn't risk him causing trouble.

'Let's see your sketch then, sir,' I said, to distract him.

He opened up his notebook and showed me. I stared at the page in awe. He'd drawn us children playing our bird game. He had us all set down perfectly on the page.

'Ah, look at little Bert, grinning away because he's learned to talk! And you've got Megs just right, hanging her head and looking worried in case she forgets she's a sparrow.' I squinted at the little bunch of children, looking for the big girl in charge of them. 'But where am I?'

Mr Rivers pointed. It was a shock. I knew what I looked like. I'd glanced at myself often enough in Mildred's mirror and in the windows in big shops, but I'd always been on my own. In Mr Rivers's picture I wasn't a big girl – I was as little and wispy as Megs, and my hair was matted and my face all lopsided.

'Oh, I look awful! Rub me out, please!' I begged.

'You'll like this sketch better, even though it's done from memory,' said Mr Rivers. He flipped the page back and I saw a picture of Mr Dolly's shop. There he was, all bent over because of his poor back, but smiling as he talked to Mr Rivers. The door through to the workshop was open and you could see a girl waving a little wooden doll around. She had a big smile on her face and somehow she looked almost pretty, in spite of her tangled hair and ragged clothes.

'I *do* like this one better!' I said. 'You're so good at drawing, Mr Rivers. You could almost be a proper professional.'

'Well, actually I am,' he told me. 'I mostly do portraits. You know, paintings of people.'

'Like the paintings of Mary, Joseph and baby Jesus in Mr Dolly's book?' I asked, awed.

'Well, probably not quite as good as those, if they're reproductions of Old Masters. But several of my portraits hang in galleries and I show at the Royal Academy every year,' said Mr Rivers.

I didn't know what the Academy was, but I was impressed by the word *royal*. 'You mean you show for the *Queen*?' I asked him.

'I suppose I do, although I don't know how often the royal feet ever step over the threshold,' he said.

'So will you paint these pictures of us playing, and me in Mr Dolly's shop, and hang them in the gallery?' I asked incredulously. 'So that all the rich folk will look at them?'

'No, these are sketches to go in a children's book.'

'Oh,' I said, disappointed.

'But think how many children will see your picture, Miss Moon. The book is by Sarah Smith and she's very popular. It will sell thousands of copies. She's written many books about little street Arabs.'

'Street Arabs?' I repeated.

'It's a stupid phrase,' said Mr Rivers, looking uncomfortable. 'I mean children in poor circumstances.'

'Oh well, that's us. We're all poor in Cripps Alley,' I said. 'Why does this writer lady want to tell stories about poor children? Why doesn't she write about rich children and all their fancy clothes and their toys and their cakes and sugar candy and plum puddings?'

'She thinks poor children are most interesting. And so do I. Though cakes and sugar candy and plum puddings sound very appealing. What do *you* eat, Miss Moon? You're very thin. Do you get three proper meals a day?'

Well, that was a laugh. Mr Rivers might have had a good education but he didn't know anything. Still, I didn't want him pitying me.

'Last night I had lamb chop and fried onions and potatoes,' I said, truthfully enough. 'I'm just naturally thin, sir.'

'It looks as if all your brothers and sisters are naturally thin too,' said Mr Rivers, peering down the alleyway.

The children had stopped playing the bird game. The boys were playing chase, not letting Jimmy Wheels join in, though he was faster than any of them. The girls were in a little huddle, arguing over a piece of knotted ribbon. Megs was sitting on the step by herself, sucking her thumb. Bert was crawling about the gutter, investigating the rubbish.

'I'd better go, sir. They always get in a pickle if I'm not there to sort them out,' I said.

'You really are a regular nurserymaid, Miss Moon,' said Mr Rivers.

'I'm just used to children, sir,' I said.

'Do you think you'll have lots of little ones of your own one day?'

'Absolutely not! I'm not even going to get married. When I'm old enough I'll go to Mr Dolly's and work there. I'll be surrounded by lots of children, but they'll be silent ones, and they'll never need their napkins changing,' I said.

Mr Rivers laughed. 'You're a card, Miss Moon. You take care of yourself as well as the other children.' He tilted my head on one side, peering at it carefully. 'It's such a gash. You must make certain it doesn't get infected. Go and give it a good wash with lots of hot water and soap, and get this Mildred of yours to put on a clean bandage,' he advised. 'Tell her I said so. And if by any chance you happen to "trip" again, perhaps you should go to my author friend Sarah Smith. She runs an establishment for destitute girls who are down on their luck – it's just off the Strand in the West End. She will protect you.'

He clearly didn't believe I'd tripped accidentally.

'Go on, little one,' he said, and gently steered me down the alley.

I didn't protest. I walked back towards our house, giving the boys a lecture as I passed, telling them they had to play with Jimmy Wheels or I'd slap them so hard about the legs they'd have to wheel themselves about too. I snatched the ribbon away from the squabbling girls and tied it on to Megs's head, and I picked Bert up and set him on my hip, poking a sodden shred of newspaper out of his mouth.

Then I turned round and looked back up the alley.

Mr Rivers was still looking at me anxiously. 'You'll do as I say, won't you, Miss Moon?' he called.

I nodded several times, and he waved and headed out of the alley. Of course I couldn't do as he suggested. Mildred would certainly whack me about the head many more times, whether I asked for it or not, but I wasn't going to go running to this strange place for destitute girls. It sounded like a genteel version of the workhouse and I didn't fancy it at all.

I couldn't even keep my wound clean. We didn't have any soap and we only had hot water when Mildred lit the copper on washdays. I couldn't dunk my head in that along with the sheets or I'd boil like a piece of beef. We didn't have any bandages, clean or otherwise, and if I told Mildred a gentleman was watching out for me she'd only think the worst and beat me black and blue.

I leaned against the wall, suddenly weary. I wished I could skip the next five years overnight. I would be trapped in Cripps Alley for such a long, long time. It was no use hoping that Mildred would sicken and die when the new baby was born, like my own poor mother. Mildred was as strong as an ox. She could have another baby each twelve-month without any problems. When she had Bert she'd given birth only a couple of hours after her first pain, and was up and about within a day, whereas Mrs Watson was flat on her back in bed for a week after she had her little Tommy.

'You all right, Clover?' It was Mrs Watson herself, calling from her doorstep, Tommy on her hip, her little girl, Alice, butting her head against her knees. Tommy was wailing mournfully, though she was joggling him up and down, trying to distract him.

'Yes, I'm fine, thank you,' I answered.

'You don't look it. That poor head of yours has swollen right up,' she said.

'I'll be as right as rain tomorrow, you'll see,' I told her.

'You're a plucky kid, Clover, I'll say that for you. And you've got a knack with all the little ones. Look at little Bert, happy as can be. My Tommy won't stop wailing. He was at it all night long and he still won't quieten,' she said. 'I'm desperate for a bit of sleep.'

'I'll mind him for you for a couple of hours, and little Alice too,' I offered. I still felt guilty about her washing being spoiled – and I loved her calling me plucky. Fancy, two people praising me in the space of half an hour! It made me feel warm and special, aching head or not.

'Oh, Clover, I couldn't possibly. You've got enough on your hands, plus you must be feeling pretty poorly,' said Mrs Watson, though she looked tempted.

'Go on, I don't mind a bit.' I set Bert back down on the pavement. 'There now, Bertie, have another little crawl. Alice, you keep an eye on him for me while I give your brother a cuddle so your poor ma can take a little nap,' I said.

I took Tommy out of his mother's arms. He was red in the face with crying and his damp little body felt hot.

'Perhaps we should loosen his shawl?' I suggested. 'It's a very fancy pattern. Did you crochet it yourself?'

'No, I got it from the used-clothes stall down the market last week – good as new.' She looked at my ragged frock. 'You ought to tell your ma to go there – you can get some lovely little outfits at sixpence a pop.'

'I doubt she'll be buying me any clothes in a hurry, new or used,' I said, rocking Tommy. I looked at his flushed little face. 'You know what, I think he's teething. Our Bert used to get those bright red cheeks. I used to rub his gums with teething jelly. I think we've still got some at home. I'll try him with it.'

'Bless you, Clover,' said Mrs Watson. 'Come and wake me in two hours then, dear.'

I was more than ready to do so because Tommy didn't settle properly, though the jelly soothed him for five minutes because it was so sweet. Bert didn't appreciate my fussing over Tommy and started crying for attention himself.

'Dear goodness, why do babies have such powerful lungs?' I said to Megs. 'You'd feel so much more obliging if they whispered sweetly.'

I'd been flattered by Mr Rivers saying I was a good little nursemaid, but I couldn't quieten poor Tommy. He was hotter than ever, his fluffy hair stuck to his head with sweat. I took the shawl off him altogether and gently blew on his face, but it didn't cool him and he was still sadly fretful.

Megs took his fancy white shawl and wrapped it over her head and round her shoulders. 'Look, Clover, I'm a bride,' she said, smiling.

'A very beautiful bride,' I said, rocking Tommy, who wailed louder than ever. 'Be a bride if you like, but I wouldn't have babies if I were you.'

'Naughty bad babies,' said little Mary smugly. She and Jenny imitated them, adding to the caterwauling. Alice hung back at first, but soon joined in their play, especially when I turned an old torn pinny into a baby for her.

Mildred was trying to nap too, and came to the door threatening blue murder if we didn't all button it immediately, but she kept her fists by her sides and had another anxious glance at my head. 'Better put some more of that ointment on, Clover,' she said.

I smeared it on, and put some on Tommy's flaming cheeks too just in case it helped. Then I carted him back to the Watson house, Alice trotting beside us clutching her pinny baby. Mrs Watson was deeply asleep in an armchair, her head nodding on one side, but as soon as she heard Tommy she sat up straight, sighing.

'He's still at it then?' she said. 'Thank you, Clover. I'll take over now I've got my strength up again. Bless you, dear.'

'I'm happy to help, Mrs Watson,' I said.

I still felt happy when we went to bed, and made up a story for all the children, whispering into the dark. It was all about a kind artist who painted our picture, which hung in a special gallery. The Queen herself saw it and took a fancy to it and invited us all to tea at the palace.

The children fell asleep one by one. I was just dropping off myself when I heard an urgent banging at the door. No one ever knocked after dark unless it was an emergency.

I jumped out of bed and ran to the top of the stairs. Mildred had the door open. I saw Mr Watson standing there, looking frantic.

'Our Tommy took a fit this evening. I ran with him all the way to the children's hospital, a good two miles away. The nurse there says it's scarlet fever and the poor little mite's unlikely to pull through. Our Tommy's been put in isolation, all alone in a little metal cot. We have to tell everyone who's gone near him because the fever's catching. The wife said your Clover nursed him half the afternoon!'

4

I **SAT DOWN AT** the top of the stairs, shivering with fear. Poor little Tommy! Was he really going to die when he was only a few months old? Scarlet fever! There had been a bout of it in the alley two summers ago. Three of the four Miles children had died of it, and their mother nearly went demented.

The fever's catching!

Would we all catch it? Oh, thank the Lord, I hadn't let

Megs hold little Tommy. But I had cradled him in my arms, rubbed my own head against his tiny hot one, put my fingers in his mouth to apply the teething jelly, even changed his soaking napkin. I couldn't have got closer to him. So was I going to catch the fever and die too?

I clasped my arms around myself. I couldn't die! Megs and all the other children needed me. How would they manage without me? I saw them all kitted out in black, their little white faces dripping with tears as they filed past my coffin. I pictured Pa wild-eyed and shaking, crying for his firstborn child. Even Mildred might shed a guilty tear and pray that no one had noticed the great gash above my eye.

What would it feel like when they screwed down the lid and took me to the graveyard and buried me under the earth? Would my spirit be able to squeeze out of my body and drift through a crack in the coffin? Would I be just a wisp of smoke, or would I assume a pale ghostly body?

I hoped I might be less scrawny, with long shining hair. And would I grow wings? I didn't want to fly up to Heaven. I wanted to stay here on earth and look after everyone. Perhaps I could be Megs's guardian angel and keep her safe and happy?

But would I actually make an angel? I hadn't always been a good girl. I had lied enough times to turn my tongue black. I had lost my temper and raged at the boys who plagued Mr Dolly. I had cracked a few heads together in my time. I had bad-mouthed Mildred. My Lord, I had even wished her dead, and meant it too.

I wouldn't be an angel. I'd be pitchforked down to hell to join the other devils. I thought of Pious Peter, who spouted hellfire every week at the Saturday market, describing the torments of the damned. My head started throbbing, as if those terrible pincers were already closing in on me. I was burning even though I was shivering. It seemed I had the fever already.

I put my head on my knees, struggling not to cry. I heard Mildred and Pa arguing down below, and then the thud of footsteps on the stairs. Mildred loomed above me in the gloom, holding a candle, an eerie white ghost without a face. I reared away from her, hand over my mouth in case I screamed and woke the others.

'That's right. Keep your mouth covered! Don't breathe on me!' she hissed.

I realized she'd tied an apron across the bridge of her nose so that it hung down like a veil. Mildred was frightened of me! It seemed so ridiculous that I burst out laughing.

'It's not *funny*, you stupid girl! You might kill us all! Why did you have to dandle that Watson baby for hours? Haven't you got your own little brother to look after? And now you're putting him in danger – all your brothers, all your sisters,' she spat.

I choked and my laughter changed to sobs. 'I won't let them catch it. I'll go away by myself somewhere,' I said.

'That's what I think you should do, in all charity, but your soft-hearted father won't hear of it. So you're to come downstairs with me now, do you hear? No creeping back to bed and giving them all the fever too. You'll sleep under the stairs now, in the cupboard. And you're to stay there all day too, while we see if the fever develops.' She stuck out a hand, dabbed at my forehead hurriedly and then gave a little scream. 'It's sticky with sweat already!'

'That's the ointment – the stuff for the cut on my head,' I said. 'The cut you gave me, Mildred, with your brass thimble.'

'Don't you dare call me Mildred. I'm your stepma, God help me. It's my duty to chastise you. Now get yourself downstairs this instant,' she said, wiping her hands on her skirts.

I had to go down the stairs in my nightgown. Pa was in the hallway, weeping.

'I'm sorry, Clover, but what else can we do?' he said. 'Try to be a brave girl. Please God it will only be for a day or so, just to make sure you haven't got the fever.'

Mildred opened the door of the cupboard under the stairs. I stood there, hesitating. I'd always feared that cupboard, hating it when Mildred sent me to rummage around for the broom or the dust rag or the dolly tub on washday. I knew there were insects creeping in the corners, and I often heard furtive scrabbling sounds. I hoped they were mice and not rats.

'Get in, child. Surely I don't have to push you!' said Mildred. 'Here, I'll fetch you a blanket and a bucket in case you need to relieve yourself.'

'It's so dark. Can't I have the candle?'

'Yes, give her the candle, Mildred,' said Pa.

'I daren't. She'll likely knock it over and start a fire, and then we'll all burn to death,' said Mildred.

'For pity's sake, we can't shut her up in the dark like an animal.'

'It's night-time. She'd be in the dark in her own bedroom,' Mildred argued. 'She has to be kept separate or she'll pass on the fever.'

'We don't even know I've *got* the wretched fever,' I cried. 'Though I expect you'll be glad if I sicken and die of it, Mildred.'

'Clover! Don't you dare talk like that to your mother,' said Pa.

'She's *not* my mother!'

'She's brought you and Megs up as her own, and never stinted. And you must admit, you haven't always been an easy child.'

'I'll say,' said Mildred. 'Now in you get!'

She pushed. I pushed back.

'You can't make me,' I said, though I knew Mildred had twice my strength.

'You don't want to give Megs the fever, do you? Or little Bert?' she said.

She had me there. I crept into the dark cupboard. Pa gave me an extra blanket and fetched a precious jar of strawberry jam from the larder.

'What are you doing, handing over that jam? It's our last jar!' said Mildred.

'She'll need something to comfort her. Try to be brave, Clover,' said Pa. 'Goodnight, dear.' He bent as if to come into the cupboard himself to give me a kiss.

'Keep away from her!' Mildred warned. 'You'll likely get it if you so much as touch her.'

Pa backed away and Mildred slammed the door shut. It was immediately as dark as if I'd tumbled down the coal hole. I hunched up as small as I could, sitting on one blanket and wrapping the other around me. I listened hard, imagining the scrabbling, the squeaking, the slow creep of the cockroaches. I pulled the blanket right over my head, clutching the jar.

I prised off the lid and stuck my finger in, then sucked up the sweetness, and it was indeed a comfort. Pa still loved me after all, even if it was just a little bit. Would he have run two miles with me in his arms when I was a baby? I thought of poor little Tommy, crying for his own ma and pa. I wished I knew a prayer for him.

My folk weren't churchgoers, for all Mildred talked of her Christian duty. Mr Dolly was a follower of Charles

Darwin and believed we were all descended from monkeys. I tried to remember Pious Peter's rants.

'Gentle Jesus, please save little Tommy. Make him get better. And please could I get better too, if I really do have the fever? Thank you. The end,' I whispered. I hoped it would be more effective if I said it out loud, but my muttering sounded very eerie in that black cupboard. I had to calm myself with several more scoops of jam.

I couldn't see what I was doing in the dark and was soon sticky up to my elbow, but it seemed the least of my worries. I couldn't stop thinking of the creeping creatures shut in the cupboard with me. Should I keep as still as a statue so that they didn't notice me? But then they might just come and crawl all over me. I moved restlessly and drummed my bare heels on the floorboards to warn them away, but after ten minutes I was so exhausted I simply lay down with the blanket over my head for protection.

I'd lost the jam-pot lid, and though I felt around for a while it seemed to have rolled into a corner somewhere and was lost. I was scared the cockroaches might glide silently up the open jar and into the jam and then I'd eat one by mistake, so I clutched the jar too, my hand protectively over the top. It was very uncomfortable and I was stifling under the blanket, but surprisingly I fell asleep almost immediately.

I was woken by footsteps pattering down the stairs above my head. I had no idea if it was morning or still the middle of the night. Then whoever it was ran to the front door and rattled the bolt, but their hands weren't strong enough to slide it open. Then I heard crying.

I edged forward on my knees until my head was against the cupboard door. 'Megs?' I called.

'Oh! Oh, Clover, where are you? I've been looking and looking for you!' Megs wailed.

'It's all right. Don't cry. I'm here,' I said.

'*Where?* Clover, I want you! I need a cuddle!'

'I'm here, darling. In the cupboard under the stairs.'

'Don't tease,' Megs said.

'I'm not teasing, it's true. I'm in here.'

'In *here*?' Megs thumped on the cupboard door and then I heard her turning the handle.

'No, stop it! You mustn't come in,' I insisted.

'But I want to. I want you. Please let me in. *Why* are you in the horrid cupboard?'

'Mildred shoved me in here.'

'Oh, I hate her! She's so cruel. I'll get you out right now!' said Megs.

'No, no, you don't understand. I have to stay in the cupboard for a while because I might have the fever and you could all catch it from me,' I said.

'The fever?'

'Scarlet fever. Little baby Tommy has it. That's why

he was so poorly. They've only just found out. So I have to stay here by myself in case I get the fever too.'

'Will you?' asked Megs, crying harder.

'I don't know. I don't feel very well but maybe I'm just frightened.'

'I'm coming in too!' said Megs. 'I don't care about the silly old fever. I don't feel well either. *Please* let me in, Clover.' She turned the handle again and managed to get the door open a crack. I pulled on it hard so that she couldn't prise it open any further.

'No, you mustn't, Megsie. We'll be able to have a big hug the very second I come out. We just have to wait a day or so,' I said.

'A whole *day*?' Megs exclaimed. 'I can't wait that long!'

I wondered how she would bear it if I died of the fever. I took hold of my hair and pulled it hard, jerking my head from side to side.

I'm not, not, not going down with the fever! I chanted inside my head.

'Clover?' Megs quavered. 'Oh, Clover, you haven't caught the fever and died right this minute, have you?'

'No, no, I'm still here, and I'm going to curl up and go to sleep. And you're going to go back upstairs and get into bed and go to sleep too,' I said.

'But I have to cuddle against you to go to sleep,' Megs protested.

'Cuddle Jenny instead,' I said. 'Off you go now.'

'You promise you'll come out when the day's over?'

'I promise,' I said, though I wasn't sure Mildred would think it long enough. I didn't know how long the fever took to develop. I curled up under the blanket again and imagined the fever spreading from my aching head down my arms and body and legs until every part of me was hot and itching.

No, no, I haven't got the fever! I'm perfectly well. I'm just hot and itchy because of this horrid old blanket. I'm NOT getting the fever. I can't get ill and die because I have to look after Megs and little Bert and all the others. I have to look after ME. I'm going to work for Mr Dolly and make beautiful dolls for lots of little girls, and I'll read all the books on his shelf and know as much as he does, and my brain will practically burst with all this knowledge and I'll have to wear the biggest size bonnet to keep it safe inside me.

Then I remembered Mr Dolly reading me passages from his special friend Mr Shakespeare. There was one lovely little song the fairies chanted. I could only remember snatches of it. *Philomel, with melody. Sing in our sweet lullaby. Lulla, lulla, lullaby.*

I sang it over and over in my head, hoping it would somehow reach Megs and soothe her. It soothed me too, and eventually I fell asleep again. I only woke when I heard Mildred thumping down the stairs.

She was a while in the kitchen, and then she came and opened the door a crack. She had her apron tied round her head again. 'Clover? Clover, are you awake? Answer me, child, for pity's sake!'

I kept quiet, just to plague her.

'*Clover!* Oh my Lord, have you gone and died on us?' she shrieked.

'Yes, and I'm going to haunt you for the rest of my days!' I said, in as ghostly a voice as I could.

'You wicked girl, don't you dare play tricks on me! Now keep away from me, right at the back of the cupboard. Here's a cup of tea and a slice of bread. You've got the jam in there with you. I'm putting them just inside the door. You take them quick.'

'Can't you leave the door open just a little, so I can have some light? I promise I'll stay at the back,' I begged. 'It's just so hard when I can't see anything at all.'

'You'll just have to put up with it,' said Mildred.

'What if I'm taken bad and need to get out?'

'You can call out.'

'But you might not hear me,' I said, panicking.

'That's true,' said Mildred quietly. She shut the door with a bang.

I felt like screaming but I put my hands over my mouth. I didn't want to give her the pleasure of knowing I was desperate – and if Megs heard it would terrify her. I moved cautiously, inch by inch, because I didn't want to spill my hot tea or set that chunk of bread spinning into a dank corner. I found the cup and drank the tea. I found the bread and ate every crumb, dipping it into my pot of jam.

Then I folded the blanket round me and tried to compose myself. Only I wasn't myself any more. I made up a story inside my head: I was a fairy-tale princess and my wicked stepmother had locked me in the castle dungeon and thrown the key down the deepest well.

5

I PLAYED MY CAPTIVE princess game on and off until her life seemed more real than my own. I started violently each time Mildred opened the door of the cupboard, shrinking from her as if she really had locked me in for ever. I lost all sense of time, not sure whether it was night or not, or how long I'd been locked in there.

'Can't you let me out now?' I begged.

'Not just yet. We have to be certain sure you won't infect the others. It's a virulent strain of fever. The Watson baby's dead already,' said Mildred.

'Baby Tommy!' I gasped.

'They've sent the little Watson girl away in case she gets poorly too.' Mildred's voice was muffled by her apron but she sounded as if she might be crying. She paused, and then blurted out, 'I know I've sometimes been hard on you, Clover. But it's for your own good. I do truly wish you well.'

I was astonished to hear her talking in that way. Perhaps she thought I was actually dying and she didn't want me telling tales to God and his angels.

I couldn't decide if I had the fever or not. I felt very strange and light-headed, but then, who wouldn't be, locked in a pitch-black cupboard for days? My head hurt sometimes, but I'd always been prone to headaches and my brow was already sore from Mildred's blows. My heart was sore too. Why hadn't Megs been back to see how I was?

I knew I'd told her not to come near me. I'd made her promise to keep away. She was simply being obedient and sensible. But surely she might have crept back once, just to make sure I was all right?

The other children had come. Jenny and Mary had both whispered to me through the door. Jenny brought Bert too. He cried when he heard my voice, and I cried too because I couldn't come out and cuddle him. Richie and Pete ran up to the cupboard door whenever Mildred took her eye off them.

I heard their feet thudding as they pushed and shoved each other, hissing, 'You go first!' 'No, you!' It was as if I'd turned into a terrifying witch and they had to dare each other to come near.

'Don't be frightened, boys! I'm still your sister Clover! I've just got to stay in the cupboard to stop you getting sick,' I called.

They squealed and ran away as if scared I was casting a witch's curse – but Pete soon crept back on his own.

'Is it really you in there, Clover?' he whispered.

'Yes, of course it is.'

'Will you promise you won't get the fever?'

'I'm trying my hardest,' I said.

'Is it just babies who die of the fever?' he asked.

'I think so,' I said, my heart beating fast. 'Poor little Tommy.'

'Mrs Watson cried and cried when they said her Tommy was dead. She said it was all her fault. They think the baby must have caught it from the shawl she bought from the clothes stall. It has to be burned now. All baby Tommy's things have to be burned.'

'The shawl?' I said. I suddenly thought of Megs draping the shawl round her head, pretending to be a bride. My heart turned over.

'If you die, Clover, will all your things have to be burned too? Can I have your boots?' Pete persisted.

'I'm not going to die, do you hear? Listen, tell me about Megs. Is she all right?'

'She keeps crying for you,' said Pete. 'She's cried so much her voice has gone all funny.'

When I heard Mildred coming I crawled to the cupboard door. I didn't care how big and strong she was. I didn't mind if she beat me black and blue. I *had* to go to Megs.

'Mildred, I'm coming out,' I said, wedging myself in the gap as soon as the door opened.

'Don't be stupid, girl,' said Mildred. 'Get back now. Don't come near me!'

'Put your apron over your face – put one over my head too if you must, but I have to come out. I've been shut in that cupboard for days and I *haven't* got the fever. Take a look at me. I'm fine. But Megs isn't. I hear she's been crying.'

'She's always crying,' said Mildred. 'No, you've to stay in there another day at least, just to make sure.'

'Please, Mildred! For pity's sake, *please*!' I tried to force my way out, but Mildred slammed the door hard on my thigh, making me scream.

'Hey, hey, watch her leg!' Pa called.

It was Sunday! He was home!

'Let the girl out now, Mildred,' he said. 'It don't seem right to keep her locked up like that. I've been talking

77

with the lads down the Admiral. They say the fever takes two days to come out, three at the most. I reckon our Clover can't have got it, not if she's still doing fine now.'

'But—'

'Let her out, I say,' Pa insisted, with an edge to his voice.

Mildred seized me by the wrist and pulled me out into the hallway. Then she let go of me sharpish. 'Dear God, she's bleeding all over the place – look!' she cried, backing away from me.

Pa was staring at me, horrified. I blinked, trying to get used to the daylight, and peered down at myself. There were clotted red stains all down my arms and smeared across my nightgown. Was this why it was called scarlet fever? Did I have it after all? I tentatively touched a red smear and then licked my fingertip.

'Ugh! Don't be so disgusting!' Mildred shrieked.

'It's jam, Mildred. It's not blood, it's strawberry jam! I must have spilled it all over myself in the dark,' I said.

'You stupid clumsy girl. How dare you give us a fright like that!'

'Calm down, Mildred. Don't get yourself so het up,' said Pa. 'Come here, Clover. Let's have a squint at you in proper daylight.'

He took me down the hall to the door and opened it. In the alley the children were playing a listless game of kick the can. They all waved and cheered when they saw me and came rushing over.

'Keep back for a minute!' Pa called, putting out his hand to stop them approaching. Then he peered at my face and neck and felt my forehead.

'She's absolutely fine,' he called to Mildred. 'No fever at all. Nothing a good wash won't cure. Clean yourself up, Clover. Thank God you've been spared!'

'Thank God, thank God, thank God!' little Mary cried, putting her hands together piously while the other children laughed at her.

I wanted to give them all a big hug, especially little Bert, who was wriggling in Jenny's arms. But I needed to find Megs first.

'Where's our Megs?' I asked.

The children looked at each other, shrugging.

'She didn't want to get up this morning,' said Jenny.

I ran back indoors and up the rickety stairs. I burst into our room and there was Megs, still in bed, huddled under the blanket, just her hair showing. She sobbed softly every time she drew breath.

'Oh, Megs, darling, it's all right. Here I am! I'm fine, truly. I haven't got the fever. And you haven't either, have you? You only wore that white shawl for a minute or so. You can't have caught the fever, you simply can't,' I said.

I gently pulled the blanket away from her. It was a shock to feel how hot and damp she was. And then I saw her face. It was blotchy and swollen, with a scarlet rash.

6

'**OH, MEGS, OH, MEGS!**' I said.

She gave another sob. Her eyes were closed, but her arms reached out and she wound them round my neck. I held her tightly, rocking her. 'My poor baby, I'm here now. I'm going to look after you. I'm going to make you better, I promise.'

I knew I was in grave danger of catching the fever from her, but I didn't care now. I didn't care about anything but Megs, though I turned on the other children fiercely when they came crowding into the bedroom.

'Get out! How could you have left Megs all alone when she's so poorly?' I shouted.

'Has she got the fever?' Jenny asked, round-eyed.

'The fever, the fever!' Mary echoed.

'Fee-va!' said little Bert in Jenny's arms, but no one laughed at him this time.

Mildred came running when she heard them. 'Have you got the fever after all, Clover? Then get away from Megs this minute!' she shouted.

'*I* haven't got it. Poor little *Megs* has it! Call yourself a mother! You were so busy keeping guard over me in that wretched cupboard you didn't even take a second glance at Megs here,' I said furiously.

'She's just grizzly – you know what she's like,' said Mildred.

'Look at her,' I said, showing her Megs's flushed face.

'Oh my Lord!' Mildred backed away and ran for Pa.

'Poor mite,' he said. 'We can't even take her to the children's hospital. They've closed the doors now that Watson baby's died. They don't want the fever to spread to all the other patients.'

'But what will we do with her?' Mildred wailed. 'She'll give us all the fever! We have to keep her separate!'

'If you try stuffing her into that cupboard under the stairs I'll kill you,' I said, knowing that Megs wouldn't be able to bear it.

'Don't you talk to me like that, missy. You'll kill me, will you? Just exactly how are you going to do that when I can knock you flying with one hand tied behind my back?' said Mildred.

'I'll wait till you're asleep tonight and then I'll get the kitchen knife and creep up to your bed and stick it straight through your heart,' I told her. 'Now go away, all of you. I'll nurse Megs here, in her own bed. The other children will have to go in with you.'

Mildred started shepherding her own children out of the room.

Pa hovered, biting his lip, looking over at Megs. 'My poor little darling,' he said. 'That kiddie means the world to me.'

He took very little notice of her these days, and hadn't dandled her on his lap since she was a baby, but I wasn't going to argue with him. I was concentrating on Megs.

I smoothed the blankets as best I could, and made her a soft pillow out of a bundle of petticoats. I smoothed her hair back from her forehead and gently blew on her face to cool her down. Then I started telling her my captive princess story, acting it out – though it was all a bit too complicated for her to follow and her eyelids kept closing.

'That's it, my Megs, you go to sleep. I think you'll feel

a lot better when you wake up. I'll sing you the lullaby song. *Philomel, with melody . . .*' I sang it softly to her and she nestled closer. I fancied I saw a ghost of a smile on her poor red face as she slept.

I tried to tell myself it was proper restorative sleep, though her breathing was harsh and she kept tossing from side to side. When she seemed settled for a few minutes I dashed off to sluice myself down at the cold tap, taking off my stained nightgown and putting on my faded dress. I soaked a rag to cool Megs's brow and filled a small bowl with bread and milk, mashing it up and adding a sprinkling of sugar.

Mildred watched me from the doorway. She snorted when she saw the sugar but didn't object out loud.

'I think you should send one of the boys to the butcher's for a meaty bone,' I said. 'Bone broth will work wonders for Megs.' I was laying down the law, but for once Mildred didn't argue.

I ran back up to Megs, praying at each step: *Let her be a little better. Please, please, just a little bit better.*

But Megs seemed worse. She was very restless, and mumbled incessantly under her breath. I couldn't make head nor tail of what she was saying. I tried to rouse her but she didn't seem properly awake even when her eyes were open.

I tried her with the bread and milk, coaxing her gently, but the spoon clanked against her teeth. When I managed to slide a morsel on to her tongue the milk oozed out of her mouth and trickled down her chin.

'Never mind, sweetheart. You're not hungry just now but we'll try again later,' I said, tenderly wiping her face.

I held the cold rag to her burning forehead and it seemed to help her a little. I climbed on to the bed beside her and put my arms tight round her to make her feel safe. I slept a little and then woke with a start when Pa came into the room.

I didn't even realize it was Pa at first. He'd tied an old muffler over his face, and with his cap set low on his brow he looked like a robber.

'It's only me, Clover,' he said. 'How's our Megs?'

I didn't need to feel her forehead. Her whole body was burning. 'She still has the fever,' I said, stroking her.

'Well, I've been right past the park over to Henderson's Buildings – someone said that's where that street doctor chappie lives. It took the devil of a time finding the right room, and folk weren't too happy to be disturbed on a Sunday, but I found him at last. He's given me his best potion for the fever. I had to pay over the odds, but I told him I didn't begrudge a penny – not if it might save my little daughter.' Pa was all puffed up and proud of himself, though his eyes were still fearful when he peered at Megs.

'Do you want to give her the potion, Pa?' I asked, leaning up on one elbow.

'No, no, you do it. I'd only spill it, I'm that clumsy,' he said, setting it down on the floor. 'You're the chief nurse now, aren't you? That's my girl.' He backed out of the room, holding his muffler tight over his nose.

'Oh dear, Megsie, they're all scared to death,' I whispered to her. 'First it was me, and now it's you. How could they ever be scared of a little scrap of a girl like you? Shall we try the potion, see if it helps any?'

I got a spoonful into her, and this time she tried valiantly to swallow, though it clearly hurt her. I sniffed the potion myself. It smelled very similar to the strawberry jam I'd had in the cupboard, just sieved and watered down, but at least it might soothe her sore throat.

I lay with her all day, changing her sodden nightgown for little Mary's clean one. Megs was a full five years older than Mary but the nightgown still fitted, though it only came down to her knees. In the evening I tried her with bone soup. Mildred had done her best, skimming it until it was clear and golden, the easiest thing in the world to slip down a sore throat. Megs managed a spoonful.

'That's it, my darling. You need some nourishment inside you. Shall we try one more little sip?' I asked, but Megs's head was heavy on my arm. She'd drifted off to sleep again.

I lay beside her, sometimes dozing too. I heard Mildred and Pa herding all the other children into their bedroom with them. It would be a terrible squash in their bed, and several of the little ones would wet the bed if you didn't haul them out and sit them on the pot while they were half asleep. I hoped Mildred would end up drowning in a sea of wee – and then prickled with shame. How could I have such mean and childish thoughts when my dearest sister was lying in my arms, fighting for breath?

I timed my breaths with hers. It made my chest ache as I panted in rhythm. 'Slow down, Megs. Breathe in, right in, fill your chest with air. Then breathe out, slowly, slowly. In . . . and then out. Try for Clover. In . . . and then out,' I murmured.

Megs was too deeply asleep to take any notice, but I went on talking to her, whispering into her ear.

'I've been helping Mr Dolly, Megs. I can paint lovely faces and make the dolls come alive! When you're a bit better I'm going to run back to Mr Dolly's and see if he'll let me make you your very own doll. Not a rag baby – a real wooden doll with a painted smile and proper clothes. Perhaps he might even let me have Anne Boleyn, my absolute favourite. Henry the Eighth had lots of wives and Anne Boleyn was his most famous one, but then he stopped loving her and had her head cut off.

'Don't worry, we're not going to be wives, you and me. When I'm grown up – and it won't be too long now – I'm going to work for Mr Dolly and make my own dolls, and I'll teach you too, and we'll have our own special little house, just for the two of us – though I dare say we'll let some of the other children come and take tea with us. Maybe even Pa. But we're never, ever letting Mildred put so much as a foot inside the door.

'I'll sell lots of dolls and so will you. We will be the Misses Moon and our dolls will be in great demand. Even the royal children will have our special dolls in their nurseries. Mr Dolly will be so proud of us. He will be too old to make dolls himself, but we will let him live with us and be like a beloved grandpapa. He will have his own rocking chair by our hearth and we will feed him bread and milk and bone soup to keep him in good health.'

I rambled on while Megs breathed in and out so shallowly that her little sunken chest barely moved. I could feel her heart beating fast. I stroked her very gently, trying to soothe her. After a very long time I fell asleep but was woken by Megs wriggling, kicking her legs.

'What is it, darling?' I asked in alarm.

'We've got so much room!' said Megs. Her throat was raspy but she sounded almost normal.

'Oh, Megs, I think you're getting better!' I said. 'We've got the bed to ourselves because you've had the fever.' I felt her forehead. She was still very hot, and when I stroked her cheeks I could still feel the bumpy rash, but at least she was properly awake now.

'I like it, just you and me,' she said.

'I like it too, Megs,' I agreed.

We cuddled close and I sang the lullaby song again, over and over. Megs's head lolled against my arm, making it ache, but I didn't move. I lay still and clung on to her.

But in the morning . . . Oh, I can hardly bear to say it. I woke up and Megs was still in my arms, but she wasn't burning hot any more. She was cold and still. I shook her gently. I shook her harder. Then I clutched her close.

'Megs, Megs, oh, my Megs,' I cried, and I started sobbing.

The door opened and Pa and Mildred peered round it fearfully.

'No!' Pa groaned and covered his eyes.

'Oh my Lord.' Mildred started crying, though she'd ignored poor Megs all her short life.

The other children clamoured behind them, but Mildred pushed them away. 'Downstairs, now, this instant,' she commanded.

'But we want to see poorly Megs!' said Jenny.

'She's not here any more,' said Mildred. 'She's gone to join the angels in Heaven.'

'No, she's not,' said Richie. 'She's lying there in our bed – I can see her!'

'*I* want to see her,' said Pete, trying to thrust his head through Pa's legs.

'Get away, all of you. Do you want to get the fever too?' said Mildred.

'Yes, go away!' I cried, desperate to be left alone with

Megs so I could whisper to her and stroke her and beg her to come back to me.

'You must leave her be, Clover,' said Pa. 'You'll catch it off her.'

'You've already shut me up in that terrible cupboard for fear I'll catch it. I haven't *got* the fever and I don't care if I do have it anyway,' I sobbed. 'I'd sooner be dead now that Megs is gone.'

'Stop that dreadful talk. I've already lost your dear mother and now your poor little sister. You can't put me through any more heartache,' said Pa. 'Can't you talk sense into her, Mildred?'

'You know she never listens to a word I say,' she snapped. 'I've tried my best with her but she's too wayward, even for me. There now, Arthur. Don't take on so.' She put her big arms round him and let him cry on her shoulder like a baby. The sight of their embrace turned my stomach. How could Pa love that great hard lump of a woman? I knew my mother had been little and soft and gentle.

'You'll be meeting our real mother soon,' I whispered in Megs's ear when the rest of the family had at last retreated, Mildred sending Jenny off to fetch Mrs Wilkes at the end of the alley to do the laying out. 'You'll fly up to Heaven and the angels will reach their arms down through the clouds and haul you up. You'll be in this magical shining land, and Mother will coming running towards you and clasp you in her arms, so happy to see you.'

I tried to believe this myself, but that vision of a happy, carefree Megs was so different from the poor scrap of a girl lying on the bed, as still and stiff as one of Mr Dolly's wooden figures. I waited in dread for Mrs Wilkes to come, knowing she'd send me away. But I heard Jenny return home wailing.

'She says she can't come, Ma! She won't go near our Megs because of the fever. She says she's got five children of her own and daren't put them at risk,' she cried.

'Oh dear Lord, what are we going to do now?' Pa said, in despair.

Mildred went out herself to fetch a midwife who also did laying out, but she wouldn't come either.

'I'll have to do it myself then,' she said grimly. 'Though Lord knows how we'll bury her. I went into the undertaker's in Harrison Road and they won't come – they say they haven't got the right facilities.'

'So what are we supposed to do? Bury the poor little girl ourselves?' Pa cried.

'The Harrison Road lot said we'd have to go to Ernest Payne's in the High Street,' said Mildred. 'But they're just for the gentry – everyone in full black, with fine horses and coffins covered in flowers. They'll cost a fortune. We can't have them.'

'Then we'll have to pawn something,' said Pa. 'My Megs isn't going to have a pauper's funeral.'

'We haven't got anything worth pawning. I don't

know – what was all that fancy talk when we first met? You were certain to be foreman, you said, making out we were going to live like gentry. And now look at us, stuck in this hovel – seven kids and another on the way!'

'Six kids,' said Pa, and started weeping.

I listened to them squabbling, hating them. I put my hands over Megs's ears, though I knew she couldn't hear them.

'I wish *I* could pay for your funeral, Megs,' I whispered. I had my five shillings in Mr Dolly's purse, but I knew it wasn't enough for a proper funeral. 'You deserve the grandest funeral ever, with folk weeping on the pavement as your carriage trundles by, all shiny black and gleaming brass, drawn by horses with purple plumes.'

I lay talking to her, but all the while she grew colder and colder. I tried wrapping another blanket round her but it had no effect. I pulled the blanket up over my own head too, wanting to shut out the rest of the world, but I still heard the front door slamming and Mildred shouting and the children crying.

It was suffocating but I stayed there, as still as Megs, until, a long time later, I felt someone pulling at me, tearing off the blanket.

'Get up, Clover! Get up at once!' It was Mildred, hiding under her apron again. 'The funeral people are here to take Megs away. You must get out of bed this instant.'

I saw a man and a woman at the door. They were

dressed from head to toe in crow black, with strange veils over their faces.

'Say goodbye to your sister, dear,' the veiled woman said firmly.

I kissed Megs on her chilly forehead. She didn't feel like my soft little sister any more. She didn't even look like her now, with her eyes glazed and her mouth open. I had to leave her with them, and then watch as they carried her down the stairs, wrapped in white cloth. It covered her completely, but one small grubby foot lolled out underneath.

The other children were watching fearfully too, held back by Mildred. The girls clung to her, and little Bert sat astride her stomach, with Richie clutching her skirts – but Pete was bolder.

'I need to give Megs back her marble!' he said, starting to cry. 'She found it – a great green glass marble with gold swirls – but I wanted it so badly I took it from her and wouldn't let her have it back. I want her to have it now. Please wait while I find it.'

'She won't be needing any marble now, laddie,' said the man, and they made their way out of the door. He paused on the threshold. 'We'll be informing the public disinfectors, missus.'

'Please don't,' Mildred begged. 'There's no need. The two girls were kept separate. And I'll scrub the whole house from top to bottom, I swear I will. For pity's sake, don't tell them.'

'It's the law, missus. It's more than my job's worth to keep quiet. It's the Sanitary Act, see. You'll get fined or sent to prison if you don't let the disinfectors do their work,' he said.

'But we can't afford it! The funeral's going to cost a fortune as it is,' Mildred wailed. 'We're clean folk. I keep this house spotless. The fever didn't *start* here. The big girl brought it into the house and gave it to her sister.'

'Doesn't matter where it came from. The room where the little lassie lay has to be purified, and all the clothes and bedding taken off to the disinfecting oven, where they'll be thoroughly cleaned of infection before you can have them back. I dare say they'll be round some time after noon to start their task. Good day to you, missus. Please accept our sympathy for your sad bereavement.'

The black ghouls departed, but within three hours the public disinfectors arrived. I'd seen them before, when there was an outbreak of scarlet fever at the other end of the alley. That time I'd backed away from these ghostly men in white, pulling their sinister handcart behind them. It was difficult remembering that, underneath their white smocks and trousers, they were only ordinary working men. The little children thought they'd be shovelled into their carts, the lids slammed on them.

Mildred and some of the other mothers found this a

useful threat. 'You quit doing that or the infection men will come and catch you,' they said. I was big enough to know this was nonsense now, but I still trembled at the sight of them. They were more rough and ready than the funeral folk.

'Keep them kiddies well away!' they told Mildred gruffly. 'Where's the sick room?'

I knew what they were about to do. I ran up the stairs in front of them and tried to snatch Megs's discarded nightgown and her hair ribbon, desperate to keep them as mementoes, but they caught me before I could hide them.

'Don't be daft, miss. They're infectious. They all have to go in the disinfecting oven,' they said, snatching them from me with their soiled white gloves and then pushing me roughly from the room.

I heard them stripping the bed, gathering up all the clothes and pulling down the ragged curtains with two quick wrenches. When they came down the stairs I saw that one even had our old rag rug under one arm.

'You've taken everything!' Mildred protested. 'Look — there's trousers there belonging to the boys, and all the baby things. Those children never had the fever, only the one, little Megs.'

'It's all infected material and has to be fumigated,' they said gruffly. 'They're mostly rags anyhow.'

'How dare you! All the kids are decently clothed. What are they meant to do now, run round naked?'

'They'll get them back again in due course, once the room itself has been disinfected,' said one man.

This was even more of a trial. They lit a sulphur fire which had to burn for a full twenty-four hours. Mildred and Pa had to have the children crowded in with them again. I couldn't bear the thought of claiming a corner of their bed and slept in a chair downstairs, thinking of Megs. Her funeral had been fixed for the Friday, but to my horror Mildred said I couldn't go.

'None of you children will be attending,' she said. 'We can't afford to kit you all out in black, not with the expense of all this wretched disinfecting. We're going to have to whitewash everywhere before they'll even let us have your old kit back, and then it'll doubtless stink to high heaven.'

'I *have* to go! Megs is my sister! She meant far more to me than she did to you or Pa!' I declared.

'Hush now. Your pa and I have to go to the funeral because we're the parents. It wouldn't look decent if we didn't. Your pa will wear his good suit and I've got my black winter coat, and I dare say I'll find a scrap of black veiling to pin on my hat,' said Mildred.

'Can't I borrow your black coat and go instead?' I asked.

'Of course not. I'm her mother.'

'You're *not* her mother, that's the whole point. I don't think you cared about her at all. *I* loved her more than anybody so I should go. I *have* to go,' I insisted.

'Hold your tongue, Clover Moon! I did my best to

95

give little Megs a mother's love.' Mildred sighed senti-mentally.

'What lies!' I cried indignantly.

'I tried with you too, but you've always been contrary, contradicting every word I say! Who do you think you are, you uppity little madam? I wonder you're not crippled with guilt! If it wasn't for you being a busybody and minding that Watson baby then Megs would never have caught the fever,' Mildred hissed.

I flinched as if she'd spat acid at me. I wanted to run up to the bedroom and cry in private but it was all sealed up and stank of sulphur. I slammed out of the house instead.

In the alley the children were playing marbles – but not Jenny, Richie, Pete, Mary or little Bert. They were huddled up together at one end, heads down. I sat beside them, putting my arms around as many as I could.

'It's so sad, isn't it?' I said softly. 'I can't take it in, can you? But we must try to be happy for Megs, even though it's so terrible for us. She's with the angels now.'

'She's not with me!' protested little Angel from five doors along. 'She's not to come anywhere near me! My ma says I must keep away from all of you or she'll give me a whipping.'

'Yes, keep away – especially you, Clover. Our ma says you'll give us the fever,' Sukey shouted.

'I haven't *got* the wretched fever,' I said, but when I approached her she actually threw a stone at me.

She was only small but she had a good aim. It hit me on the temple, where my head was still sore from Mildred's blows. It hurt a lot, but my feelings were hurt even more. These children were my friends. I'd played with them since they were babies, telling them stories and making up games and giving them little treats, and yet now they were all turning on me as if I were a bogeyman.

Maybe I was. I didn't seem to catch the fever myself, but perhaps I simply passed it on to others. I stood up and stepped away from my siblings. Bert wailed and held up his arms, wanting a cuddle, but I didn't dare pick him up now.

'You look after him, Jenny, just in case,' I said.

I set off up the alley and into the street. I knew people here were unlikely to know about poor Megs and the fever, but it seemed as if they were backing away from me, dodging out of arm's reach, their heads turned. I started to think I was doomed to wander the streets alone for ever, with not a soul talking to me. I'd march on and on and on, day after day after day, until I reached the sea, and the three ships would sail away from me and I'd walk on though the waves while the fish swam away from me in terror.

I didn't know where I was walking, but my feet did. Down Winding Lane, round the marketplace, along the High Street, into Merchants Lane, past the draper's, the coffee shop, the stationer's, to Dolls Aplenty. But I didn't go in. I stayed outside, looking at the wooden dolls in the window. I stared until I could still see their black eyes and pink cheeks and red lips when I closed my eyes. I longed to shrink to doll size so that I could clamber in and pose with them, and be a stiff wooden creature without a heart.

7

THEN I HEARD THE tinkle of the shop bell and
Mr Dolly's gentle voice.

'Good day, Clover. Aren't you coming in to see me?'

I covered my mouth with my hands. 'I can't, Mr Dolly!
You mustn't come any nearer! I might infect you with
the fever!' I said urgently.

'My dear child! What are you talking about?'

'It's true. There's scarlet fever in our alley. Little baby

Tommy died of it, and I was looking after him, and our Megs dressed up in his shawl and she caught it too – and now . . . now Megs has died and I don't see how I can manage without her!'

'Oh, my poor child,' said Mr Dolly, and he came right out of the door, limping towards me.

'Please get back! I couldn't bear it if I gave it to you too,' I said.

'Have you any symptoms of the fever yourself, Clover?' Mr Dolly asked urgently. 'Do you feel hot? Do you have a headache or a sore throat? My Lord, what's that dreadful gash on your forehead?'

'That's nothing to do with the fever, that's just where Mildred hit me,' I said.

'That dreadful stepmother? Why doesn't your father protect you?'

'He doesn't see her do it.'

'He must know! He's got eyes in his head, hasn't he?'

'Yes, but he doesn't want to know,' I said. 'Mr Dolly, I must go. I shouldn't have come here.'

'You must come inside and let me look after you. I'm pretty sure you *don't* have the fever – and it's not of enormous consequence to me if you do. I'm old now. I've lived enough life already.'

'But what if children come to your shop with their parents or nursemaid to choose a doll? Couldn't they catch it if I've been inside?'

'I doubt it – but perhaps you're wise to be cautious. Well then, we'll take a little walk together where no children go. I'm not sending you away while you're in such distress. Wait here a moment. Promise you won't run away?'

He dodged back inside his shop, and after a minute returned with a big yellow silk scarf patterned with orange stripes.

'There we are,' he said, turning his shop sign to CLOSED and locking the door. 'I've never taken to this scarf. Too fancy by half. So you pop it round your face like a flamboyant little highwayman so there's no possibility of spreading any germs and we'll toddle off.'

'But you can't close your shop now. You might miss another customer like Mr Rivers,' I protested.

'I don't think there will ever be another Mr Rivers,' said Mr Dolly. 'I haven't had a single customer in the shop today. The last purchase was on Saturday, and that was a penny doll's-house doll. Now tie the scarf and come along.'

I did as I was told.

'You wear that scarf with style, dear. If you had a pistol in your pocket I'm sure you could make your fortune,' said Mr Dolly.

'I *need* a fortune,' I said sadly. 'Megs is having a grand funeral on Friday but Mildred won't let me go because I haven't anything black. Do you think my five shillings would be enough to purchase a set of mourning clothes? Just a hat and a dress and a coat – and maybe a pair of black boots, because the soles of my old brown ones are flapping. I daren't go to the second-hand stall because that's how poor Mrs Watson's baby caught the fever – from the shawl she bought there.'

'You could buy a plain black bonnet, but it wouldn't stretch to a coat, let alone a frock and new boots. Can't you dye an outfit black, dear?' Mr Dolly asked.

'I haven't really *got* an outfit, not one that's suitable,' I said, too embarrassed to explain that I simply had the ragged dress I stood up in. The only other garment I could call my own was my nightgown, and that had been confiscated by the disinfectors.

'Well, we'll have to put our thinking caps on,' said Mr Dolly.

He scratched his head as if he were wearing one already, not looking right or left so as not to catch anyone's eye. His wore his white hair past his shoulders, and his faded scarlet velvet cloak seemed more suitable for opera-going, so folk might well have stared even if he hadn't had his huge hump. He was a very small man to start with, and his crooked back made him hunch over and lean heavily on his carved cane.

Uncouth little boys called after him, and adults muttered horrid words and imitated his jerky gait. Mr Dolly took no notice, walking as briskly as he could in his black patent boots. I hurried along beside him, hoping he hadn't seen or heard them, though that seemed impossible. When we reached the marketplace some hateful urchin threw a rotten tomato at his back. Mr Dolly turned as best he could, shook the tomato disdainfully off his cloak and carried on walking.

'It's very fortunate that both the missile and the cloak are red,' he murmured. 'The stain shouldn't be very noticeable.'

I burned for him. I seized my own tomato from the gutter, turned towards the laughing boy and aimed. I caught him full in the face, which was very satisfying.

Mr Dolly tutted at me, but he still smiled. 'I think I should take you with me for protection every time I go for a stroll, Clover. I had no inkling you had such devastating aim!' he said.

'I thought you said we were going somewhere quiet.'

'We are, my dear. Come with me.' He led me down the lane from the marketplace and then up the steep slope towards the great grey church of St Anne's, with its strange coloured windows and long thin spire.

'I thought you weren't a religious man, Mr Dolly,' I said.

'You're right, Clover. I have no faith, but that doesn't mean I don't find solace in a churchyard.' Mr Dolly was panting with the effort of climbing the hill. He leaned even more heavily on his stick.

'Perhaps you might hold on to my shoulder while the

road is so steep?' I suggested. 'Though I'm scared I might contaminate you.'

'I told you, dear, I don't mind the thought of dying,' Mr Dolly wheezed, standing still to catch his breath. 'It's a shame I am not a churchgoer. It would be pleasant to believe in a carefree eternal life in Heaven.'

'Do you find your own life so very hard?' I asked.

'I'm used to it now, but when I was your age I was very unhappy.' Mr Dolly spoke calmly, though there were tears in his eyes. We went through the lych gate and walked between the great yew trees. He sat down gratefully on an old wooden bench and struggled to catch his breath.

'My parents were ashamed of me and sent me away to school when I was very young,' he said, wiping his eyes with a handkerchief.

'Ashamed? Because – because of . . . ?'

'Because I was born a hunchback,' said Mr Dolly matter-of-factly.

'How cruel and stupid of them!' I declared.

'Perhaps. But I received a good education and a love of learning. It was a relatively humane establishment. It was the other boys who were the problem. If I'd had your fiery spirit I'd have fared much better. I was too meek and craven. I always longed to find a friend.'

'*I'm* your friend, Mr Dolly,' I told him. 'You're my best friend now that Megs isn't here.' I started crying too.

'Oh dear, forgive me for being such a self-pitying old

fool. I'm snivelling over times long gone while you're going through fresh agonies,' said Mr Dolly, passing me his handkerchief.

It was a struggle to wipe my nose while wearing the yellow silk scarf.

'Take it off now.' Mr Dolly felt my forehead, looking carefully at my face. 'You seem healthy enough to me, though that cut will be a while healing. If there really is an afterlife I can't see that stepmother of yours growing wings. She'll be writhing down below, with all the other wretched devils.'

'If only my own mother hadn't died,' I said.

'Can you remember her, Clover?'

'Yes. She was good and kind and sweet and gentle. At least, I think she was. I seem to remember her holding me in her arms, singing to me. But perhaps that's just fancy. I make up so many things and they seem so real that it's hard remembering what's true and what isn't. Yet when something terribly true happens, like Megs dying, it doesn't seem real at all. There's a part of me that thinks she'll be back at home, sucking her thumb on the doorstep, waiting for me.'

Mr Dolly waited patiently beside me as I willed it to be true. I could see Megs stroking her nose as she sucked her thumb. I saw her short straggly hair sticking up at the back where she'd lain on it. I saw the patches in her pale print frock. I saw her skinny, mottled legs, scabs on

105

the knees because she fell over so frequently. I saw her old brown boots, both soles flapping so they could no longer be padded with newspaper. But as soon as I thought of her boots I remembered that little grubby foot dangling.

Mr Dolly waited until I had stopped sobbing.

'I'll miss her so,' I said. 'Did you have a special sister, Mr Dolly?'

I wondered if he'd made dolls for her when they were children. Perhaps they played games together, and that was why he understood girls and their concerns so perfectly.

'No, I had brothers,' said Mr Dolly, in the tone he'd used for the boys at his school. 'But when I was grown up I always longed for a little girl.'

'Were you ever married?'

'It's hardly likely, is it, my dear,' said Mr Dolly sadly.

'If I were older I would want to marry you, Mr Dolly,' I said. 'You're the loveliest man I've ever met.'

'I shall treasure that remark until my dying day.'

I looked about me at the old tombstones, so moss-covered you couldn't read who lay underneath.

'Will Megs be buried here?' I whispered.

'I think the new graves are behind the church.'

'She won't like it at all. She'll be so lonely. I'll have to come and visit her every day,' I vowed.

'Is your mother buried here?'

'I don't know. Pa's never taken me to see her. He'll rarely talk about her.'

'Shall we take a little stroll and see? Then we can imagine her looking after your sister when she's laid to rest here.'

This was such a comforting idea that I ran up and down the rows of recent gravestones at the back of the churchyard reading every one. I hoped Mother would have a beautiful white marble angel spreading her wings above her grave, or even a small cherub. But when I eventually found her I saw that she didn't even have a proper gravestone with an elaborately carved loving message. She had a small flat rectangular stone inscribed with her name, Margaret Moon, the date of her birth and the date of her death.

'Oh!' I said, thrilled to have found her but horrified to see such a paltry memorial stone. It was almost like a gravestone for one of Mr Dolly's penny specials.

I knelt down, trying to work out the shape of Mother's coffin underneath.

'Do you think there might be room to bury Megs here?' I asked Mr Dolly.

'I should think so.'

'I need to be there for her funeral! Then I can ask the men who dig the grave. I *must* be there – but I can't turn up in this ragged dress,' I said, plucking at it in despair.

'I'll see what I can do, dear,' said Mr Dolly. 'When is the funeral?'

'On Friday.'

'Then come and visit me on Thursday. I'm not promising I can work a miracle, but I'll do my best,' he said.

'You are the kindest man in the whole world,' I said fervently.

I didn't quite know what he was proposing. Was he hoping that another customer like Mr Rivers would miraculously appear? But even if he did, Mr Dolly needed every penny of the sale himself. I'd seen the bills piling up by his cash box, noticed the gaps in the tiles on the shop roof, shivered in his damp unheated rooms. He was as poor as my own family, maybe even poorer.

I had every faith in Mr Dolly, but all the same I decided not to be too hopeful. Instead I busied myself tidying Mother's grave, pulling up weeds and brambles, not caring when my hands got scratched. I saw that other mourners had left vases of flowers on top of their loved one's grave.

I decided that no one would really mind too much if I took one small flower out of each arrangement. I gathered them quickly, adding daisies and buttercups growing wild in the tussocky grass. I found an old ginger ale bottle tossed into the shrubbery. It wasn't quite right for a vase, but it was the best I could do. I filled it with rainwater from a pail and then set my purloined bouquet in front of Mother's meagre gravestone.

'There, dear. That looks very pretty,' said Mr Dolly.

I didn't want to go home again. When we got back to Dolls Aplenty Mr Dolly invited me in, but I was still worried about polluting his shop with germs. I dawdled on the way home, keeping my scarf over my nose, though folk stared. I pretended I was a real highwayman and selected people at random, pointing two fingers at them in place of a pistol.

Your money or your life! I shouted inside my head, and soon collected imaginary fistfuls of silver, enough to provide mourning outfits for the whole family. I even kitted out little Bert in a black dress and coat and tiny black button boots. We could attend the funeral and mourn Megs in appropriate style. I could also afford to take a white silk dress with matching silk slippers to the undertaker's so that Megs could be dressed like a little angel.

But when I turned into our alley all my imaginings seeped out of my head. I looked at our doorstep, where Megs had always sat. It was empty.

The sight was so painful that I doubled up as if I'd been punched in the stomach.

There was a sudden clatter on the cobbles and Jimmy Wheels bowled up to me. 'Have you got the bellyache, Clover?' he asked.

I straightened up slowly, shaking my head. 'I'm just sad, Jimmy,' I mumbled.

'Because your Megs is dead?' Jimmy was used to

siblings dying. His ma had tried to have a healthy child but none had made it much past babyhood.

I nodded. 'I don't suppose your ma has any mourning clothes she could lend me?' I asked hopefully, though Jimmy's mother was twice my size.

'She hasn't got any now. She pawned them after the last baby died. She can't bear to go to funerals no more,' said Jimmy. 'Why have you got that snot rag tied round your face, Clover?'

'So I can't give anyone the fever,' I said.

'Have you got it then?' Jimmy bravely propelled himself forward and peered up at me. 'Can't see any red rash.'

'I think I must be all right,' I said. 'What about Mrs Watson and her little girl? Did they get the fever too?'

'Can't say. They've gone away. She had the hysterics when the infection men took all the baby's clothes so her old man packed her off to relatives in the country. Don't even know if they'll be back for the funeral. So when's your Megs getting buried then?'

'Friday. I don't even know if I'll be going because I haven't got any black clothes, though Mr Dolly says he'll try to help me,' I said.

'Mr who?'

'Well, he's Mr Fisher really. The man who makes all the dolls. He has a shop in Market Street. Have you ever been that far?' I asked, because I'd only ever seen Jimmy scooting up and down our alley.

'Do me a favour!' he said indignantly. 'I've been all over, even up west with all the toffs. I heard tales and wanted to see what it was like for myself. Made a fortune that day too. Some old girl took pity on the poor little crippled boy and gave me sixpence when I wasn't even asking for it. So I asked all sorts and they coughed up royally. Had to stick all the cash down my jumper, and it didn't half dig in during the long trek home. Still, I wasn't complaining. Of course I know the Dolls Aplenty man. He made me my chariot.' He thumped the sides of his wheeled board proudly.

'Mr Dolly did?'

'Yep, before that Ma used to drag me about in an old pram and I hated it because I felt like such a baby. She used to park me outside his shop window when she did her errands, so's I had something to look at. The bloke with the crooked back used to come out of his shop and chat to me. Then one day he gave Ma this piece of wood, all smoothed and varnished, with wheels at all four corners. "See if your Jimmy takes a shine to this," he says. "It'll give him a bit of independence." So we tried it out when we got home and I was off, like a dog after a rat. Don't know what I'd do without it now,' he said.

'He's a lovely man, my Mr Dolly,' I said.

'Yeah, he is. Me and Ma think the world of him now,' said Jimmy Wheels.

If only Mildred felt the same way!

The house was empty when I got home.

'She's gone off down the park with all the kids because they were driving her mad cooped up indoors, and we're not allowed to play with them in the alley,' Sukey told me importantly. 'We're not allowed to play with you either, Clover.'

'That's stupid. I haven't got the fever. And even if I *had*, you couldn't catch it from me because I've got this scarf on, see?' I said.

I kept Mr Dolly's scarf tied over my nose even inside the house because it still stank of sulphur. It smelled of burning too. Mildred hadn't put enough liquid in the stewpot and it had started to blacken. I added water and flour for thickening, fished out the worst of the burned mutton and cut off the crusty bits. I fried up a couple of onions too to give the stew a bit more flavour. Mildred was a hopeless cook.

She wasn't the slightest bit grateful when she came home, the children straggling behind her.

'You been cooking onions?' she said, sniffing. 'I was saving them to fry up with a bit of bacon for your father. You're always interfering, Clover. Where have you been all day anyway, leaving me to cope with everything when you know I'm poorly?' She rubbed her swollen stomach significantly.

I slumped at the table. The children came and stood near me, still a little wary. I reached out my arms for Bert, and he allowed Jenny to place him on my lap, though he didn't snuggle up to me as usual. I looked at each and every one of my brothers and sisters. I cared for them all, especially baby Bert, but none of them were anywhere near as dear to me as Megs.

The boys were joshing each other, squabbling over some silly stick they'd found, and Jenny and Mary were playing a complicated clapping game. I couldn't credit it. Weren't they missing Megs at all? I didn't have the energy to be angry with them. I bent my head so they couldn't see the tears in my eyes.

Perhaps Mildred saw. She was still patting her stomach as if trying to soothe the baby inside. 'Tell you what,' she said. 'If this baby's a girl we'll call it Megs.'

I knew she was trying to be kind to me for once. I also knew I hated the idea. Megs was the name of my own dear sister, taken away from us and still not even buried.

'We're not calling any new baby that!' I said. 'It's *Megs's* name.'

'Suit yourself,' said Mildred huffily. 'Well, don't just sit there like a wet weekend. Get the table laid and them kiddies washed – they're all over mud from the park. And I'm sure our Bert needs changing.'

Bert was indeed feeling very soggy. He was starting to relax, though he still didn't seem very sure I was his old Clover. He reached up and started pulling at my scarf with his chubby hand.

'No, Bert, she has to leave it on for a few days, just in case,' said Mildred. Then she peered more closely. 'What is it you've got wrapped round your face?'

'A pair of bloomers,' I said irritably, and the children giggled.

'Don't try to be smart with me, miss.'

'Well, it's a scarf, obviously, so I can't give any of the children the fever, though I keep *telling* you, I haven't got it,' I snapped.

'It's not your scarf though.' Mildred had been keeping her distance from me, but now she came up close. 'It's silk, that is. Where did you get a gaudy gentleman's handkerchief like that? You didn't nick it out of some old boy's pocket, did you?'

'No I blooming well didn't!' I protested.

'So how did you get it?'

'Someone lent it to me,' I muttered.

'Someone! It was that horrid old hunchback, wasn't it?' Mildred said triumphantly. 'That doll man.'

'He's not horrid. He's the kindest, loveliest gentleman ever!'

'He gives me the creeps. Haven't I told you to keep away from him? You're asking for another hiding,' said Mildred. She had the large ladle in her hand and looked ready to strike me with it.

'Don't you dare!' I said fiercely. 'There's already folk wanting to report you for bashing me about the head with that brass thimble.'

'I've a right to discipline my own child,' she said.

'But I'm not *your* child, and I'm so glad I'm not too. I hate you, Mildred Moon,' I said recklessly.

The other children stared at me round-eyed and then looked at Mildred, waiting for her to attack me.

She shook her head, her mouth open. 'That's all you can say? That you hate me? After all I've done for you! I've fed you and clothed you and taught you and corrected you and wasted whole weeks of my life arguing with you, and that's the gratitude I get!' Mildred peered around at the other children. 'Do you hear that? This is how she repays me!'

'It's your own fault I hate you,' I said. 'You've been so cruel to me.'

'You wicked girl! Am I cruel, like she says?' she asked the children. 'Or am I a kind, loving mother who only wants the best for all of you?'

They blinked at her.

'You're a kind, loving mother,' Jenny blurted.

'Thank you, Jenny,' said Mildred.

'Kind mother,' Mary echoed quickly. 'And loving – I forgot loving.'

'Kind and loving mother,' said Pete and Richie in unison.

And even little Bert joined in. 'Muvver! Muvver!' he said.

Mildred smiled triumphantly. 'You see, Clover?'

I saw that the children were scared of her and willing to parrot any nonsense, but there was no point arguing. I badly wanted Megs beside me, slipping her hand in mine, showing me she was on my side.

I held on to Bert, but when Pete and Richie went back to arguing about their stick he wriggled to be set free so that he could lay claim to it too. During the few days I'd been locked in the cupboard under the stairs he seemed to have stopped being a baby and become a little boy. He didn't really need me any more. Nobody needed me now. I didn't have any full blood relatives left, apart from Pa.

He was late getting home from work, and when he eventually arrived he smelled of beer. He wasn't usually a heavy-drinking man, stopping after a tankard or two, but tonight his voice was slurred, his steps unsteady. He didn't feel like eating and spurned the boiled mutton, not even fancying Mildred's bacon.

She was annoyed and nagged him, telling him he was a selfish drunken sot wasting good money on beer when the family had only pennies to live on.

'For pity's sake, hold your tongue,' Pa moaned, clasping his head. 'I'm grieving, can't you see? I've lost my little girly, my own sweet Megs.'

'Oh, Pa,' I said, rushing to him and flinging my arms round his neck. 'Don't worry. *I* understand. I'm missing her so much too.'

He pulled me on to his lap and held me close. It was years since he'd held me like that and it felt so good and comforting.

'Don't you go making a fuss of that wicked girl,' said Mildred furiously. 'She's been impossible today, flouncing off without so much as a by-your-leave, then coming back here and yelling abuse at me. She deserves a whipping.'

'Stop shouting, woman, you're making my head ache,' said Pa. 'And don't be so hard on our Clover. She's got a loving heart and it's broken in two because she's lost her sister.'

I took hold of his hand and squeezed it tight.

'There now, pet,' he said. 'Bless you for wearing that scarf. It's a shame to hide that pretty face but I suppose we can't be too careful.'

'It's not *her* kerchief. She's been hanging around that nasty crookback doll-maker yet again, after all I've told her,' Mildred exploded.

'Oh, Clover!' said Pa reproachfully. 'You're not to spend your time with the likes of him. He fills your head with all sorts of nonsense. What sort of man is he anyway, making dollies for little girls? Now, you're to be a good girl and stay in the alley where your mother can keep an eye on you.'

'She's not *my* mother,' I said.

'Quit that,' said Pa, and he tipped me off his lap.

8

PA WENT OFF ME after that. I couldn't do anything right. He wouldn't change his mind about my going to the funeral.

'You can't go, not if you haven't got the right clothes. You'll shame us,' he said.

'I might be able to get proper clothes,' I said.

'Don't talk daft. And stop nagging at me in that shrill voice. You're staying at home minding the little ones while your mother and I are at the funeral,' he said. 'And if you say another word against her I'll give you a good hiding.'

I held my tongue but inside my head I was making plans. On Thursday I started up a game of hide and seek in the alley. The other children were allowed to play with us now that we still seemed to be in good health. Sukey and the twins and Angel and Jimmy Wheels and Daft Mo all joined in, though Mo never really got the hang of it. When it was his turn to hide he simply pulled up his shirt and hid his head, thinking that if he couldn't see us then somehow we wouldn't be able to see him. He didn't seem to mind being tagged straight away so it didn't matter.

I waited until they were all absorbed in the game, and Jenny was the seeker. She was always slow at finding anyone, especially hampered by Bert, who had chosen her as his pair of arms for the day. He was behaving like a saucy lad with two eager lady friends, playing Jenny and me off against each other.

Normally I felt hurt when he rejected me, but now it suited me. As soon as everyone else had hidden themselves in doorways and behind coal bunkers and the boys had hitched themselves up a drainpipe on to our roof, I ran quietly down the alleyway. Pete and Richie spotted me from their rooftop and cried out, but I didn't turn round. I ran out of the alley and into the street. Then I went on running, making for Mr Dolly's.

I hoped the boys wouldn't tell on me straight away. Sooner or later the children would realize I wasn't hiding. There would be a hue and cry and Mildred would find out. She'd know in an instant where I'd gone, and doubtless I'd get another hiding, but I didn't really care. The worst thing in the world had happened to me and nothing else could hurt me as much.

I was out of breath when I reached Dolls Aplenty. I didn't even pause to look at the window, though I saw there was a new display of dolls in a schoolroom setting. I burst straight in through the shop door – and then saw that Mr Dolly had a customer, a stout young mother in very unbecoming bright violet, with an even stouter small daughter in sickly pink, with pink kid boots to match. She had obviously spent last night in curl-papers because her hair was in tight glossy ringlets. She shook her head constantly to show them off.

Mr Dolly smiled at me but held up one finger to show he had to attend to his customers before he could talk to me. They took a very long time, wanting to examine practically every doll in the shop, even demanding that Mr Dolly disrupt his window display to let them examine each 'pupil' and the schoolteacher herself.

Mr Rivers had been almost as exacting, but he had been very polite and was simply trying to find the most perfect present for his daughter. Perhaps Mrs Violet Dress was intent on doing the same, but little Miss

Sickly Pink didn't seem particularly interested in anything, saying that she didn't really care for old-fashioned wooden dolls, and would much prefer a proper French china doll with a trousseau of silk dresses.

'Ah, but I have fine china dolls too, little missy,' said Mr Dolly politely, though he caught my eye for a second, making it plain what he really thought of spoiled Sickly Pink.

He brought out Hyacinth and Violet and sat them side by side on the counter, but the child still wasn't impressed.

'Their dresses are the wrong colours,' she said, shaking her ringlets dismissively. 'I want them to have pink dresses exactly like mine.'

I wondered if she wanted the dolls to increase in girth and sprout ringlets from their china heads too. There was clearly no pleasing her, even when Mr Dolly produced a pink silk doll's dress from a drawer and assured her it would fit either doll.

'I dare say it would, but can't you see it's entirely the wrong shade of pink?' she said pertly.

'Oh, bless you, Araminta!' said her mama fondly. 'The child is so exacting. She's got such style already.'

I thought Araminta had the exact opposite of style. I snorted before I could stop myself.

Mrs Violet Dress glanced over her shoulder at me, looking pained. 'Mind your manners, little girl!' she said sharply.

I knew I should bob her a curtsy and say sorry but I didn't feel like it. Instead I looked over at the shelf of dolls, pursing my lips and pretending to whistle.

'Insolent little brat!' she said, catching hold of Araminta by her satin skirts and pulling her close as if I might contaminate her. If she knew I'd been in contact with the fever she'd expire on the spot.

'No, no, that's my dear friend Clover. She's a tremendous help to me,' said Mr Dolly.

'You befriend street children?' said Mrs Violet Dress. 'Dear, dear, I think we had better leave straight away, Araminta.'

They swept out, skirts rustling, Araminta's ringlets flying up and down.

'I'm so sorry, Mr Dolly,' I said, hanging my head. 'Oh dear, I've cost you a customer, and clearly a rich one too.'

'I don't want that horrid woman's money. And that child was such a spoiled madam I'm sure she'd never have chosen any of my dolls. But never mind those two creatures. How are you, my dear? Still well? No signs of fever or rash?'

'No, none,' I said.

'I'm so relieved! You do feel well, don't you? You look very wan.' Mr Dolly looked at my face anxiously.

'I have an ache here,' I said, touching my chest. I'd been dimly aware of it for some days. It was like a constriction. At night it was sometimes hard to breathe.

'Mr Dolly, do you think I have something wrong with my heart?'

'Yes, I do,' he said gravely.

'Is it failing?' I asked, frightened.

'It's not failing. It's broken, my dear. I know just how much that little sister meant to you. But you are young and in time your heart will mend, I promise you.'

'I'm not going to forget Megs though, not ever,' I said.

'Of course you're not. And are you still sure you want to attend her funeral?' asked Mr Dolly.

'Of course, but Mildred and Pa forbid it. I can't see why it matters so much that I haven't got the right clothes. They say it wouldn't be respectful but I think that's nonsense,' I declared.

'I do too – but I've done my best to make sure you can go,' said Mr Dolly. 'Come with me.'

He led me behind the counter, opened the door to his workshop and pointed upwards. I saw all his half-finished dolls pegged to the line, but there was also a padded hook at the end of the row, with a set of clothes swinging from it. It was an outfit too large for even the biggest doll but too small even for little Mr Dolly. A black outfit. A wondrously cut, seemingly brand-new, black cord coat with brass buttons, with a black cotton frock to go underneath and even knitted black stockings. On the floor underneath was a pair of soft black boots.

'Oh, Mr Dolly!' I cried, and I burst into tears.

'There now, I think those poor pink eyes of yours are sore enough already,' he said, finding me yet another handkerchief.

It was harder than ever to stop – now I was howling with gratitude as well as grief. I only stopped sobbing when Mr Dolly made us both a pot of tea and forced me to take a few sips from his proffered cup.

'I wish I had cake to offer you, my dear, but perhaps you'd fancy a slice of bread and butter?'

I shook my head, but he insisted. 'In fact, I'll make you two. You've always been a slight child, but now you're desperately thin,' he said, circling my wrist with his bony fingers. 'Look at you! I'll swear you've got smaller wrists than most of my dolls.'

I was worried I was depriving him of his supper, but the bread and butter tasted wonderful. I'd hardly eaten since Megs died. When I'd finished the last mouthful I wiped my fingers very carefully on Mr Dolly's handkerchief and went to examine my funeral outfit.

'How did you magic it, Mr Dolly?' I asked in awe, stroking the fine black cord. 'Are they brand new?'

'Oh yes, my dear. I went straight to Whiteley's of Bayswater and asked them to supply me with their very best mourning outfit,' said Mr Dolly. He chuckled when he saw that I believed him. '*I* made them, Clover. Long ago I used to wear a voluminous black cape, but then I had an unfortunate encounter with a bunch of lads who thought it hysterically funny to throw a can of pigswill at my back. The cape was ruined, though I sponged it all evening.'

'Oh, Mr Dolly, how dreadful!'

'Ah well, such things happen. Especially to me. And perhaps it was just as well, because I did rather resemble a huge black bat when I was wearing it. Anyway, I salvaged what I could and occasionally used it to make a sturdy coat or cloak for one of my dolls. It was a little tricky fashioning a pattern for you, dear, as I didn't have your measurements, but I took a guess and I think it will fit quite well. I cut you a fancy beret too. I thought you'd prefer it to a conventional bonnet – I'm not much of a milliner in any case.'

'And the dress and the stockings and the boots?' I asked breathlessly.

'The dress was a simple cotton print from a bolt of material I use for my standard penny doll. I simply steeped it in a ha'p'orth of black dye – that, and the felt I've used for your boots. They're very flimsy, I'm afraid. Let's hope it doesn't rain tomorrow. I've made the soles from the stoutest cardboard I could find.'

'And the stockings?' I touched them, looking at the even stitches. 'Did you make the stockings yourself, Mr Dolly?'

'Oh, they were the easiest task. I'm used to tiny needles and knitting with silk thread for many pairs of little wooden feet. It was a joy to use real needles and two-ply wool. I must say I'm proud of my knitting skills. Look how finely I've turned those heels,' said Mr Dolly, holding a stocking in either hand and making them twirl comically.

'You must have worked day and night on my outfit,' I said.

'Well, I must say it's just as well my dolls are made of wood, else many would be shivering by now. They've been waiting days to be decently clad.'

'You are the dearest, kindest, loveliest man in the whole world,' I said, and I reached up and kissed him on either cheek. 'These clothes are worth fifty shillings, not five!'

'No, no, the five shillings is still yours, Clover. The clothes are a gift. I shall be highly offended if you insist otherwise,' said Mr Dolly.

He packed up the clothes in brown paper, folding them neatly over the beautifully fashioned felt boots so that the parcel wasn't too bulky. I still didn't know how to get it home without Mildred spotting it.

She'd guess that Mr Dolly had made me my outfit and stop me wearing it. She seemed determined to prevent me going to the funeral. I needed to hide the clothes and then put them on secretly in the morning. I planned to run to the church by myself, and skulk at the back if necessary. Mildred could hardly make a scene at the actual burial. She couldn't start shrieking at me while poor Megs's coffin was being lowered into the earth. So where, where, where could I hide my precious parcel of clothes?

I used to have hiding places in our bedroom. I'd stow things behind the curtain or tuck them amongst Bert's baby blankets or stuff them in an old cushion. But the infection men had taken the curtains, the blankets, the cushion. Our bedroom was bleak and bare.

I couldn't think of anywhere downstairs to hide the parcel. I wondered about the privy, but it was so dark and disgusting out there, and the floor was often wet. I could try the yard, but what if it rained in the night?

I was so wrapped up in my worries that I didn't look where I was going. I stepped on something small and skittery, and then something bigger that started squealing.

'Oi! Watch where you're going, Clover Moon!' It was Jimmy Wheels, who had been quietly playing marbles by himself until I'd blundered into him. 'I'll have a blooming great bruise on my side now from where you kicked me!'

'I'm so sorry, Jimmy. I didn't see you,' I said, squatting down beside him.

'What's that you've got in that parcel?' he asked.

'Oh, just some butcher's meat for tomorrow,' I said quickly.

'That's never butcher's meat.' Jimmy gave it a poke. His finger was sharp and the paper tore a little. 'That's clothes,' he said. 'Black clothes. For your Megs's funeral.'

'Ssh!' I said, peering around to see if any of the other children were lurking. 'Mildred mustn't find out. She doesn't want me to go.'

'So where did you get them then?'

'Stole them,' I said.

'You never!'

'Yep – I went to some other child's funeral and there was this girl all dressed up in black, and I waited till they were all praying and jumped on her, hand over her mouth to stop her squealing, and took her in the bushes and tore off all her clothes and bundled them up for myself,' I said.

'My legs might not be any good, but my brain's in full working order,' said Jimmy, laughing. 'You got them from the Dolls Aplenty man, didn't you?'

'Yes, I did – but you won't tell, will you?'

'Cut my throat if I do,' said Jimmy, miming it.

'Trouble is, I don't know where to hide them. If Mildred sees them she'll snatch them off me and I'll doubtless end up in that blooming cupboard again,' I said.

'Give them to me. I'll stow them with my stuff,' said Jimmy.

'Would you really? Won't your ma find them?'

'She'd not say a word. She doesn't like Mildred any more than you do. Ma don't think it's fair – she's got all the love in the world and she's only got half a child to give it to, and Mildred's got a whole houseful of kids and doesn't seem to care for any of them. I'm glad she's not *my* ma.'

'Well, she's not mine either. You wait, Jimmy. I'll be out of here soon enough,' I vowed.

'Good on you, Clover. Give us these clothes then. And what will you do – come calling for them tomorrow?'

'The minute Mildred and Pa leave for the funeral I'll rush over to yours. They'll be going the long way round in the funeral carriage, and they always go slow to show respect. I'll nip along the back alleys and be at the church first.'

'That's the ticket, Clover. You show them,' said Jimmy.

I handed my precious parcel over. He clutched it carefully to his side and wheeled himself off to his house. His ma had fashioned a little ramp out of a plank of wood and nailed it to the front step, so as long as Jimmy gathered enough speed he could wheel himself up and in through the open door.

I was scared of entering my own front door. The children had stopped playing hide and seek ages ago, and were now lolling about the house, with Mildred snapping at them, giving the boys a clout about the head for good measure.

She glared at me. 'Where did you get to then, Clover? The kids said you just disappeared. They've been up and down the alley calling for you. Did you go and see that doll man even though I expressly forbade it?' she demanded, her fist clenching.

I opened my eyes wide in an expression of innocence. 'Of course not. I went for a walk by myself because I was feeling so sad about Megs,' I told her. 'I ended up at the church and I went inside and tried to say a prayer.'

'Don't give me that rubbish,' said Mildred, but she looked disconcerted, almost as if she believed me.

I told the same story to Pa when he came home from the factory, reeking of drink again. He nodded blearily, seemingly fond of me again. I nestled close to him and told him I'd been to the church.

'And I found where my mother's buried,' I whispered in his ear. 'Pa, could our Megs be buried there too? There's not much room but she's only little. Please ask if Megs can be squeezed in beside her.'

Pa nodded. 'I thought of it before you did, Clover. I've already given my instructions to the funeral director. Megs is to be buried in our family plot, as it were. They say she might have to be put atop your ma, but I figure neither would mind that, eh?'

'Oh, Pa, that would be even better!' I gave him a big hug, not minding the smell of drink now. 'You're the best pa in the world!'

'And you're the best girl,' said Pa. His voice was slurred but still distinct.

Jenny and Mary had been trying to persuade Bert to walk, but now they let go of him. They frowned at Pa, while Bert sat down hard on his padded bottom and complained bitterly.

Mildred's face contorted. 'You're all best girls,' she said, evenly enough, but the look she threw me was venomous.

I'd always known she disliked me. I would have to have been a fool not to realize this. When I was small she smacked me frequently, and these days attacked me even more violently. I fingered the wound on my forehead. She hadn't hurt me simply because she wanted to teach me a lesson or thought me a bad child. She actively hated me.

It made me shiver inside. I knew there was nothing I could do. I could behave as meekly as possible, forever doing her bidding, but she'd still go on hating, simply because I was me. Of course, I hated her too, but it still seemed shocking that my stepmother clearly wished me as dead as poor Megs.

I thought of the big book of fairy tales that Mr Dolly had read to me in instalments between customers. I loved the story of Snow White best of all, fascinated by the seven little dwarfs who cared for her so devotedly. There was a colour plate of all seven – small, smiling, hunched over men in strange outfits, very much like Mr Dolly himself. I wanted to look like Snow White. We both had hair as black as coal, but the girl in the picture had pearly skin, full lips as red as cherries, and a beautiful blue silk gown. My face was sallow, my lips were thin and colourless, and my dress was in tatters.

Now I turned Mildred into Snow White's wicked stepmother. It was easy enough. I could just imagine her commanding a woodcutter to take me into the woods to cut out my heart. I saw her buying the rosiest apple in the market, injecting it with the deadliest poison, and then tempting me with it.

I didn't know what to do. I didn't have a handsome prince to come to my rescue. I had to rescue myself, but I didn't know how.

9

THE NEXT DAY I woke early, before anyone else was stirring. I crept downstairs and out to the privy, and then stripped off my nightgown and washed myself thoroughly at the tap, even my tangled hair, using a handful of Mildred's carbolic washing crystals. They stung my skin and the water was icy, but I was determined to be spotless for Megs's funeral.

I hated putting my dirty old dress back on, but I had no choice. I was as helpful as I could be, suddenly terrified that Mildred might push me back in the cupboard for no reason. I got the range going and set the big kettle to boil, and then laid the table. By the time Mildred stumbled downstairs to the privy, nightgown taut against her stomach, hair hanging over her face, I'd cut the bread and laid out butter and a new pot of jam as well as the usual bowl of dripping.

'Butter and jam for breakfast?' Mildred snapped when she came back, her nightgown wet down the front from splashing her face under the tap. 'Do you think we're made of money?'

'It's not for us kids. It's for you and Pa, to keep you going through the funeral. It'll be an ordeal,' I told her.

Mildred peered at me, twisting her hair up into a bun and stabbing pins in it. 'What are you up to, Clover?' she asked suspiciously.

'Nothing,' I said.

'If you're still angling to come too, the answer's no. Look at the state of your dress! And it's barely decent, hardly covering your knees,' she pointed out.

It wasn't *my* fault! I was the eldest so I didn't get hand-me-downs. I'd been begging for new clothes for the last six months but Mildred never took any notice. Still, I held my tongue, knowing she was spoiling for a fight.

'I'll go up and get Bert changed,' I said. 'He's doubtless sopping wet.'

I was right about that – and Pete had wet himself too. Jenny liked to play the big sister so she could boss the little ones about, but she was hopeless at looking after them and making sure they had a wee before bed.

I tipped the rest of the children out of the bed, hung the damp sheet over the banister and set about changing the boys. Pete was subdued, hanging his head in shame, especially when Richie started teasing him for being a big baby, but Bert was in a boisterous mood, flailing at me with his fists and kicking his legs when I laid him on his back.

'Hold *still* and stop waving that little sausage at me,' I said, struggling to pin a dry napkin on him.

The children laughed and Bert joined in, crowing delightedly as if he'd done something very clever. I tickled him and he laughed even harder, his face pink with merriment. When I set him upright again he held out his arms for a proper cuddle.

'Oh, so you're my friend now, are you?' I said, hugging him to me, realizing how much I'd missed having his warm little body snuggling up to me.

I hugged all the others in turn, but somehow none of the hugs felt right. I wanted *Megs*. I loved all my half-brothers and -sisters, but not the way I loved my own sister. I thought of her now, lying flat on her back in her coffin, so cold and lonely.

'What's the matter, Clover?' Pete asked.

'Don't be silly, Pete. She's upset about Megs,' said Jenny. '*I* keep crying for her.'

'Why isn't she back yet?'

'She's in Heaven,' said Mary. 'I won't get sent to Heaven, will I, Clover?'

'Not until you're an old, old, old lady,' I said.

Mary giggled at the idea of being old and started hobbling around the bedroom, her back stooped.

'Oh, Mary, don't!' said Jenny. 'You're walking just like the crookback dolly man.'

Pete and Richie laughed and started doing the silly walk too.

'Stop it!' I said fiercely. 'You're not to mock like that. It's very unkind. Mr Dolly's a lovely kind man. He can't help the way he walks.'

'He's scary,' said Jenny, shuddering. 'Ma says he gives her the creeps and she'll give you what for if you go to his shop again.'

'I don't care what Mildred says. She's not *my* ma,' I said, starting to brush Jenny's hair a little too vigorously.

'Ouch! You're hurting. I'm going to tell Ma you said that,' Jenny threatened.

I took hold of her. 'You won't really tell, will you, Jenny?' I asked.

'I *could*,' she said, wriggling. Then she smiled at me. 'But I won't.'

'That's a kind girl. Come on then, all of you. Let's go and get breakfast,' I said.

'What sort of breakfast will Megs have now she's in Heaven?' Mary asked.

'I don't know. Maybe . . . manna?' I said. I didn't know what it was, but Mr Dolly had once used the phrase 'manna from Heaven' when he shared a cold meat and pickle sandwich with me.

'What's manna? Is it bread and jam?'

'I don't think so.'

'Then Megs won't like it. She only likes bread and jam,' said Mary, and her face crumpled. 'I want Megs to have bread and jam!' she wailed.

Mary had never seemed especially fond of Megs, and I'd seen her pinch Megs's slice of bread off her plate when she wasn't looking, but now she seemed truly upset.

'Poor Megs,' said Jenny. 'Perhaps they'll make special bread and jam in Heaven just for her.'

Mary seemed comforted and I smiled at Jenny approvingly.

Richie and Pete were less kind.

'You're daft, you two. Megs is dead. She can't eat nothing any more,' said Richie.

'She's dead like that cat we found up the alley. She'll be all stiff now, with maggots,' said Pete.

Mary started wailing again and Jenny joined in.

'Stop it, Pete! Button your lip!' I said. 'You're upsetting the girls.'

He was upsetting me. I had pictured Megs dead and cold but still herself, looking as if she'd simply fallen asleep. But now I had the most grisly images in my head. I shook it violently to try to get rid of them.

'Oh Megs, oh Megs, oh Megs,' I mumbled, as if it were a magic spell and I could somehow summon her back from the dead.

'Megs!' said Bert. He beamed because he'd said a new word. 'Megs! Megs!' He looked disappointed when I didn't pick him up and kiss him and make a fuss of him. 'Megs,' he kept repeating, as if perhaps I hadn't heard.

I thought how thrilled Megs would have been to find that she was the first sibling Bert had named. I resolved to tell Bert all about Megs as he was growing up. I would remind him again and again that he'd had a wonderful sweet sister. I could even say she was an angel now, with great white wings to spread over him and keep him from harm.

There was an impatient shout from downstairs.

'Come on, that's your ma. Breakfast. Bread and dripping. Now!' I said, shooing them out the room.

They ran downstairs in a rush, but stopped in shock at the kitchen door. Pa was sitting at one end of the table, Mildred at the other. Pa wasn't in his usual rough blue shirt and grey trousers. He was wearing his wedding suit. I think he'd only worn it three times before. Once to marry my mother. Then again to bury her. And once to marry Mildred. It had seldom hung in his wardrobe. It spent most of its life in and out of the pawn shop.

Mildred's costume was another pawn-shop regular – a black jacket and skirt and the cream lace blouse she'd worn at her wedding. I think the jacket and skirt might once have been her mother's because they were cut in a strange way and were much too small, especially the skirt, which she'd had to leave unfastened. Her wedding blouse no longer fitted either. Her great chest strained at the stitches, threatening to burst right out.

It was hard to keep a smirk off my face, but Pa was looking at her as if she were still his new bride.

'You look proper handsome in that get-up, Mildred,' he said softly.

I couldn't believe it. There he was, drooling over her the very day of Megs's funeral – and she looked a total sight anyway.

'Doesn't your ma look splendid, Clover?' he said, making it worse. 'She's still a fine figure of a woman.'

I managed a cursory nod because I didn't want to risk a row before they left for the funeral. I didn't even murmur that Mildred wasn't my ma. She gave me a little nod back and offered me the jam. I spread it on my bread, though the sickly sweet taste reminded me of the cupboard.

I continued to act the docile daughter, clearing the dishes and wiping a damp rag round the children's sticky faces. Pa went out to the privy twice, saying his stomach was in a state. Mildred had a cheap brass fob watch from the fancy goods stall pinned to her jacket. When it showed twenty past nine she stood up, adjusting her skirt and checking her hair.

'We'd best be going,' she said. 'They'll be here at half past.'

There wasn't room for the funeral carriage and its fancy horses to turn down our alley. Pa and Mildred had been told to wait in the street.

'You be good now, children, and think of your poor sister,' said Mildred. 'Keep an eye on them, Clover.'

'Of course I will,' I said.

Pa actually gave me a kiss. 'I'll make sure the little lass is buried with her mother, I promise,' he said in my ear.

They set off, Mildred's hand tucked firmly through Pa's arm. We watched from the doorstep. Some of the alley folk were out in the street, watching too. The adults nodded in respect, though the children carried on playing, swinging on a rope from the gas lamp. Old Ma Robinson dabbed at her eyes with her apron. Peg-leg Jack stood still and saluted when Pa and Mildred passed.

Pa shuffled along, bent over, scarcely noticing, but Mildred tossed her head and walked with mincing steps, clearly enjoying being the centre of attention. She took a new handkerchief from her sleeve and dabbed at her eyes, as if she were crying.

'I can't see no horses!' said Richie. 'I thought there was going to be a grand carriage and horses with plumes.'

'They'll be waiting outside the alley,' I said.

'I want to see them!'

'Me too, me too!' said Pete.

'We want to see the horses too, don't we, Mary?' added Jenny.

'Well, look, you take them all to see the horses, Jenny. Take Bert too. I'm going to slip out to do some errands, so you keep an eye on all the kids till I get back, all right?' I took hold of Jenny and looked at her. 'You will see they're all right, won't you?'

'Course I will,' said Jenny, shrugging me off impatiently. She put Bert on her hip, took Mary's hand and lumbered off with them, the two boys running ahead.

I ran too – down the alley to Jimmy Wheels' house. I saw him waiting for me. His pa and ma were out doing their shift at the sauce factory. They just rented the downstairs back room. I'd never been inside before. I'd expected it to be similar to our place, with a few sticks of furniture, rags and rubbish in the corners and a dirty old rug on the floor. But this room was pretty and pin neat. The walls had been whitewashed, the floor scrubbed and polished, the rug newly knotted in gay reds and purples. The bed against the wall was carefully made, with a patchwork quilt in bright colours that matched the rug, and there were pretty curtains at the window – simple limp white cotton, but tied with red and purple scraps of ribbon. Jimmy's bed was the most touching. It had a special quilt with animals stitched in a pattern – a lion, a tiger, funny little monkeys and a big grey elephant.

'Oh, Jimmy!' I said. 'I love your quilt!'

'Ma and Pa took me to the zoological gardens one Sunday when I was little. Well, I'm still little now, ha ha. See that Jumbo? I fed him a bun. His trunk didn't half tickle! Ma made me a quilt to remind me of that day.'

'I expect my ma made me a quilt once,' I said quickly. 'Jimmy, have you got my parcel?'

'Parcel? What parcel?' he said, and then burst out laughing when he saw my face. 'Course I've got your flipping parcel. Here it is.' He wheeled himself over to his bed and pulled the brown paper parcel from underneath.

'Right. I'd better be quick. Turn your back and no peeping!'

I pulled off my old dress and slipped on the black one. It smelled a little strange from the dye, but it felt beautiful, crisp and fresh. I tried on the coat and it fitted perfectly. It had lovely details: little brass buttons and carefully fashioned pockets. I crammed the floppy black beret on my head, setting it at an angle. Then I pulled on both stockings, eased my feet into the felt boots and tied the laces. I straightened up, smoothing my clothes.

'My Lord!' said Jimmy, staring at me.

'I told you not to peek!' I said self-consciously. Then, 'Do I look all right, Jimmy?'

'You don't look a bit like you, Clover. You look like a toff!' he said. 'You'll do your Megs proud.'

'Oh, Jimmy, you're a true pal.' I bent down and gave him a kiss on his cheek.

'Leave off!' he said, scrubbing at it, but he looked pleased.

I thanked him again and then ran off. I couldn't go the quickest way – *up* the alley – because the children would still be there, and Mildred and Pa might very well catch sight of me. Instead I ran *down* the alley and went the long way round to the church.

It meant going along Whitgift Road and Jacob's Lane, both terrifying territory. Cripps Alley and Market Street were genteel by comparison. I had to tread very carefully in my beautiful felt boots because half the folk who lived there relieved themselves wherever they fancied, especially when drunk. And I had to dodge quickly past any man or lad who stared at me. The women worried me too. I'd heard tales of them shadowing a well-dressed child, luring them into the lane with the offer of a toy or sweet, and then suddenly tearing off all their clothes to sell up Monmouth Street. I'd normally nothing to fear in my dirty rags, but now, in Mr Dolly's fine outfit, I really did look a swell.

I ran like the wind – easy now that I was wearing my light felt boots instead of my old broken ones with their flapping soles. By the time I got to the church I was so winded I could barely speak and my new black dress was sticking to me. There was no sign of any funeral carriage or black horses. The church bells were tolling dolefully.

A vicar was standing in the porch in his strangely feminine garb of long frock and white pinafore. 'Hello, little girl. Have you come for the funeral of Margaret Anna Moon?'

For a moment I didn't even recognize Megs's name. No one ever called her that at home. It was a wonder Pa had even remembered it.

I nodded.

'Are you family or friend?' the vicar asked.

'I'm both,' I said, because I was Megs's sister *and* her best friend.

'Well, sit either side,' said the vicar, giving me a little pat on the shoulder.

I walked into the church apprehensively. I'd had a peep inside several churches but I'd never visited one properly. I was in awe of the huge room, the wooden pews, the big gold cross at the end and the stained-glass windows reflecting pools of red and yellow and blue on the stone floor. It smelled of damp and candles and the heady scent of flowers.

I saw two great vases of white lilies beside the altar and wondered who could have provided them. I knew that Pa and Mildred had had a conversation about flowers. Pa had wanted to have flowers for Megs's coffin – maybe just a small posy of roses – but Mildred had talked him out of it, saying it was a waste of money because you couldn't even take them home with you to get the benefit.

I sat right at the side where the coloured light from the windows couldn't fall on me. There were two old ladies in dusty black whispering together a few rows back. They had big old-fashioned bonnets on, misshapen from years of wind and rain. I peered round at them, trying to see their faces. Did they live in the alley? They didn't look familiar. They weren't Megs's friends, I was pretty sure of that. Could they perhaps be distant family, invited by Pa? Could they be unknown aunts? They looked too elderly.

My heart suddenly started beating wildly. Could one of these ladies be my mother's mother – my grandmother? Pa had told me he'd lost touch with her and thought she was dead. Had he made enquiries and found her and given her the sad news that her little granddaughter had passed away?

I couldn't stop myself edging along the pew towards them. 'Oh please, ma'am, ma'am, would you mind telling me why you're here?' I asked, looking from one to the other, wondering if I could detect a faint family likeness.

They peered at me from under their ragged bonnet fringes.

'We're here for the funeral, of course,' said one.

'So did you know our Megs?' I asked.

'Who's that, child?' said the other.

'My sister Megs. Margaret Anna Moon,' I said urgently.

They still looked blank.

'It's her funeral!'

'Oh dear, we're so sorry. Please accept our condolences,' said the first.

'Was she a slip of a thing like you? Tragic!' said the other.

'But why are you here if you didn't even know her?' I demanded.

'We love a good funeral, dear. We always come here. The vicar always conducts such a dignified ceremony.'

'He'll do your sister proud, my dear.'

I backed away from these two crows, sitting there so placidly, treating Megs's funeral as if it were entertainment. I went back to the shadows of my side pew. Then I heard a horse whinny and the sound of carriage wheels on the stony path outside. They were here.

An unseen organist started playing a melancholy dirge. I waited for what seemed like an age. Then at last I heard footsteps. I held my hand up to my face and peered through my fingers. Six tall gentlemen in black were proceeding very slowly up the aisle, carrying Megs on their shoulders. It was a heart-stoppingly small coffin. Any one of the men could have carried it unaided, but they plodded along as if they were supporting at least twenty girls.

Pa and Mildred walked behind, heads bowed so they didn't even glance in my direction. Mildred matched her steps to those of the men bearing the coffin, but Pa tried to walk with his usual gait and she had to keep restraining him. An usher showed them to their pew, right at the front of the church. The coffin was laid down slowly. The vicar stood to one side, waiting to start the proceedings. He waited. We waited.

I realized he was waiting for further mourners. But this was all there were – Pa, Mildred and me, and two ghoulish old women here to pass the time of day. I wished I'd been bolder and brought all my brothers and sisters with me, whether or not they were wearing the right clothes. I should have brought all the children in our alley – I could have filled several pews. They might look ragged and behave restlessly, yawning and fidgeting and kicking their heels, but each one of them would have known Megs, and perhaps they'd have cried genuine tears when they said goodbye to her.

The funeral started. There were two Bible readings and a couple of hymns, although Pa and Mildred didn't know them and the old women were only prepared to be spectators, so the vicar sang solo, loudly and not very tunefully. Then he went up the steps into his pulpit and started talking about Megs.

He spoke of little Margaret Anna, a happy, obedient little maid who had laughed and skipped throughout her brief life. We mustn't be sad that she was taken from us at such a young age. We must picture her laughing and skipping in Heaven.

I glared at him from my shadowy pew. It was clear that he didn't know a thing about my sister. She rarely laughed – only when I tickled her. She never skipped. She simply wasn't that sort of a child. She sat on a step and sucked her thumb, waiting for me.

Next there was another hymn and prayers, and then the service ended with more organ playing. The six coffin-bearers returned and took Megs back down the aisle. After hesitating uncertainly, Pa and Mildred shuffled after them. The old women dabbed at their noses, seemingly overcome. I stood and marched past them, hating them, hating Pa and Mildred, hating the undertakers, hating the vicar, hating this whole bizarre, expensive ceremony that had nothing to do with my own dear Megs.

I was so angry that I forgot to skulk in the background. Mildred turned and saw me. For a split second she didn't recognize me in my new black finery and gave me a sickly smile. Then it froze on her face. She nudged Pa and he turned too. Mildred muttered something, her face flushed. She started towards me, her arm lifted, ready to give me a clout, but Pa grabbed hold of her. He looked at the vicar, at the coffin-bearers, and whispered urgently. He was clearly telling Mildred she couldn't give me a hiding at my own sister's funeral, not in front of everyone.

She beckoned me instead. 'Clover dear,' she said in a strangled voice. 'Good Lord, look at you! My, what a surprise!'

'Don't she look fine, Mildred?' said Pa.

'Oh yes, she does indeed. Do tell us where you got your outfit from, Clover.'

'Oh, I – I got it off a clothes stall in the market,' I said.

'Of course you did,' said Mildred.

'Well, they were a lucky find,' said Pa, not realizing she was being sarcastic.

The vicar turned, clearly wondering why we were chatting at such a solemn stage in the proceedings. Pa and Mildred walked on together and I followed in their wake. There was a newly dug hole in the shade at the side of the church and I bit my knuckles, terrified that this might be intended for Megs's grave. Perhaps Pa hadn't really bothered give instructions about Mother's grave.

I wondered what I could do. Megs would be so scared and lonely by herself in the shadows. The coffin-bearers marched on, slowly but steadily, and I cleared my throat, ready to cry out – but to my intense relief they went past the hole and walked on round the church.

'Where are they going?' Mildred hissed. 'There's the hole! They've gone straight past it.'

'I've asked for Megs to be buried with her mother,' Pa murmured.

'So she's buried here?' said Mildred. 'You never said! Do you come and *visit* her?' She flushed, actually seeming jealous of someone long dead.

'Just occasionally,' said Pa.

My heart soared. I had never realized Pa made these secret visits to Mother. Perhaps he would let me go with him next time. Pa and me, and Mother and Megs, a little family again.

The vicar was frowning at us, so we walked the rest of the way in silence. There was Mother's grave, with a fresh hole right beside it, as requested. We stood by the mound of earth while Megs's coffin was lowered in very slowly and respectfully. Then the vicar indicated that Pa should shovel a spadeful of earth on top of the coffin. Pa did so, his hands shaking. As the earth pattered down he burst out sobbing.

Mildred put her arm round him, shielding him. I looked down at the grass and saw a patch of clover. I seized a fistful and scattered it on top of the coffin.

'There you are, Megs. It's clover. A little bit of me is down there with you,' I whispered. I looked at the modest little headstone beside her. 'Look after her, Mother.'

I stayed whispering to her until the vicar at last took hold of my arm.

'Come away, child. Your sister is at peace now.' He led me over to Pa and Mildred. 'Take your comfort from each other,' he commanded.

Pa wiped his eyes with the back of his hand and thanked the vicar.

Mildred joined in too. 'Thank you kindly, my dear sir,' she said, trying to speak like gentlefolk.

'My heart goes out to you in your time of grief,' he said. 'But don't forget, you still have your other daughter.' He patted me on the shoulder.

Mildred smiled tightly. 'Oh, I won't forget,' she said. She let go of Pa and seized hold of me instead. She bent close, as if about to kiss me. 'Just wait till I get you home,' she hissed.

10

SHE HUNG ON TO me as we walked away from the church. Pa had only been able to scrape together enough money for the carriage to the church, so we had to go home on foot.

'How *dare* you disobey me, Clover!' said Mildred. 'I told you to stay at home and look after the others. What sort of a sister are you? How can you leave a helpless little baby?'

'Bert's not a baby any more. And Jenny's good with him. He's just as happy with her now,' I said.

'Don't be cross with the little lass, Mildred, not now. Let's do what that nice vicar gent said and try to comfort each other,' said Pa, still sniffing. 'You didn't mean any harm, did you, Clover?'

'You're too soft with her. She can't go on like this, doing whatever she damn well pleases. Look at her, flaunting herself in that get-up!' said Mildred, pulling at my black velvet beret.

'She just wanted to pay her respects. What a clever girl you are, Clover, finding such fine duds down the market,' said Pa.

'Oh, very clever,' said Mildred. 'She never got them clothes from a market stall! You might fool your father, Clover Moon, but you don't fool me. They were specially made for you, weren't they?'

'Don't be silly, Mildred. How on earth would our Clover get enough cash to go to a dressmaker?' said Pa, bewildered.

'She didn't go to no *dress*maker. No, she went to a *doll*-maker!' Mildred gave me another shake. 'You went whining to that creepy little crookback, didn't you, even though we expressly forbade you to go near him ever again.'

'Don't call him that! He's a fine, lovely gentleman and he truly cares for me!' I retorted.

'Oh yes, I dare say he does. A crippled old man and a little girl. It's disgusting,' said Mildred vehemently.

'It's not, it's not! He made these clothes for me because he knew how badly I wanted to go to Megs's funeral. Mr Dolly's just like a father to me,' I blurted out.

'Just like a father?' said Pa, going red in the face. It had been an unfortunate phrase for me to use. 'You've got a father already!'

'Yes, I know, of course I have, and you're a lovely father, Pa. I just meant that Mr Dolly cares about me in a fatherly way,' I stammered.

'Mr Dolly! Don't you go giving that old man silly nicknames. You're to do as your mother says and keep well away. There's all sorts of talk about that one,' said Pa.

'Ignorant, hateful talk!' I insisted, so angry I lost all caution. 'By people who think nothing of mocking a poor man for his misfortune. I shall still see him whenever I like, and when I'm old enough I shall go to be his apprentice, so there!'

'You'll do no such thing! You'll get a job in the factory, same as us,' said Pa. 'Now stop the nonsense, Clover. It's a difficult day for all of us and I know you're sorely troubled, but you're to put any idea of working with that doll man out of your head. He might have meant it kindly when he made you these clothes, but we don't want charity from the likes of him, thank you very much.'

'It gives me the shivers to think of him stitching away at all this stuff,' said Mildred. 'You're not keeping them. You don't need a fancy black outfit. You'll probably never wear it again, and those silly soft boots will be worn out in a couple of weeks. I'm going to take the lot up Monmouth Street. I reckon I'll get ten shillings – it's quality stuff and fancy stitching.'

'You're not laying a finger on them! They're mine!' I protested, trying to wrench myself free of her.

'I'm your mother and what's yours is mine,' said Mildred.

'You're *not* my blooming mother!' I shouted, so loudly that people in the street turned and stared at us.

'Hold your tongue!' Mildred hissed. 'How dare you make a spectacle of us when we're all dressed in mourning!' She turned to Pa. 'Do you see what I mean? She's completely out of control. She's needs to be disciplined. If you're too weak to do it, then I'll take over. I'll give her what for if she goes gallivanting off to that crookback again! I'm not having her neglecting the kiddies no more. Poor little mites, left on their own. No wonder poor little Megs got sick.'

'How dare you say that!' I couldn't stop my tears now. 'You know that's not true. I always looked after Megs.'

'I'm going to make sure you stay home and look after the children now. I'm getting a little cane tomorrow. We're going to start learning you proper.'

'You don't say "learn", it's bad grammar. It's "teach"!' I retorted.

'Then I'm going to teach you good and proper, you snobby little brat,' said Mildred. 'You're due a right hiding! Just you wait!'

'Pa, you won't let her cane me, will you?' I said, taking his arm.

'I don't know, Clover. I don't know what's got into you. It's not right, you turning your nose up at Mildred and me. You won't be told! Mildred's right, it's all down to you hanging round that freak.'

'He's not a *freak*!' I cried.

'There now! Here you go again, with all the argy-bargy. I won't have it. I dare say he can't help the way he was born but he could certainly do something more manly than making dollies. He's been a bad influence on you all along, teaching you this reading lark and filling you with fancy ideas. You need to have some sense knocked into you. You've got to be taken down a peg or two. Maybe a caning's the answer.'

He really meant it. As I looked at him he stopped being Pa. He turned into a stooped, balding man with bloodshot eyes and a red circle round his thick neck where his collar was rubbing. He reeked of last night's

157

drink and his usual stale smell – he never washed properly, simply doused his head under the tap to wake himself up in the morning. He just wanted a quiet life. He didn't really care about me.

Mildred certainly didn't care about me either. The day Pa brought her home and told Megs and me she was our new mother she was all false smiles. She gave Megs and me penny buns to get us to like her, but it didn't work. We knew she didn't like us, and we didn't like her. And now I hated her, especially as she was looking at me triumphantly, feeling she'd got the better of me at last.

There was no point arguing any more. I pressed my lips together and trudged down the road in silence.

'There now,' said Pa uncomfortably. 'We're not meaning to be hard on you, Clover. You just need to see reason. Now, let's all get home and check on the little ones and have a nice cup of tea,' he said. 'I'm parched with all this grieving.'

Mildred patted his arm. 'It's a dreadful thing when a parent has to bury a child. Thank goodness we have a new little one on the way.'

As if Mildred's new baby could ever replace Megs! I was anxious about the other children, knowing that Jenny might not keep her eye on Bert all the time. He'd often crawl into a corner and try to catch a shiny beetle and eat it. Pete and Richie needed careful handling to stop their tussles developing into real fisticuffs, and little Mary was forever trying to turn a cartwheel and was likely to tumble down and hit her head. But when we got home the children were playing a game of hopscotch, little Bert clutching a stick of chalk in his fist and giving it little licks as if it were sugar candy.

'Watch Bert, Jenny. He shouldn't eat chalk,' I said, snatching it away from him.

Bert protested bitterly, and arched away from me when I tried to pick him up to comfort him.

'There now, you've upset him,' said Jenny. She gave him a hug and Bert snuggled up to her. 'Here, darling, come to Jenny. He's been such a happy boy all the time you've been gone.'

I stood staring at them. Jenny didn't really mean it unkindly. I knew Bert was just playing one of us off against the other in his baby way. I was currently out of favour but he still needed me, didn't he?

I'd carried each and every one of my brothers and sisters round with me and tried to be a little mother to them. They all loved me for it, and whenever they were in trouble they ran to me, not Mildred. They all still needed me. Or did they?

Perhaps they'd all get along perfectly without me. Pa didn't care about me any more – he'd said he thought a caning would teach me a lesson. He'd gone indoors to change out of his good suit, and Mildred said she was exhausted after the walk and thought she'd have a little lie down. Pa said he might join her.

'That's it, dear. Make the most of your day off,' she murmured.

My stomach turned over at the thought of them together. They didn't even seem to be grieving for Megs any more. I had a dread of going into the house now – even with everyone crowded round it would seem so empty without her. It wasn't home any more.

What was the point of staying here now, when no one really loved or needed me, not even little Bert? All I had to look forward to was a caning – probably many of them.

So why didn't I run away?

I sat down on the step, wondering where I could go. I longed to take refuge with Mr Dolly, but Mildred and Pa would guess I'd gone there. They'd come after me and drag me home – and hurl abuse at poor Mr Dolly too. I couldn't do that to him.

I could try and get a job on one of the market stalls, but they'd find me there too. I'd have to go further, where no one knew me. How would I earn enough for my keep? I knew that thousands of children younger than me managed to scrape a few pennies together each day by selling flowers or matches. If they didn't have proper beds to go to at night they curled up in doorways, with sacking for blankets. I'd seen them myself and pitied them.

I'd also heard lurid tales of what could happen to these children. Whenever I particularly annoyed her Mildred said I'd go to the bad. I didn't want to be bad. I wanted to be good. I simply wanted a different life. But if I ran away from home I'd be destitute.

Miss Sarah Smith's Home for Destitute Girls!

Mr Rivers's words suddenly echoed in my head. I sat there, hugging my knees. I could walk there right this minute. My heart beat hard beneath the black cotton of my dress.

'Clover? What you pulling that funny face for?' Richie called.

'What?'

'Aren't you playing? You're tops at hopscotch,' he said, sitting beside me.

'I can't, not in these boots. I don't want to spoil them,' I said.

'Take 'em off then. And all that other stiff black stuff. You don't look like you any more,' said Richie.

'If I do then Mildred will snatch the lot and take it up to Monmouth Street where all the second-hand clothes shops are. I'm keeping everything on, thanks very much! Here, give us that chalk and I'll draw you a picture on the paving stones.'

If I really *was* going to make a run for it I wanted to play with the children first and leave them with a happy memory of me.

First I drew a big animal with a wolfish grin and a wagging tail because I knew that Richie was desperate for a dog of his own.

'Oh, I love him! He's mine, isn't he, Clover?' he said.

'No, he's *my* dog and I'm calling him Tiger,' said Pete.

'You can't call a dog Tiger, daftie! He's mine and he's called Savage, and he'll bite all the other dogs but he'll lick me,' said Richie.

'I don't like dogs,' said Mary. 'They bark and they hurt you.'

'I know what you like,' I said. I drew a big plate of buns – cream buns and cherry buns and iced buns.

'Oh, buns!' said Mary, laughing as she recognized them. She reached out and pretended to pick one off the plate. 'Yum yum, all mine!'

'Don't be silly, Mary – you can't eat chalk buns,' said Jenny.

'Shall I draw something for you, Jenny?' I asked.

She shrugged. 'I'm busy with Bert,' she said, holding him up so that just the tips of his toes touched the ground. 'Come on, Bertie, walk for Jenny!'

Bertie kicked his legs in the air but let his knees buckle whenever Jenny lowered him.

I drew a girl with long curly hair a little like Jenny's, wearing a fancy dress and a hat with flowers.

'Yes, I want a dress and a hat just like that,' said Jenny, smiling in spite of herself.

'I want one too,' said Mary, still munching pretend buns. 'But I want it all pretty colours, not black like yours, Clover.'

'Yes, but mine's black for Megs's funeral,' I said.

'Was it very sad?' said Jenny.

'Yes, dreadfully,' I said.

'Did you see her go up to Heaven?' asked Mary.

I shook my head.

'Did you see her dead in her coffin? What did she look like? Did she turn into a skellyton?' asked Pete.

'Stop it. No!'

'But she's in the ground now, isn't she? That's what buried means, isn't it?' said Richie.

'I'm not being buried ever,' said Mary. 'I wouldn't like it.'

'Perhaps it's just like being tucked up in bed at night,' I said. 'Let's think about Megs like that.'

'I don't want to think about her at all, not if she's a skellyton – she'll frighten me,' said Pete.

'I keep telling you, she's not a skeleton,' I said. 'Think of her in a nice clean nightgown, her hair brushed, her eyes closed, a little smile on her face because she's having a happy dream.'

I tried desperately hard to conjure up this picture of Megs too. I imagined kissing her. Then I gave each of my siblings a real kiss.

The boys grimaced and rubbed their cheeks but I knew they didn't really mind. Mary smiled and gave me a rather wet kiss back.

Jenny kissed me warmly. 'Do you want to hold Bert now?' she offered.

'Just for a minute.'

'Here, Bert, go to Clover.'

I took him, and this time he didn't wail. He grinned at me too, dribbling down his chin. 'Co-va,' he said. 'Co-va! Co-va!'

'Oh, Clover, he's saying your name!' said Jenny.

'Yes, he is! Oh, Bert, bless you! Clever boy! I'm your Clover. Don't forget me, will you? Clover!'

'Co-va!' Bert repeated.

I gave him one last kiss and squeeze and then set him back on Jenny's lap. 'Bye then,' I said softly.

'Where are you going?' Jenny asked.

'Oh, just for a walk,' I said.

'You'd better not go back to Mr Dolly's. Ma will beat you if you do,' she warned.

'Don't worry, I'm not going there,' I said. I gave them a little wave.

'You won't be long, will you?' Mary asked, helping herself to another pretend bun.

'I might be quite a while,' I said, and then I started walking quickly away.

I heard them calling after me but I didn't look back, or I knew I'd weaken. I hurried down the alley.

Old Ma Robinson was sitting on an upturned orange crate, smoking her pipe. She waved to me. 'Well, don't you look a little Miss Fancy Pants,' she said, chuckling.

I ignored her – but then Peg-leg Jack caught hold of me. He was only just out of bed, smelling strongly of sleep and last night's beer, his hair tousled and his eyes barely focusing – but they filled with tears at the sight of me.

'My Lord, it was your little sister's funeral today,' he said, looking me up and down. 'I meant to go and pay my respects. Dear little kiddie, though she would never say boo to a goose. You'll be feeling bereft without her.'

'I am, oh, I am,' I said, wondering that the only person who seemed to understand and show true sympathy was this drunken old sot.

'Bless you, dear. Well, may the little one rest in peace. I shall drink to her today. Little . . . what was she called now – Peg?'

'Megs. Her name was Margaret Anna, but we all called her Megs, Mr Jack,' I said. 'Thank you for asking after her.'

I detached myself gently from his grasp and got to the end of the alley. I heard the high thin voice of Jimmy Wheels behind me and the grind of his wheels on the cobbles, but I didn't hang around to speak to him in case Mildred was up again and looking for me.

I was halfway along Winding Lane, walking quickly, when I heard Jimmy's voice again, and a rush of wheels. There he was, bowling along like the wind, a small parcel balanced on his board.

'Lord's sake, Clover, are you deaf?' he yelled.

I stood still so he could catch me up.

'Where are you off to in all your black finery?' he asked breathlessly, rearing up as far as he could to see the expression on my face. 'Are you going to see Mr Dolly?'

'I daren't. Mildred's threatened me,' I said.

'She's a right one, your stepma. So, where are you going then?' he demanded, his face pink from hurrying, though his hands were black from bowling himself along the grimy streets.

'I – I just thought I'd take a walk. Get a bit of fresh air,' I said.

Jimmy said a very rude word. 'You lying toad, Clover Moon – you're running away!' he said.

'All right, maybe I am. But don't you go back and blab on me,' I said.

'What do you take me for? I'm on your side. Hey, you'd better have this. It'll keep you warm at night.' He pulled something blue and woolly out of his shirt, folded small.

'What is it?' I shook it out and saw that it was a beautifully crocheted shawl. 'I can't take your ma's shawl!'

'It's *my* shawl. She wants me to put it round my shoulders because she's scared I'll get a chill. Only I'd look a right berk, wouldn't I? You take it, Clover. I want to give you something. You've always been good to me,' said Jimmy earnestly.

'Oh, Jimmy, you're the best.' I knelt down and gave him a big hug.

'Watch out, you'll squash me to bits,' he said, laughing. 'Go on, get off then! Good luck!'

I gave him a last kiss, clutched the shawl and ran off. I followed my usual route down Market Street because I couldn't leave without saying goodbye to Mr Dolly.

11

IT WAS A LITTLE foolhardy because it was the first place Mildred and Pa would look for me, but I couldn't just disappear. Mr Dolly would think that something bad had happened to me. Maybe he'd even think I'd got the fever after all.

I went bursting into his shop, making him jump as he sat behind the counter, stitching a tiny doll's nightgown. He gave a double take at my appearance.

'Clover! My dear, you look splendid, even if I do say so myself!' he exclaimed. 'The clothes fit you perfectly. I take it you attended your sister's funeral after all?'

'Yes, I did.'

'And it all went well? Your stepmother wasn't too vexed?'

'Well, she was, but she couldn't do anything in the church. It was a very quiet funeral, and I wish Pa had purchased flowers for Megs's coffin because it seemed so bare, but there were the most beautiful lilies and they made the church look lovely,' I said.

'Oh, I'm so pleased,' said Mr Dolly.

There was something strange about the way he said it, and the smile that flickered on his lips.

'Mr Dolly! Did *you* send those lilies?'

'I wanted to send a wreath but I thought that might not be wise. Your parents would be curious, and if they thought it was from me they would doubtless be indignant. Then I had the idea of sending two bunches of lilies for church decoration. I do hope that was the right decision.'

'Yes, it was a wonderful idea. Now whenever I think of Megs I shall remember those lovely flowers and fancy I'm breathing in their sweet smell,' I said, my voice wobbling a little.

'It must have been such an ordeal for you today,' said Mr Dolly. 'Come into the back room and I'll make you a cup of tea – and I dare say a slice of plum cake wouldn't go amiss? I bought some specially, just in case you decided to pay me a visit.'

'Oh, I'd love a cup of tea and especially some cake, but I'm afraid I daren't stay long. I've come to say goodbye,' I said, clasping his hand.

'Goodbye? Oh, Clover, have you been forbidden to visit me?' asked Mr Dolly, looking stricken.

'Well, Mildred has long since forbidden it, but that's of no import,' I said. 'I never mind what she says. I hate her. I'm not going to be her little drudge any more. And I'm not going to start at the factory either.'

'Of course not! You're just a little child!'

'I'm eleven now, and the girls in our alley generally start there at twelve. You start on the vegetables because there's no skill and you don't need any strength. You just cut up onions and tomatoes all day long,' I said.

'But you're such a bright girl, Clover! You can read and write beautifully. If you have to work you could surely obtain a junior position in an office or shop, where there are some prospects.'

'I don't think Mildred and Pa want me to have prospects,' I said. 'They want me to be the same as them.'

'But we aren't all the same. That's the point. Look at my dolls. If you give them a cursory glance they all seem the same. They all have wooden heads, painted faces and jointed limbs, but we both know there are so many differences. Some are bold little creatures who want to run and dance and kick. Some are shy, retiring girls who like to sit demurely. Some are little beauties with big eyes and glossy rosebud lips. Some are dear Plain Janes with sensible, homely heads on their shoulders,' said Mr Dolly.

'That's me. I'm a Plain Jane all right,' I said.

'Nonsense. You're the pick of the bunch, the cleverest, sweetest, most dazzling lily in a field of brassy dandelions,' said Mr Dolly. '*Please* have some plum cake.'

I couldn't resist, though I kept glancing round anxiously whenever I heard footsteps passing the door. 'I'm so scared Mildred will come for me,' I explained.

'Perhaps it would be a good thing. I could try to persuade her to see common sense,' said Mr Dolly.

'The Queen herself couldn't make Mildred listen,' I said. 'That's why I'm running away.'

Mr Dolly choked on his own slice of cake. 'You can't run away!'

'I have to. I hate it at home. It's never going to be the same without Megs.'

'I know you feel like that right this minute. It's only natural on such a sad day. But don't forget you have all those other brothers and sisters – and I hear from my little pal Jimmy that half the children in your alley depend on you,' said Mr Dolly.

'They don't really need me any more. And I won't be there for them anyway if I'm stuck in the sauce factory. I have to leave,' I said resolutely, finishing my cake.

'Here, let me cut you another slice! Where are you planning to go then, Clover? You're still a little girl. You can't just walk off into the streets of London with no one to take care of you,' said Mr Dolly.

'There are many children who find themselves in that situation,' I pointed out.

'And look what happens to the poor mites! They are preyed upon by brutal adults and end up in the gutter,' said Mr Dolly. 'I couldn't bear it if you suffered the same fate.'

'I will be properly looked after, I promise you. I have a plan. I am going to seek out a lady called Miss Sarah Smith.'

'The Sarah Smith who writes children's books?'

'Yes – have you heard of her? She runs some sort of home for girls in need. I'm sure she will take care of me.'

'You have her address?'

'It's just off the Strand,' I said.

'So who told you about this benefactress?' Mr Dolly asked, still doubtful.

'Mr Rivers. You know – he bought Marigold for his little girl.'

'Oh, that gentleman,' said Mr Dolly, looking a little reassured.

'Yes – he told me to seek her out if I ever felt the need. You know what swell gentlemen are like. He fussed because he saw that my head was cut,' I said.

'Badly cut too. You'll have a nasty scar,' said Mr Dolly sadly. 'I should have confronted the wicked soul who did it.'

'Then you'd have ended up with a matching blow or worse, so what would have been the point?' I said.

He flinched, and I realized I hadn't been very tactful.

'I'm sorry, Mr Dolly, but you know it's true. But anyway, we don't have to bother about it any more because I'm going to see Miss Smith and she'll take me under her wing,' I said. 'Mr Rivers assured me that she'd look after me.'

'Well, she certainly has a reputation for protecting children. I read an article about her in the newspaper. You know the exact address?'

'Yes, of course,' I said, not quite truthfully. 'I dare say it's only half an hour's walk,' I added, guessing wildly.

'I think it'll take longer than that. Are you sure you know the way?'

'Yes! Well, if I get lost I'll ask. Don't worry, Mr Dolly, I'll be perfectly fine,' I assured him. 'I *must* be off now or Mildred will be out looking for me. Thank you very much for the plum cake, it was delicious.'

'You must take the rest. I'll wrap it up for you. Wait just one moment.' He wrapped the cake in paper, and then added a large wedge of cheese too.

'No, Mr Dolly! Surely that's for your supper!' I said.

'You can have a little munch on your journey to sustain you. And you'll need something to drink too. Ah, I believe I have a stone bottle of ginger beer in my larder!' He bustled about collecting my feast together and put it in a small sack. I put Jimmy's blue shawl inside too, and slung the sack over my shoulder.

'There! I feel like one of the fairy-tale heroes, off to seek my fortune!' I said. 'A sack is much more practical than a red spotted handkerchief on a stick.'

Mr Dolly fetched the little embroidered purse containing my five shillings. 'This is your money, Clover.' Then he emptied his cash box of coins and tipped them into the purse too.

'No, Mr Dolly, I can't take all your money!' I protested.

'I absolutely insist. I wish I could give you more, but I've already banked Mr Rivers's five-pound notes. Still, this will be more than enough for a hansom to the Strand. You'll find the cab stand up the street, then turn left and go round the corner. It'll save wear and tear on those boots – they're not made for walking.'

'You have been truly good to me, Mr Dolly. Now that Megs is dead I think I love you more than anyone else in the world,' I said solemnly.

'Dear child,' said Mr Dolly, his blue eyes watering. 'I love you very much too. I shall miss you dreadfully. I do hope we can meet again one day.'

He held out his hand. I shook it solemnly – but then put my arms round him and hugged him hard. He patted me a little awkwardly, sniffing.

'Clover, I know you're a very grown-up child, for all you're so little. I wonder ... you've never asked, but would you perhaps like a doll as a small companion in your new life?'

I breathed in sharply. 'Oh, yes please, Mr Dolly. Are you sure? You've already been incredibly generous.'

'I've fashioned an outfit from several scraps, given you a few morsels of food and a handful of change. Hardly lavish. Clover, it would give me immense pleasure if I knew that one of my doll daughters was living with you,' said Mr Dolly. 'Which will you choose? Hyacinth or Violet?'

'May I choose another doll instead?'

'But they are my two finest. Perhaps they're not quite as grand as the French beauties in Cremer's window in Bond Street, but they're just as good as any of the German china dolls,' said Mr Dolly.

'Yes, I know, and they're much more beautiful than the French dolls,' I said, though I had never been to Cremer's – or indeed Bond Street. 'But could I perhaps have one of your wooden dolls – quite a small one, though not the tiny ones that live in a doll's house? Could I have ... Anne Boleyn?'

'Of course you can,' said Mr Dolly, 'if you're really sure she's the one you want the most.'

'I'm certain sure,' I said.

Mr Dolly went into the back room and came out with Anne Boleyn, newly attired in a jade print dress to match her green eyes and a red cloak the colour of her glossy cheeks. He pressed her into my hands. I held her close, and one of her small wooden hands touched my wrist as if she were stroking it.

'Keep safe, Clover dear,' said Mr Dolly.

'I will – of course I will. You mustn't worry about me.' I held Anne Boleyn in my right hand, slung my sack of provisions over my shoulder, gave Mr Dolly a quick kiss on the cheek and then walked to the door. I opened it cautiously, looking for Mildred, but there was no sign of her.

'Goodbye!' I said, and then ran off quickly.

The sack was a little cumbersome and the ginger beer bottle banged uncomfortably against my back. I held Anne Boleyn with a stiff wrist, as if carrying a fragrant bouquet, because I knew her small wooden limbs were fragile and I didn't want to crush her clothes. I certainly couldn't run easily now, and after ten minutes I had to resort to an ungainly hobble.

I looked for the hansom cab stand but couldn't see one. I had clearly failed to follow Mr Dolly's directions. Had he said go up the street or down? Turn left or right? It had seemed so simple at the time but now I couldn't remember.

I stood there dithering, starting to panic. How could I be lost in such a short space of time? I held Anne Boleyn tight and told myself to calm down. I didn't really need a cab, did I? I could walk to the Strand easily enough. I peered down at my boots and raised each foot in turn to examine the soles. They still seemed sturdy. Yes, I would walk to Miss Smith's establishment and save all the money in the purse for my future needs.

I stopped the first kindly-looking woman I saw, timidly plucking at her skirts. 'Excuse me, ma'am, but could you possibly give me directions to the Strand?' I asked, trying to speak as correctly as possible.

She laughed at my little speech. 'You what, love? The Strand? What, where all the theatres are? Well, I see you're in your best bib and tucker. What show are you going to see?'

'I'm not going to see a show. I'm looking for a certain lady who advises young girls,' I said with all the dignity I could muster, because I knew she was teasing me.

'Oh, bless the child! Wouldn't you like *me* to give you some advice? That would be to run along home to your mother!' The woman laughed at her own joke.

'I would if I could, but sadly my mother is in her grave, and my little sister too,' I said.

She suddenly realized the significance of my black outfit. 'Oh my dear, I'm so sorry. There's me having my little carry-on, and there's you with a breaking heart, mourning your loved ones! So, you need to go to the Strand, dear? Well, I don't rightly know the way, because I have to admit I've never been there myself, only heard of it, but it's up west, isn't it? Stands to reason, because Hoxton's east, right? So go that-a-ways,' she said, pointing. 'Make for Clerkenwell – then, when you reach . . . Bloomsbury, is it? . . . then it's a little bit south, as far as I can make out. Yes, we're east, so go west, and then south. Just don't go north and you should be fine,' she said. 'God bless you, child. I'm sorry for the loss of your dear ones.'

I thanked her and set off again. I walked a very long way along dreary roads that seemed to stretch out for ever, but at least I knew I was in Clerkenwell, because that was the name of the road. I certainly wasn't up west yet because the folk in the street looked ordinary enough. I was expecting silks and satins for the ladies and top hats for the toff gents in the Strand. I was worried that I might be chased away the moment I got there, but glancing in the windows at my reflection I saw that in Mr Dolly's outfit I looked positively genteel, and my hair shone in the sunshine.

Despite my smart outward appearance I was feeling weary now, worn down by worries far heavier than my sack. I'd stopped looking for Mildred over my shoulder every minute, but now that fear had eased a little I kept thinking of Megs. Try as I might, I could not picture

Mother under the earth, reaching out her arms and drawing Megs to her bosom. Megs would be so lonely lying there. I wondered if I should go back home after all, take my punishment from Mildred, start the daily drudgery of factory work, suffer anything at all so long as I could go to that churchyard every day and whisper reassuringly to my poor sister.

And what about Jenny and Richie and Pete and Mary and Bert? My little Bert, who might be crying for me this very instant. What of all my friends in the alley? What about Jimmy? And what about dear Mr Dolly? How could I bear not to see him any more?

I turned round more than once, but after a few paces turned resolutely westwards again, knowing that I *had* to take this new opportunity. It was surely long past lunch time now, so I stopped in a big green square, sat on a bench and munched on my cheese and plum cake. I started off thinking I would nibble a quarter of each and prudently save the rest for later, but I found I was so ravenously hungry from grief and exercise that I ate the lot, and drained my bottle of ginger beer.

'My, that went down quick,' said a gaunt-looking man with thinning grey hair. He was sitting on the other end of the bench, writing in a small notebook. I'd been so intent on my own thoughts that I'd scarcely noticed him. He was wearing a shabby jacket and the fine cord of his trousers was rubbed pale, especially at the knees, and though his boots were of good quality they were unpolished and down at heel. He spoke in a gentlemanly manner, but he looked poor. Perhaps he was hungry too. Maybe he'd been hoping that I might offer him a few crumbs of cake or a morsel of cheese.

'I'm so sorry, sir, I've eaten everything. But perhaps you'd like to lick up the crumbs . . .' I said, offering him the paper wrapping. My brothers and sisters always fought over the last crumbs of any meal we were sharing.

However, the man seemed taken aback. He laughed uncertainly. 'I'm peckish, child, but not *that* hungry,' he said. His pale face coloured. 'Did you think I was a *beggar?*'

'No, of course not,' I said hastily, though I had wondered.

'Oh dear, oh dear, you *did*! No, child, I'm just a poor poet, starving in my garret – well, not literally, but pretty near. I don't suppose you care for poetry . . .' He didn't look as if he expected me to say yes.

'Oh, I do!' I assured him. I was very impressed. I'd never met a poet before. Mr Dolly spoke of all the writers of his volumes in awed tones, as if they were gods. He worshipped poets most of all and told me tales about them. They lived in exotic places amongst mountains and lakes, or even abroad in Italy, though Mr Dolly's favourite poet came from London. He knew some of his poetry by heart, and often recited a very long *Ode to a*

Nightingale. I didn't really understand it. There seemed to be very little about nightingales – just some man feeling sad and rather wishing he were dead. I remembered the worrying part about men having sparse grey hair and being spectre-thin. I suddenly blinked at the poet.

'I'm glad you like poetry,' he said, holding out his hand to the sparrows fluttering all around us. 'Why don't you give the birds a little feast of your crumbs?'

I scattered the crumbs and they pounced on them, jostling for morsels.

'You like birds, sir?' I said.

'Yes, I do. There's nothing as determined and lively as a London sparrow,' he replied.

'And I expect you like nightingales too.'

'Well, yes,' he said, surprised. 'Though doesn't everyone marvel at a nightingale's song? Especially when it "singest of summer in full-throated ease".'

I knew that phrase!

'I know which poet you are, sir!' I said triumphantly.

'I rather doubt that. I am scarcely published,' he said.

'But I know a gentleman who knows lots of your poetry by heart and it means a great deal to him,' I said.

'Really?' said the gentleman eagerly.

'You're Mr Keats!'

He stared at me. 'Mr Keats?' he echoed.

'Yes, and you're very romantic, Mr Dolly says, and you write about Nature. That's the countryside.' I paused. The poet was choking with laughter.

'I'm not John Keats, you silly girl! How could I be? He died many years ago, for a start. Plus he was an undoubted genius and I'm beginning to think I'm just a wretched hack who can only write doggerel,' he said, sobering.

'Oh. I'm sorry.' He clearly thought me very ignorant, which was humiliating. I was used to knowing more than anyone else, but perhaps I didn't know very much at all compared to other folk. I'd been longing to go to Miss Smith's institution to show off my reading and writing skills. What was I going to do if all the girls there were cleverer than me?

'I'm sorry too,' he said. 'Sorry that I can't make a decent living for myself, let alone my poor wife and daughter. Still, I couldn't betray my artistic spirit. Never do that, child, do you hear?'

I didn't properly understand – he was talking in a very grand way, clutching his heart and gesturing wildly. But I nodded all the same. 'I won't, sir. Definitely.'

'So what is your most heartfelt desire for the future?' he asked.

I tried hard to manufacture some sort of answer. Until recently I'd been so busy living in the present I hadn't even thought of the future. 'I'm not quite sure . . .'

Did *I* have an artistic spirit? I was certain I wasn't a poet. I didn't know enough grand words and I couldn't make them fit neatly together, line after matching line. But perhaps I was a little artistic . . . I'd been surprised by how easy it was to chalk little pictures on the pavement. 'I think I want to be an artist,' I said grandly. I certainly knew I wanted to be an artist more than a factory girl.

'Another noble creative profession,' the poet said approvingly. 'Have you had any instruction, child?'

'Not yet, but maybe Miss Sarah Smith will instruct me,' I said. 'I'd better be on my way. Do you think I'm anywhere near Bloomsbury, sir?'

'Near it? You're *in* it!'

'Then which way is south?' I said, standing up and shouldering my sack. I wiped my hand on it before picking up Anne Boleyn, not wanting to get any cake crumbs on her.

The poet stood up too, and spun round. 'Devil if I know,' he said. 'I've no sense of direction.'

'I'm looking for the Strand.'

'Ah. I can help you there.' He spun me round too. 'That way, through St Giles. Keep going and you'll find you're there,' he said.

He didn't seem to make much sense, but I hoped he was at least sure of the direction. We waved goodbye to each other and I set off, refreshed. The soles of my feet were starting to burn a little because there was very little padding in the felt boots, but they looked so attractive I didn't mind. The sack was much lighter now I'd consumed my cheese and cake and discarded the ginger beer bottle. Anne Boleyn bounced along in my hand, looking about her with her bright green eyes.

'We're really up west with all the fine folk now,' I told her.

But the folk didn't look especially fine – bent-over office clerks and errand boys and milliner girls carrying great round hatboxes. I walked on, and the streets got smaller and darker and much more crowded, and the folk were just like the ones in our alley, only poorer still, in really ragged clothes, and most of the children went barefoot. I held Anne Boleyn tightly, feeling bewildered.

I found myself in a street of second-hand clothes shops, with ancient greatcoats and limp christening robes and faded satin dresses and patched calico nightgowns all hung higgledy-piggledy from the door frames, and old women and little children sitting on stools outside their shops, busily sewing and patching. I shrank back, terrified that one of these limp garments might have fever lurking in its folds.

'Don't look so feared, dearie,' said one ancient old crone, smiling at me toothlessly. 'Nice bit of material on your back, I see. I'll give you a sixpence for your cap and a whole shilling for that coat. Can't say fairer than that. Come on, it's nearly summer – you won't be needing them no more.' She stood up and hobbled towards me, actually putting her misshapen old hands on my lapels.

'Get off me! My clothes aren't for sale,' I insisted, prising her fingers off.

I hurried along the street, walking in the middle so that none of the stallholders could touch me. Several children ran after me, mimicking me and calling me names – but I could handle little kids. I turned round suddenly, pulling a terrible face and waving my hands in their faces, and they shrieked and shrank back.

One bigger lad was bolder, and actually pulled my beret right off my head, twirling it round his forefinger while the others laughed. I knew how to deal with big lads too. I pretended to cry, distracting him, and then whipped my foot out and kicked him hard where I knew it would hurt. I only had felt boots on, but he still doubled up and lost his grip on my hat. It went flying through the air, and I caught it neatly, returned it to my head and marched on.

I went up and down a maze of lanes, all such dirty dwelling places that our alley seemed palatial by comparison. I twice saw girls empty chamber pots and buckets out of the window straight into the street. After that I kept looking up fearfully. There was one man lying motionless in all the mire. I don't know if he was dead or simply dead drunk. No one seemed to care, simply skirting round him, and a gang of half-naked urchins kept galloping over him as if they were horses and he a fence.

I felt sure I must have mistaken my way. This hellhole couldn't be the West End. Miss Sarah Smith couldn't possibly run a respectable home for girls anywhere near here. I tried to retrace my steps, but it seemed I was in a filthy maze, destined to wander round and round until I dropped.

I clutched Anne Boleyn so tightly it was a good job she was made of sturdy wood. If she were wax she would have melted. I was aware of a distant cheeping sound, as if a vast flock of birds were flying overhead, though the sky was empty. Then I turned another corner and understood.

I was standing in a great street market of caged songbirds, all clustered together and stacked one above the other, singing out in sorrow at their captivity. I knew which were starlings and recognized the bright yellow of canaries, but couldn't tell a lark from a finch. One man had a long cage strapped round his neck, with four birds on perches that he'd somehow trained to dip their beaks into their bird-feeders simultaneously, like comical toys.

There were larger birds in bigger cages – hens attempting to peck any passer-by and great hissing geese. I skirted my way round these, and nearly stumbled into a bran tub of mealworms, still alive and writhing horribly. There were cages chock-a-block with rats, all scrambling over each other, while fierce terriers barked at them hysterically, eyes bulging.

I dodged past them all, shivering in disgust. It was better at the end, where there were more dogs in cages. I saw perky mongrels of varying shapes and sizes, funny lap dogs with little button noses, and large dogs with soft fur and soulful eyes. They were too big to be caged, and were kept tied to railings. Some stood abjectly, heads drooping, and some barked incessantly, but one big golden dog snuffled when he saw me, and ambled over to sniff me.

I put Anne Boleyn in my sack, worried he might bite off her little stick hands or feet, but the dog was docile, rubbing his large head against my coat, leaving a pattern of golden hairs behind.

'He's taken a fancy to you, miss, and that's for sure,' said the dog-seller, a man with a large cap and a very ruddy face. 'Be your friend for life, that one.'

'And I'd be his friend,' I said.

I'd never been a particular friend of any dog before. There were often strays haring up and down the alley, ready to make a nuisance of themselves, and Peg-leg Jack had his noisy terrier, but there were no calm gentle beauties like this golden boy.

'What's his name?' I asked, scratching his ears, which he seemed to enjoy tremendously.

'His name, miss? Why, he's . . . Brutus,' said the dog-seller.

He'd probably made the name up on the spot. It seemed a harsh one for such a sweet-natured animal.

'Hello, Brutus,' I said nevertheless, and the dog pressed against me, seemingly delighted that we were on first-name terms.

I stopped feeling quite so scared and lonely. I knelt down and laid my head against his back, putting my arms right round him.

'There, what a picture! It's as if you were soul mates already. Take him home with you, miss. It'd break my heart *and* his if you didn't take him away with you,' said the dog-seller, and he nodded and winked towards several of his mates, encouraging them to agree with him.

I knew he was simply trying to sell his dog but I went on hugging Brutus, wondering if I could possibly keep him as a companion. It would be so marvellous to have a dear friend with me. I could share my food and bed with him and he would be my devoted companion. Whenever the ache for Megs got too much to bear, Brutus would be there to hug and hold for comfort.

Would Miss Sarah Smith object if I brought a dog with me? I was sure I could train him to lie by my feet during lessons. The other girls would probably be delighted. He would act as a guard dog too, protecting us all from danger.

'How much is he?' I asked.

'Well, seeing as you two have taken to each other I'll be generous. He's a very special breed, with a lovely nature as you can see, and if you took it into your head to go hunting you'd find him a great retriever. I dare say some folk would fork out a fortune for him, but I'll give you a bargain price. Ten shillings! Can't say fairer than that, can I, lads?'

They all nodded their heads and declared the price extremely generous. Ten shillings! I had my five shillings and Mr Dolly's loose change. I fumbled in the purse. Count the coins as I might, I couldn't make them add up to ten shillings.

'I don't suppose you could reduce the price a little?' I asked.

'Come on, now, miss, don't waste my time. I could get a sovereign for him easy, not to say a guinea. Reduce from ten measly shillings? You've got a cheek!'

The chorus of lads shook their heads and echoed him. I stood up and stroked Brutus's strong back. I wished he was even bigger so I could climb on that back and let him carry me far away.

'I'm afraid I can't afford ten shillings,' I said.

'There now, don't look like that. Don't break my heart! I've got my own little girls to look after. I have to make a living, sweetheart,' he declared, shaking his head and clicking his teeth, and a couple of the lads shook and clicked too. Brutus seemed determined to join in the performance. He butted against me with his big head and looked up at me pleadingly with his soulful brown eyes.

'Oh, I want him so!' I said.

'Then you must have him, my duck. You're clearly made for each other. I can't stand between girl and dog, not when there's already such a bond between you. Tell you what. I'll knock a bob off. Nine shillings! Can't say fairer than that. I'm giving him away without a penny profit. Don't you think it a generous offer, boys?' he asked.

They nodded and cheered and patted him on the back and then looked at me expectantly.

'I'm sure it is a very generous offer, sir, but I'm afraid I simply haven't got enough money,' I said.

'Come on, now, child, don't play games with me. Look at you, with your smart little outfit. It must have cost a pretty penny,' he said.

'It was a gift, sir.'

'And *I'm* giving you a gift, letting you have Brutus cut price. He's got a lovely nature and will make a loyal guard dog. How can you resist? Especially when I can hear the tin clanking in that purse of yours,' he said.

'I've only got seven and six, and I should keep some of that for emergencies. I simply can't afford your lovely dog,' I said.

'Then what are you doing wasting my time?' he said, looking disgusted. 'Be off with you. Brutus – to heel, sir!'

Brutus took no notice, leaning against me lovingly. The man jerked his lead, yanking him so hard he choked.

'You're hurting him!' I protested.

'It's nothing to do with you. He's not your dog,' said the man, and he wouldn't even let me give Brutus one more stroke to say goodbye.

I trailed sadly away, hoping that Brutus would realize I wasn't deliberately rejecting him. I turned down a dank little alleyway, wanting to get away from the reek and din of the birds and dogs. Two of the lads ran after me. For one mad second I thought the dog-seller had relented and was going to let me have Brutus for my pocketful of change. But then one lad pinioned my arms while the other pulled the purse from my pocket. Then they gave me a shove into the gutter and left me lying there in the filth.

12

I **WAS SO STUNNED** I couldn't move. I lay there, feeling like a fool. How could I have been so stupid, flashing my purse about like that? I wasn't some country bumpkin fresh from the pigsties. I lived in London, for goodness' sake. I should have known better. It was my own fault I'd lost every single penny, all of it from dear, generous Mr Dolly, which somehow made it worse.

What about Anne Boleyn and Jimmy's shawl? Oh my Lord, both were missing. I started crying then, unable to bear the loss of my two dearest possessions, my *only* possessions – but when I got to my knees and stood up unsteadily I saw the sack lying crumpled in a corner. I ran over to it, but it was empty.

I started howling, blundering about in a stupor until I stepped on something soft. I gasped, terrified it might be some animal, but then I came to my senses. It was my beautiful blue shawl, balled up and cast aside. I clutched it to me and then started searching, hoping the lads might also have thrown away a little wooden doll.

I wandered along the alleyway, feeling the loss of Anne Boleyn almost as keenly as that of my sister, and then at last I spotted a scrap of red and green in the gutter. I darted forward and snatched her up, my own dear doll. Her face was still smiling, her little wooden limbs intact, her cloak and dress still spotless.

That was more than I could say for my own clothes. I was shocked when I came out of the dark alley into the sunlight. I had smears all over my coat, my stockings were torn and one of my felt boots was ripped at the side. I leaned against the wall, feeling sick. Oh, how I longed for Megs to come along and comfort me, winding her thin arms round my neck, rubbing her soft cheek against mine.

What would Miss Sarah Smith think of me now, filthy and torn? Perhaps she'd take one look at me and send me packing, not wanting a dirty ragamuffin besmirching her establishment. After all Mr Dolly's care and time and patience my beautiful outfit was ruined.

I wanted to go and search for those two boys in the crowd and punch them hard, but what little common sense I had left prevented me. No matter how well I fought, two big boys were much stronger than me, and they'd likely have friends who would join in. I'd be left worse off than ever – this time they might trail my shawl in the filthy gutter or stamp on Anne Boleyn out of spite.

So I made my way wearily away from the market, not even giving beautiful Brutus a second look. I imagined him padding along beside me on his big soft paws, teeth bared, ready to sort out any ruffian who so much as glanced at me, but it was hard work picturing him when I was so cast down. Every step I took made the rip in my boot a little bigger, and I wanted to weep at the sight of my coat. My dress was stained too, with the hem hanging unevenly below my knees.

Now that I was in a much bigger street I looked around for a horse trough, wondering if I could find a rag and dab at the stains, but I couldn't see one anywhere, though there was a constant stream of horses pulling cabs and carriages and huge omnibuses. I saw a boy holding a big broom and sweeping a clean path for the ladies when they made their way over the crossing. He wore a filthy shirt and ragged trousers, and no boots at all. When he ran, the soles of his feet showed hard and black, and the palm held out for a penny payment was black too from handling all the coppers. He didn't risk putting his money in his torn pocket. He had a worn leather purse hanging on a string about his neck. The purse looked very full.

Whenever a horse paused to lift its tail he dashed out into the street, busily sweep-sweep-sweeping with the big broom, though his arms were not much thicker than Anne Boleyn's stick limbs and seemed just as likely to snap. I judged him to be a year or two younger than me, and maybe a little simple – because his mouth hung open as he toiled and his eyes were dull.

I had always got on splendidly with simple children. Daft Mo treated me like a second mother and always came to me if he were troubled. Perhaps I could befriend this poor boy, and then maybe he'd spare me a penny.

I stood at the edge of the pavement and he came up to me.

'Was you wanting to cross, little lady?' he asked, bobbing his head at me.

'No thank you,' I said, smiling at him.

He could tell from my accent that I was no lady, just another London child like him.

'Then what you staring at?' He eyed me up and down. 'You look a real guy in them clothes.'

195

'Yes, I know. Some hateful boys pushed me over and stole all my money. I was wondering, could you possibly spare me just one penny so I could find a public washroom and clean myself up a little?'

'Not blooming likely! Them pennies are my earnings,' said the boy, putting one grimy hand protectively over his purse.

'Just *one* penny? Please?' I begged.

'If I don't take every single coin back to my master he'll beat me,' he said. 'And if you don't quit plaguing me *I'll* beat *you*!' He raised his filthy broom in a threatening manner.

'Hey, hey, you little varmint, are you threatening this young lady?' It was a lady herself speaking – a beautiful lady with shining auburn hair, amazing blue eyes, pink cheeks and a crimson mouth. All the women I knew were pale, with lank hair, dressed in muted shades of grey or brown or blue, whereas this lady wore a tartan silk dress with checks of emerald and scarlet, and a green jacket that fitted snugly over her chest. Her boots were equally astonishing – bright red leather laced with black ribbon, very pointed, with little heels.

Perhaps she wasn't *quite* a lady, given that she was wearing such a bold outfit. She didn't sound like a lady either, because when she saw the state of my dress she started swearing at the crossing sweeper, thinking he'd whacked me with his filthy broom. He dropped his broom, hung his head and started to cry. Perhaps he was simple after all.

'He didn't do it!' I said quickly. 'He just didn't like me begging.'

'You was begging off *him?*' said the lady, looking astonished.

'I just wanted him to spare me a penny so I could go and wash off all this filth,' I said, shaking my skirts. 'It was two thieving lads up in that songbird lane. They pushed me over and stole my purse with all my money.'

'Oh, you poor mite. Stop your bawling, varmint. There's still no call to go threatening a little lady, even if she's after your money. You want to be popular with all the girls, don't you?'

He nodded, scrubbing at his eyes.

'So you've got to learn to treat them nice, see. If they ask for money and you ain't got it or don't want to give it them, you don't try to whack 'em with your broom. You say, "So sorry, my dear, but I'm a bit short of tin at the moment," and then there's no hard feelings. You remember!' she insisted.

'Yes, ma'am,' he said.

'Now, if you will kindly sweep a clear path for us, seeing as that poor old nag has just gone and relieved herself, I will see about rewarding you myself,' she said.

The boy scurried about his business, and as we passed him the lady gave him two pennies for his trouble.

She saw me looking wistfully. 'Don't fret, I'm taking you somewhere you can clean up for free, Miss Woeful. What's your real name then?'

'Clover. Clover Moon,' I said. 'Thank you very much.'

'Think nothing of it, dear. Us girls have to help each other out, don't we? I'm Miss Thelma, dancer by profession.'

'A dancer!' I said, impressed. 'I haven't got any profession yet. Mildred was all set to make me start work at the sauce factory but I didn't want to.'

'You start work? You're just a baby! And you don't want to work in any factory either, toiling twelve hours a day with your back breaking. Who's this Mildred then?'

'My stepmother.'

'Oh. I had one of those,' said Thelma. 'We've got a lot in common, you and me. My stepmother made my life a misery. I couldn't stand her.'

'I can't stand Mildred,' I said. 'That's why . . .'

'Why you're running away?' Thelma guessed anyway.

'Well, she's one of the reasons. And also it's because of my sister,' I said, my voice starting to wobble. 'We only buried her today and I can't bear the thought of being at home without her.'

'You poor little kid,' said Thelma, and she put her arm round me a little gingerly so that her own clothes wouldn't get stained. 'So these are your funeral clothes, eh? Nice styling and such neat little stitches. Don't you worry, we'll get you mopped up in no time. Here we are!'

She'd been hurrying me along the pavement, and now stopped outside a gigantic building with a red carpet up the steps and gold doors.

'Oh my! Is this a *palace*?' I gasped.

'Looks like it, doesn't it? But it's just a theatre, dear. The Gaiety. *My* theatre. We'll give you a little wash and brush up inside,' said Thelma.

'Are you sure I'm allowed?' I said anxiously.

'Course you are. You're with me.'

'But it looks all shut up.' I looked up the stairs. The gold doors seemed securely locked and bolted.

'We don't go up *those* stairs. They're just for the crowd. The artistes have their own door,' she said proudly. 'Follow me.'

We went round the side of the theatre. I expected an even better door for the artistes, gold again but possibly studded with crystals. The peeling green paint of the wooden stage door was a disappointment.

There was an old man sitting in a small office whittling a stick with his knife. He grinned broadly when he saw Thelma. 'You're very early today, Miss Thelma! And who's this with you? A little sister?'

'She's a new little pal, Ronnie. And you're my *old* pal, aren't you? You won't object to my bringing her backstage for a little wash and brush up?'

'You can bring in a whole orphanage so long as you keep me as a pal,' said Ronnie, winking at her.

Thelma winked back. I wondered if this was a special theatrical greeting and did my best to wink too, which made old Ronnie chuckle.

The theatre was surprisingly shabby inside, with lino on the floor and narrow bare stairs, but I loved the dancers' dressing room. There were mirrors on all the walls and little shelves scattered with glorious potions and powders, and racks and racks of costumes in exotic colours: short swishy tulle skirts in buttercup yellow and crimson and turquoise blue; little black satin bloomers with matching skimpy bodices edged with gold fringing; and long flounced scarlet dresses plus white petticoats with scarlet ribbons. There were fancy pairs of shoes scattered all over the floor as if engaged in a complicated two-step: pink satin ballet shoes; black patent laced boots; and scarlet boots with black ribbon like the ones Thelma was wearing.

I knelt down, marvelling at them all. I wished Megs could see them too. She had always ached for pretty clothes, especially a pair of fine new boots. She'd always had to inherit my worn-out ones, and they were second-hand when *I* got them, so they were falling to pieces, the heels worn right down and the soles flapping. Even after all that wearing the leather stayed hard, and Megs's feet were especially tender so she always had angry blisters.

I stuck my hands in a pair of the scarlet boots. They were as soft as gloves.

'Dancers' boots,' said Thelma. 'Especially light, with soft soles. They wear out fast, but the management always coughs up for replacements. They like us girls to look smart.' She smiled at herself in the wall of mirrors, striking an attitude, and a dozen sister Thelmas struck simultaneous poses too.

My own reflection appalled me. I looked so thin and pale, with livid weals on my forehead. My cap was lopsided and my beautiful black clothes were ruined.

'Don't look so tragic,' said Thelma. 'Strip down to your shift in the water closet through there and have a good wash in the basin. Then I'll give your clothes a quick scrub.'

I hesitated. I was used to whipping my clothes on and off in front of my brothers and sisters, but I felt very shy in front of Thelma. I stood still, clutching Anne Boleyn and the sack.

'Here,' said Thelma, taking them from me, shaking her head fondly. 'So you still play with dolls, do you?'

'She's a special gift. I don't exactly play with her,' I insisted.

'Well, Dolly here looks as good as new. Which is more than I can say for her mother,' said Thelma. 'Come on, let's skin a rabbit.'

She undid all my buttons, unlaced the boots, and had me shivering in my grubby shift in seconds.

'There now! My, you *look* like a little rabbit – though you certainly wouldn't feed a family of four. Go and wash yourself quick. There's plenty of soap. The management looks after us girls well. There's some theatres that herd you all into one room the size of a cupboard with no washing facilities whatsoever, yet they dock your pay if you don't look fresh as a daisy.' She chattered on as she took a damp rag and sponged both my boots.

I went into the water closet. I stared around the little room in awe. There was a white china sink with shining taps and a cake of pink soap in a little dish. A large white towel hung on a brass hook and there was a pile of small clean face cloths on a little table, with a big raffia basket containing a few used ones. Best of all there was a large lavatory with a hanging chain and wooden handle and a polished mahogany seat. There was even a blue-and-white pattern down inside the pan – tiny figures crossing odd little bridges in an oriental country.

We didn't have a china sink at home, only a tap, and Mildred rarely bothered with soap. We didn't have towels or face cloths, just old rags. We certainly didn't have a magnificent indoor lavatory with a decorative pattern, we had the outside privy, and it always smelled and looked disgusting.

I filled the sink and washed myself all over, even though I'd had a proper wash that morning. It already seemed weeks ago. The soap was soft on my skin. Then I used the lavatory, though it seemed dreadful to pee all over the pattern. There was even a roll of paper to wipe myself with.

When I came out of the water closet Thelma was sitting cross-legged on the floor, her sleeves rolled up and her jacket unbuttoned, stitching away at my torn boot like a tailor.

'Oh, Thelma, can you mend it?' I asked.

'Well, I'm giving it a go. The stitches will make the felt pucker but it should hold for a while. They're flimsy little boots, though very pretty, only really good for indoor wear. The soles are nearly worn through already. You'll have to patch them with cardboard. Can you sew?'

'A little bit.' I'd turned up dresses for Megs because she was so small, using hasty tacking stitches until Mr Dolly showed me how to hem neatly.

'Well, you finish off your boot while I set to work on your clothes. Dear Lord, did those nasty boys *roll* you in the gutter? They're in a right state!' said Thelma, clicking her tongue. 'But your saucy beret is as good as new.' She tried it on, tipping it to one side at a jaunty angle. 'Very French,' she said, admiring herself in the mirror.

'It suits you,' I said.

'Yes, it does, doesn't it?' she said complacently. Then she looked at me. 'You're shivering, poor little mite. You'd better have my jacket.'

'No thank you, I have a shawl,' I said, proudly producing it from my sack.

'Oh my, very fancy.' Thelma sifted through my clothes. 'Oh dear Lord, I'm going to get that muck all over my own outfit if I'm not careful!' she declared.

'Then please let me do it,' I said.

'No, little rabbit, I'll manage,' she said. 'I'll just have to strip off too.'

She was nowhere near as shy as me. She had her jacket and dress off in a trice, her fingers undoing each button, hook and eye so speedily that I couldn't help staring.

'We have three costume changes in the show,' she said. 'You have to be quick about it or you find yourself going onstage in your drawers. And how the crowd would love that!'

Her underwear was extraordinary. I had no idea that grown-up ladies wore such amazing laced corsets. I'd seen Mildred without her dress but she simply wore her old threadbare shift, plus a petticoat on Sundays. Her large chest flopped loosely like a pillow down her bodice. Thelma's chest was firmly pushed into place by her corset, beautifully arranged like two peaches on a plate. Her petticoat was frilled and trimmed with pink lace to match the little rosebud sewn at the top of her corset.

I wondered if I would ever be able to wear such beautiful clothes.

'Do you earn lots of money as a dancer, Thelma?' I asked her as she fetched lavatory paper, more rags, the violet soap and a bucket of water.

'Not really, dear, not for all the hard work we do. But I get by. I do a turn at midday at a dining club – a little solo act that goes down well with the gentleman, and they pay a bit better,' said Thelma, spreading my clothes out on the floor and then setting to work, scraping and rubbing and scrubbing.

'Oh, Thelma, you're doing such a good job!'

'Well, I know what I'm doing, dear. I worked in a laundry when I was fourteen, and they teach you all the tricks. Couldn't stand the work though. My hands were always scarlet, the colour of me fancy boots, and in the winter when I had chilblains I was near screaming,' she said.

'So you left?'

'Yes. Though it was a case of out of the frying pan into the fire,' said Thelma.

'What do you mean?'

'Well, I went into service, didn't I, forging me own reference. It was hard work too, but I didn't feel boiled to death like a lobster every day, and the missus seemed nice enough. And the master. Too blooming nice, he was. He quite turned my head and then I was a little fool.' She gave me a sideways glance. 'Do you get my meaning?'

I nodded.

'Yes, well, I won't dwell on what happened next. They weren't good times, I tell you, but I tried to keep my spirits up. One day I was dancing in the street when the barrel organ was playing, and this gentleman stopped me and said I had natural talent and was quite a looker and why didn't I try my luck on the stage? Of course I thought he was having me on, but he was actually a producer, would you believe.'

'So now you're a famous dancer!' I said.

'Well, I wouldn't go that far, dear. I'm not a solo act, just one of a line of dancing girls. But I earn my keep and you can't say fairer than that.'

'Do you think I could ever be a dancer too?' I asked. I'd done my own share of twirling round to barrel-organ music and taught Megs and Jenny and little Mary several fancy steps.

I wondered if I dared show Thelma – but she was shaking her head at me.

'You're not really the right type, dear. The management like dancing girls big in all senses of the word. You're always going to be the small, scrawny type, little rabbit,' she said, rubbing away at my coat.

'Oh dear,' I said, sighing.

'Don't look so down-hearted. You seem like a clever girl to me, if a bit naïve. Are you good at your lessons?'

'I don't rightly know, as I've never been to school. I've always been kept at home to look after the little ones.

But I can read and write and I know quite a lot, I suppose, because Mr Dolly's forever telling me things.'

'Mr Dolly?'

'He's the loveliest gentleman ever, and so very kind to me. He gave me Anne Boleyn.' I nodded to her, sitting on the floor beside me. 'He makes wonderful dolls and he's very learned and extremely kind, especially to children, but just because he's a little crooked in his person, with a poorly back, folk laugh at him and say dreadful things. Why do people have to be so horrid?' I asked passionately.

'Who knows? They just are,' said Thelma.

'But some people are very kind. *You're* very kind, Thelma. I'm so grateful to you.'

'Bless you, sweetheart, all I'm doing is cleaning up your clothes, and that's no trouble. You got that boot stitched yet? Better try it on to make sure it still fits.'

It was a little too snug at first, squeezing my ankles, but the felt was so soft it stretched as I wandered around the dressing room, examining all the paints and powders and fingering the bright clothes hanging from the racks. My boot was almost as good as new, though now it had a jagged line of stitches on one side. Thelma went on soaking and scrubbing and smoothing my clothes until she shook them out and spread them before me on the floor.

She bobbed a curtsy to me. 'Well, ma'am, cast an eye on your pretty outfit and see if I've made a difference,' she said, pretending I was a lady and she my maid.

'Oh my goodness, you've made all the difference in the world!' I said. 'You're magic, Thelma!'

'There now, I've just cleaned them up a bit, that's all. They're still a bit damp. Leave them to dry a little,' she said, arranging the coat and dress over the backs of chairs. 'Here, we'll do a bit of dancing now to keep you warm. I'll teach you our opening number.'

It was the funniest dancing ever, all wiggles and bold moves and high kicks. Mildred would have died to see me showing my drawers but I was too out of breath laughing to care about being immodest.

Wait till I show Megs! I thought for an instant – before I remembered.

'What's up?' said Thelma. 'Have you got a pain?'

'It's Megs,' I said. 'My sister Megs. Oh, I miss her so.'

'What did she die of?'

'Scarlet fever,' I said.

'Oh!' said Thelma, and took a step backwards.

'But I haven't got it, I swear I haven't. Megs caught it from a shawl.'

Thelma's eyes widened as she stared at my present from Jimmy.

'Not this shawl, I promise,' I said hastily.

'Dear God, you know how to startle a girl,' said Thelma, fanning her face. 'So none of your family caught the fever too?'

'No. Mildred shut me in the cupboard, just to make sure.'

'She shut you in a *cupboard*?'

I didn't point out that it was the reasonably big cupboard under the stairs. I enjoyed seeing Thelma outraged on my behalf.

'She didn't let me out for days,' I said.

'Oh my, what a witch! Didn't your pa say anything?'

'He just does what Mildred says, mostly.'

'Then you're better off without them. You don't need family, Clover, not when you've got friends,' Thelma declared.

13

'**ARE YOU REALLY MY** friend, Thelma?' I
asked.

'Of course I'm your friend, you ninny,' she said, smiling
at me. 'Let's have a cup of tea, eh? And there's a baker's
two doors along from the theatre. Fancy a muffin?'

'Oh yes!'

My dress was still pretty damp and my stockings
wringing wet, but my coat was dry on the inside so I

slipped it on and found my way back to the stage door. Ronnie and I gave each other another wink, and then I ran along to the baker's shop with two pennies from Thelma clutched in my palm.

She'd told me to say they were for her, and as soon as I said her name the rosy-cheeked baker slipped a cherry tart into the paper bag on top of the muffins.

'Oh dear, I've only got two pennies,' I said.

'That's all right, love. A little treat, seeing as it's for Miss Thelma,' he said.

I went back to the theatre triumphantly, winked yet again at Ronnie and ran up the stairs. I got lost at the top and wandered along several corridors without finding the dressing room. I thought I'd found the right door at last, but found myself looking at a stout gentleman in a striped dressing gown applying powder to his large purple nose. We stared at each other in horror.

'Oh my Lord, a peeper!' he said. 'Be off with you, you nasty little urchin!'

I ran away, mortified. Thank goodness I ran the right way this time, though I only dared open the door when I heard Thelma singing away to herself.

'Hello, ducks,' she said. 'Kettle's boiling away on the spirit stove. I'll make the tea.'

'Thelma, I went into the wrong room and saw a strange man in his dressing gown!' I said.

'You saucebox!' said Thelma. 'Don't look so worried. I expect it was only Arnie, our operatic singer. Did he have a big nozzle?'

'Yes, and he was powdering it!' I said, amazed that a man should do such a thing.

'He was simply getting ready for the show. He comes in hours early so that the other fellows don't rag him. Arnie looks like a comic turn, so he primps for hours to make himself appear more dignified. He gets through tubs of green powder to make his nose less red, bless him, and it's rumoured that he squeezes that great belly of his into a lady's corset. Perhaps that accounts for his strangulated tone when he starts up all that Italian trilling.' Thelma put her hands on her chest and started singing falsetto as she made the tea.

I couldn't see any plates, so I tore the paper bag in two and set a muffin on my half and the other muffin and the cherry tart on Thelma's.

'We're sharing it, silly,' she said, dividing up the tart.

'But the baker put it in the bag specially for you,' I told her.

'Yes, he's a little gone on me,' said Thelma complacently.

'Is he your sweetheart?'

'Hardly! He's a dear soul but I'm setting my cap at someone a little grander,' said Thelma, waving my beret in the air with a flourish. 'I've got several gentlemen vying with each other to take me out to dine after the show, all proper toffs.'

As we tucked into our muffins and tart she told me about each one. One was called Sam, one Arthur and one Geoffrey, and they often sent bunches of roses to the dressing room and waited for her at the stage door.

'And which do you like best?' I asked, wondering what it would be like to have three gentlemen vying for *my* attention.

'Oh, they're all much of a muchness,' said Thelma. 'They seem sweet enough lads, but they've got no real style or breeding. No, there's this other fellow who sometimes comes to see the show. We don't know his name but us girls call him Lord Handsome, and he certainly is. Lovely clothes, very dashing, with truly gentlemanly airs. He always wears a cloak and carries a cane. He's got dark curly hair, beautiful aristocratic features and dark eyes – oh, such dark eyes. He sits in a box, and when we come on stage he leans forward as if to single me out, looking just at me with those dark eyes of his. They say he really is a lord. I do hope he is! Imagine if I was to be Lady Thelma one fine day!'

I was a vivid imaginer myself and I thought Thelma might be telling a fairy tale, but I smiled politely all the same and pretended to be very impressed.

Thelma nibbled her half of the cherry tart with her sharp little teeth, biting into the syrupy black fruit with such enthusiasm that a little syrup trickled down her chin.

'Dear, dear, look at me, dribbling like a baby,' she said, giggling. 'Never mind! When Lord Handsome makes me his bride I shall have my maidservant come running with a fine lace handkerchief so I can mop myself up in a moment.' She wiped her chin with the back of her hand. 'Do you want to see the show tonight, little rabbit? I dare say I can slip you in somewhere. You can see me dance my little tootsies off and peer up at the box to see if Lord Handsome is there.'

'I'd love to see the show, but perhaps I'd better find Miss Sarah Smith's place first or I won't have anywhere to sleep tonight,' I said. 'Unless . . .' I paused hopefully, wondering if Thelma might actually invite me to share her digs as she'd already been so friendly to me.

'I wish you could stay with me,' she said, understanding. 'But I don't actually have my own place. I'm staying with some of the other dancing girls – there are actually three of us in the bed and one on the couch, so it's uncomfortably crowded as it is.'

'Oh no, that's quite all right,' I said hurriedly. 'Do you have any idea what the time is, Thelma?'

'Well, it's nowhere near show time or some of the other girls would be drifting in. Run down and ask Ronnie. He has a clock in his office. It's his job to sign us all in, and if anyone's late he's meant to report us to the management – but he's not a snitch,' said Thelma, licking away the last of her cherry tart.

I did as she suggested, counting the doors this time and taking note of each twist and turn and flight of stairs, not wanting to risk another encounter with Arnie and his powdered nose.

I found Ronnie again, my head on one side and my eye already shut.

'I'm sorry to trouble you, Mr Ronnie, but I wonder if you could tell me the time?'

'Certainly, little miss.' He craned his neck, looking up at a clock in the corner, hidden from my view. 'It's five past the hour.'

'Five past which hour?' I asked. Five past three? Five past four?

'Five minutes past five,' said Ronnie.

'Oh my Lord!' I gasped. I thanked him and then flew back to Thelma. 'It's five past five! I had no idea it was so late. I meant to find Miss Sarah Smith long before now. What shall I do if her establishment is closed?'

'Hey, hey, calm down. No need to get in such a state. She'll keep her doors open at all times if she's rescuing girls off the street – stands to reason. Here, your dress is barely damp now. Let's pop it on you and make you all spick and span,' she said.

I folded my shawl and put it in my sack. I tucked Anne Boleyn in too. Thelma had been so kind to me that I wondered about giving her one of my precious possessions as a present. But they were so dear to me, given by such special friends. Besides, the shawl was plain wool, and blue. My new friend clearly preferred a fancier style of dress. Anne Boleyn was bright and fancy, but Thelma was many years past playing with dolls. And I couldn't give away the parting gift of the man who meant more to me than my own father.

Thelma was busy brushing my hair and then setting my black beret on at the right angle.

'I know!' I said. 'Would you like my hat, Thelma? I don't really need it now and I think it suits you more than me.'

'Oh, don't be silly, dear. I can't take your beret!' said Thelma, though she looked tempted.

'Please take it. You've been so very kind to me,' I said.

'Well, that's very sweet of you, little rabbit.' Thelma put the floppy beret back on her auburn hair and smiled at herself in the looking glass. 'Yes, it does suit me, even though I say so myself. I'll have to get myself a striped blazer to go with it. It'll look very dashing.'

'Perfect for when Lord Handsome takes you out walking of a Sunday,' I suggested.

'Are you teasing me, saucebox?' said Thelma, laughing. 'Now, I've got half an hour to spare. I'll come and help you find this Miss Smith's establishment.'

'Will you really? Oh, you're an angel, Thelma!' I said.

So we set off together to find Miss Sarah Smith's Home for Destitute Girls.

'What number is it in the Strand?' Thelma asked.

'I don't have the number, I'm afraid,' I told her.

'But it is definitely on the Strand?'

'Well, I don't think it's *on* the Strand,' I said. 'I was told it was just *off* it.'

'Yes, but off it *where*? A lane that actually runs off the Strand?' Thelma asked yet again.

'Probably,' I said.

'Or simply in the surrounding area?'

'Perhaps,' I said.

'And you don't even know which side of the Strand – south towards the river or north towards Covent Garden?'

I shook my head hopelessly.

'Oh my, little rabbit, you don't make life easy, do you?' said Thelma, but she didn't give up on me.

We went out of the theatre and on to the Strand. The crossing-sweeper boy stared at us, and I stuck my nose in the air. We walked the length of the Strand from Waterloo Bridge to Charing Cross, darting up and down the maze of narrow streets that bordered the Thames, peering hard at every nameplate and asking almost every soul who passed if they happened to know where Miss Sarah Smith's establishment might be.

Thelma asked for me at first, but her request caused comments and quips from the gentlemen: 'Destitute, are we, my dear? Don't despair, I'll happily share my lodgings with you.' I soon took over and gabbled out my question. But whichever one of us asked, there was always the same answer. No one seemed to have heard of Miss Smith or her institution.

At Charing Cross we crossed the Strand and started walking back again on the other side of the road. There were more little lanes to explore, but it still seemed a hopeless task. We heard clocks chiming the quarters, and Thelma speeded up until she was almost running.

'Oh Lordy, I'll have to go back to the theatre soon or I won't have time to change,' she said at last. 'Ronnie will fill in the attendance book for me, but if I'm not on stage in the right outfit when the curtain goes up then I'll lose my job. They sacked a girl on the spot last week when she was only a few minutes late. Her ma had been taken bad with her heart and she'd simply been trying to help, but the management wouldn't listen.'

'Go back now, Thelma. I'll carry on looking by myself. Please! You absolutely mustn't lose your job,' I said.

'But I hate to think of you wandering back and forth like a lost soul searching for this place that no one's ever heard of,' said Thelma, looking worried. 'I'm beginning to wonder if it even exists. It was definitely the Strand? There's a place called Strand-on-the-Green. Could it be over there?'

'I don't know! Mr Rivers just said the Strand.' I hadn't been concentrating properly. I'd never in a million years imagined that I would run away – I'd needed to look after Megs.

I started thinking of my other sisters too, gentle Jenny and pert little Mary. Mildred was softer with them, but she still cuffed them when she was in a bad temper. She was even fiercer with Richie and Pete, beating them if they grew too rowdy. They were such silly boys, forever egging each other into mischief, but they weren't bad lads. And what about dear baby Bert? What was I thinking of, leaving that poor little mite? Jenny seemed able to handle him, but she didn't really have my knack, for all Bert had favoured her recently.

Perhaps I'd been truly wicked to walk out on all of them. If I were a truly good person I'd go back now and take my punishment.

But if I went back now I'd never have the courage to leave again. In a few years one of the big lads would start courting me and I'd end up in one room with a husband and babies of my own, trapped for ever.

I had to make the break now. I wanted a proper education and training. I needed to find Sarah Smith's place. It was my only chance.

'You go back to the theatre, Thelma. I'll keep looking for it. I'll find it. Mr Rivers wouldn't have made it up. He said just off the Strand, I'm sure he did.'

'Well, we're nearly back at the Gaiety now. Let's just run up and down one last lane, and then, if we still don't have any luck, you're blooming well coming back to the theatre with me. You can watch the show and then I'll bed you down in the dressing room, and we'll start looking again in the morning. It's not safe to be wandering around on your own, especially when it gets dark. Drury Lane's just up there!' Thelma warned.

'What goes on in Drury Lane?' I asked.

'It's Gin Palace City, where all the bad girls hang out. *They* wouldn't do you no harm – they'd like as not make a fuss of you – but you get all the riff-raff gentlemen sniffing around, and I wouldn't put it past some of them to prey on a little rabbit like you.' Thelma put her arm round me protectively.

We looked up at the next lane, which was very small and dark.

'Little St Giles Lane,' I said.

'It's little, all right. Never even noticed it before,' said Thelma. She wrinkled her nose. 'It's a bit whiffy too. Perhaps we won't bother with this one. Don't look like there'd be a respectable girls' home in a dive like this.'

Even so I took several cautious steps into the lane, squinting up at the tall blackened buildings overhanging the narrow street. There was a brass plate on one of the doors. It shone brightly, clearly given a daily polish, which seemed strange in such a grimy street.

'Come on, Clover,' said Thelma, pulling at my coat.

But I took a step nearer so that I could read the engraving on the brass plate.

THE SARAH SMITH
HOME FOR DESTITUTE GIRLS

'Look!' I whispered.

'Oh my Lord! You're right, girl. This is it. I'd never have dreamed they'd have such a place here. Well, go on. Knock!' said Thelma.

I reached out a hand but I couldn't make myself grasp the polished knocker. I knew Thelma urgently needed to get back to the theatre and I desperately needed a bed for the night. But my hand wouldn't move. I was suddenly terrified.

'Give it a good old rap.' Thelma sighed, seized the knocker herself and rapped loudly several times.

'Ssh!' I said, stepping back from the doorstep in alarm.

'Well, we want them to hear us, don't we?' said Thelma. When no one appeared immediately she knocked again, even louder.

'Thelma!' I gasped. When the door opened I hid behind her.

A very small, elderly lady scarcely as tall as me peered at us through her spectacles. She glared at Thelma. 'Be off with you!' she commanded, though she only came up to Thelma's splendid bosom.

'I beg your pardon! That's no way to talk to a lady,' said Thelma indignantly.

'You're certainly no lady!' said the tiny woman. 'How dare you come battering at our door, disturbing all my young girls. You've no business coming here dressed up like a dog's dinner and flaunting yourself. Are you trying to lure my girls into your evil ways, is that it?'

'How dare you!' said Thelma, flushing deep pink. 'Don't you go telling *me* I've got evil ways! I'm a hard-working, decent girl, a dancer at the world-renowned Gaiety Theatre, I'll have you know!'

'A dancer at the theatre!' said the lady, unimpressed. 'Well, you're certainly not welcome here. This is a decent God-fearing establishment.'

'Yes, and I think God himself would be a-feared of you, you sanctimonious old trout!' Thelma retorted. 'I wouldn't step over your doorway if you paid me a thousand pounds. I've simply brought this poor child here because she's nowhere else to go.' She stepped to one side.

The woman blinked at me in surprise, taking in my black mourning clothes. 'Oh my,' she said. 'Well, you should have said sooner, miss. Hand her over then!'

I clung to Thelma, not at all sure I wanted to go in.

'I'm sorry, I really have to scarper now, little rabbit,' said Thelma. 'But come and find me at the theatre if you really can't stick it here.' She thumbed her nose at the tiny lady and ran off, her bright skirts rustling, her scarlet boots pounding the pavement.

I stared after her helplessly.

'Well, don't just stand there, child,' said the lady. She seized hold of my wrist and pulled me inside her establishment.

14

SHE **SLAMMED THE FRONT** door and then took a key from her pocket and locked it. I couldn't get out now!

'My goodness me,' she said. 'I'm afraid that young woman is not at all a suitable companion, child. What were you thinking of?'

'She's my dear friend,' I insisted.

'Then you're not a very wise little girl, and it's just as well you've taken refuge here. How did you hear about our establishment?'

'My friend Mr Rivers told me about you,' I said.

'About *me*?'

'Yes. You're Miss Sarah Smith, aren't you?'

'Don't be ridiculous. I am Miss Ainsley, the warden and head teacher,' she said grandly, tossing her head as if she were six foot tall instead of less than five. 'And your name is . . .?'

'Clover Moon,' I said.

'Clover Moon *and* . . .?'

'And I don't think I want to be here,' I said, clutching my sack for comfort.

'I meant that you should say, "Clover Moon, *Miss Ainsley*," for that is my name and that is how you should address me. And how can you say you don't want to be here when you've been standing in this hallway for scarcely a minute! Come with me, child.'

'No, I really mean it. I think I made a mistake coming here. Please can I go now?' I asked.

'Please can I go, *Miss Ainsley*!' she said, confusingly. 'No, of course you can't.'

'Am I a prisoner then?'

'Silly girl! Of course not. You came here of your own free will, did you not?'

'Yes, but now I want to go because I don't like it here!' I said.

'You're barely inside the front door. How can you possibly judge?' said Miss Ainsley.

I peered around the bleak, bare hallway with its narrow strip of carpet and dim gaslight. The only thing you could say for it was that it was clean. The smell of carbolic was so strong it made my eyes water.

'It smells!' I said, wrinkling my nose.

'There's no need to be so rude. We teach our young girls to be polite.'

'You weren't polite to my friend Thelma!' I retorted.

'She is clearly not a suitable friend for you, child. But I'm sure it isn't your fault that you're not more discerning. You cannot help the way you've been brought up. We are here to help you. Now follow me, if you please,' said Miss Ainsley.

I wondered about trying to snatch the front-door key out of her pocket, but she was formidable, for all she was so small. I found myself following her meekly. As we passed a staircase I saw faces peering through the banisters, staring at me and whispering amongst themselves. One girl stuck her tongue out at me. So much for politeness! I waggled my own tongue vigorously back. Then I saw a little child at the end who made me catch my breath. She was small and scrappy, with short wispy hair and great big eyes. She was so like Megs that my heart turned over.

'Please, who is that little girl – that one up there?'
I asked Miss Ainsley.

'You'll be able to meet the other girls at supper. You
must be interviewed first, and we will have to attend to
your person too.'

'What do you mean?' I said, alarmed.

'Ssh now. Enough questions. I hold to the view that
little girls should be seen and not heard,' she said, turning
and nodding at me.

'I'm not a little girl, I'm eleven. And if I don't ask any
questions I won't get any answers,' I said.

'Now you're being impertinent. One of our rules here
is that you learn to respect your elders and betters.'

She was clearly my elder but I didn't feel she was my
better at all, though I decided it might be wise not to
press the point. She took me into a small room at the end
of the corridor, again unusually bare, with just a table
and two stark wooden chairs. There was an accounts
book and a pen and inkwell on the table. That was all.
No ornaments, no knick-knacks, no velvet cloths or lace,
no potted plants, no needlepoint cushions, no pictures on
the walls.

Megs and I used to sneak off, exploring the streets
near the church where she now lay buried. Richer folk
lived there – some even seemed to have a whole big
house to themselves. We'd creep up the garden paths
and peep in between the cracks in the lace curtains. We

marvelled at all the fancy stuff crammed into each room. We played we were grand ladies, choosing furniture for our own big house, though we were often chased away by angry maids waving brooms and brushes at us.

This was a big house and yet they had less stuff than we had at home. Mildred took great pride in her mantelpiece clock, even though it had long since broken, and the twin china dogs that guarded it on each side. On the wall we had a picture of the Queen cut from an illustrated paper. Once, when Pa was in a silly mood, he had made all us girls curtsy to the black-and-white Queen, and then *he* did a curtsy too, which made us all laugh.

I'd once loved Pa with all my heart. I still loved my brothers and sisters. Was I really better off in this strange bleak house with no family at all?

Miss Ainsley pointed to one of the chairs and I slumped down on it, suddenly realizing I was exhausted.

'Come now, sit up straight – head up, shoulders back,' said Miss Ainsley, hitching herself up on to the chair opposite. She opened the large accounts book to a blank page in the middle, dipped her pen in the ink and then looked at me enquiringly.

'What was your name again, child?' she asked.

'Clover Moon.'

'You should say, "Clover Moon, *Miss Ainsley*." Please try to remember. You say you are eleven years old? Give me your birth date.'

'I don't rightly know,' I said truthfully. 'Pa said I was born in the winter near Christmas, but he doesn't remember the date.'

'Surely your mother knows?'

'My mother died,' I said flatly.

'Is that why you're wearing mourning now?' she asked, in a slightly gentler tone.

'Mother died when I was small. I'm in mourning for my sister. She was only buried today,' I said, my voice wobbling.

'That's very sad for you, dear. But try not to be sad for long. Your sister will be happy playing with the angels in Heaven now,' said Miss Ainsley.

I was sure Megs would sooner be down on earth playing with me, but I didn't argue.

'Is that why you're here?' asked Miss Ainsley. 'Can your father no longer look after you?'

'Pa hasn't ever really looked after me,' I said.

'But did he actually turn you out of the house? I have to be clear. We cannot accept girls if they are still wanted at home.'

'I'm not wanted,' I said.

'You're sure this is the case?' Miss Ainsley persisted.

'Look,' I said, and I pushed my hair back and showed her the weals on my forehead.

'Oh my goodness,' she said. 'He did this to you?'

'My stepmother. But he knew. And he didn't stop her. They don't want me. They didn't even want me to go to my sister's funeral. They didn't want her either.' I started crying. I wasn't crying for myself, I was crying for Megs. They hadn't even noticed she had the fever. She might have died in her bed before they'd realized anything was wrong. I was the only one who had loved Megs. And she was the only one in the family who had truly loved me.

'There there.' Miss Ainsley looked uncomfortable at my tears, but she felt up her sleeve and brought out a white handkerchief. 'Here now. Mop your face, dear. Well, it seems we have grounds enough to accept you into our small community. Let me continue taking your particulars, Clover Moon. Have you ever attended a school?'

I wiped my face, blew my nose and shook my head.

'You must say, "No, Miss Ainsley," if the answer is negative,' she said, busily writing. 'Don't look so despondent. We will give you intensive lessons here, and within a few months I'm sure you'll be reading simple stories and able to pen a short letter. Most of our girls make excellent progress.'

'I can read!' I said. 'I can read great long complicated stories. I haven't ever written a letter, but I'm sure I could if I tried.'

'Are you *sure* you can really read and write, Clover?' Miss Ainsley asked. She passed me a spare sheet of paper from the back of the book and gestured to the pen and ink. 'Show me.'

I'd never used a proper pen and inkwell before. Mr Dolly had always given me pencils. I had a little difficulty getting the right amount of ink on the pen nib. First I didn't get enough, so that no words came out on the paper at all, and on my second attempt I overdid things and made a great blot on the page. Miss Ainsley didn't comment, but I saw her raise her eyebrows.

I gritted my teeth, dipped the pen again and started writing:

I am Clover Moon and I am eleven years old. Mr Dolly taught me to write. He is an excellent teacher.

I was prepared to write a whole page praising dear Mr Dolly, but Miss Ainsley cut me off.

'That's enough, child. You do indeed have a very clear hand, and you spell well too,' she said. 'How about Arithmetic? Are you equally competent at your sums? Do you know your multiplication tables?'

Mr Dolly had failed to introduce me to them, and when Miss Ainsley wrote a series of figures in a special pattern I didn't know how to make sense of them. I felt foolish and hung my head, but when she asked how much change I would have if I bought two tuppenny-ha'penny cakes and one penny bun and gave the baker a shilling, of course I could tell her at once that I'd have sixpence change.

'But what sort of cake costs tuppenny-ha'penny?' I asked, puzzled. 'Is it a little cake or a big cake? Cherry tarts only cost tuppence and they're the best kind of little cake, but all the big family-sized cakes – seed cake and fruit cake and Victoria sponge – they all cost at least threepence, sometimes much more.'

'Are you being impertinent, child?' Miss Ainsley asked sharply.

'No, I'm just telling you,' I said.

'It's not your place to tell me anything. I am the adult. It is my place to instruct you,' said Miss Ainsley. 'You might be bright at lessons, Clover Moon, but you still have a great deal to learn.'

She continued to test me. I stopped seeming bright. I faltered in Geography. Mr Dolly had frequently entertained me with stories of extraordinary lands with vast deserts and dense jungles, and I could name every creature in his picture book of exotic animals – but I couldn't name a single capital of any country for Miss Ainsley. I didn't shine in History either. I could chat for hours about the Tudors – and of course name every one of Henry the Eighth's wives – but I didn't know the date when any monarch came to the throne.

My needlework didn't pass muster either. I could alter an outfit to fit my sisters, but when Miss Ainsley took a woollen stocking from the table drawer and asked me to start darning the heel I couldn't handle the clumsy needle and had no idea how to patch the hole neatly.

She seemed most shocked by my ignorance of the Bible. I'd seen tattered copies when the Bible-thumpers came down our alley shaking their tambourines and telling us we were all damned unless we changed our wicked ways. The alley folk were insulted and told them in no uncertain terms to clear off. The boys even threw rubbish at them. Richie and Pete thought this great fun.

I'd heard of God and Jesus Christ, but mostly because folk round our way used holy names as curse words.

'Don't you know any Bible stories? Not even Noah's Ark? Or Daniel in the Lion's Den? Or the most important story of Adam and Eve and how this world started?' Miss Ainsley asked incredulously.

I shook my head. 'My friend Mr Dolly told me many wonderful tales, but he didn't have much time for the Bible. He said he didn't care for a god who allowed little children to be crippled,' I said.

Miss Ainsley breathed in deeply. 'You seem to have a knack for picking the wrong kinds of friends, child.'

'Mr Dolly is the most perfect friend. He's always been extremely kind to me and taught me everything I know,' I insisted.

'But with no system whatsoever. He can't have used proper schoolbooks,' said Miss Ainsley.

She was right. Mr Dolly had bought one specially when he first started teaching me, but we both agreed it was very boring.

'I shan't know which class to put you in,' she continued. 'In many respects you belong with the very little girls, for all your fancy penwork. Ah well, tomorrow we will try you in the middle class and see how you get on. Now, let us get you organized. You need to wash and put on some respectable clothing.'

I stared at her as if she were mad. 'I've *had* a wash today. *Two* washes, actually. And I'm extremely respectably dressed.'

'It's one of our rules that all our girls wear uniform, Clover. It's to stop any bad feeling if one girl is more finely dressed than another. It's a very attractive uniform, specially designed by Miss Smith: a fresh blue cotton frock, with a navy reefer jacket for chilly days. *I* never had such a stylish outfit when I was a girl.'

'I have to wear black. I'm in mourning,' I said, wrapping my arms round my black dress and coat.

'Yes, I know, but you have to wear uniform even if you're in mourning.'

'Does it say so in the rules?'

For the first time Miss Ainsley looked uncertain. 'No, it doesn't. I don't think this situation has arisen before. I shall have to consult with Miss Smith tomorrow,' she said, pronouncing the name with reverence, as if she were referring to the Queen.

'Can't you consult with her now?'

'No, of course not. Miss Smith only comes to the home in the morning – when she can manage it. She is an extremely busy lady. She writes her books, she's a governor of the Foundling Hospital, she serves on various committees and she does a host of good works. We are so lucky that she still considers this establishment her top priority. *You* are lucky, Clover Moon. There are many thousands of poor waifs in desperate circumstances on the streets of London, suffering dreadfully. Many die, like your poor sister. Many suffer a fate worse than death, like your so-called friend.' She sniffed and shook her head.

I clenched my fists. 'Please don't talk about her like that, miss.'

'Miss *Ainsley*. I can see you're very attached to that person, but it's obvious she's a most unsuitable friend for a little girl.'

'How can you say that when you don't know her at all?' I asked.

'I know the type, child. There are many similar debauched girls who come flocking round this area. We have tried taking in some of the younger ones to see if we can instil in them a moral sense and purpose, but it nearly always proves disastrous. Miss Smith feels that our offices should be right in the centre of vice-land, within reach of any female in dire need, but for once I cannot help feeling that she might be mistaken. When they have spent an evening in one of those dreadful gin palaces, girls sometimes carouse outside our building, entertaining wretched men in our doorway, and when I tap on the windows and remonstrate they scream the most dreadful abuse at me.'

'Thelma wouldn't carouse,' I said, though I wasn't really sure what the word meant.

'She insulted me in the most vulgar way,' said Miss Ainsley. 'I fear she wasn't a true friend at all. She was only befriending you to get you into her clutches so she could corrupt you too.'

I couldn't bear the thought that Thelma had only been kind to me for an evil purpose. I knew she was a true friend. 'That's bleeding nonsense!' I said hotly.

Miss Ainsley gasped.

'I mean, that's nonsense, Miss Ainsley,' I tried, more meekly.

'I think you had better soap inside that dirty mouth when you take your bath, Clover Moon,' she said.

She went to the door and opened it. 'Sissy!' she called.

After a minute or so a tall girl in the regulation blue print dress came walking briskly along the corridor, her boots squeaking on the polished lino. 'Yes, Miss Ainsley?' she said.

'Please take this girl to the washroom, Sissy. Cast an eye over her clothes, especially the seams. If it seems clean enough and you're sure it's not infested, we will allow her to wear them for a month as she is in mourning for her sister. And keep an eye on her. She looks meek enough, but she's a contrary little madam with a mouth like a sewer,' said Miss Ainsley. 'Off you go.'

I stood up and clutched my sack.

'And take that dirty sack from her. It's in a disgusting state,' said Miss Ainsley, wrinkling her nose.

Thelma had scrubbed my clothes but we'd both forgotten my sack, and it was undeniably stained from my tumble in the alley. Nevertheless, I clasped it to my chest passionately.

'You're not taking my sack away!' I declared. 'Never! It's got my most treasured possessions in it.'

Miss Ainsley rolled her eyes. 'Dear Lord, must you turn everything into an argument, Clover Moon? I haven't the energy to deal with you any longer. Take her away, Sissy, please.'

'Certainly, Miss Ainsley. Why don't you go and ask Maude to make you a nice cup of tea? She's on kitchen duties this week,' Sissy said cheerily. She patted my shoulder. 'Come on, little 'un.'

'I'm not little, I'm eleven,' I insisted. 'I'm just small for my age.'

'Yes, you're a tiny scrap,' said Sissy.

'My friend Thelma calls me little rabbit,' I said.

'That's a sweet nickname.'

'She's a sweet lady. But *she* called her horrible names,' I said, nodding at Miss Ainsley as she left the room.

'Ssh! You mustn't be rude to Miss Ainsley.'

'*She* was rude to *me*,' I said.

'I dare say. But she means well. She's just trying to teach us right, see. She had her work cut out when I first fetched up here!' said Sissy. 'But you'll get used to her ways soon enough, Clover, I promise you.'

'I don't *want* to get used to them.' I looked longingly down the hallway to the locked front door. Then I looked up at Sissy. She seemed surprisingly obliging. 'Sissy, I don't really want to stay here any more. Do you have a key? Would you let me slip out without letting that Miss Ainsley know? This place isn't a bit how I expected. I really don't like it here.'

'Everyone feels like that at first, Clover. Try a few days first.'

'I don't want to! *Please* let me out.'

'Do you want to go home?'

'No! I want to find my friend Thelma. She says I can stay with her. That Miss Ainsley says horrid things about her, but she's truly kind and lovely and she'll look after me,' I said.

'I'm sure that's right, Clover, but I can't let you go, not if Miss Ainsley doesn't approve,' said Sissy, taking my hand. 'Come on, let's go upstairs.'

'So we're prisoners and Miss Ainsley is our jailor and keeps us locked in all the time?' I asked bitterly.

'We keep the door locked for security, that's all.'

'And we're never allowed out?'

'Of course we are! We have walks in the park, under supervision. And I dare say I could go anywhere I choose, as I'm a pupil teacher now,' said Sissy proudly. She kept hold of my hand and coaxed me gently upstairs as she spoke. 'You wait and see, Clover. I think you'll be really happy here.'

'No I won't,' I said. 'I shall hate it.'

'Then if you still feel like that in a week or so, you will have to talk to Miss Smith and see if she can help you,' said Sissy.

'Is she very severe like Miss Ainsley?'

'No, she's absolutely marvellous. We all love her.' Sissy opened a door upstairs. 'Don't we all love Miss Smith, girls?' she cried.

The girls in blue print dresses and pinafores who had peeped at me through the banisters were now gathered in this room, sitting at a table or lolling on battered sofas, drawing, sewing and reading. They all nodded enthusiastically in response to Sissy's question – apart from one strange, wild-looking child lying flat on the carpet, her face in a cushion. The little one with short wispy hair was half hiding behind the sofa. She had very big brown eyes that reminded me painfully of Megs.

'There now, Clover!' said Sissy. 'This is the junior sitting room. The seniors are next door. I won't bother to introduce you to everyone properly just now because it will simply be bewildering, but you'll get to know us all very quickly. There are fourteen of us – fifteen now that you're here too.'

'Temporarily,' I said.

Sissy took me into the large washroom at the end of the corridor. There were three baths in cubicles, a row of washbasins and three doors.

'See – we have indoor water closets,' said Sissy, opening one of the doors. I stared at the scrubbed seat and dangling chain.

'You pull it and everything gets flushed away!' she explained. 'Isn't it wonderful! We only had the filthiest shared privy at home, and it smelled so. Aren't we lucky to have such luxury?'

'I've seen water closets with pictures all the way down the pan,' I said loftily. 'These are just ordinary.'

These water closets smelled of such strong disinfectant that my eyes watered.

'Oh, don't cry,' said Sissy, looking concerned.

'I'm not crying,' I told her. 'I never cry.'

'Shall I help you take off your clothes?' she asked, running a bath for me. Steam rose all around us. The water looked alarmingly hot, almost boiling.

'I'm not a baby. And I don't need a bath, I'm clean as clean.'

'Yes, you certainly look it. You should have seen me when I first came here. I was so grimy I looked like a little chimney sweep. And my hair was in such a state I had to have it all chopped off. *I* wasn't a baby, but I bawled my eyes out then.'

'Is that why the little girl with the big eyes has got such funny short hair?' I asked.

'Oh, you mean Pammy, poor little mite. Her brute of a father snipped it all off with shears to punish her, and then he couldn't bear the sight of her and put her out of the house,' said Sissy.

'Oh, how dreadful!' I said. 'I had a little sister a bit like Pammy. She was only buried today.'

'Oh, you poor lamb,' said Sissy, and she put her arms round me.

I suddenly started crying, silently at first, but then in great gasps and gulps.

'That's it, have a really good cry. Let it all out. There now,' said Sissy.

We sat on the edge of the bath together, and I howled and howled while she held me. She didn't try to undress me and coax me into the bath. She just held me and stroked

241

me until I quietened down at last. Then she gave me a handkerchief and I did my best to mop myself up.

'I didn't cry before. I didn't think I could,' I said jerkily.

'I know, I know. Sometimes you have to be so brave and tough that you daren't let yourself cry, and then you find you can't, even when your heart is breaking,' said Sissy. She paused. 'I had a little sister too. My Lil. She died two years ago.'

'Does it still hurt as much?'

'Yes. It hurts terribly. But you get used to it. And it helps to live here, where I can look after the other girls. It's not so lonely.' Sissy leaned over and put her hand in the bath water. 'Oh my Lord, it's practically cold. What a waste of hot water.'

'If I really have to have this bath I'd sooner it was cold. I don't want it hot – it'll hurt me.'

'You wait, Clover. A hot bath is bliss. We take it in turns once a week. It's my favourite time,' said Sissy, letting out the cool water. 'We'll run the hot tap all over again for you and you'll see. It's absolute bliss.'

I was still very wary. I hated taking off my clothes in front of her, even my shift. Then I screamed when I put a foot in the water because it really was piping hot. But I gradually got used to it and stepped right in, and then very slowly lowered myself up to my shoulders. Then I lay back, my head resting on the porcelain. Sissy was right. It was bliss.

I felt all the sore bits of me soften and relax. I lay there with my eyes closed and very nearly fell asleep. Everything that had happened today whirled round and round in my head, very like a dream. I vaguely heard Sissy tiptoe out of the washroom. Then she was back, holding something that smelled of violets.

'Here. Miss Smith gave it me for my birthday. I'll let you use it just this once instead of that old carbolic,' she said, handing me a soap dish.

There was a small cake of deep purple glycerine soap. I sniffed at it rapturously. 'Oh, Sissy, it smells beautiful!'

'Don't it just! Exactly like violets – and I should know because I used to sell little violet posies.'

'Do you think Miss Smith might give *me* a cake of soap? Oh, but I don't know what day my birthday is!'

'She'll help you choose a special day. She makes everyone's birthdays special. She makes a cake too, with cream and icing, not just sponge like the one Cook bakes.'

'She doesn't sound a bit like that Miss Ainsley,' I said, rubbing violet soap on my arms and breathing in deeply.

'I've bought you shampoo for your hair too,' said Sissy. 'Not as special as the violet, but it still makes your hair shine when it's dry.'

She helped me lather my hair and then rinse it so clean it squeaked. When I got out of the bath at last I found I was bright pink all over. Sissy gave me one towel, very thick and warm, and rubbed my hair with another.

I winced a little when she rubbed the cut on my forehead. She looked at it and shook her head.

'Was that your pa? Mine used to hit me when he'd had a few,' she said matter-of-factly.

'It was my stepmother,' I said.

'Ah. So you didn't get on?' asked Sissy, giving me a clean shift from the airing cupboard.

'She hated Megs and me. She was all right with the others, more or less,' I said, wriggling into the shift. It felt so soft and smooth compared to my own crumpled grubby one. I held it out, examining it. There were no tears, no patches. It looked almost brand new. 'It's lovely,' I murmured.

I thought how Megs would love a shift like this. Hers were always hand-me-downs and desperately ragged. She'd skip about like a little fairy in this one.

'Wait till you put on your dress,' said Sissy, fetching a blue frock from the cupboard and shaking out the folds.

It looked very fresh and pretty, but I bent down and clutched the black dress Mr Dolly had stitched so lovingly for me. 'I need to wear this one. Miss Ainsley said I could as I'm in mourning,' I said.

'All right, if she says so,' said Sissy. 'Better put a pinafore on top to keep it clean.'

I struggled into the dress and pinafore, and pulled on my stockings and felt boots.

Sissy looked at them. 'They're beautifully made but they're not very sturdy. Why don't you keep them for best?' she suggested. 'I'll find you a pair of our boots. You'll like them – they're really soft leather.'

I thought of Thelma. 'Are they red?' I asked hopefully.

'Red!' Sissy laughed. 'You're kidding me, aren't you? Red boots indeed! You don't get *red* boots.'

'Yes, you do. My friend Thelma has the most beautiful red boots,' I said.

'Then she must be a very saucy girl,' said Sissy. 'Well, you're not getting red boots, especially as you're in mourning! Black boots, that's what you want.'

She fetched me a pair from a boot cupboard. I wrinkled my nose at them, though they were far finer than any boots I'd ever had at home.

'Pop them on, silly,' said Sissy.

These boots were certainly soft on my sore feet. They were burning because the cardboard Mr Dolly had used had worn very thin already. I cradled my felt boots protectively and then shoved them into my sack quick while Sissy was searching for a hairbrush.

She still spotted what I was doing. 'You can't put them in there, chickie. We've got to throw that sack away. Miss Ainsley said.'

I muttered a very rude word about Miss Ainsley.

'Language!' said Sissy. 'Come on, give us that sack.'

'Never!'

'Why are you hanging on to it, you funny girl? It's only an old sack and it's all covered in muck.'

'It's got my precious things in it,' I said. 'I need to keep them all together.'

'But not in that dirty old sack. I'll fetch you a clean pillowcase, how about that? You can keep your stuff in that.'

'All right,' I said cautiously.

Sissy reached right up to the top of the airing cupboard and brought down a small pillowcase. 'Big enough?' she said.

I nodded. 'And I can really keep all my things?' I asked her.

'Yes, though it would be silly to trail them round with you all day. Perhaps you'd better keep your pillowcase of treasures on your bed, or you can hide it in your bedside locker. Come on then, let's see what you've got. Give us a peep.'

'No, it's private,' I said, but I let her fumble gingerly in the sack.

She fished out my boots and shook her head at them.

'What else have you got in here then?' she asked, feeling around inside the sack. 'This is like a Lucky Dip at a bazaar! Hold on, what's this? It's like a little person! Here's its head, and stiff little arms and legs. Is it a doll?'

I nodded shyly, wondering if she'd tease me for treasuring a children's toy, but she gasped in delight.

'Oh my, what a lovely dolly!' said Sissy. She picked up Anne Boleyn and examined her admiringly. 'She's got such a sweet face – and look at her clothes!' She lifted her frock. 'She's even got lace edging her drawers, bless her! Oh, our Lil would have given anything to have a doll like this. Did she belong to your little sister then?'

'No, she's a special present to me from my dear friend Mr Dolly. He makes the most beautiful dolls in the world. He let me choose whichever one I wanted, and I chose Anne Boleyn. And I'm keeping her for ever and ever,' I said.

'Of course you are!' said Sissy. 'And you're keeping this shawl too. It matches our uniform. It's lovely – so evenly crocheted! Who made it for you?'

'My friend Jimmy gave it to me,' I said. 'His mum made it for him because he can't run around so he feels the cold – but he said I needed it more.'

'It sounds as if you've got some wonderful friends, Clover. I promise you'll make lots more here,' said Sissy, brandishing a large hairbrush. 'Here now, let's get the tangles out of your hair.'

'I can do it. I'm not a baby,' I said again, but I was finding it heady stuff being cajoled and persuaded and humoured.

I'd been the one mothering Megs and Jenny and Richie and Pete and Mary and Bert and Jimmy Wheels and Daft Mo and the twins and little Angel – and all the other kids in the alley. I'd been doing it ever since it was just Megs and me. It seemed so strange to be like one of the little ones here.

15

I WAS ONE OF the middle girls at Miss Sarah Smith's Home for Destitute Girls. I stared at them all as we ate supper. We were sitting at a long trestle table in the dining room, seven on one side, seven on the other, with Sissy and Miss Ainsley at each end. There were several girls as old as Sissy, tall, with big chests and small waists and wide hips. They whispered together, mostly ignoring me, though Sissy kept nodding at me encouragingly and checking to make sure I had enough vegetable soup and bread and cheese and milk.

It was plain food, but plentiful. I watched the way the other girls held their spoons and chewed their food, grateful that Mr Dolly had delicately helped me with my table manners. I thought I had no appetite, but once I'd forced a mouthful down I found I was ravenous. I was a little too eager using my spoon, so that I spilled a little soup. A very pretty, long-haired girl raised her eyebrows and nudged her neighbour, while I blushed. The girls around me all started whispering and pointing at my soup puddle. Miss Ainsley frowned at them. Muted conversation was clearly the older girls' privilege.

The littlest girls were at the four corners of the table, so that Sissy or Miss Ainsley could attend to them. There was one curly-haired child only Mary's age, and another about five with long hair and little spectacles. They spooned their soup and sipped their milk like little ladies, but the wild, dark-haired girl seemed unable to eat properly at all, though she looked older than the others. She lifted her bowl of soup and drank it down in several gulps, even though it was served piping hot; she bolted her bread and cheese, barely swallowing; she spilled half her milk down her front she drank so carelessly. Sissy gently remonstrated with her and mopped her up as best she could, while the child growled at her and tried to fend her off.

Little Pammy only nibbled a morsel and drank two sips of milk. I longed to encourage her – although she was at the other end of the table from me. I tried to catch her eye and smile reassuringly, but she only stared sadly at her plate.

We'd said a prayer at the start of the meal (I didn't know the words but clasped my hands and muttered, copying the others) and then we said an entirely different prayer of thanks at the end too. Everyone joined in except two. The wild child licked her bowl and then tried to lick everyone else's as well, and slapped at Sissy's arms when she tried to restrain her. Pammy slid slowly under the table until only the tufts of her hair were visible.

Then Miss Ainsley clapped her hands and we all had to take our cups and plates and bowls and cutlery to the kitchen. There was a lady there wearing a curious mob-cap and a white apron down to her boots, directing all the girls and smacking the heads of the naughty ones who stuck their fingers in the jam jar or tried to tear a chunk of bread from a loaf. She was as tall and fat as Miss Ainsley was small and thin. Perhaps she sampled her own bread and jam all day long.

She gave me an appraising look. 'So what's your name then, missy?' she asked.

'Clover Moon.'

'I'm Mrs Grant, the cook. You certainly look like you need feeding up. Suet pudding twice a day for you!'

I wasn't sure whether this was a treat or a punishment, but it seemed like a good idea to suck up to the person in charge of our food.

'Thank you very much, Mrs Grant,' I said, thinking she'd like me to add her name to every sentence like Miss Ainsley.

'Ooh, Miss Manners,' she said, mocking me. 'Just call me Cook, that'll do.'

I couldn't win! Sissy was trying to get the wild child to put her crockery in Cook's big sinkful of hot soapy water, but she threw her dish down on the stone flagged floor instead.

'The little vixen!' said Cook, and swiped at her.

The wild child screamed and tried to hit her back.

'No, Jane, you mustn't do that!' Sissy said, trying to catch hold of her arms.

Wild Jane clearly felt she must, and whirled her arms like a windmill, screaming her head off. One of her fists hit Pammy on the shoulder, and she winced but didn't make a sound.

'Oh, poor thing! Did she hurt you?' I asked, trying to put my arm round her.

Pammy seemed more worried by my gesture and backed away rapidly.

'It's all right, Pammy. Hey, you're not frightened of me, are you?' I said softly.

She hunched her shoulders and wouldn't look at me.

'Pammy's a bit shy, that's all,' Sissy panted, still struggling with Jane.

I was used to children having tantrums. Daft Mo had often fought for no reason, and tried to bite the other kids if they taunted him. I had learned how to hold him until he quietened.

'Try standing at her back and grabbing hold of her round her waist. Like this,' I said, seizing Jane.

She screamed even louder but couldn't reach round to hit me.

'There now. Got you tight! Calm down,' I said, and then I walked round and round the kitchen with her, trying to distract her. I spoke right into her ear to make myself heard above her racket. 'It's all right, I've got you safe. I'm Clover. And here's Sissy, who's so kind and looks after you. And here's Pammy, and she's got her hands over her ears because she doesn't like that noise you're making. And here's Cook, and she looks cross with both of us. And here's a pot of jam and it looks good to eat. I wonder if Cook will let you have a little spoonful if you stop that silly screaming?'

'I will not! I've never heard such a thing! You don't reward a child for dreadful behaviour. That one deserves a good beating. She's like a wild animal,' Cook declared. 'Get her out of my kitchen!'

'Come, Clover, come, Jane,' said Sissy, herding us out. 'Come out, everyone, and leave poor Cook in peace.'

She led us all up the stairs to the little girls' sitting room. 'There now, girls. Time for our Bible reading,' said Sissy.

I kept hold of Jane, so that when I squeezed on to a corner of the sofa she ended up sitting on my lap. I thought she might struggle to free herself, but she stayed where she was, and after a while I didn't have to hold her so tightly. She let herself go limp, flopping against me.

'I wouldn't have Mad Jane on *my* lap,' said the pretty girl next to me. Her voice was surprisingly stuck-up and grated on my ears. She might have had beautiful long yellow hair like a fairy princess but her blue eyes were mean, and I didn't like her. 'She wets, you know.'

The other girls on the sofa sniggered. Jane snuffled angrily and started sucking her thumb.

'She isn't going to wet on me, are you, Jane?' I said. 'She's my friend now.'

'That one doesn't know how to have friends,' said the princess girl. 'She's like a wild animal. She should be locked up and kept in a cage.'

'She's loopy,' said the girl next to her, who had very neat plaits and a prim expression. She tapped her forehead to make her point.

'Girls! Don't be unkind. Settle down,' said Sissy, opening up her big Bible. She stood in front of us a little self-consciously, found her place in the book and started reading.

I stared at her, astonished. Sissy was nearly grown up, the most senior of all the girls, and yet she read like an infant, pointing along the lines and often hesitating, having to have several stabs at the longer words. It was very difficult to make sense of what she was reading, especially as it sounded so strange and old-fashioned.

The girls fidgeted, yawning and nibbling their nails and pleating patterns in their pinafores. Jane reached up and took hold of a strand of my damp hair. I thought she was going to pull it, but she stroked it and then rubbed it against her nose like a comfort blanket.

'There now,' I murmured, touched.

Sissy nodded at us, smiling, and then laboured on with her text. She speeded up a little, and then at last shut the big book with a satisfying soft thud.

'Right, you little ones, let's go and start getting ready for bed,' she said. 'Elspeth, Moira, Pammy, Jane, jump to it. Jane? Bedtime!'

Jane clung to me, her fist tight round my lock of hair.

'Slide her off your lap, Clover,' said Sissy.

I wriggled and tried gently pushing, but Jane seemed stuck to me. 'I'd better come with her,' I said.

'That's very kind of you. She's taken such a shine to you! You're very good at soothing her,' said Sissy. 'I've tried and tried, but nothing I do seems to work.'

She rounded up Elspeth and Moira and little Pammy while I carried Jane. We all went to the washroom.

Elspeth and Moira were reasonably independent little girls. Elspeth had little pinch-marks on her nose when she took her spectacles off to wash round her face. Moira washed so vigorously that the front of her curly hair got soaked. They didn't use the water closet. They sat companionably side by side on chamber pots, singing a nursery rhyme.

Sissy wiped Pammy's face and fists with a flannel and then sat her on a chamber pot too. Pammy didn't struggle but her face screwed up, and she shut her eyes tight when she was on the pot, perhaps hoping we couldn't see her if she couldn't see us.

Jane struggled dreadfully, even though she seemed to have taken a shine to me. She badly needed her face wiping – she had soup and milk smeared all round her mouth – but when I tried to wash her she started screaming again.

'Ssh now, Jane. Don't act like I'm murdering you,' I said. 'We've got to get your pretty face clean.'

'Jane's not pretty!' said Moira.

'She's Plain Jane,' said Elspeth, and they both giggled.

'Don't be unkind. She's pretty. You're all pretty,' I said. I smiled at Pammy in particular, but she still had her eyes shut.

I wished I could look after her, but I had my hands full with Jane. She utterly refused to let me wash her face.

'All right, *you* do it,' I suggested.

Jane snorted but seemed to like this idea. She did indeed wash her own face, squeezing the flannel a little too tightly so that water dribbled down her chest. She went on rubbing nevertheless.

'There, good girl. I think you're clean as clean now. Give me the flannel back,' I said.

Jane shook her head. Then she suddenly shoved the flannel into *my* face and gave me a good scrubbing.

'Hey, Jane, stop it! I've only just had a bath,' I said.

Jane carried on, of course, while Moira and Elspeth laughed so much they nearly fell off their pots.

I was very damp and exhausted by the time I got the flannel out of her hand, and then there was another royal struggle to get her to sit on a chamber pot.

'She usually utterly refuses,' said Sissy. 'I put her in a napkin at night, and even then she always needs her sheets changing in the morning.'

'How about trying her on the lavatory?' I asked. Mary had always refused to go on the pot but didn't mind me holding her over the privy.

'The little ones always have pots,' said Sissy. 'I think the lavatory frightens them.'

'Yes, you can fall right in the water,' said Moira.

'Down, down, down, with all the fishes,' said Elspeth.

Pammy said nothing but she looked as if she agreed.

'Shall we try, even so?' I said.

Sissy didn't look keen, shrugging her shoulders.

'Come on, Jane. You're going to be one of the big girls,' I said, carrying her into the water closet.

She clung to me tightly, hiding her face when she saw the lavatory. Perhaps she really *was* frightened.

I closed the door so we were shut inside in private. 'I'll go first and show you how it works,' I said.

I sat her on the floor with difficulty and used the lavatory myself while Jane watched me in surprise.

'Now it's your turn,' I said, pulling down her drawers and lifting her on to the seat. 'Come on, tinkle tinkle – it's easy.'

And she did!

'Well done, you clever girl!' I said. 'Now I'll hold you up and you can pull the chain.'

Jane did so, and laughed when the water swooshed.

'There! You're really one of the big girls now,' I said.

I'd thought her so wild that I wasn't sure she could understand much, like Daft Mo – but when I praised her for being a big girl a huge, unexpected smile lit up her face. She looked like a real child, not a frantic animal.

When I led her out, still smiling, Sissy had the other three little ones lined up in clean nightgowns, having their hair brushed. She looked astonished. 'My, my! Did she really go?' she asked.

'Tinkle tinkle,' said Jane proudly, making them all laugh. Even Pammy looked amused.

Jane thumped her chest. 'Big girl!' she announced.

'Yes, you are a big girl, sweetheart. Good Lord, Clover, you've certainly got a way with children. I take my hat off to you,' said Sissy, miming removing a bonnet. 'I'm so glad you came to the home. You're going to be so handy here!'

I was pleased – but I still didn't want to stay in this strange place. I resolved to await my chance in the morning and then make a bolt for it. They couldn't leave the front door locked twenty-four hours a day. And wasn't there a *back* door – out of the scullery beyond the kitchen? I'd be off like a shot at the first opportunity, back to my friend Thelma.

She might even come knocking for me in the morning to make sure I was all right. I'd have to stay alert, seize my chance and knock little Miss Ainsley flying if I had to. I'd rush out of the door, and Thelma and I would run off triumphantly, and then . . . and then . . .

I could see I'd have to spend the night here first. I hoped I could sleep in the little girls' dormitory. Jane certainly did her best to insist that I actually share her bed, but this time Sissy wouldn't weaken.

'Don't be silly, Clover. You can't squeeze in with the little girls, for all you're so small! You'll be in the dormitory with the other girls your age.'

There were three rooms for the girls: a small nursery for the four little girls, a larger dormitory for the ten- to fourteen-year-olds and a bedroom for the older ones to share.

Sissy showed me her own private room, allotted to her because she was a pupil teacher. It was not much bigger than a cupboard but fresh and dainty, painted a pale rose-pink. Sissy smoothed the fancywork coverlet on her meagre bed, blew a speck of dust off her small looking glass and rearranged her floral china jug and basin with immense pride. She had one real rose in a blue medicine bottle, its petals filling the room with fragrance.

'You're showing such promise already, Clover. *You* might have a room like this one day. Isn't it pretty? Miss Smith said I could paint it any colour I wanted.'

'It looks lovely,' I said.

Megs and I had always longed to have our own bedroom. At home we had lain in each other's arms at night and fantasized about a pretty place just for us. We'd wanted a quilted coverlet instead of our coarse blanket, a looking glass and a china jug and basin, just like Sissy's. The walls of our old bedroom weren't painted at all, just stained plaster, and when I'd tried to draw a picture above our bed with chalk, the colours had smeared and spoiled immediately. We'd longed for flowers too, because our bedroom smelled really bad – of damp and cockroaches and boys' feet and used chamber pots.

I wished I could have a room like Sissy's, a place to keep pretty and private and paint any colour I liked. The walls were so smooth. Perhaps I could save up for some proper paints and a brush and do a portrait of Megs on the wall. I could picture it now: I'd have her sitting on the floor with her arms round her knees, her head on one side, smiling shyly at me. I'd work slowly, with a fine brush, making it such a true portrait that it would look as if Megs were really there in the room with me. I'd see her first thing every morning when I opened my eyes and last thing every night when I drifted off to sleep.

I could cover my bed with Jimmy Wheels' mother's soft blue shawl – and maybe find a china washbasin with a blue floral pattern. Forget-me-nots would be perfect. I'd sit Anne Boleyn on the windowsill with her back to me so that she could stare out with her bright green eyes.

Oh, I so wanted a room like that! But I had to go along to the girls' dormitory instead. It was torture. We all visited the washroom first, splashing our faces with soap and water and taking it in turns to use the three water closets. One poor plain lumpy girl had some kind of stomach upset and was in the closet for a long time. The princess girl giggled and went to listen at the door, her golden hair rippling down her back. Her small eyes glittered maliciously.

'Listen to the sounds Millie's making! She's utterly disgusting!' she exclaimed in her niminy-piminy voice.

The other girls gathered round, and they all started making vulgar explosive noises. When poor Millie emerged she went scarlet in the face to see they'd all been listening.

The princess girl sniffed the air and held her nose. 'Oh, the smell, the terrible smell!' she said, pretending to faint.

The others copied her too, while Millie hung her head in shame.

'Don't be so hateful!' I said. 'We all do that at times and we all leave a smell. It's not her fault!'

'And who exactly are you?' said the princess girl, tossing her beautiful hair over her shoulders.

'I'm Clover Moon.'

'Well, I suggest you mind your own business, Clover Moon! Who do you think you are, new girl? If you think the Millie-pig is so sweet, *you* go in the WC right this minute and breathe in her delightful fumes,' she said, and she seized hold of me and started pushing me into the cubicle.

I pushed back. She was a head taller than me, but I was stronger than I looked, and my arms were hard as iron from doing all the chores and lumbering little children about. I'd have pushed *her* in the water closet, but the others joined in and I couldn't beat a whole bunch of them.

I got shoved right inside. It was horrible. I put the hem of my dress over my nose and used the lavatory myself as quickly as possible. I pulled the chain and then attempted to open the door. It wouldn't budge. I'd unbolted it but it was somehow stuck. I put my shoulder to the door and pushed hard, but it still wouldn't move. Then I heard giggles. They must be leaning against it.

'Go away, you idiots!' I called. 'Get out of the way!'

More giggling.

'Ah, don't you like it in there, after all?' said the princess girl. 'Fancy that!'

They muttered outside.

'You show her, Mary-Ann,' someone said.

'Mary-Ann, Mary-Ann, I'll stick her head down the lavatory pan,' I chanted.

'You'll have to get out first,' said Princess Mary-Ann.

'I'm blooming well coming out now!' I said, banging hard on the door. I tried another shove, but it still wouldn't budge. 'Oi, Mary-Ann, you with the long yellow hair! Let me out this minute, you hateful rat-face!'

There was a gasp at that. It was clear that none of the others dared call her names. I tried kicking my way out, and the door did move an inch or so because I'd taken them by surprise. I kicked again, harder, but this time they held it firm.

'This is ridiculous!' I said. '*Let me out!*'

More muttering. Someone said that perhaps they ought to let me out now or Miss Ainsley might hear, and then they'd all be in trouble.

'I'm not letting her out *ever*,' said Mary-Ann. 'Not unless she truly grovels and begs me.'

'Then we'll wait till doomsday!' I retorted through the door, though I was starting to panic now. It wasn't just the smell, it was the lack of space. It was like being back in that dark cupboard again, as if the walls were gradually inching inwards against me, the low ceiling pressing right down on the top of my head.

'*LET ME OUT!*' I yelled again, hoping Sissy might hear me.

'Oh, she's getting really frantic now!' said Mary-Ann triumphantly. 'If we let you out you have to crawl on the floor and lick my feet, do you hear me, new girl?'

'I'll bite your toes off one by one and then spit them at you,' I said. 'Millie? Millie, are you there? Run and get Sissy!'

'Oh, you're set on snitching to Sissy, are you?' said Mary-Ann. 'Well, hard luck. Millie's not going to help you, are you, Millie-pig?'

'No, Mary-Ann,' Millie muttered, sniffling.

'Oh, Millie!' I said. It was all her fault I was stuck in the wretched water closet.

Then I heard gasps and a sudden scuffle of feet.

'Whatever's the matter, girls? Why are you being so tardy tonight? You should have been in your beds ten minutes ago. Get to your dormitory at once!' It was the clipped tones of little, shrunken Miss Ainsley.

'Sorry, Miss Ainsley,' they all chorused as they went out of the room.

I hoped she'd follow them, but I heard her stepping over to the water closet.

'Who's in there?'

'It's me, Clover,' I said, feeling ridiculous.

'Well, come out at once, Clover Moon!'

I tried the door. It opened immediately. I stepped out and shut the door behind me, breathing deeply.

'Whatever's the matter?' Miss Ainsley asked irritably.

'I . . . I couldn't get out,' I said.

'Don't be silly, girl. It's a simple enough latch,' she said. 'Now go to the dormitory, get changed into a nightgown, say your prayers and get into bed, quick sharp.'

'A nightgown?'

'A gown that decent folk wear at night,' she said.

I was clearly indecent because I'd never worn a gown in bed in my life. I just kept my shift on, and so did Megs and Jenny. Little Mary wore her vest and the boys their combinations. On washdays, when they were still damp and un-ironed, we wore nothing at all, and had great night games pretending we were naked savages on a desert island.

Miss Ainsley was delving in the astonishing cupboard, which seemed to contain enough linen for the whole of London. She took out a long, loose white robe, carefully ironed, with a white trim on the collar. If asked to guess I'd have identified it as a wedding dress.

'I'm to wear this dress in bed?' I asked.

Miss Ainsley nodded curtly.

'Do *you* wear one, Miss Ainsley?' I asked, wondering if this were possible as she was so very small. Surely it would trail across the floor and bunch up unbearably under the covers?

She went pink. 'You must learn not to ask personal questions, Clover. Yes, of course I wear a nightgown – and a nightcap too.'

I pictured this and had to press my lips together hard to stop myself sniggering.

'Off you go then,' said Miss Ainsley, making a little fluttering gestures with her tiny hand. 'I'll be in to check on all you girls in five minutes flat.'

'Miss Ainsley, do I absolutely have to sleep in that dormitory? Couldn't I possibly sleep in the nursery? I don't need a cot – I will quite happily curl up on the floor. I could be very useful if Jane is upset or needs her sheets changing, and I could keep an eye on the other three girls. Sissy says I'm very good at looking after them,' I said.

'I dare say you are, but you must sleep in a proper bed in the dormitory with the other girls your age,' she said firmly.

'I don't think they like me very much,' I mumbled.

'Nonsense,' Miss Ainsley responded briskly. But when she saw my face she stepped nearer and actually patted my shoulder. 'Don't look so anxious, Clover. You'll make friends soon enough.'

'I'm not sure I want to make friends.'

'You must learn to get along with the others, dear. Mary-Ann is a very popular girl. I'll ask her to keep an eye on you,' she said.

'Please don't!' I said, and hurried out of the washroom.

16

MY HEART BEAT FAST as I walked towards the dormitory, nightgown in one hand, pillowcase in the other. I wasn't used to being tormented by other children. I had grown up Queen of Cripps Alley. I was the one all the other children looked up to and admired. I sorted out the squabbles, chastised the bullies, dandled the babies.

I was the oldest child in the alley apart from Daft Mo, and he didn't count because he had the mind of a five-year-old. There were grown girls and boys of course, but they were all out at work at the sauce factory or down the market. A few boys were apprenticed as upholsterers or plasterers, or worked as pot boys in the tavern, and poor Georgie now worked with his pa in the night-soil business. Several girls were kitchen maids, and pretty Sarah worked in a grocer's and sneaked all kinds of goodies home to her family.

Of course they had once played in the alley, and they were all older than me, but because I'd always looked after Megs and the others they accepted me as one of the big ones, even though I was half their size.

I'd never really had a friend my own age. I didn't know how to manage it. I wanted to be with the four little ones or with Sissy in her private room. I did not, not, not want to be in a dormitory with Mary-Ann and all her hateful allies.

I heard them chattering excitedly behind the door. I thrust it open, my chin in the air, determined not to let them see I was frightened. The girls looked eerie in the flickering candlelight, ghostly in their long white gowns. They were all gathered round one of the beds but their backs were to me and I couldn't see what they were doing.

'She's here!' said one, and they all sprang away, sly grins on their faces.

'You took your time in the WC, Clover Moon,' said Mary-Ann, and the others sniggered. She put a jug down on her bedside locker and started brushing her long hair.

'Oh, let me brush your hair for you, Mary-Ann,' said a dark girl with a short bob and fringe. 'It's so beautiful. I'd give anything to have hair like yours.'

'Me too! Me too!' said the others, even Millie. She seemed pathetically keen to praise Mary-Ann, in spite of everything.

Mary-Ann smiled complacently and gave the brush to the dark girl, as if bestowing a very special favour.

'You have the loveliest hair I've ever seen,' sighed the dark girl, brushing slowly.

'Your hair is lovely too, Julia,' said Mary-Ann. 'It suits you having it cut in that bob. Perhaps I might try my hair in that boyish style.'

Julia and the others all protested, just as Mary-Ann had intended. I rolled my eyes.

'Why are you pulling that silly face, Clover Moon?' she asked. 'I think you'd better see to your own hair. If you've come straight off the streets you'll have lots of little creepy crawlies hopping about in that tangled black mop.'

'My hair's as clean as clean. I washed it here this very evening. *You're* the little creepy crawly, biting and stinging. Do you know what you do with creepy crawlies? You take a cake of carbolic and you go *thump-thump-thump* until they're squashed to a pulp. And watch out for *your* hair. How do you know I won't go looking for a pair of scissors? When you're fast asleep I might creep over to your bed and go *snip-snip-snip*, and then you'd have a boy's haircut, like it or not!'

The other girls squealed.

'Don't think you can threaten *me*, Clover Moon!' said Mary-Ann.

'I shall threaten you all I like,' I told her.

'So that's the way you want to play it, is it?' she said, grabbing her brush back from Julia.

'I'll play any way I want and I'll make sure I win.'

I wasn't sure at all. Mary-Ann was a head taller than me. I wasn't sure I could hold my own in a fight, especially if she used her hairbrush as a weapon. And it wouldn't be just Mary-Ann. All the other girls would wade in on her behalf, even Millie. I would be flattened before I could tug one lock of her long hair.

But I couldn't back down now. I made myself march right up to her, hands on my hips, looking as fierce as I could. Mary-Ann tossed her hair back elaborately. It gleamed in the candlelight and crackled slightly from all the brushing.

'I think it's time you were put in your place, new girl,' she said, and she raised her arm, gripping her hairbrush tightly.

But then the door opened and Miss Ainsley stepped into the room. The girls scurried over to their beds.

'What on earth is the matter with you tonight, girls? Why are you being so disobedient? I might have to report you to Miss Smith in the morning.'

'Oh, please don't, Miss Ainsley. We're so very sorry. I promise we've said our prayers – and now, look, we're in bed already,' said Mary-Ann, and she jumped straight into her bed, all the other girls copying her.

'Very well. I will give you just one more chance,' said Miss Ainsley. 'Come along, Clover, you're not even undressed. Get into your nightgown immediately!'

Reluctantly I started unbuttoning my dress and wriggling out of it. I heard smothered giggles.

'No, no, *under* your nightgown, you silly girl,' Miss Ainsley hissed. She clearly cared for modesty more than Sissy did.

I had to use my nightgown like a tent. It was incredibly difficult getting changed that way but I managed it at last.

'Now say your prayers,' Miss Ainsley commanded.

'You mean the ones we said at supper?' I asked.

'No, we said grace and then we gave thanks. I had better teach you the Lord's Prayer in Bible Study tomorrow morning. But for now, simply put your hands together, kneel down by your bed, shut your eyes and pray to our dear Father to teach you to be a good kind hard-working girl,' said Miss Ainsley.

I knelt down by the unoccupied bed – the one the other girls had been gathered round, giggling. I clasped my hands. I shut my eyes. The room had gone very silent around me.

'Dear Father,' Miss Ainsley prompted.

'Can't I talk to him silently inside my head?' I asked.

'Very well,' she said.

At least this wouldn't give the other girls another reason to laugh at me. *Dear Father*, I said silently. I didn't know how to continue. Father? I thought of Pa in his work clothes, with his muffler round his neck and his old cracked boots; Pa sleeping in the only armchair, snoring with his mouth open; Pa having a good scratch with his shirt tails flapping and his braces down; Pa leering at Mildred, patting her big behind in a way that made my stomach turn.

I didn't need a Miss Ainsley to tell me that these weren't holy images. I tried to think of a truly kind pure man. I thought of Mr Dolly in a long white nightgown to make him look more holy.

Dear Father, I thought I was a good kind hard-working girl, though Miss Ainsley clearly thinks otherwise. I don't like her. I especially don't like Mary-Ann. But Sissy is lovely, and I quite like Jane, for all she's so wild, and I want to get to know little Pammy properly because she reminds me of Megs. Oh, I miss my Megs so much. Will you please look after her if she's up in Heaven with you, and tell her that I love her dearly and always will and miss her so terribly.

I found there were tears trickling down my cheeks.

'Into bed now, Clover,' said Miss Ainsley quietly.

I sniffed and got into my strange new bed. It felt . . . wet. Soaking wet, right through to the mattress. So that's what they'd been doing. Mary-Ann had poured water from her jug into my bed.

She was staring at me. They were all looking at me, waiting. I opened my mouth to tell tales on them, but in our alley sneaking was the worst crime of all. Besides, I couldn't prove it was Mary-Ann. Miss Ainsley might not believe me anyway. Someone else would get the blame – probably poor Millie.

So I said nothing at all and lay still in my cold, soggy bed.

'Blow out your candles,' said Miss Ainsley.

There was sudden darkness and the smell of burned candlewicks.

'Goodnight, girls,' said Miss Ainsley.

'Goodnight, Miss Ainsley,' they chorused.

She went out of the room, her long skirt sweeping the floor as she went.

I waited in the dark. The other girls waited too, until the sound of Miss Ainsley's boots had receded.

'I hope your bed is comfortable, Clover Moon,' Mary-Ann called, and they all spluttered with laughter.

I said nothing.

'It's a good job you were so long relieving yourself in the WC. You wouldn't want to accidentally wet your bed in the night, would you?' said Mary-Ann.

I put my hands over my ears.

'Miss Ainsley comes and inspects our beds in the morning, you know. Oh, the shame of any of us ever having a wet bed. You have to parade up and down the dormitory with your stinky wet sheets over your head as a punishment,' said Mary-Ann.

I didn't know whether she was making it up or not. I didn't have the heart for a further slanging match. I was exhausted after my long, sad, adventurous day. I lay shivering in my soaking sheets, half dozing, while Mary-Ann's voice droned on like a mosquito.

I slept for an hour or so and then woke up, shaking. I thought I'd had the most terrible dream. I reached for Megs but I couldn't find her. My hands scrabbled over my icy soaking sheet – but there was no one there.

No Megs. I gave a great sob, but then I heard someone turning over restlessly in another bed. I remembered I was in a dormitory of hateful girls. I put my fist in my mouth and choked back my sobs.

I ached for Megs. I ached in my head and I ached deep in my bones. I'd hoped the sheets might dry from the heat of my body but they seemed wetter than ever. They would still be sopping in the morning. I thought of a bed inspection, the public humiliation, the sniggerings of Mary-Ann and the others. They'd spread the news that the new girl had wet her bed all round the home. Sissy might get to know. She wouldn't laugh or mock, she was far too kind, but she might suggest putting a napkin on me, and then I'd truly die of shame.

I curled into a tight ball, desperate for some kind of comfort. My precious pillow of possessions was stowed in my bedside locker. I wanted Anne Boleyn. She was too small and stiff and spiky to cuddle closely, but I longed to hold her, to stroke her shiny head and touch her little wooden limbs. Did I dare fumble in the locker for her?

But what if Mary-Ann spotted her in the morning? She'd laugh her head off at a girl my age owning a doll. Maybe she'd snatch her from me. Maybe she'd play catch with her, throw her around the room, tear her clothes, even stamp on her. I'd better keep Anne Boleyn hidden in her pillowcase no matter what.

The pillowcase made me think of the linen cupboard in the washroom. If they stored pillowcases there they might store sheets too. Clean dry sheets.

I sat up and peered around the dark room. I could just about make out each bed. The girls seemed to be lying still now. Several were snoring, and Millie was murmuring something but seemed deeply asleep nevertheless. I slid my legs out of bed and stood up slowly, praying the bed wouldn't creak.

I waited, holding my breath. Then I folded the blanket and put it on top of my locker, and felt the top sheet. It was a little damp – and the bottom sheet was wringing wet. I stripped them off as silently as I could and felt the mattress. Oh thank the Lord, it had a rubber sheet wrapped round it. There was a little pool of water but I mopped it with the top sheet until it was dry. Then I bundled both sheets up into my arms and crept as quietly as possible out of the dormitory.

The door had been left ajar so it was easy enough to slip outside. It was even darker in the hallway, but I remembered how to get to the washroom. There was no lamp there, but I felt my way to the cupboard and then explored the linen with quick hands. I found two clean sheets easily enough, and then another nightgown, because mine was clinging damply to me.

I changed into the dry gown and balled it up with the sodden sheets. I didn't know what to do with them. I wandered around the washroom, seeing if there was anywhere I could hide them. I tried the window to see if I could throw them out, but it was nailed shut. After searching further I found a wicker basket and shoved them inside in a sodden heap.

I decided to use the water closet again – after Mary-Ann's taunting I was terrified that I really might wet the bed, though I hadn't had an accident since I was a tiny girl, when Mildred first came to live with us. She'd thought I was simply too lazy to use the pot and had smacked me hard every morning. She said it was for my own good – I had to stop being such a dirty girl.

I was sad to have left all my brothers and sisters. I was sad to have left Pa. But I was glad, glad, glad that I was rid of Mildred at long last.

I scurried back to the dormitory. Everyone still seemed fast asleep. I took my clean sheets and silently spread them out, tucking them in neatly and putting the blanket on top. Then I climbed into bed and pulled the sheets over my head. For a few moments they seemed wet too, but it was only their cold crispness. It wasn't long before the bed warmed up. I felt warm too, but I still shivered. I slept eventually, though every time I turned over I woke up again because the bed felt so empty.

At last it was daylight and Miss Ainsley came knocking at our door. 'Wake up, girls! Rise and shine!'

There was a chorus of sleepy groans and murmurs.

'Did you sleep well, Clover?' Miss Ainsley asked.

'Not very well,' I said.

'Well, I dare say it will feel a little strange here at first, but you'll soon settle in. Now jump up, dear, and turn your covers down to air while you go along to the washroom. Come along, girls, all of you. Out of bed!' she said.

They all stumbled out of their beds and threw their covers back. I got out too, and slowly and deliberately pulled my top sheet right back. Miss Ainsley glanced at it. Every girl in the room stood very still.

Miss Ainsley brushed the bottom sheet with the back of her hand and then gave me a little nod. 'Off you go then, Clover,' she said. 'And the rest of you! What are you staring at?'

Mary-Ann didn't just stare. She blatantly felt my bed, looking bewildered. I smiled at her and then marched off to the washroom in my clean dry nightgown.

She caught hold of me when I was in there. 'So how did you pull that trick?' she asked, frowning. 'Those sheets were sopping! How could they be bone-dry now?'

'I wonder,' I said.

'No, don't mess with me,' said Mary-Ann, taking hold of my arm. 'Tell me how you did it!'

'Magic!' I said.

'What?'

'Look at my eyes. What colour are they?'

'Green.'

'Exactly. Witch's eyes. Everyone knows that. And I'm a witch. I can work all kinds of spells. So watch yourself, Mary-Ann. Don't *you* mess with me,' I said.

I pulled myself free, went into the water closet and slammed the door. I wondered if she'd try to trap me inside again, but the door opened easily enough when I came out.

They were all standing still, staring at me.

'Are you really a witch?' Millie quavered.

I nodded.

'Of course she's not,' said Mary-Ann, but she didn't sound certain.

'Do another spell then,' said Julia, the girl with the dark bob.

'Yes – make toads come jumping out of Millie's mouth,' said Mary-Ann.

Poor Millie squealed and covered her face, retching.

'I don't do silly party tricks like that,' I said scornfully.

Just then Sissy came into the bathroom. Jane was in her arms, screaming and kicking, Elspeth and Moira on either side, and little Pammy trailing behind, sucking her thumb.

'Oh Lordy, Jane's having a real roarer this morning,' said Sissy, struggling with her. 'Can *you* try to calm her down, Clover?'

I went over and took hold of her clenched hand. 'Hey, Jane. It's me, Clover,' I said, having to shout above her screams. 'What's all this noise?'

But there was no noise. As soon as she recognized me Jane stopped yelling. Her eyes still streamed with tears but she clamped her lips together and reached out for me. I took her from Sissy, holding her tight, and Jane crowed triumphantly, though she was still jerky with sobs.

'There now,' I said. 'Are you going to use your pot like a good girl?'

Jane shook her wild hair.

'Well then, I'd better take you into the water closet,' I said.

'Tinkle tinkle!' said Jane, laughing shakily.

I pushed in front of a whole queue of girls from my dormitory and took Jane inside. She refused to climb on to the seat herself, insisting I lift her up, but then performed perfectly. We emerged from the water closet hand in hand, Jane walking demurely, utterly composed, with a proud smile on her face.

'*That's* the sort of trick I do,' I murmured to Mary-Ann and Julia. 'But beware. I have learned the Black Arts too.'

'Do you think we're stupid?' said Mary-Ann, but she took a step backwards as I passed her, her hands going to her hair, as if I might really conjure a pair of scissors from mid-air and start snipping at her golden locks.

I breathed out as I turned my back on her. For the first and only time in my life I felt grateful to Mildred for calling me a little witch so often. She'd given me such an effective idea. My black mourning clothes were also useful. Mary-Ann and Julia whispered away while we had breakfast – creamy porridge with a little sugar sprinkled on top, so much nicer than the burned slop Mildred made. By the time our bowls were clean every girl in the home thought I wore black because I was a witch, and even the big girls were peering at me warily.

'What tales have you been telling?' Sissy asked me in the kitchen.

'Tales?' I said, trying to sound innocent.

'They're all saying you're a witch and can do magic spells. You're a bad girl to spin them such silly nonsense!' she said, but she was smiling.

'I can't help it if they're stupid,' I said. 'And *you* said I worked magic on Jane.'

'And so you did. Please keep it going – you make my life much easier. Just stop scaring the rest of the girls!'

'I won't. Well, not much. Sissy, don't tell them it's all play, will you?' I asked anxiously.

'Not for the moment,' she said. 'I can see it's a very useful ploy. I remember what it was like to be a new girl here. There was a lot of unwelcome joshing. But don't worry about it too much, Clover. You'll soon settle in and be one of the girls.'

I didn't *want* to be one of the girls. I was still seriously thinking of making a bolt for it, but I was no longer sure that Thelma was my best bet. I didn't want to go home either, though I longed to give little Bert a cuddle again. I missed Mr Dolly most of all, though I knew I couldn't be his little apprentice. He thought I should continue my education, so perhaps I should try hard to learn here.

I didn't get off to a good start. First of all we had Bible Study and I proved a total dunce, ignorant of everything. Miss Ainsley taught me the Lord's Prayer and I learned that quickly enough, though I was baffled by everything else. She spoke reverently about Jesus, and told a story about huge crowds gathering to hear Him speak. She said there were only five loaves and two fishes to feed this multitude, yet Jesus shared the food out so that everyone had enough to eat.

This was clearly impossible. Of course, it depended on the size of the loaves and fishes. I wondered if they might be gigantic loaves baked as big as a house, and fish as vast as whales, but when I asked Miss Ainsley she shook her head.

'Please don't ask out loud like that, Clover. If you have a question, put up your hand,' she said. 'And don't be silly, child – how could you possibly have giant loaves? Where would you get an oven that huge? And there were no *whales* in the Sea of Galilee! They were perfectly normal-sized loaves and fishes.'

I put my hand up.

'Yes?' said Miss Ainsley, sighing.

'But it wouldn't be possible, Miss Ainsley, even if the crowd only had one mouthful each,' I said.

'You're missing the point, Clover. Don't you see? It was one of Jesus's miracles,' she said.

I put up my hand again. She looked really exasperated. I was surprised. Mr Dolly had always delighted in my questions and said it was a sign of a lively mind. Miss Ainsley would have clearly preferred a dull one.

'What is it *now*, Clover? You must learn not to interrupt so much – unless there's something you truly do not understand,' she said.

'But I *don't* understand. What *is* a miracle?'

'What is a miracle, *Miss Ainsley*. How many times do I have to tell you? A miracle is . . . like magic. An amazing supernatural gift,' she said.

'Oh!' I said, enlightened at last. 'So Jesus was a witch?'

I thought Miss Ainsley was simply cross because I'd once again forgotten to say her name. I was astonished when she took hold of me and said I must go to the washroom and rinse my mouth out with soap this instant because I was a wicked blasphemer.

'Go this instant! Scour your tongue! Never, never, never say such words again!' she cried, in a passion.

I trailed off to the washroom. She wasn't there to supervise me, so I didn't do much scouring. In fact I didn't see the point of making myself sick with soap, so I simply rubbed a little at the corners of my mouth to make a convincing froth. Then I returned and quietly apologized to Miss Ainsley to see if it would calm her down. She nodded and pointed for me to return to my desk, as if talking to me further might contaminate her.

Julia leaned towards me. 'Did the soap make you gag?' she whispered.

'Of course not,' I whispered back. 'Witches absolutely love to eat soap, it's one of our favourite treats.'

'You're mad!' she said uncertainly.

'Ssh!' said Miss Ainsley, and started telling us about Jesus's parables. This seemed to be another word for a short story, but I didn't like to check with Miss Ainsley in case this was another blasphemous supposition.

It was a relief when the clock ticked round to ten o'clock and we could move on to another lesson, Writing. Mary-Ann was in charge of giving out notebooks and inkwells and blotting paper and very worn pens. She gave me a particularly scratchy pen and an inkwell silted up with someone else's blotting paper, but I felt I might prove myself good at writing.

However, we weren't allowed to write our own thoughts and ideas. Miss Ainsley copied out a long passage on the blackboard in her pinched copperplate and we had to copy it, word for word, Capital for Capital, comma for comma. It was a very tedious passage too – about a girl being wilful until her mother whipped her severely to teach her a lesson.

I didn't want to copy a story like this. I wanted to imagine the girl seizing the whip from her mother and lashing *her* severely because I didn't think any parent should beat a child, but I had just enough sense to see that this would aggravate Miss Ainsley. I'd end up having a whole cake of soap stuffed down my throat.

So I copied the nasty tale in the even, round hand that Mr Dolly had taught me, wondering why the other girls were sighing and groaning and shaking their hands as if they hurt. I craned my neck to see Julia's notebook and was surprised. She was sharp enough, but her penmanship was appalling, wavering up and down and sloping this way and that. She'd missed out some of the words and inserted several twice over, so that her passage didn't even make sense.

When I peered around it seemed that Julia was one of the most competent pupils. Several girls were still getting to grips with the first sentence, bent over their page with their pens clutched like drumsticks. Mary-Ann's writing climbed upwards as if her words were trudging up a mountain, and she'd made three big blots already.

Miss Ainsley wandered around, tutting and sighing and pointing out mistakes. She paused as she peered over my shoulder. I hoped she might praise me for my work. Mr Dolly always told me I was a very clever girl, and if he thought I'd tried extra hard he'd reward me with a peppermint. But Miss Ainsley was less encouraging. She simply sniffed and walked away without saying a word, though I was sure I hadn't made a single mistake.

I was finished long before the others and had nothing else to do. I turned the page and started drawing instead. I'd never drawn with pen and ink and made a few blots myself, but after several attempts I had drawn a passible portrait of Miss Ainsley in the classroom. I made her even smaller, dwarfed by the desks on either side. In fact I turned her into a little mouse, eyes beady behind her spectacles, her sharp nose twitching, a tail peeping out under her too-long skirts.

Julia glanced at my notebook and then burst out laughing. Miss Ainsley looked up. I tried to rip the page out of my book and scrunch it up but I wasn't quick enough. She snatched it, smoothed it out and stared at it.

'How dare you, Clover Moon! Go and stand outside the classroom in disgrace,' she demanded.

The other girls gasped. This was clearly considered a dire punishment.

I put my hand up and cried, 'But it's only a drawing, Miss Ainsley!'

'Put your hand *down!*' Miss Ainsley insisted, to my bewilderment, tearing my drawing into tiny shreds. 'You are not allowed to draw in your handwriting notebooks, especially not unpleasant caricatures. Outside this instant!'

17

I **STOOD OUTSIDE IN** the dismal corridor. I told
myself I didn't care. I'd finished my copy-writing
anyway. And it was pointless to boot. This home for
destitute girls wasn't going to teach me all the things I
wanted to know. If this was schooling then I hated it.
I thought of Mr Dolly's patience, his interest, his
encouragement, and longed for him.

I longed for Megs too. Our mother had given me a

good-luck name but it seemed like a grim joke now. Was it lucky to be here in this horrible home with cruel girls and alarming teachers and incomprehensible rules – while poor little Megs was miles away, lying in her fresh grave beneath the yew tree, all alone?

I so hoped being dead was just like sleeping. What if she were still awake inside her poor cold body? She'd be so frightened, so lonely, so desperate for comfort.

I closed my eyes and tried to talk to her inside my head.

I'm here, Megs! I'm still thinking of you and I always, always will. Don't be scared, darling. Imagine my arms around you, holding you tight. I'm stroking your hair, kissing your cheek, whispering in your ear.

'Oh dear, are you feeling that miserable?' said a voice.

A woman had come silently along the corridor and was now standing beside me. She was tall and held herself very erect, though she was quite elderly. She had long, wavy white hair arranged neatly in a snood. Her dress was black too, of a soft satin material that hung beautifully. Her hands were very white and carefully manicured, but she had ink stains along the forefinger of her right hand, showing she did a lot of writing.

'Yes, I am very sad, Miss Smith,' I said, wiping my eyes with the cuff of my dress.

'Here, my dear.' She took a lace handkerchief from

her sleeve and offered it to me. 'Have a good mop and blow. So, you know who I am. And as a matter of fact, I know who you are too. Miss Clover Moon?'

I nodded, mopping and blowing obediently. I didn't know what to do with the used handkerchief. Should I hand it back to her?

'I should pop it in the laundry basket in the washroom later,' said Miss Smith. 'Now, perhaps you'd like to tell me why you aren't in your classroom, Clover.'

'Miss Ainsley sent me out,' I said.

'Yes, I gathered that. Have you been very naughty?'

'I didn't mean to be!'

'Perhaps I'd better go and have a word with Miss Ainsley,' said Miss Smith. 'Stay here, Clover.'

She went into the classroom. I watched through the window as she talked quietly with Miss Ainsley, having to bend down low so that they could speak face to face. Miss Ainsley still looked very indignant, nodding her head emphatically. The other girls were listening of course. I saw Mary-Ann nudging Julia. Miss Smith looked very grave.

I was in serious trouble.

I don't care, I don't care, I don't care. I don't care even if they whip me, like the girl in the stupid story on the blackboard. I can stand any beating after living with Mildred all these years. I wish I was a real witch and could cast a spell on them. I hate them all.

291

It wasn't true. I liked Sissy, I liked Jane, I liked Pammy. And I liked Miss Smith too. She had seemed kind. But now she would think me dreadful.

She patted Miss Ainsley on the shoulder and then walked out of the classroom.

'Well, you've certainly made an unfortunate start with Miss Ainsley,' she said. 'You'd better come with me, Clover Moon.'

I felt my breakfast porridge stir uneasily in my stomach. *Was* she going to whip me? I trudged miserably behind her to a room at the end of the corridor. I followed her inside and she shut the door on us ominously.

It was a small room and sparsely furnished, but it wasn't bleak like the rest of the house. There was a bookcase full of books with green and red and deep blue covers. On a large desk with a green lamp, letters and papers and several registers were neatly stacked.

'Are they *your* books, Miss Smith?' I said quickly, pointing to the bookcase.

'No, they're not *by* me. I think it would look very vain if they were out on public display,' she said.

'Oh, I'd like to have seen one,' I said.

'I think you're trying to distract me,' said Miss Smith. 'But I'll let you have a quick peep.'

There was another door to one side, behind her desk. She opened it and I peered inside a secret little room. On another bookcase was a row of books with gold lettering and curly decorations on the spine, clearly children's books. There was another desk too, with a pen and inkwell, a blotter and an open manuscript book covered in neat handwriting. There was also a picture hanging on the wall. It showed children playing chase in an alleyway. There was something familiar about the delicate lines and soft shading.

'That's one of Mr Rivers's drawings!' I exclaimed.

'You are absolutely right! So how do you know that? You can't possibly read his signature from the doorway,' said Miss Smith.

'I know just how he draws! Mr Rivers came down Cripps Alley and drew all of us. He drew my sister! My little sister, who's only just died. I'd give the whole world to see *that* drawing again, it was so like her!' I said. 'I miss her so.'

I had to use the already damp lace handkerchief again. Miss Smith shut the door to her inner sanctum, guided me to a chair, sat me down and waited quietly until I'd finished weeping.

'There now,' she said. 'If you're going to carry on crying I'm going to need a handkerchief as big as a sheet to cope with your tears.'

'I'm sorry,' I mumbled, sniffing.

'I understand how distressing it must be to lose your sister. My own sister is very dear to me. I am pleased that Miss Ainsley is allowing you to wear your beautiful mourning dress for a while. It was very kind of her because we have strict rules that all girls must wear uniform while they are here. But I don't think you are repaying poor Miss Ainsley with polite and grateful behaviour!'

I sniffed again and bent my head.

'I hope that's a sign of remorse,' Miss Smith said. 'Poor Miss Ainsley. She is very shocked. She is such a good woman and she tries her hardest to help all the girls who come here, but she has declared you one of the most challenging she has encountered so far. She is worried that you might be a bad influence on the others.'

My head shot upwards. 'That's so unfair! I have been a positively *good* influence on Jane – just ask Sissy!'

'Yes, I know. Sissy says you have a very calming effect on poor Jane. She says you have a remarkable way with the little ones. I'm sure you'll prove a very capable assistant for her. But first you must learn to get on with poor Miss Ainsley,' said Miss Smith.

'I tried! I put up my hand whenever I spoke to her. I kept saying her name, even though she obviously knows her own name so it seems pointless,' I said.

'Miss Ainsley is simply trying to teach you normal classroom etiquette. All the girls have to learn how to conduct themselves when they come here. Now tell me, did you really say to Miss Ainsley that our dear Lord

Jesus was' – she lowered her voice to a whisper – 'a *witch*?'

'Well, she kept telling us about these miracles and said it was like magic and so I thought he might have been. I didn't realize she'd get so upset,' I said.

'You truly didn't intend to be blasphemous?'

'No. Well, I don't actually know what blasphe-thingy is,' I admitted, shame-faced.

'It's not a crime to be ignorant, Clover. You're clearly intelligent and articulate, and your writing skills are exemplary. I've just been looking at your test downstairs. But you have a great deal to learn about Our Lord. I suggest you pay attention in Bible Study and stay humbly silent while absorbing new knowledge.' Miss Smith looked at me. 'Clover?'

I sat still.

'Clover, are you listening to me?'

'Yes, Miss Smith. But I'm practising being humbly silent,' I replied.

Miss Smith stared at me and then smiled, shaking her head. 'I have no idea whether you are being obedient or impertinent, but I'll give you the benefit of the doubt. However, I *do* know that you drew a very unkind caricature of poor Miss Ainsley in your notebook and it upset her very much.'

'I didn't mean to upset her. It was a *good* portrait, very like,' I insisted.

'Oh, come, Clover. Miss Ainsley told me you portrayed her as a *mouse*!'

'But it was a fully-clothed, very sweet little mouse, simply with Miss Ainsley's features,' I insisted. 'I thought she might find it amusing.'

I hadn't thought any such thing, I'd only been intent an amusing myself, but I didn't like Miss Smith being severe with me. She was frowning now, and her look made me wriggle on my chair.

'Yes, well may you squirm, Clover. You know perfectly well that it's unkind to mock someone's appearance. Miss Ainsley is very sensitive about the fact that she's a short in stature.'

'I didn't mean to mock her. I hate it when folk are teased because of the way they look. My dearest friend Mr Dolly has a very crooked back and I can't bear it when people call him names. And Jimmy Wheels is my other good friend, and his legs don't work properly so he has to shunt himself around on a board with wheels – that's how he got his name – and the children in our alley used to torment him, but I soon put a stop to that,' I said.

'Well, I'm glad to hear it, Clover. I can see that you are a good kind girl at heart. You remind me of another tempestuous child I've taken under my wing,' said Miss Smith.

'A child here?' I asked, wondering if there might be another girl in the dormitory who could possibly turn out to be a friend.

'No, no, she lives in another institution but I visit her from time to time. I take her out to tea occasionally. Her name is Hetty. I think you'll like her. Shall we make a special bargain, Clover? If you apologize profusely to Miss Ainsley, work diligently at Bible Study, help Sissy with the little ones and do your best to get along with the girls in your dormitory, I will invite you out to tea too. Is that a deal?' asked Miss Smith. She held out her hand for us to shake on it.

My arm wavered. My fist was clenched.

'Oh dear! You're clearly hesitating,' she said.

'Could I possibly beg an extra favour?' I asked.

'It depends what it is.'

'Can I have a peep at Mr Rivers's picture in your secret study every now and then? I know it's not a sketch of Megs, but it reminds me of her, and the way we all played together in the alley,' I said.

'Of course you may come and look at it whenever you feel the need,' said Miss Smith. 'Now, I dare say the other girls are having their mid-morning break. You'd better run and join them.'

I still hesitated. I didn't know how to thank her. When Mr Dolly had been especially kind to me I'd kissed him on the cheek, but I could see that this was out of the question with Miss Smith. Instead I bobbed her a clumsy curtsy and then made for the door.

'Clover?' said Miss Smith as I was on my way out. 'One last thing!'

'Yes, Miss Smith?'

'If you were naughty enough to do a caricature of me, which animal would you choose?'

I looked at her long white locks, her big brown eyes, her long nose, her large stature. I thought of Mick the Milk with his cart and his faithful friend Daisy, who snickered softly whenever any child offered her a stump of carrot.

'I think I'd draw you as a big white horse,' I said.

'Clover Moon! You're incorrigible!' Miss Smith exclaimed, but when I closed her door I heard her laughing.

I didn't wish to join the other girls at their play. I crept into the dormitory, went to my cupboard and felt carefully for Anne Boleyn, unwrapping the shawl and then tipping her gently out of the pillowcase on to my bed. She was as bright and perfect as ever, even after her hazardous adventures.

I held her close, stroking her smooth head, then shaking my own hair forward so that it looked as if she'd suddenly grown long black hair.

'Oh my! Do you think it suits you, Anne Boleyn?' I asked.

She tossed her head from side to side, considering, then told me she thought it would be too much trouble having to brush it every day.

'You're absolutely right,' I said. 'Perhaps I'll cut off all my hair and then I won't have to brush mine either.'

I thought of poor little Pammy, whose brutal father had cut off her hair.

'Do you think I'll ever make friends with Pammy, or will she always shrink away from me?' I asked Anne Boleyn.

She said I would definitely become her friend but it would take time – Pammy's heart wasn't easily won because she was sad.

'You're very wise, Anne Boleyn. Much wiser than me,' I said.

Anne Boleyn smiled graciously.

'Do you think I'll ever make friends with all the girls in this dormitory?' I asked.

Anne Boleyn swivelled in my hand, looking at each and every bed. Her little painted eyebrows seemed to twitch when she looked at Mary-Ann's bed. She said that I would become friendly with most of the girls, possibly even Julia, but she very much doubted I would ever wish to be friends with Mary-Ann.

'You're the wisest little doll in the world!' I said, delighted with her. 'Can I ask you another question?'

Anne Boleyn lay down on my bed saying she was rather fatigued and needed a little rest.

'Just one more. It's the most important. Miss Smith has made a bargain with me. I've got to be good and work hard and not annoy that tedious Miss Ainsley, and if I do all this, she'll take me out to tea. Do you think I should keep the bargain – or run away again? I don't really like it here but I can't think of anywhere else to go. I don't want to wander the streets. I can't think of any way to earn my living. I definitely don't want to be a crossing sweeper. I'd like to be a dancer like Thelma, no matter what Miss Ainsley thinks of her, but I'm too small and thin. So what should I do, Anne Boleyn?'

She thought for a long while and then asked what kind of tea.

'What kind of *tea*?'

She wondered whether Miss Smith might treat me to a plate of buns – iced buns, currant buns, jam buns, cream buns, buns of every shape and variety – all the buns I could ever wish for.

I laughed. 'All right, Anne Boleyn. I'll keep my side of the bargain for a month and we'll see if the buns are worth it. Though it will be a struggle being good, when half the time I have no idea I'm actually being bad.'

But I did my best. When I heard the bell ring I went back to the classroom and swept Miss Ainsley a proper curtsy.

'I'm so sorry, Miss Ainsley. I'm very foolish and ignorant and don't know how to behave in school, but I shall try my best to be a dutiful pupil from now on,' I said, trying to sound as sincere as possible.

I didn't convince my fellow pupils. Mary-Ann and Julia groaned, mocking me, but Miss Ainsley looked at me earnestly.

'I say unto you, that likewise joy shall be in Heaven over one sinner that repenteth, more than over ninety and nine just persons, which need no repentance,' she said. 'It's a quote from the Bible, Clover. Our dear Lord of Forgiveness spoke truly and beautifully so I shall try to follow his example.'

I didn't know how to reply, so I curtsied again and went to my desk.

'You creeping toad,' Mary-Ann whispered.

'Don't remind me of toads,' I whispered back, miming toads spilling out of my mouth and then pointing at her meaningfully.

'I don't believe your witchy nonsense,' she said, and she reached out with her boot and kicked at my stool.

She took me unawares, so that I tumbled off it. I leaped back immediately, worried that I would be in trouble yet again – but Miss Ainsley had been watching.

'Mary-Ann! I saw that! Poor Clover, she could really have hurt herself, taking a tumble like that. How could you be so unkind when she's trying so hard to make amends for her behaviour? That's not like you at all!' she said reproachfully.

'I'm so sorry, Miss Ainsley,' said Mary-Ann, scowling. 'I didn't mean to. My foot just jerked all by itself. Please forgive me.'

'Very well, dear. But take care you don't do it again,' said Miss Ainsley.

I turned round. *'Now who's a creeping toad!'* I mouthed.

It was clear that Mary-Ann and I were always going to be enemies. However, I did my best to make friends with the other girls. It was hard work because they were all Mary-Ann's little followers, but whenever she went off arm in arm with Julia I made myself agreeable to the others. I drew them caricatures and sang some of Peg-leg Jack's saucy sea shanties. They laughed and tried to draw too and learned the rude choruses, but whenever Mary-Ann and Julia strolled into the sitting room they shut their mouths and shunned me all over again.

Then one day Sissy asked me if I could possibly look after the little ones for the afternoon because Cook had cut her hand badly and needed her help making pastry for the pies for supper. I was happy enough to oblige and miss my session of Needlework, which I hated.

I was supposed to be supervising the little girls' sewing. They were each assigned a square of canvas, a skein of wool and a fat needle. They were supposed to work rows of cross-stitch, but they were all fingers and thumbs, and Jane kept trying to poke the others with her needle.

'No wonder this is called cross-stitch,' I said. 'Let's do something else instead. Something that we'd all do.'

'I'd like to make the pies for supper!' said Moira, who was very round and keen on her food.

I thought about taking four little girls to the kitchen. They'd get in Sissy's way and make a terrible mess and I couldn't trust Jane near any of Cook's knives.

Could we *pretend* to make pies? I'd once stolen some flour from Mildred and mixed it into dough so that Megs and I could make pretend biscuits. I'd given one to Mr Dolly and he'd shown me how to make dough angels with wings and little wiggly curls. He'd taken them to be baked in the big oven at the cake shop, and then he'd painted them and hung them in his shop as decoration.

'Wait here a minute and be as good as gold or we'll all be in trouble,' I said. 'Do you hear me, Jane?'

'Tinkle tinkle,' said Jane.

'No – no tinkling in here! I'm just going to charge to the kitchen and back,' I said. 'Be good and I'll sneak you a handful of raisins.'

Sissy was whirling around the kitchen, Cook's big apron round her waist, rushing from larder to work table and back again.

'Sissy, I wonder if I could possibly—?'

'Oh, Clover, I'm in a terrible flap, dear. Could it wait? Why aren't you with the little ones? They're all right, aren't they?'

'They're fine, it's just that I wanted ...' I looked meaningfully at the larder.

'Take whatever you want,' said Sissy, barely listening as she frantically rubbed lard into flour in an enormous bowl.

I took a small bowl, a few ounces of flour in a bag and a handful of raisins and then bolted for the door, knowing that Sissy wouldn't approve if she knew what I was planning. But I thought it would be such fun for the children, and good for them to do something different.

I ran back to the nursery room, clutching my stolen goodies. On the way I saw two big girls carrying Mary-Ann to our dormitory.

'What's up with Mary-Ann?' I asked.

'She just fell over. She does that sometimes,' one girl said, rather vaguely. 'She needs to sleep now.'

Back home Mildred had often pushed me over deliberately, but I never needed to go to bed afterwards. I was pretty sure Mary-Ann was making a fuss about nothing. Perhaps she hated sewing as much as I did, and this was a clever ruse to avoid it. She'd probably spend the rest of the afternoon sitting in bed brushing her famous hair. I worried that, alone in the dormitory, she might get bored and start making mischief. I didn't want a soaking bed again. And what if she went poking in my bedside cupboard? What if she pulled out my pillowcase and discovered Anne Boleyn? What if she tried to hurt her? She could tear her dress! She could snap off her tiny wooden fingers! She could pull her legs out of their wooden sockets! She could saw right through her thin wooden neck with a kitchen knife, re-enacting her Tudor beheading.

I decided to follow her to the dormitory and rescue Anne Boleyn, but one of the big girls barred the door.

'Off you go!' she said, shooing me.

'But I need something from my cupboard!'

'You'll have to do without. Mary-Ann needs peace and quiet,' she said.

I had to give up and return to the little girls. I could hear them clamouring at the end of the corridor, calling my name imperiously. I sighed and went to the nursery.

I shared out the raisins one by one, making the girls pretend to be little birds opening their beaks.

'That's it, all fed,' I said.

'More!' Jane demanded.

'No, we're going to make pastry now.'

'Pies!' said Moira, clapping her hands.

'No, not boring old pies. We're going to make little pastry angels! Watch and I'll show you how!'

I fashioned one quickly – head, body, wings, little face, curls. Elspeth and Moira marvelled, which was very satisfying. Pammy wouldn't look. Jane snatched my angel, and then squashed her and cried.

'You don't need to cry, Jane. You can make your own angel,' I said, dividing up the rest of the dough and handing a quarter to each little girl. Elspeth and Moira made passable angels, though they were rather round and lumpy – they'd need very strong wings to enable them to fly. I showed Jane six times over how to fashion a head and a body, but she couldn't get it, and tried to eat the raw dough instead. I had to take it away from her, which made her scream and drum her heels on the floor.

I decided to let her lie there until she'd calmed down, and tried to get Pammy's attention instead. She hunched up in a ball and wouldn't look up at me or down at the dough I'd pressed into her hands.

'Lovely squishy dough,' I said, trying to make her knead it. 'And we can make shapes with it, Pammy. Little angels. You know what an angel is, don't you? I have a sister, Megs. She looks a bit like you. She's an angel now.'

Pammy looked vaguely interested for once. She peered around as if looking for Megs.

'No, she's not here. She got the fever and died so now she's an angel up in Heaven. She wears a long white dress and flies through the sky with her big feathery wings,' I said. I flapped my own arms. 'Yes, she flies like this.'

'She's dead,' Pammy said.

It was the first time I'd heard her speak. She had a gruff little voice that made my heart turn over.

'Yes, she's dead, but she can fly up in the clouds,' I said.

'My ma's dead,' said Pammy. She said it matter-of-factly, but a tear trickled down her cheek.

'So is *my* ma. Perhaps they're friends up in Heaven, and they both take care of Megs,' I said. 'Shall we make a dough ma?'

Pammy nodded and tried fingering the dough. She frowned and gave it to me. '*You* make it,' she said.

'You can do it if you try,' I said, but I fashioned the head and body and wings all the same.

Jane had calmed down now. She started pulling at me but I gently shrugged her off.

'Wait, Jane. I'll make you an angel too, but I'll just finish Pammy's first,' I said.

I gave Pammy a darning needle and encouraged her to poke two eyes and a smiley mouth on the dough face.

'She's smiling!' she said.

'Yes, she is. Did your ma have curls? Shall we make her some? You can do that bit. Just roll a weeny bit of dough and curl it round and stick it to her head. That's the way,' I said.

Pammy did her best. Then she took another wisp of dough and tried to stick it to her own head. 'I've got curls,' she said.

'Lovely curls,' I said, giving her chin a fond little pinch.

This was too much for Jane. She clenched her fist and battered the dough mother into a blob, and then tried to do the same to Pammy, hitting her hard.

Pammy screamed, Jane roared and Elspeth and Moira cried. Miss Ainsley came rushing into the room.

'Goodness me, this place is like a bear garden!' she cried. 'I thought you were meant to be looking after the little ones, Clover. Why aren't they doing their cross-stitch? And what on earth is that nasty grey stuff smeared all over the lino?'

'I'm so sorry, Miss Ainsley,' I said, hastily trying to scrape it all up and put it in the bowl. I didn't want her telling tales on me to Miss Smith when she next paid a visit. I wanted to be taken out for tea!

I tried to get the little girls to help me, but all four continued wailing.

'Oh dear goodness,' said Miss Ainsley, going from one to the other. 'Stop this silly noise, girls! I thought you were supposed to be so good with little children, Clover. I can't see much evidence of it so far. I don't think we can trust you to look after them again!'

'Oh, that's not fair, Miss Ainsley. We've been getting along splendidly, haven't we, girls?' I said.

Elspeth and Moira nodded, but Jane was too far into her tantrum to see reason and Pammy went and hid in the corner, clutching the mangled remains of her angel.

'What's that you've got in your hands, Pammy?' Miss Ainsley asked. She peered closer and must have spotted her pastry curl. 'And dear Lord, it's all over your hair too!'

She plucked it out of Pammy's sparse wisps. Pammy wept bitterly.

'Please stop! I won't have this silly shrieking! It's very bad for my nerves,' said Miss Ainsley. 'Dear goodness, what a day! First Cook cuts herself, then Mary-Ann has one of her turns and now you little girls get into a terrible pickle.'

'What's the matter with Mary-Ann, Miss Ainsley?' I asked.

She looked stricken. 'Never mind, dear. Off you go now. See if you can make yourself useful elsewhere. I need to get these little ones calmed down before supper.'

At least she didn't seem too cross with me – but what was all the mystery about Mary-Ann? I took the bowl of angel remains and slipped along to the dormitory. There were no big girls on guard now, so I opened the door and crept inside. The curtains were drawn so it was very dark, but I could just about make out Mary-Ann lying in her bed. She was breathing deeply and seemed asleep.

I went to my own bed and checked under the covers, but it was bone-dry. I opened my cupboard very slowly so that it wouldn't creak and felt for my pillowcase. It still had the soft shawl inside and I could feel Anne Boleyn there too. I felt her head, her body, all four limbs. Thank goodness she seemed intact. I shut her up again, then crept cautiously to Mary-Ann's bedside and peered down at her.

She had her hands pressed to her forehead as if she had a terrible headache, and when she turned in her sleep she gave a groan.

'Mary-Ann?' I whispered. 'Are you really ill?'

What if she had the fever? I reached out gingerly and put my hand on her forehead. She wasn't burning, but she groaned again.

'Does it hurt bad?' I asked.

'Dreadfully,' she murmured. She sounded unlike herself, young and scared.

'Shall I get Miss Ainsley?'

She shook her head and then started crying.

'There now,' I said. I knelt beside her bed. I couldn't help feeling sorry for her, even though she'd been so hateful to me. I smoothed back her long hair and then stroked her forehead. 'Does this help?'

'A little,' she murmured, still crying.

'Try not to cry – it will make it worse,' I said, wiping her face with a corner of the sheet. 'There now. Go back to sleep.'

'Are you . . . Clover?' she asked warily.

'Yes, but don't worry. I'm not going to put a spell on you,' I said.

'You can if you want. Make my head better!'

'I'll try.' I kept on stroking and murmuring, 'There now. Go away, pain. I'm soothing it away.'

Mary-Ann's breathing slowed and she relaxed. I tried taking my hand away and she didn't murmur or groan. I picked up the pastry bowl and crept silently out of the room.

18

THE NEXT MORNING MARY-ANN seemed almost normal, though she was very pale. She didn't say a word about our encounter, so neither did I. I wondered if she even remembered it because she'd seemed half asleep, but later that day, when we bumped into each other on the stairs, she gave me a tiny nod of acknowledgement.

She was different after that. She was still the boss of the class, she still picked on the weaker girls, she still said cutting things – but not to me. She didn't make friendly overtures, she left me alone, but she didn't seem to be my enemy any more.

Occasionally when she was spending the whole day at the home Miss Smith gave us middle girls a lesson. She didn't teach Bible Studies or Reading or Writing or Arithmetic or Needlework or General Housecare. She didn't write on the blackboard and set us copying in our notebooks. She simply talked to us, calling her lesson 'Travel'.

We stayed sitting at our desks, but Miss Smith took us travelling the world, telling us about the huge hot lands of Africa and India, the frozen climes of the Arctic and Antarctic, the thick jungles and vast deserts and endless seas that made up the world. She told us about intrepid women missionaries who went to spread God's word in heathen lands, and fearless female explorers like Isabella Bird and Mary Kingsley and Marianne North.

I especially liked the sound of Marianne North, who journeyed all over the world and painted all the exotic plants and had recently set up her own art gallery in Kew Gardens.

'Oh, how I would like to do that!' I exclaimed.

The other girls mocked me, laughing that a girl from the gutters of London could fancy herself a grand lady artist and traveller, but surprisingly Julia said, 'Though actually Clover really is very good at drawing.'

Everyone looked at Mary-Ann, expecting her to be furious that Julia of all people should stick up for me. Even Julia looked uncertain, wishing she'd kept her mouth shut, but Mary-Ann simply nodded.

When class was finished I followed Miss Smith back to her office, asking her if I could possibly look at Mr Rivers's picture again. I stared at the children skipping in the alley and imagined Megs and me joining in the game.

'You're missing your break time, Clover,' Miss Smith said gently.

The children in the alley faded back into the picture. I stared after them wistfully.

'You look very sad, dear,' said Miss Smith.

'I am, Miss Smith. It hurts so. I miss my Megs all the time. We were all in all to each other.'

'I understand,' she said. 'And I think Jesus understands even more. I hope you pray to him every night.'

I prayed to Megs instead, having private little chats to her inside my head when we knelt beside our beds.

'But in spite of your natural grief, you seem to be settling in,' said Miss Smith. 'Is that right?'

I thought about it. For the first few days I'd looked longingly at the front door. Once I'd even let myself out silently and run down the alleyway, but then I'd stopped, unable to think where to go. Thelma had made it plain I couldn't stay with her.

I'd thought of trying to find my way back to Mr Dolly, but what would I do if Pa and Mildred came looking for me there? I couldn't bear the thought of being dragged back home, though I often missed the children, especially little Bert. So after walking up and down the Strand feeling lost and frightened I returned to the Sarah Smith Home for Destitute Girls. I'd have been done for if Miss Ainsley had opened the door, but thank goodness it was Sissy. She'd pulled me indoors quickly and given me a hug. She told me she'd tried to run away several times when she first came to the home because she'd found the rules and routine so difficult.

'But a couple of days back on the streets trying to sell flowers soon changed my mind,' she said. 'Heaven knows what might have happened if I hadn't come back. And now look at me, one of the staff! You're a bright girl, Clover, brighter than me. You'll get on even better. You'll love it here too, you'll see,' she'd said.

I didn't love it here. I didn't want to end up in Sissy's place. I wanted to be an artist or an explorer or a doll-maker – any or all of these things. But I couldn't be any of these things *now* so I answered Miss Smith's question with a nod.

'Yes thank you, Miss Smith, I am settling in,' I said.

'And you have made friends with the other girls?'

'I suppose I have,' I said. 'I'm even sort of friends with Mary-Ann. Miss Smith, why is she here? She's not at all like us other girls. She talks like a lady.'

'Yes indeed, she does,' said Miss Smith.

'Then why is she destitute?'

It was Miss Smith who hesitated. 'I wonder if I can trust you with this information, Clover. It's very private.'

'I won't tell a soul, Miss Smith, I swear,' I said.

'Our girls come here for various reasons, most of them tragic. You have been very understanding with Jane. She's not quite right in the head and consequently finds it hard to behave herself. Her family abandoned her. And poor little Pammy was very cruelly treated because she is a little backward,' said Miss Smith.

'Yes, but Mary-Ann's not wild or backward.'

'I'm sad to say her family had her locked up in a lunatic asylum,' Miss Smith said gravely.

'A lunatic asylum? But that's where they put mad people!' I exclaimed.

'Yes, it is. And asylums are very grim places,' said Miss Smith.

'She's not mad though,' I insisted.

'Of course she's not. But she suffers from a condition which makes her have occasional seizures. She falls down and becomes insensible and then has to rest afterwards.'

'That happened to her recently! And then she had a very bad headache and I tried to soothe her,' I said.

'That was kind of you, Clover.'

'But she was all right the next day. Not a bit mad,' I said.

'Some people think that seizures are a sign of the devil, that sufferers are possessed. This is clearly nonsense, but even well-educated, God-fearing folk sometimes think like that. When Mary-Ann grew older and her seizures became worse her family consulted their priest, who unfortunately advised incarceration. She was locked up and put under restraint – a terrible experience for anyone, let alone a little girl. She spent nearly a year there – until while having treatment one day she seized an opportunity to break free. She climbed out of a window and ran away. It took her many days of wandering and suffering before she reached London, but then some kind soul directed her to our door,' said Miss Smith.

'My goodness!' I said. 'Poor Mary-Ann. So will her seizures ever stop?'

'I don't think so. I have taken her for a consultation at Miss Garrett Anderson's New Hospital for Women and Children, where they were very sympathetic but could not really help. Life is going to be difficult for Mary-Ann, but she is a very determined and resolute child,' said Miss Smith.

'She's certainly that!' I agreed.

'I think the same could be said for you, Clover. But I have been hearing good things of you.'

'Even from Miss Ainsley?'

'Miss Ainsley feels you are a little too impulsive at times, but she can see you're trying hard to conform to our ways. And Sissy speaks very highly of you. So as you have kept your side of the bargain I must keep mine. Perhaps you would like to come out to tea this Saturday?'

'Oh, I would absolutely love that! Do you think we could possibly have buns – or would that be too expensive?'

'I think my funds will stretch to a plate of buns, and maybe a plate of cakes too,' said Miss Smith. 'I'll ask my little friend Hetty as well. So, make sure you're spick and span and waiting downstairs at three o'clock this Saturday.'

She looked me up and down. 'Perhaps you might like to wear a fresh cotton dress for the occasion?'

Miss Ainsley had let me wear Mr Dolly's black mourning outfit every day so far, but the dress was getting very stained and creased now, though I'd done my best to sponge it. I fingered the worn folds anxiously, not sure what to do.

'You can still wear your smart black coat, dear. We'll have your black dress laundered and then you can keep it carefully folded in your bedside cupboard and wear it again if you really feel the need,' said Miss Smith.

So on Saturday I wore a blue dress. Sissy found me one that wasn't too big and wasn't too small. It was a novelty to have a new dress that fitted perfectly and was such a pretty colour. It still couldn't make *me* look pretty. I was too small and scrawny and my face was pinched, even though I'd put on a little weight now I was having regular good meals. But I was as clean as clean nowadays, with pinker cheeks, and my hair was well-brushed and shiny, though it was sparse compared with Mary-Ann's.

My black coat still looked very smart, if a little sombre, but my felt boots had hardly any soles left. I had to wear my ordinary boots, but I polished them until they shone.

The girls in my dormitory raised their eyebrows when they saw me all dressed up.

'Going out to tea, Clover?'

'Is Miss Smith taking you?'

'So you're Miss Smith's little pet now?'

'Stop that nonsense,' said Sissy, breezing into the dormitory. 'You know perfectly well that Miss Smith doesn't have favourites. She's taken you all out to tea at some time and I dare say she will again. Now stop lounging around the dormitory, it's a waste of your free Saturday afternoon. As it's such a lovely sunny day I'm taking the little ones for a walk in St James's Park. You can come too if you promise to walk two by two and behave yourselves.'

There was a squeal of delight and they rushed around getting ready.

Sissy put her arm round me. 'You look very fine, Clover – quite the little lady. Go and wait for Miss Smith downstairs. Have a lovely time,' she said.

'I will,' I said, though my tummy had tightened into knots. I'd been so looking forward to going out to tea with Miss Smith, but now I rather wished I was going out for a walk with Sissy and the other girls instead. I wasn't sure if I could make polite conversation all afternoon. And what exactly would this teashop be like? Would it be very grand? What if I spilled tea all down myself? Would I have to use a knife and fork if we were just eating buns and cake?

I'd had difficulty using cutlery at the home. I'd been used to eating with my hands before, but here we had to cut everything neatly and hold the fork and knife properly. Mary-Ann had mocked me when I first used a spoon. What if all the people in this grand teashop laughed at me too?

'It will be all right,' Sissy whispered reassuringly, as if she could read my mind. 'There's no need to be scared. You couldn't make a worse fool of yourself than me when *I* was first taken out for a meal by Miss Smith. It was before I even lived at the home, when my own dear sister Lil was still alive, and my pa. I'd met up with Hetty on the streets and—'

'Hetty? I'm going to be having tea with this Hetty,' I said.

'Yes, I guessed Miss Smith would introduce you two. You'll love her, Clover. Anyway, Miss Smith took us both to this fancy restaurant and I got all unnerved and I couldn't read the flipping menu, and then, when the meal came – a huge great amazing meat pudding – I stuck half of it in my napkin on my lap to take home to Lil, and the gravy seeped right through and started dripping down my legs! Dear Lordy, I couldn't get out of there fast enough,' said Sissy, laughing.

'Well, I'm definitely not going to order meat pudding. I want buns and Miss Smith said there might also be cake,' I said.

'There you are then. You can eat buns and cake without fussing,' said Sissy. 'But run downstairs right this minute. It was chiming three when I came into the dormitory. You'll be keeping Miss Smith waiting.'

I flew down the stairs so fast my boots slipped and I tumbled down the last three steps on my behind.

'Goodness, Clover, have you hurt yourself, child?' Miss Smith hurried towards me, looking concerned. She had a strange-looking girl with her, wearing the oddest old-fashioned clothes – a floppy white cap, a brown stuff dress with a white apron, and enormous boots much too big for her. She pulled a face at me and I jumped up quickly, feeling like a fool.

'I'm fine, Miss Smith,' I said, smoothing my skirts hurriedly. 'I'm so sorry to have kept you waiting.'

'That's quite all right. I can see you've been dressing very carefully. You look delightful, dear. That blue really suits you,' she said.

I felt my eyes pricking with tears. Nobody had ever said I looked delightful before, not even dear Mr Dolly. If we'd been alone I'd have taken her hand and squeezed it, but the strange girl was staring.

'This is Hetty, Clover. I'm sure you two are going to be great friends,' said Miss Smith.

I wasn't so sure about that, for all everyone's insistence. Hetty was eyeing me up and down. She didn't look too sure either.

'Come along, girls. I thought we'd go to the Northgate Tearooms in Piccadilly,' Miss Smith said.

'Oh lovely, my favourite,' said Hetty, and as we went out into the alley she took hold of Miss Smith's hand. 'Then might we go to the stationer's nearby? I have very nearly finished writing in the notebook you so kindly bought me.'

'Perhaps,' said Miss Smith. 'If you're a good girl.'

'Miss Smith, I'm always good,' said Hetty, laughing.

I doubted that! The alley was narrow and there was no room for me on the other side of Miss Smith. I had to tag along behind. Hetty had long red plaits bouncing on her back, so tightly tied it was a wonder her blue eyes didn't pop right out of her head.

I wondered why she wore such strange clothing. People stared at her, and when we walked along the Strand someone pointed and said, 'Look at that foundling child!'

Hetty stuck her nose in the air, acting like she hadn't even heard, but she went pink. She looked back to see if I'd heard.

'This is the Strand, Clover,' she said slowly, as if I were daft in the head. 'It's very busy, isn't it? You mustn't mind all the carriages and cabs. You'll get used to the traffic soon enough.'

'I'm used to it already,' I said. 'And I know the Strand very well. See that theatre over there? My dear friend Thelma dances on the stage there.'

Miss Smith blinked a little at that, but didn't seem as shocked as Miss Ainsley.

'She dances on the stage?' Hetty repeated. She let go of Miss Smith's hand and walked in step with me. 'Tell me, does she wear a pink sparkly dress and fleshings?'

'No, she wears all different colour dresses with amazing red pointy boots with ribbons,' I said.

'Red pointy boots with ribbons!' said Hetty, glancing down at her own clumsy footwear. 'Oh, how I wish I had red boots!'

'Me too,' I said. 'Though I have a beautiful pair of fine felt boots specially made for me. I'd have worn them today, but I have to save them for best. They were made to go with my coat.'

'Yes, I can see it's finely styled,' said Hetty. It was sunny but with an autumnal bite to the air, and she was shivering in her short sleeves. 'Pity it's so plain though. And black.'

'It's plain and black because I'm in mourning,' I retorted.

Miss Smith was listening to both of us attentively. 'Clover's family were stricken with scarlet fever. She lost her little sister.'

'That's so terrible. I've lost a brother, and I felt so bad when he died. And what about your mother? She didn't get the fever too . . .'

'She died long ago, when I was little.'

'Oh, you must miss her so,' Hetty said.

'Yes, I do,' I said, truthfully enough, because I'd felt the lack of my real mother throughout my childhood.

'I know just how you feel,' said Hetty. 'It's the worst thing in the world to lose your mother.'

Miss Smith was looking at her sympathetically. 'Hetty has lost her mother too,' she said.

But when she was momentarily distracted by a flower girl on the steps of a big church, Hetty came close to me. 'I *had* lost my mother – but now I've found her again! It's a secret though. You won't tell, will you?'

'I promise,' I said, touched that Hetty trusted me with such an important secret. I licked my finger. 'See my finger wet.' I wiped it on my dress. 'See my finger dry.' Then I drew my finger across my neck. 'Cut my throat if I tell a lie!'

We shook hands solemnly. Miss Smith looked round and saw us.

'I see you two are friends already,' she said, smiling. 'Look, girls, this is the great church of St Martin-in-the-Fields.'

We looked. I couldn't see St Martin and there were no fields anywhere in sight, but I tried to look impressed, and Hetty did the same. We decided we preferred the four great bronze lions in Trafalgar Square. Hetty wanted to climb on them but Miss Smith wouldn't let her. She hurried us towards Piccadilly and the tearoom and we skipped along, though Hetty stopped once, catching sight of herself in the plate-glass windows of a large shop.

'Oh my Lord, I look such a guy,' she said. 'You're so lucky to have fancy clothes, Clover.'

It was the first time in my life that anyone had envied *my* clothes.

'You should have seen me a few weeks ago. I wore old rags and my boots were so worn out the soles flapped,' I said.

'I wish these blooming boots would wear out,' said Hetty, stamping her big foot. 'And my frock has no doubt been passed down from foundling to foundling for the last hundred years at least!'

'Do you have to wear that get-up all the time?'

Hetty nodded. 'But when I'm grown up I shall wear silks and satins and smooth velvets in beautiful bright colours. I am going to be a writer and I shall publish books and make sacks of gold so I will be able to afford a fine dress for every day of the week,' she declared.

Miss Smith raised her eyebrows. 'Where are my sacks of gold, hmm?' she asked, laughing. 'I doubt I've earned half a sack throughout my entire career! But at least I've made a comfortable sufficiency, enough to treat two dear girls on their best behaviour.'

And treat us she did, taking us into a beautiful tearoom with golden doors and window frames, and a burly gentleman standing to attention on the steps to welcome customers and keep away the riff-raff. The walls were papered rose pink, with a deeper rose carpet on the floor. The tables were covered in white damask cloths and there were gold chairs with rose velvet cushions.

'Oh my!' I said, looking about me in awe.

'Oh, we go to all the finest tearooms, don't we, Miss Smith?' said Hetty, sitting at the nearest table and lolling back in her chair, examining the menu, totally at ease.

I still felt flustered, particularly when a waiter tried to take my coat. I held on to it for dear life, sure he was trying to steal Mr Dolly's masterpiece. Miss Smith whispered that he only wanted to hang it up for me, and promised he would give it back at the end of our meal, but I still clung on determinedly.

'I don't blame you, Clover. If I had a fine coat like that I'd want to keep my eye on it,' said Hetty. 'Now, which tea are we going to drink? Do you fancy Earl Grey or Darjeeling or Gunpowder or Orange Pekoe or Rose Petal?'

I thought she was making up these strange names – surely tea was tea. I wasn't sure she'd be able to read the fancy writing anyway, but when she passed me the menu I saw the listed teas for myself.

'My goodness!' I said. 'I think I'll have Rose Petal! Then my drink will match this lovely room.'

'And I'll have Gunpowder, and if anyone strikes a match my tea will explode!' said Hetty.

Miss Smith chose Earl Grey, the dullest. Hetty and I were a little disappointed when our teapots arrived. Hetty expected her tea to be fizzing ominously but it seemed perfectly tranquil, and I'd hoped my tea would be pink and fragrant but it looked an ordinary brown, though it did smell a little of roses.

The food was far more astonishing. Miss Smith ordered a plate of sandwiches for us to share. I expected a hunk of bread with dripping or jam. Instead there were slithers of soft snowy bread without any crust containing mashed-up egg or grated cheese or pink ham, all delicately garnished and set out on the plate in such a beautiful pattern that it seemed criminal to take one.

But Miss Smith bade us eat up, so we did, and each filling was delicious. I thought she had forgotten her promise of cakes and buns and had chosen sandwiches instead, but as soon as the sandwich plate was gone the waiter brought us a plate of strange pale-gold morsels that were perhaps cakes, perhaps buns.

'These are scones,' said Miss Smith. 'And see these little pots of jam and cream? We spread these on the scones.'

Hetty wasn't quite as knowledgeable as she made out because she set about slathering cream and jam on the top of her scone. Miss Smith didn't say a word, but I saw that she split her own scone in two and applied the cream and jam to the inside. I did my best to copy her but found my knife had a will of its own, and I ended up with very sticky fingers. Even eating the scone itself was rather a challenge. The jam and cream oozed out whenever I took a bite and I ended up spilling it down my coat, which was upsetting.

Miss Smith saw me rubbing at it with my napkin. 'Don't worry, I'll clean it for you when we get back to the home,' she said quietly.

'It's all right, my friend Thelma showed me how to sponge a coat,' I said quickly.

'You're obviously a very messy eater, Clover!' said Hetty, cheerfully licking her own jam and cream off the top of her scone as if it were a penny ice cream.

The scone was so delicious it was worth the embarrassment of spilling it. I was starting to feel wonderfully full. The waiter returned to give us fresh pots of tea – *and then he brought a huge silver cake stand.*

'Would you like me to describe the cakes for you?' he asked.

Hetty and I nodded, speechless.

'The top plate comprises pink iced sponge cakes with a butter-cream layer and a crystalized rose as decoration, choux éclairs filled with fresh cream and topped with coffee icing, and meringues, also filled with cream and garnished with blackberries and slices of peach. The middle plate has refreshing lemon tarts and cherry pie in a shortcrust pastry sprinkled with icing sugar, and chocolate gateau with piped chocolate cream and a layer of raspberry jam. The third plate has your specially requested buns, iced pink and white and yellow. I hope you enjoy them, madam, little misses,' said the waiter, scarcely drawing breath.

For a full minute Hetty and I were speechless, staring at the sweet splendour in front of us.

'Help yourself, girls,' said Miss Smith.

It was so difficult to choose!

'Could we possibly have two, Miss Smith?' I whispered.

'You may have as many as you like. Just don't give yourselves a tummy ache,' Miss Smith told us.

She selected a pink cake, ate it in four neat bites and then started on a coffee éclair. So Hetty and I started tucking in too. I'd asked Miss Smith for buns and she'd taken the trouble to order them specially and I very badly wanted buns, but I knew what buns tasted like. I'd never had a pink sponge cake or an éclair or a fruit meringue or lemon tart or cherry pie or chocolate gateau, and I was already quite full.

I thought of Sissy trying to take her meat pudding away with her. I'd have even less success attempting to stuff a cake or two into my napkin.

Hetty reached out for the chocolate gateau, the biggest cake on the stand – so I did too. Miss Smith touched the little silver forks by our china plates, indicating that we should use them to eat the gateau. It seemed an odd idea and I'd already had a battle with the knife, but I did my best. Hetty didn't bother. She simply picked up her gateau in both hands and started munching away. By the time she'd finished she had smears of chocolate all round her mouth and on her cheeks, and I dare say my face needed a good wash too.

'Perhaps you'd better run to the ladies' room, girls, and splash your hands and faces,' said Miss Smith, pointing to the back of the tearoom.

We ran off together, winding our way through the tables. Some of the grand ladies stared at us haughtily, but we didn't care. We peered at ourselves in the great glass mirror in the washroom and laughed out loud, before splashing ourselves liberally. Then we used the water closets, which were far grander than the ones at the home. The chains even had gold handles.

'Do you think they're *real* gold?' I breathed.

'Maybe!' said Hetty. 'My, aren't they amazing? At the hospital we just have privies. It's awful if you get picked to clean them!'

'What's it like there?' I asked.

'It's horrible. I hate it. I especially hate the matrons – they're so cruel and strict.'

'Why are you in a *hospital*? You don't seem at all ill,' I asked.

'It's just called a hospital. We're not sick. Well, we all had the influenza once, but that's all. We're there because our mothers couldn't look after us. I know it broke my mother's heart having to leave me there. So what's it like at Miss Smith's home? *She's* not in the least cruel or strict,' said Hetty.

'No, she is lovely,' I agreed. 'But we are taught by Miss Ainsley, and she is very particular and quite strict. She once sent me out of the room in disgrace but she's not cruel. She doesn't beat us and I suppose she tries to be fair.'

'What are the other girls like?'

'Some of them were very mean at first, but they're nicer now. And the little ones are sweet, and I especially like the oldest girl, Sissy,' I said.

'Oh, Sissy!' said Hetty. 'I like her too. She was so kind to me. You're lucky to have her as a friend.'

'Can't you come and live in Miss Smith's home too?'

'Oh, how I wish I could! But I have to stay in the hospital until I am fourteen, and besides, I get to see my dearest mother in secret and that helps me bear it there,' Hetty told me. 'She's my very special secret friend. I'm not friends with the other girls there now. And I'm deadly enemies with Sheila.'

'Can we be friends, Hetty?' I asked.

'Oh yes, I'd like that,' said Hetty, and we gave each other a hug. Then we ran back to Miss Smith and started anew on the cakes. I ate a pink cake and a coffee éclair and a lemon tart and a meringue and a cherry pie, and then flopped back in my chair, my stomach stretched to bursting point.

The buns stayed untouched. I stared at them anxiously. I wanted them so much – but I knew I was in danger of being sick then and there if I ate another morsel. Miss Smith saw me looking at them. Hetty was peering hopefully at the remaining cakes.

'I will ask the waiter to bring a cake box and you two girls can take some back with you,' she said.

'Could I perhaps have the last lemon tart and maybe the cherry pie because – because I know someone who would especially appreciate them,' said Hetty.

'You can have all the cakes if I can have the buns,' I said.

So we walked out of the tearoom with two full cake boxes, big smiles on our faces and big tummies under our frocks.

There was one extra wonderful treat. Miss Smith took us to a magnificent stationer's shop down a little alleyway and allowed Hetty to choose a new notebook for her journal.

'I'll have this lovely sapphire-blue one,' said Hetty. 'To match my eyes!'

'Would you like to start keeping a journal too, Clover?' Miss Smith asked. 'Perhaps you could choose a green one to match *your* eyes?'

I hesitated, carefully looking inside all these wonderful notebooks, relieved I'd washed my hands thoroughly.

'Do they all have lined pages?' I asked.

'Oh no, miss. We have notebooks with blank pages too. They are generally used for sketching,' said the stationer.

'Oh, I would love a sketchbook!' I said. 'A sketchbook like Mr Rivers's!'

'Did you fancy a green volume, miss? How about this one?'

He showed me a beautiful deep green marbled notebook. I opened it with trembling hands. The pages were creamy smooth and blank.

'This one?' said Miss Smith softly. 'And perhaps a packet of coloured pencils too?'

'Oh, Miss Smith, you truly are an angel!' I said.

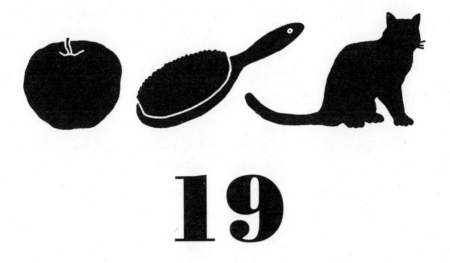

19

BACK AT THE HOME I had six buns to give away – two pink, two white and two yellow. I wondered about cementing the uneasy truce with Mary-Ann by giving her one of the buns – but then I'd have to give one to Julia too, and all the other girls in the dormitory would start clamouring.

I went to the nursery instead. Sissy was there with the little ones, reading them a story, but they didn't seem to be listening properly. Sissy read aloud so slowly, her usual lively voice a monotone. Jane was muttering under her breath and fidgeting, Elspeth and Moira were poking each other and giggling, and little Pammy seemed fast asleep, her head on her knees.

She woke up soon enough when I opened my cake box.

'Who would like a bun?' I asked.

'They'll be having their supper shortly!' Sissy protested, but she let them select a bun each. Elspeth and Moira both chose pink.

'I want pink!' Jane yelled, predictably enough.

'I should choose the white – it has jam inside!' I whispered in her ear, so she grabbed a white bun.

'Would you like a white bun too, Pammy?' I asked.

Pammy nodded and held her hand out for it nervously, as if it might bite. She had to be persuaded to have the first nibble, but soon she was wolfing it down as eagerly as the others.

'You must have a bun too, Sissy,' I insisted.

'Then you'll only have one left for yourself,' she said.

'But I've already had sandwiches and scones and cake. Oh, Sissy, the tea! Miss Smith is so kind and generous. Look, she's bought me a sketchbook too, and a packet of pencils.'

'There, I bet you're glad you came here now,' said Sissy, persuaded into having a bun after all.

I reflected as I ate my own bun. The primrose yellow icing was sweet, but inside the soft bun there was a large dollop of sharp lemon curd. It was the most delicious combination I'd ever tasted and I licked my fingers appreciatively. I *was* glad I'd come. I'd still give anything to have Megs back, but without her my home in Cripps Alley meant nothing to me.

At our lunch-time recreation the next day I took my sketchbook and a pencil and went to sit in the window seat to catch the light. I drew Megs from memory, copying Mr Rivers's style a little, using delicate lines and adding shading to make her look more real. I made several false starts, but at last I managed to capture a reasonable likeness. She was there on the page staring back at me, sucking her thumb, her eyes huge in her tiny pointed face, her hair like dandelion fluff.

I lightly stroked her little pencilled face and fondled her fluffy hair. I was filled with a strange mixture of joy and sadness. It was magical that I could conjure her up on the page, but dreadful to remember I'd never see the real Megs ever again.

The girls came crowding round to see my drawing and seemed impressed.

'Draw *me*,' Mary-Ann demanded.

I flattered her as I sketched, exaggerating the curls and length of her hair and adjusting her features, making her eyes much bigger, with long lashes, so that she looked like a real fairy princess. Mary-Ann smiled at herself, thrilled.

Now every recreation time I had a queue of girls lining up to have their portraits sketched. Millie was the last to get hers done, and I tried extra hard with it, elongating her little squashed-up face and giving her a fancy new hairstyle.

'Is that really me?' she breathed when I showed her.

In truth it wasn't really a proper likeness but I nodded solemnly all the same. Millie stared at the page, her plain face glowing. 'Me!' she repeated happily. 'Me!'

I sketched the four little girls too. Elspeth and Moira were enthusiastic, both managing to sit still long enough for me to capture a likeness. Jane was another matter.

'Draw me, draw me – me, me, me!' she demanded, but she couldn't keep still for a single second. In the end I drew her running wildly round and round the room, arms out, legs leaping, hair flying out behind her, deliberately blurring her features to show that she was moving fast. It was unmistakably her and Jane kept pointing at it, roaring with laughter.

'Now Pammy,' I said.

She shook her head, putting her hands over her face, making it impossible. I had to sketch her a few lines at a time when she didn't realize I was watching her, and then she didn't seem to like her portrait – though I'd given her longer hair and made her look less lost and lonely.

'It's you, Pammy. Don't you look pretty?' I said, but she shook her head vehemently.

I tried drawing as a way of helping the four little girls to read. Sissy had tried to teach them their A B C but with no success. Jane wouldn't listen, Pammy wouldn't look, and even Elspeth and Moira couldn't seem to understand that the black squiggles Sissy wrote on their pages had any meaning.

'Could I try something, Sissy?' I asked. 'I just need to nip to the kitchen.'

'I don't think dough letters would be a good idea,' she said quickly.

'No, this won't make any mess whatsoever,' I promised.

I ran downstairs to the kitchen where Cook, now totally recovered, was making a large apple crumble.

'Could I please borrow an apple for five minutes, Cook?' I asked politely.

'Borrow it, missy? I think you mean eat it – and you'll be sorry, because it's a sour cooking Bramley and you'll be doubled over with stomach ache for the rest of the day.'

'I'm not going to eat it, I swear,' I said, grabbing it quickly.

I ran upstairs and produced the apple. Of course *Jane* wanted to eat it, so I wasted a lot of time persuading her that it wouldn't taste nice. She didn't agree, so eventually I let her have one small bite. She screwed up her face, shuddered and spat it out immediately.

'Nasty apple!' she said.

'Yes. I told you! But clever you for knowing that this is an . . . ?'

'Apple,' said Jane.

'Yes, apple. Now, I'm going to draw the apple for all of you. Watch!' I took a bright green crayon, sketched a big round apple on the page and let them take turns at colouring it in. They weren't very good at it, of course, and went over the lines, and inevitably the pencil lead got broken, but it was soon sharpened.

'Now, we're going to write the word *apple* underneath. Watch me do it. *A-p-p-l-e.* What does the word say?'

'*Apple*,' said Elspeth and Moira.

'*Apple*,' said Jane, after much prompting.

Pammy didn't say anything at all, but she did look at the picture and the word.

'Now let's write the word *apple* again on a fresh page. I'll write it first. Then you take turns copying it. You can each choose a different colour.' I wrote the word *apple*. Then Elspeth. Then Moira. Then Jane made an attempt, though her letters went wildly up and down and looked like scribbles. I tried to encourage Pammy to have a go. I put a coloured pencil in her hand but she wouldn't close her fingers round it.

'Never mind. Maybe you'll try to do some writing tomorrow,' I said. 'Let's read our words now. Elspeth, what does this say?' I pointed to her word.

'*Apple*,' she said.

'Yes! Well done. It says *apple*!' I said, making a big fuss of her.

Moira read her word. Jane *shouted* her word at the top of her voice. Pammy didn't read but she looked at the four words that said *apple* on the page as if she knew what they were.

'The word *apple* is made up of all these letters. The one at the beginning is *a*. *A* is for *apple*. Remember!' I said.

The next day I took a brush and gave each child's hair twenty strokes. I counted each one aloud – they might as well learn their numbers too! I wasn't sure Pammy would let me brush her hair but she stayed still when I attempted it. I brushed very carefully indeed because she still had big patches of bare scalp, though there were now little fine downy hairs growing.

'You're going to have pretty curls soon, Pammy,' I assured her.

Then I drew the brush and had each child draw some bristles. It became a very, very bristly brush, but still recognizable. I had them tell me what it was, and then I wrote the word *brush*, and three of them wrote the word too. Then we read the word.

'*Brush!* And the letter at the beginning of the word is *b*. *B* is for *brush*.'

Just before bedtime I gave them another impromptu lesson because I happened to see a big white cat prowling in the little back yard. I bribed him with a sliver of cheese, picked him up in my arms and rubbed my cheek against his furry head until we'd properly made friends, then lugged him indoors and up the stairs.

Elspeth and Moira and Jane were all desperate to stroke him. I took Pammy's hand and tried to make her touch him too but she clenched her fists.

'What is this lovely furry creature called? Is it a . . . dog?' I asked.

'It's a cat!' said Elspeth, giggling.

'Of course it's a cat. Shall I draw it?'

'Oh my goodness,' said Sissy, bustling in. 'What's a cat doing here?'

'He's part of our reading and writing lesson, Sissy,' I said.

'Well, can't it wait until tomorrow? It's nearly bedtime.'

'But the cat might not be here tomorrow. Please, Sissy! Just this once can they be a few minutes late for bed?' I cried, and the little girls begged too.

'Well, Miss Ainsley isn't going to be at all pleased if she finds out,' said Sissy. 'But very well, go ahead, Clover. I can't quite see how puss here is going to help, though. I've heard all the girls in your dormitory say you can do magic tricks. Have you taught him to miaow the alphabet?'

'Don't laugh at me, Sissy. You watch! Who's going to hold the cat on her lap to keep him still while I draw him?'

Elspeth and Moira wanted to be picked. Jane was desperate, shouting, 'Me, me, me!'

'Ssh, Jane! If you're going to hold him you have to be very quiet and still or you'll frighten him. Do you think you can manage that?'

Jane nodded emphatically. I wasn't so sure but decided to take a chance. I put the cat on her lap and she stroked him carefully, making sure not to ruffle his fur the wrong way. The cat fidgeted anxiously at first, but then settled down and started purring.

'He likes me!' Jane whispered.

'Yes, he does!' I said, sketching quickly, just in case the cat changed his mind.

'He doesn't need to be coloured in because he's white, and the page is white, but you can each draw a whisker,' I said.

Pammy didn't draw one, but she watched the others.

'And what shall we write underneath our drawing of the cat?' I asked.

'The word *cat*! Can I go first after you?' said Elspeth.

'Of course. *Cat* is just a little word, *c-a-t*. *C* is for *cat*. There now, Elspeth, you copy it out. Then you, Moira.

Then you, Jane. And how about you having a try, Pammy, to show Sissy how clever you are?'

Pammy still wouldn't join in, but the other three wrote their words. Then I turned the page and wrote the word *cat* and each girl read it aloud.

'Excellent!' said Sissy, clapping her hands.

'And now, which word is this? It starts with an *a*,' I said, writing it out carefully.

'*Apple!*' they chorused.

Then '*Brush!*' And finally '*Cat!*'

'Oh, you're such clever little things!' said Sissy. 'I couldn't read till I was a great girl of fourteen, and I struggled dreadfully at first.'

She gave each child a hug and then she gave me one too. 'You've worked wonders with them, Clover. Well done!'

'I still can't get Pammy to do anything,' I said, quietly so that she wouldn't hear.

'Perhaps she just can't manage it. She's clearly had such bad treatment before she came here, poor pet,' said Sissy. 'Maybe she has something wrong with her head now and can't think properly.'

'Maybe,' I said, but I wasn't going to give up on Pammy yet.

The next day I was ready to start on the letter *d. D* is for ... It suddenly came to me. But could I trust the girls? Could I trust *Jane*? She'd been gentle with the cat, after all. I could usually manage her now, and even divert her when she had a tantrum. But there were other times when she took me by surprise. She'd already torn up one of my drawings when she got bored and wanted attention.

I decided to risk it all the same. I ran to the dormitory, bent down by my locker and carefully pulled out my pillowcase. I felt inside my shawl and gently unwound Anne Boleyn. I hadn't had the chance to look at her properly for a while. I was overcome with fresh love for her glossy face, her delicate limbs, her perfectly fitting dress. I kissed her shiny black hair, her red cheeks, her tiny fingers. They were so carefully carved. I thought of Mr Dolly whittling away with such patience day after day with only his dolls for company. I ached to see him and reassure him that I was safe and starting a new life that was safe and in many ways agreeable.

'I'm going to introduce you to four little girls, Anne Boleyn,' I whispered. 'One is very boisterous but you mustn't be frightened. She means well, and I will keep hold of you so that she can't hurt you.'

Anne Boleyn smiled back at me, reassuring me that she was made of wood. China dolls might smash and wax dolls might crack but wooden dolls were made of sturdier stuff.

I held her tight and hurried back to my four small pupils. I held her behind my back as I walked into the room.

'Today we're going to learn the next letter of the alphabet, *d*.' I made the sound *der*. 'Can you girls think of anything that starts *der*?'

'*Dog!*' said Elspeth.

'Yes, well done. That's brilliant. But we haven't got a dog here at the home, and I don't think one's going to jump into the yard the way the cat did. Try again. *Der, der, der.*'

'*Door!*' said Elspeth.

'You're so clever! *D* is for *door*. But perhaps it would be a bit boring to draw a door. It's a very dull design. I was thinking of something prettier. How about *d* is for *doll*?'

Even Elspeth looked baffled.

'Haven't you ever had a dolly? Maybe a rag baby? I used to make them for my sisters at home,' I said.

My four had clearly never had a big sister to make a doll for them.

'A doll is like a little toy friend. I have a very special doll. Would you like to see her?'

Elspeth and Moira and Jane nodded.

'But you have to sit very still and you can't snatch at her because it might hurt her very badly. Will you be good, well-behaved girls?'

Elspeth and Moira nodded. So did Jane. Pammy put her head on one side this time, almost as if she were agreeing.

'Then come and say hello to four new friends, Anne Boleyn,' I said, and I brought her out from behind my back.

All four girls gasped and smiled.

I made Anne Boleyn do a little dance in the air, her arms outstretched. 'Do you like her?'

All four nodded.

'Would you like to take turns holding her?' I asked. I took a deep breath. 'Jane, you were so gentle with the cat yesterday. Would you like to hold Anne Boleyn first to show the other girls how to do it?'

'Oh, *yes*!' said Jane.

I passed Anne Boleyn over.

'Hello, Anne-Blin,' said Jane.

'She's saying *Hello, Jane*, but she's got such a tiny doll voice you probably can't hear her,' I said.

Jane bent her head as if she were listening. 'I *think* I hear her,' she said. 'You're pretty, Anne-Blin. You want to be Jane's dolly, don't you?'

'She's just teasing you,' I said quickly. 'She'd like to be your doll but she knows she's mine. Now you've made friends, can you pass her to one of the other girls, please, so they can make friends too?'

'She says she wants to stay with me,' said Jane.

'Well, she can't,' I said firmly. 'Choose which girl she's going to next, Jane.'

'Well then – Pammy,' said Jane artfully. She waved Anne Boleyn at Pammy. 'Want to hold her, Pammy?'

She waited, already sure of the answer. But Pammy was looking straight at Anne Boleyn. She held out her hands.

'There, Jane! Pammy wants to,' I whispered, scarcely able to believe it.

'No she doesn't,' said Jane, hanging on tight to Anne Boleyn.

Pammy was almost touching Anne Boleyn now, her little fingers outstretched.

'Come on, Jane, you can see how much Pammy wants to hold her,' I said.

'She has to say so,' said Jane.

Oh no, it was all going wrong! Pammy hadn't spoken since Jane flattened her dough angel. There was going to be a tug of war any minute. Anne Boleyn's eyebrows were raised and her mouth was in a little O of alarm.

But Pammy opened her mouth and said clearly, 'I want to hold the dolly!'

'There!' I said, scarcely able to believe my ears.

Jane frowned and pouted, gripping Anne Boleyn hard.

'You clever girl, Jane. You've made Pammy speak,' I said. 'Well done! You're so kind. Anne Boleyn wants to kiss you and then she wants to jump into Pammy's arms so she can have a cuddle with her too.'

Jane sighed but let me help Anne Boleyn kiss her. Then she unclenched her fists so that I could hand my doll to Pammy.

'There, Pammy. Can you say thank you to Jane?' I asked.

'Thank you,' Pammy mumbled. Her hands shook as she held the doll. She made little rocking movements with her arms. 'My dolly,' she said.

'She's *my* dolly, but I'll share her with all you girls,' I said. 'Now I'll draw her for you.'

I drew her quickly while Pammy rocked Anne Boleyn. Jane frowned at her but didn't try to snatch her back. Elspeth and Moira were as good as gold, patiently waiting their turn. I let them draw Anne Boleyn's eyes, one each. Then I asked Jane to draw her nose and she made a little dash with my pencil. It was a rather lopsided nose, but it didn't really matter.

'Now, Pammy, if you hand Anne Boleyn over to Elspeth perhaps you'd like to draw her mouth?' I suggested.

Pammy didn't look very keen on this idea but she managed to pass her on, and tried to hold the pencil. It was a bit of a struggle for her, so I put my hand over hers to guide it.

'We'll give her a really smiley mouth, shall we, as she's so happy she's having such lovely cuddles,' I said.

Together we drew Anne Boleyn smiling from ear to ear. Then I wrote the word *doll* and all four girls did their best to copy it. Jane's writing wavered right off the page and Pammy's was just a tiny scratch – but it was a start! And when I asked the girls to read the four words they'd learned so far, they all said them aloud.

When they read them to Sissy later she was so impressed she fetched Miss Ainsley.

'All right, girls, let's read the special words we've learned so far,' I said.

'A is for *apple*,' said Elspeth.

'B is for *brush*,' said Moira.

'C is for *cat*,' said Jane. 'Miaow, miaow!'

'D is for *doll*,' said Pammy.

'Oh my!' said Miss Ainsley, and clapped her hands. 'Well done, Clover. You've worked wonders.'

It felt so good to be praised! That evening, after the little girls were all tucked up in bed, I did one more portrait of Anne Boleyn. I spent much longer drawing her, giving her neat features and colouring her in very carefully, even each little flower on her frock. I tore the picture out of my notebook and then another page to write a letter.

I knew how to do it properly because Miss Ainsley had given us several classes on letter-writing. I wrote my new address carefully in the top right-hand corner, and then the date. I was about to put *Dear Sir* – but it seemed such a formal way of addressing Mr Dolly, so I decided to write the letter my own way.

Dearest Mr Dolly,
    Remember me, your special friend Clover?
I miss you, but you mustn't worry – I am

mostly happy here, though I'm still sad when I think about dear Megs. I do some learning and I do some teaching too. The little ones love learning 'd' is for 'doll' because they can play with Anne Boleyn. Thank you so, so, so much for giving her to me. I hope you are well and your poor back not too sore.

Miss Ainsley had suggested we finish with *Your esteemed servant* but that sounded wrong too.

Love from your friend Clover

I added a little green four-leaved clover beside my signature.

I put the letter with the drawing, and in the morning I went to Miss Smith's office, asking her if I could possibly have a big envelope and a postage stamp. Then I wrote the address on the front:

Dolls Aplenty,
Market Street,
Hoxton

and Miss Smith let me go down the alley to the Strand to the big red pillar box. It was the very first letter I'd ever sent and I felt very grand and grown up.

20

I DIDN'T FEEL LIKE the grimy, ragged girl from Cripps Alley any more. I was this new neat Clover who wore a pretty blue frock and taught the nursery girls.

'You've blossomed, Clover,' said Miss Smith when I encountered her on the stairs. 'I haven't seen you for a little while. You haven't needed to come to my office to look at Mr Rivers's picture recently.'

'I've done my own drawing of Megs,' I admitted shyly.

'I'm sure it's very like her. You're talented, dear. But I hope you still admire Mr Rivers's work?'

'Oh yes, very much!' I said.

'That's just as well because he's coming here later this morning. He's bringing his portfolio with him, and we'll be discussing his illustrations for my new book. I thought you might like to say hello to him,' said Miss Smith.

'Oh, yes please!' I said eagerly.

'I should show him your sketchbook if I were you. I think you'll find he'll be very impressed.'

'Really?' I said, blushing.

'Run off to your morning classes now. I'll send for you when Mr Rivers is here,' she said.

I skipped off to the classroom. 'Good morning, Miss Ainsley. I'm sorry I'm a little late,' I said politely.

She shook her head at me but didn't chastise me. I couldn't say she really liked me any better and I didn't care for her either, but we'd learned how to get along together. I settled down to copying from the board an extremely dull passage about the conduct of young ladies. It was so tedious that we were all soon fidgeting, and Miss Ainsley found it necessary to add at the bottom of the blackboard: *Young ladies should never yawn in public or scratch their heads!*

Then we switched to a deadly Arithmetic lesson, adding and subtracting pounds, shilling and pence. I could calculate sums in my head in an instant because I'd been doing the family shopping down the market for years, but writing all the figures in columns muddled me and I had to count on my fingers to check I'd got it right.

I kept stealing glances at the clock. It was nearly half past eleven. Surely that was 'later this morning'. Where was Mr Rivers? Was he here already? I waited and waited and waited, watching the thin black hand of the clock creep slowly round to the top. When the two black hands overlapped at exactly twelve noon Miss Ainsley gave us a nod.

'Gather your books together, girls, and go and have your lunch.'

The morning was over! Perhaps Mr Rivers hadn't turned up. Or perhaps he'd been to see Miss Smith and was now gone.

I'd so wanted to show him my sketchbook. Perhaps Miss Smith had suggested it, and he'd said he couldn't be bothered to peer at a child's scribbles. No, he wouldn't be cruel and scornful. He was a lovely kind man. That daughter of his was so lucky, having her father search all over London for the perfect doll. If my pa had all the money in the world I knew he would never take the trouble to buy me a present, even though once I'd been his pet.

I wondered if he were missing me now. It must be so strange for him to lose two daughters in quick succession.

354

How were Jenny and Richie and Pete and Mary and little Bert? And dear Jimmy Wheels?

They didn't seem quite real now, more like characters I'd read about in one of Mr Dolly's story books.

'Clover? Clover, stop your daydreaming!' Miss Ainsley gave me a little shake. 'Did you not hear me, child? You are not to go to luncheon with the other girls as usual. You are to join Miss Smith and her visitor in her office. She's just sent word.'

'Oh, how wonderful! Thank you, Miss Ainsley!'

I went flying to the dormitory and saw that Mary-Ann was there, lying on her bed. 'Oh dear, are you poorly again?' I whispered.

'No, this time I have a stomach ache,' she said. 'It's a girls' thing. You're too little to understand.'

I understood perfectly. You couldn't grow up doing the weekly washing in Cripps Alley without knowing.

'Oh well, I hope you feel better soon,' I said.

I bent down by my bedside cupboard and took out my pillowcase of special possessions. Mary-Ann was watching me intently. I wasn't sure what to do. If I simply took my sketchbook and stowed my pillowcase back inside she *might* just creep over and investigate the contents when I was gone. I'd tried to keep Anne Boleyn a secret from all the girls in my dormitory. I didn't know if I could trust Mary-Ann now. We weren't bitter enemies any more, but neither were we bosom friends. If she discovered my doll she might tease me. And then there was my special packet of crayons. Mary-Ann had commented on them sourly, saying she supposed I was Miss Smith's special pet now. Might she be tempted to try them out herself, deliberately breaking the carefully sharpened points?

I picked up my pillowcase and took it with me, just to be on the safe side.

'Where on earth are you going with that pillowcase?' Mary-Ann asked. 'And why is it all lumpy? What's it got inside it?'

'It's just old bedding for the laundry basket,' I said.

'Aha! It wouldn't be *wet* bedding, by any chance?' she said.

'No, it wouldn't! It just needs to be changed. It's your girls' thing,' I said, and I clutched the pillowcase and hurried out of the dormitory, running to Miss Smith's office.

'Ah, Clover dear, come in,' she said, opening the door. 'Come and say how do you do to Mr Rivers. I believe you two are old friends.'

He stood up and held out his hand as if I were a true lady. I dropped a little curtsy and then shook his hand solemnly. Miss Ainsley would have been proud of me for once!

'Sit down, Clover. Bring that chair nearer to my desk. Mr Rivers and I are having a picnic lunch here while we discuss work. Would you like to join us?' asked Miss Smith.

'Oh yes please!' I said.

I knew from the thick smell wafting up the stairs that the girls were having onion soup, my least favourite meal. It reminded me of Mildred, who had served it up frequently.

Miss Smith, Mr Rivers and I had dainty little pork pies, salmon patties, a selection of cheeses, a bunch of hothouse grapes, a plate of iced sponge cakes and a glass jug of lemon cordial.

'What a feast!' I said enthusiastically.

'Indeed it is!' said Mr Rivers, tucking his big spotted handkerchief in over his waistcoat.

He was looking much smarter, with no paint smears on his jacket or trousers, and properly polished boots. His suit was a maroon cord, his waistcoat a deep midnight blue with a red floral design, and his boots were pointed with silver caps. He looked like a dandy!

He was eyeing me up and down too. 'My, my, Clover, I scarcely recognize you! You look ravishing,' he said.

'I could say the same for you, sir,' I said.

I meant to be polite, but it made him burst out laughing. 'Oh, I have to make a big effort with my appearance when I come to see Miss Smith. She's a highly influential lady. I need her approval for all my little sketches, or her esteemed publishers won't pay me a penny!'

'Nonsense,' said Miss Smith. 'I'm extremely lucky to have such an important artist prepared to illustrate my humble story books. I'm sure Clover will agree with me. She particularly admires your drawings, Mr Rivers.'

'Yes, Miss Smith says you used to come to look at the sketch in her inner sanctum practically every day when you first came to the home,' said Mr Rivers. 'But I expect that was simply for comfort. Miss Smith has explained that you've suffered a most terrible loss.'

I nodded. 'My sister Megs died,' I murmured.

'The frail little girl with the big eyes? This one?' Mr Rivers reached into his large pocket, found his own sketchbook and flicked through the pages. 'Here.'

I looked at the picture he showed me. I suddenly couldn't swallow my mouthful of salmon. I stared at the drawing. I thought I'd caught Megs's likeness well enough, but this was her true portrait. I'd been such a fool to think I could draw well. My picture of Megs was just a nursery scribble compared to Mr Rivers's living likeness.

'It's her. It's truly her,' I whispered. I remembered Mr Dolly's book of great painters. 'Oh, Mr Rivers, you're an Old Master!'

'Hardly, Miss Moon, but I'm delighted with the comparison. I wish other people felt the same, and then it wouldn't be so hard to get portrait commissions,' said Mr Rivers.

'I think you'd get plenty of commissions if your patrons wanted to be painted warts and all, like Oliver Cromwell,' said Miss Smith. 'That's why I'm wary of commissioning a portrait myself. A lady of my advanced years welcomes a little flattery. I wouldn't like your paintbrush to emphasize my wrinkles and wattles. And I shall certainly never require a portrait from you, Clover, as you see me as an old horse in a bonnet.'

Mr Rivers burst out laughing, and then apologized profusely.

'I don't, Miss Smith, not at all!' I protested. 'You asked me which animal you reminded me of, did you not?'

'So you're another little George Washington, are you?' said Mr Rivers, chuckling. 'He was an American president who chopped down a cherry tree.'

'Yes, he chopped it down with his hatchet, and then admitted he'd done it and said he couldn't tell a lie!' I finished triumphantly. 'Mr Dolly told me all about him.'

I hadn't been particularly impressed with the story. I thought George Washington a little simple. If he'd grown up in Cripps Alley he'd have learned that you save yourself an awful lot of beatings if you lie until your tongue turns black.

'Is Mr Dolly your name for the splendid chap who runs the doll shop? He's been like a private tutor to you, Miss Moon,' said Mr Rivers. 'So did he teach you how to draw too? Miss Smith has been singing your praises to me.'

'No, Mr Dolly didn't teach me. No one did. I just found I could do it,' I said. 'But nowhere near as well as you, Mr Rivers.'

'Have you got your sketchbook in that great big bundle?' he asked. 'Let me see!'

I delved into the pillowcase, feeling amongst my mourning clothes, stroking Anne Boleyn as she slumbered in the shawl, and at last found the sketchbook right at the bottom.

'There's no need to carry all your possessions around with you, Clover. You look like Father Christmas with his sack of toys,' said Miss Smith, shaking her head.

'Here's my sketchbook, Mr Rivers,' I said. 'My drawings are truly very bad. Please don't feel you have to compliment them.'

'Let's have a look at them, then!' He took my book and started flicking through the pages. Then he slowed down and looked more carefully. 'Oh, Clover Moon!' he said.

I hung my head. 'They're terrible, aren't they?'

'Terribly *good*! Well, you could do with a little instruction. Your perspective is a trifle odd, and you don't know much about shading, but your figures are full of life and show great promise,' he said.

If he'd told me they were perfect I'd have known he was lying, but he seemed to think I really did have promise.

'Do you think I might be an artist like you one day, Mr Rivers?' I asked.

'Well, there are certainly many ladies who love to paint and draw, but not many who are professional artists. However, Lady Butler exhibits at the Royal Academy and is especially feted. I believe the Queen has purchased one of her paintings,' said Mr Rivers.

'Did she have any instruction?' I asked.

'Oh yes, she was a pupil of the famous Italian painter Bellucci,' said Mr Rivers.

This gave me an extraordinary idea. 'Oh, Mr Rivers, could I be *your* pupil?' I begged.

'Come now, Clover!' said Miss Smith, shaking her head. 'Of course Mr Rivers can't agree to any such thing.'

'Well, I don't see why I can't pop along to the home occasionally and give Clover a little lesson. If that's all right with you, Sarah?'

'I'm not sure about just one of my girls being singled out in such a way. I don't think that would go down well. Perhaps you could give a general drawing lesson to everyone?' she suggested.

'Oh dear Lord, that will be a bit of a challenge! I can't keep my own daughters in order. I'll be hopeless with a huge class of girls. The little ones will bawl, the middle ones will tease and the older ones will run rings around me,' said Mr Rivers. 'I only want to teach Clover!'

'Well, Clover herself will help you keep them all in order, especially the little ones. She has a true knack with small children,' said Miss Smith.

'You're a formidable woman, Sarah Smith. You always end up getting your way,' said Mr Rivers, eating a pork pie in three big bites. 'Very well, very well! Count me in as the home's new drawing master if you really must. Do I get any payment?'

'How about five pork pies per session?' said Miss Smith, smiling.

'It's a deal,' he said.

They continued to tease each other in affectionate fashion throughout our picnic lunch. I stopped listening. I even stopped eating, though the food was truly delicious. I just sat with Mr Rivers's sketchbook on my knee, communing silently with Megs.

'You may have the picture if you'd like it,' Mr Rivers said gently. 'I will have to send it to the publishers, but when they've reproduced it in Miss Smith's new book I shall claim the sketch back and bring it to you immediately. Would you like that?'

'Oh, I would absolutely love it. So Megs's picture will actually be in a book?' I asked incredulously.

'I will give you your own copy when it is published,' said Miss Smith. 'I can see it means a great deal to you, so perhaps you'd like me to dedicate the book to Megs? It could read, *In Memory of Megs Moon.*'

'Really and truly?' I said, so overwhelmed my voice was a squeak.

'Really and truly,' said Miss Smith.

This was far better than a headstone in a church-yard. My Megs would be in her own book, thousands of copies of the same book, to be read all over the country. Children far and wide would see Megs's portrait, read her name and think of her. And I would hold her book every day and look at her portrait and feel she was truly with me.

'Don't cry, Miss Moon!' said Mr Rivers.

'I'm crying because I'm so happy!' I sniffled.

At that exact moment there was an urgent knock on the door.

'Come in,' Miss Smith called, sighing.

Sissy put her head round the door. She looked pink and agitated. 'I'm sorry to bother you, Miss Smith, but there's a telegram boy come to the door,' she said.

'Oh dear goodness,' said Miss Smith. 'Bring him up to my office at once, please, Sissy.'

'Yes, Miss Smith. But – but it's not for you.' Sissy nodded at me. 'He says he's got a telegram for Clover here.'

'For *Clover*?' said Miss Smith. She looked at me. 'Who would be sending you a telegram, Clover?'

I shook my head, baffled. 'I don't know,' I said.

I'd seen telegram boys speeding along the road, but none had ever come calling down Cripps Alley, where folk found it hard enough to find the price of a stamp, let alone a telegram.

'We'd better have him brought up here straight away,' said Miss Smith.

We waited, my heart beating so fast I had to put my hand on my bodice to try to calm it down.

'Telegrams can sometimes bring good news, not bad,' said Mr Rivers, trying to be comforting.

'I think it's probably a simple mistake,' said Miss Smith. 'Try not to get too anxious, Clover.'

It seemed as if an age went by before Sissy returned with a red-faced boy in navy uniform.

'Here he is, Miss Smith,' she said, nodding at the boy. 'Go on then.'

'Telegram for Miss Clover Moon!' the boy bellowed, as if he were in the street.

'Quieter, boy!' said Miss Smith. 'This is Clover Moon. Please read her the telegram straight away.'

'BEWARE! MILDRED CAME LOOKING AND SNATCHED YOUR LETTER! SO SORRY. MR DOLLY.'

'What does it mean?' asked Miss Smith.

The telegram boy shrugged his shoulders. 'Don't ask me, miss. My job is just to deliver telegrams, not tell you what they mean.'

'Hey, hey, don't take that tone with the lady,' said Mr Rivers.

'Pardon me, sir, but I'm just telling it straight. Will

there be a reply?' The boy looked at me and I shook my head weakly. 'Then I'll be on my way.'

'I'll see him out,' said Sissy, glaring at him.

I was left in the room with Miss Smith and Mr Rivers. I shut my eyes, my hands over my mouth. I thought of the address I'd written clearly at the top of my letter to Mr Dolly. Mildred couldn't read properly herself, but for a small price she could easily find someone at the market to decipher it for her. Then she'd come and drag me back. My forehead throbbed.

'Clover?' Miss Smith said softly.

I opened my eyes. She was leaning towards me, her long face kind and concerned.

'Clover, who is Mildred?'

I couldn't speak.

'I think I know. She's the brute of a woman who scarred your forehead, isn't she?' said Mr Rivers.

I managed a tiny nod.

'There's no need to be frightened, Clover,' said Miss Smith. 'You are safe here. No one can hurt you.'

'Mildred might,' I murmured. 'She's my stepmother and she hates me. I have to go right now, before she finds me!'

'Calm down, Clover. You're not going anywhere. We will look after you.'

'But she'll come here!'

'Then I will deal with her, and if necessary call a police constable to take her away,' said Miss Smith.

'And I will protect you too,' said Mr Rivers, though he looked a little anxious.

'She'll make me go back to Cripps Alley!'

'No, she won't, not if she's already washed her hands of you. You told Miss Ainsley you were turned out of your house by your father and this woman,' said Miss Smith calmly.

'Yes, but I wasn't exactly telling the truth,' I said, in agony. 'I ran away! I'm not really destitute. They wanted me to stay – but Mildred was going to cane me to teach me a lesson. I can't go back, not now. I couldn't bear it!'

'Of course you can't go back to such a monster!' said Mr Rivers. 'You can stay here until you're fully grown, can't she, Sarah?'

But Miss Smith was looking very grave. 'Not if she has a living parent who lays claim to her. I'm afraid it's the law. I have to be very particular on this point. I have tried to save girls from unfortunate families before, and the authorities have threatened to close the home down altogether if I persist.'

'Then the law is ridiculous! It can't possibly be right to return this child to a woman who clearly terrifies her. I can't believe this of you, Sarah! You of all people! The champion of waifs and strays!'

'Please don't shout at me, Edward. I agree it would be terrible to let Clover go, but I cannot change the law. There's nothing else I can do.'

'Then let her run away now, before she comes!' said Mr Rivers.

But it was too late. There was such a banging at the front door that we heard it even up in Miss Smith's office.

'Open up, open up! You've stolen our girl away from us!'

Mildred was already here.

21

'**IT'S HER! MILDRED! OH** please, let me hide from her!' I cried.

'For pity's sake, Sarah, can't you see the child is terrified of this woman?' said Mr Rivers. 'Don't let her into the house!'

But we heard the front door opening and Miss Ainsley remonstrating. But even formidable little Miss Ainsley was no match for Mildred. We heard her shouting and then thundering up the stairs.

'Sarah! She'll be up here in an instant!' said Mr Rivers, seizing hold of me protectively.

'Calm down, Edward.' Miss Smith was whiter than usual, but her manner was unruffled. 'Why don't you take Clover into my private study while I conduct the interview with this lady?'

'I had better stay to protect you,' Mr Rivers offered, very pale too.

'Nonsense. I am used to dealing with agitated women,' said Miss Smith. 'You look after the child. Only come out of the study if I call for you. Take your things with you, Clover.'

I grabbed my pillowcase and Mr Rivers took my hand. We went through the door behind Miss Smith's desk, into her writing chamber beyond. There was only one chair. Mr Rivers sat down heavily and I leaned against the wall, trembling.

We heard the door to Miss Smith's office opening.

'I'm so sorry, Miss Smith, but this . . . person insists on seeing you!' It was Sissy's voice, sounding outraged.

'Yes, I blooming well do insist!' said Mildred. 'You're the lady in charge of this girls' prison, are you?'

'How do you do?' said Miss Smith coolly. 'I am Miss Smith and this is my refuge for destitute girls. It is certainly not a prison. It is a private home. Now how exactly can I help you, Miss . . .?'

'It's Mrs to you, Mrs Moon. I'm a good, God-fearing woman and I made sure Mr Moon and I were decently wed. I've come about my eldest, Clover,' said Mildred.

'*She's not my mother!*' I mouthed at Mr Rivers, and he patted me reassuringly.

'Clover Moon?' Miss Smith repeated vaguely, as if she hadn't heard my name before.

'Don't try and pull the wool over my eyes! I know she's here. I seen the letter she wrote to that horrid little cripple doll-maker. It's all his fault. He lured her away from her own family, filling her up with all kinds of fancy nonsense. I always knew he was up to no good. Heaven knows what he's done to that poor innocent girl, the evil little monster!'

'How *dare* she!' I whispered.

'I'm afraid I have no acquaintance with the gentleman,' said Miss Smith.

'He needs locking up! He stole her away and brought her here, and now she's writing to him telling him she loves him, and she's only eleven years old! I knew it! I've been backwards and forwards to his shop, trying to get the truth out of him, but when I tackled him he just came out with a whole pack of lies. But this time I barged past him into his workshop and there was this letter on his desk, all squiggly writing that makes your eyes cross, but I saw this little picture, a green leaf thing, and it suddenly clicked. She'd drawn a clover leaf, like some secret signature – I knew it had to be from her. I got the letter-reader down the market to spell it all out for me, and I was that incensed I had to come straight here to collect her. Don't sit there all po-faced looking down your nose at me, Madam Muck. You give the girl back, or I'll fetch a policeman and have you arrested for abduction!'

'I don't abduct little girls, Mrs Moon,' said Miss Smith, her tone icier now. 'They come here of their own free will. I give them shelter and food and education until they're ready to make their own way in the world. Meanwhile this is their home.'

'Our Clover's got a home back with me and her pa and her little brothers and sisters. They all miss her so. They've wept buckets since she was taken away, and her pa's not himself at all. It's come so hard, especially since our second eldest died of the fever. Oh, how I miss that poor mite! And it was the last straw when our Clover got snatched away,' said Mildred, and she started sobbing.

'She didn't shed a single tear for Megs!' I whispered. 'She's just play-acting.'

'I can see how grieved you are,' said Miss Smith dryly.

'My heart's fair torn apart!' Mildred declared. 'It shows what a motherly soul I am because them two girls aren't even mine by birth. But when I married their father I took them on without a word of protest and I've been a loving parent ever since.'

'You say you have your own children too, Mrs Moon?'

'Six fine sturdy little dears, fair and handsome. There's a new little one now, young Sammy, and dear Lord, he's got a right pair of lungs, that one, bawling night and day. That's why I have to get our Clover back, see. She's got a knack with the young 'uns. I need her at home to look after them. I'm fair worn out with trying. I might look strong but I'm weakened with childbirth. You've no idea how it takes it out of you, you being a single lady. My insides feel like they're fair dropping out of me at times,' Mildred whined.

'But surely Clover would be out at school all day?' Miss Smith enquired.

'School? We don't bother with no schooling! What's the point? That doll-maker learned her all that rubbish and look what it did to her. She gave herself airs and looked down on us all – especially me, her own mother! She needs to be taken down a peg or too, that one. Knocked into shape,' said Mildred, her voice hardening.

'Knocked into shape?' Miss Smith repeated quietly.

'Well, in a manner of speaking.' Mildred suddenly sounded cautious. 'I don't mean I'd really give her a caning. Well, only if she said something very bad. That girl's got a wicked tongue on her. She needs to be a bit more respectful to me seeing as I'm her mother. Spare the rod and spoil the child, that's what they say, don't they? And that one's spoiled, I'm telling you.'

'You're telling me a great deal, Mrs Moon,' said Miss Smith. 'It makes me want to do the right thing. But I'm afraid I cannot help you in your quest. I believe a child called Clover Moon might have spent a night or two here. I will check the record book. However, I'm afraid she did not settle. I cannot tell you where she is now.'

'Oh, Miss Smith is brilliant,' Mr Rivers whispered in my ear. 'Note how wonderfully evasive she's being, so she doesn't have to tell a downright lie!'

But Mildred was no fool.

'You can mouth off at me in that niminy-piminy way, but I know you're up to something. I reckon our Clover's here, hidden away. Maybe you're in league with that doll-maker and set about procuring young girls and starting them on the path to ruin,' said Mildred.

'I find your suggestion offensive, madam,' said Miss Smith. 'Kindly leave these premises immediately or I will call a constable. There's a police station two minutes away, in the Strand.'

'Is that the case?' said Mildred. 'Well, I'll save you the trouble. I'll go myself. *I'll* bring a constable back here, and get him to search the house from top to bottom and drag my daughter out, do you hear me?'

Miss Smith didn't reply.

'*Do you hear me?*' Mildred repeated, and she thumped something hard.

'Oh my Lord, is she hitting Miss Smith?' Mr Rivers gasped, and he leaped up and ran to the door.

I ran too, but when we reached her office Mildred was gone. We heard her thundering downstairs, still yelling. Miss Smith was sitting very still behind her desk, her hands clasped.

'Did that female demon hurt you?' asked Mr Rivers, taking Miss Smith by the shoulders and peering anxiously into her face.

'No, no. She hit the table, not me,' Miss Smith said, sounding stunned.

'I'm so sorry, Miss Smith,' I said, starting to cry.

'My poor lamb, it's not your fault.' She reached out and put her arm round me. 'But what are we going to do? I dare say she'll be back with a constable in tow – and then the law is on her side.'

'Can't Clover stay hiding in your private chamber?' asked Mr Rivers.

'If Mrs Moon makes enough fuss they'll search the premises,' said Miss Smith. 'They've done that before. And then they'll close the home down, and where will all the other girls go?'

'*I'll* go,' I said.

'I'm trying so hard to think of somewhere safe to recommend,' said Miss Smith – and then, to my shock

374

and horror, she started to cry too. 'I can't let you simply wander the streets, child. I know all too well the kind of danger you'd be in.'

I knew too. I thought of the boys who'd pushed me into the mire and stolen my purse, the men who'd leered and said crude things. The only man who had ever protected me was dear Mr Dolly, but I couldn't go to him now because Mildred would find me there.

Where could I go? Could I get some kind of work so that I had a roof over my head and food every day? What could I do?

Then it came to me. I looked at Mr Rivers. He seemed in a helpless daze, looking from Miss Smith to me. I doubted he'd think of it himself. I couldn't waste time hinting. I had to come out with it straight away.

'I know where I can go,' I said. 'I'll come and live at your house, Mr Rivers.'

They both stared at me.

'Clover, Mr Rivers has children of his own. He can't possibly adopt you, dear,' Miss Smith said gently.

'No, no, I don't want to be his daughter! I'll be his servant,' I declared.

'But you're still a child,' he said, stunned.

'I'm eleven. I could even be twelve – Pa was never clear about my birthday.'

'You're still much too little to cook and clean – and I have cooks and maids already,' said Mr Rivers.

'I'll look after your children! You said yourself I was like a little nursemaid with all the young 'uns in our alley. And I'm brilliant with the little ones here, aren't I, Miss Smith?'

'Yes, you are,' she said. 'Clover has a way with even the most troubled of our little girls, and she's teaching them to read.'

'That's wonderful, but you see I already have a nurse for the children, Clover,' Mr Rivers said gently. 'I couldn't possibly replace her. She's been with our family for many years. I'm very sorry.'

I took a deep breath. I couldn't give up on my only chance. All my life I'd been waiting for my good luck to start. Perhaps I had to *make* it happen.

'I dare say your nurse could do with some willing help,' I said. 'And if she's been with your family for years, then perhaps she's getting elderly now and would like a rest occasionally. I'll not need a proper wage, just my keep. And you can't say you can't afford it – I've seen you happily paying a fortune for a china doll for your daughter.'

'Clover, that's enough!' said Miss Smith.

But Mr Rivers started laughing. 'My, you're one determined girl, Miss Clover Moon. Very well, I'll take you under my wing for now and try you out as a little nurserymaid.'

'Oh, bless you, Mr Rivers! I promise you won't regret it! I can go with him, can't I, Miss Smith?'

'Well, if Mr Rivers is certain,' she said. 'It's all very irregular, but given the circumstances it can't be helped.

I shall stay in touch with you, Clover. I still feel responsible – and I've grown very fond of you in the brief time you've been here.'

'And I'm very fond of you, dear Miss Smith,' I said, and I dared to give her a bashful hug.

'Well. So that's settled.' Mr Rivers shook his head a little as if he couldn't quite believe it had all happened.

'If you've finished your business with Miss Smith could we go now, Mr Rivers? Immediately? Before Mildred gets back with the constable?'

'Yes, of course,' said Mr Rivers, jumping up. 'We certainly don't want to encounter Mildred.'

I realized there was no time for any goodbyes, not even to my special nursery children.

'Could you tell the girls – especially Jane and Pammy – that I'll miss them dreadfully and try to come back and see them one day,' I implored Miss Smith. Then I scrabbled in my pillowcase, unwound Anne Boleyn from her shawl and brought her out into the open. She looked so fresh and pretty that I had a sharp pain in my chest – but I knew what I had to do.

'Please can you let the little ones play with her occasionally so long as they're very careful?' I said.

'That's very generous of you, dear. I'll make sure they look after her,' said Miss Smith. 'Take care, Clover. You'd better make haste now.'

Mr Rivers picked up his portfolio. I clutched my pillow-case and took hold of his other hand, steering him towards the door. We went along the landing and down the stairs. Mary-Ann was standing at the door of the dormitory. She looked astonished when she saw me with Mr Rivers. I waved at her and she waved back.

Sissy was downstairs comforting Miss Ainsley, who was still quivering from the aftereffects of Mildred.

'Goodbye, Miss Ainsley. Thank you for everything you've taught me. And goodbye, dearest Sissy. Make a special fuss of Jane and Pammy, won't you,' I said in a rush, and then we were out in the alleyway.

'Oh my goodness,' I said, not knowing whether to laugh or cry.

I still had hold of Mr Rivers's hand. It didn't seem quite appropriate given that I was now his servant, but I hung on to it all the same.

'Well, Miss Moon, we'd better go to the cab stand on the Strand,' said Mr Rivers.

'Do you live far away, Mr Rivers?'

'In London, but several miles away, and we're both too burdened to walk,' he said. 'And I don't know about you, but my legs are still wobbly with shock. Your stepmother sounds a most terrifying creature. I'm rather glad I didn't actually clap eyes on her.'

We came out of the alleyway into the bright bustle of the Strand – and there, shouting at the crossing sweeper to clear a path for her, was Mildred herself, with a burly constable beside her.

'It's her!' I breathed. 'Oh my stars, that big woman with the red face. It's Mildred.'

'Hide behind me!' said Mr Rivers.

I did so, while delving into my pillowcase. I brought out the blue shawl and wrapped it quickly round my head, hiding my long black hair. Mildred suddenly darted across the wide street, the policeman behind her. She walked right up to me and I felt my head spin and my feet falter – but she carried on, striding towards the alleyway.

She hadn't recognized me! She'd seen a girl in a clean blue dress with a shawl about her head, holding the hand of a gentleman. I'd lived with her since I was three years old, but a different dress and shawl had rendered me invisible. I wasn't any kind of daughter to her. I was just a pair of hands and a punch bag.

I hung on to Mr Rivers and he squeezed my hand tightly.

'Well done, Clover. Quick thinking! And thank goodness too! She looks even worse than I'd imagined. But you're free of her now. I've rescued you,' he said proudly, as if it were all his idea.

I'd had to *badger* him into rescuing me, but it didn't matter now.

'I feel safe with you, Mr Rivers. And I promise you, I'll be the best nursemaid in the world,' I said.

We crossed the road and Mr Rivers found a cab. As we were getting in I saw a flare of vivid purple, a flash of red boot.

'Oh goodness, is that Thelma?' I cried.

'Thelma?' Mr Rivers looked anxiously at her. 'Is she your . . . sister?'

'A special friend,' I said, waving to her.

'Well, strike me pink, it's young Clover!' said Thelma. She looked at Mr Rivers. 'Who's this gent, then? You sure you know what you're doing, Clover girl?'

'Quite sure, Thelma, I promise,' I said.

'Because you're much too young for a Lord Handsome,' she said.

'Oh no, this gentleman is my employer,' I said grandly.

'Well, good for you, girl. Glad things have worked out. Take care now. And you, Mr Toff, take good care of this little kid, right?'

'Certainly,' said Mr Rivers, startled.

Thelma nodded and set off, hips swaying, boots tip-tapping.

Mr Rivers raised his eyebrows. 'She's another young lady I won't forget in a hurry!' he said. 'Right. Let's be on our way before we have any further encounters!'

He told the cabbie to take us to the Lion House in Melchester Road.

The *Lion* House? 'Oh, Mr Rivers, do you live in the zoological gardens?' I asked hopefully.

He laughed at the idea. 'I'm afraid I don't, Miss Moon, much as I'd like to. No, it's simply the name of my perfectly ordinary house.'

I was disappointed, but I liked the idea of living in a road instead of an alley, and 'Melchester' had a lovely gentle sound. I murmured it again and again as we bowled along street after street. I was a little afraid we might be heading towards Hoxton, but Mr Rivers assured me we were going in entirely the opposite direction.

We proceeded westwards and I stared out at all these amazing streets that I hadn't even known existed. We passed the gates to a park, and then turned right and I saw the street sign. This was Melchester Road! And, oh my goodness, the houses were all as grand as palaces – great four-storey red-brick beauties with gables and arches and enormous windows. These houses were the very opposite of ordinary!

The hansom cab stopped outside the biggest of them all, with a fancy iron gate flanked by two huge stone lions on pillars. I jumped out of the cab and stroked first one lion, then the other. They had great carved manes and beautiful faces with big eyes. They reminded me a little of Brutus, the dog in the market.

'Do they have names?' I asked Mr Rivers.

'What? The lions? No, they just mark the name of the house,' he said, pointing to the brass nameplate which said THE LION HOUSE.

'Then I shall name you,' I whispered to the lions. 'Lion on the left, you shall be Brutus – and lion on the right, you can be Rufus. I hope that pleases you.'

I imagined them nodding their great white heads approvingly, tongues lolling.

Mr Rivers was watching me. 'You really are still a little child,' he said. 'Oh dear, I do hope this is going to work out. Come along then.'

I followed him up the steps. The door was painted green – almost the colour of clover! It had a great brass knocker in the shape of yet another lion. I hoped Mr Rivers would let me have a good rap, but as we stood before the door, it opened as if by magic, and I saw a maid wearing a frilly white cap and apron and a long black dress.

'Good afternoon, sir,' she said. Then she saw me. I smiled at her anxiously but she didn't smile back. 'Is this young person with you, sir?'

'Certainly, Edie. This is Miss Clover Moon. She has come to join our household as a young nurserymaid,' said Mr Rivers grandly.

'Really, sir?' she said. 'Does the mistress know?'

'She will soon enough. Come in, Clover, and see your new home.'

I followed him into the most sumptuous hallway clad in turquoise tiles and decorated with great china vases and embroidered hangings, like a scene from Mr Dolly's copy of *The Arabian Nights*.

'Papa's home!' a little boy shouted from upstairs, and then he climbed on to the wide banister and slid all the way down, landing with a bump on his bottom.

'Algie!' Mr Rivers remonstrated.

'Didn't hurt, didn't hurt!' Algie cried, though he was red in the face.

'Papa, Papa!' Two more children came running after Algie, a chubby little girl and a delicate boy with long hair almost to his shoulders.

Mr Rivers picked each one up in turn and hugged them hard. 'Hello, my monkeys! What have you been up to? Making mischief, I'll be bound,' he said.

'Have you brought us a present, Papa?' they demanded. 'Something to play with?'

'I've brought you the most excellent present, and you can play with her all you want. Allow me to introduce you to your new little nurserymaid!' He pushed me forward. 'This is Miss Clover Moon. Isn't she delightful?'

The children looked at me in disappointment. Edie sniffed.

'Haven't you brought us anything *else*, Papa?' Algie demanded.

'Something to eat?' asked the little girl hopefully.

'Clarrie! You're practically bursting out of your pinafores as it is!' said Mr Rivers, but even so he produced a paper bag from his pocket.

Clarrie delved in eagerly, and squealed when she discovered a twisted stick of barley sugar. The boys clamoured for one too, snatching at the bag.

'I believe Nurse doesn't care for the children to eat sweetmeats before their lunch, sir,' said Edie.

'So don't tell Nursie, monkeys!' said Mr Rivers. 'Now I need to get to work in my studio. I'll leave you to herd Sebastian and Algie and Clarrie back to the nursery, Clover. You can introduce yourself to Nurse.'

He sauntered off, rather to my dismay. The children were all sucking barley-sugar canes now, getting lamentably sticky.

'There'll be trouble if they touch any of the furniture,' said Edie. 'Well, I suppose they're your responsibility now.' She smiled maliciously.

I tossed my head at her and tied my shawl firmly in place. 'Come along, children. I want to see your nursery,' I said. 'Have you got any dolls? I think *one* of you has a very special doll called Marigold.'

This took them by surprise. 'How on earth did you know that?' they clamoured, tugging at my arm, my skirts, my pillowcase.

'That would be telling,' I said as I steered them up the stairs. I nodded at Edie triumphantly, showing that I was in charge.

'Yes, but *how*?' Algie persisted.

'Perhaps I have magic powers!' I said. 'See my green eyes? I could be a witch.'

I heard a chuckle from the landing. There was a girl a little older than me sitting in the window seat. She had long shiny brown hair tied with a dark green ribbon and she wore an embroidered grass-green smock. She was swinging her long bare legs, not even wearing shoes. She had a large storybook balanced on her lap.

'Are you saying you're a witch?' she asked.

'I could be,' I said. 'And *you* could be Beth and have a doll called Marigold.'

She laughed at me. 'You're not a very clever witch then. I'm not Beth. She's in the nursery, tucked up on the chaise longue because she's not very well. I'm Rose and I'm too old for dolls. Who on earth are you?'

'I'm Clover.' I wondered if I should call her Miss. Should I even bob her a curtsy – or tell her to go and put some shoes and stockings on? I dithered, distracted by her book. It was hard to read the print upside down, and it was arranged in a strange way, in little short sections.

She saw me peering. 'Do you like poetry?' she asked.

'Maids don't read poetry!' said Algie dismissively. 'Papa says she's our new nurserymaid. We don't want one, do we?'

'Algie!' said Sebastian. 'You'll hurt her feelings.'

'I *do* like poetry!' I said, stung. It wasn't quite a lie. I'd loved my stolen nursery-rhyme book, and that was poetry, wasn't it?

'Can you do magic tricks if you're a witch?' Clarrie asked. 'Can you magic more sweets?'

'Nurse isn't going to want her either,' Algie retorted.

'Oh, bother Nurse,' said Rose.

'I'd better go and introduce myself to her,' I said.

'In a minute,' said Rose. 'Come to my room first. I'll show you my books. Come on, Clover. Not the rest of you though. You've all got sticky hands. Go and wash!'

She waved them away and took hold of my hand as if we were friends! I still wasn't sure how I was going to get on in this strange Lion House, but I knew one thing. I liked Rose very much indeed – and she seemed to like me.

AUTHOR'S NOTE

Poor Clover was very badly treated by her stepmother. We can all understand why she ran away, but it must have been very frightening to wander the streets of London – a very dangerous place for a young girl who was all alone. Life in the nineteenth century was extremely harsh for a large number of children. Many experienced cruelty and neglect from uncaring or desperate parents. They were forced to work long hours, or left to beg in the streets, often starving and in need of medical attention.

Thank goodness there were a few concerned and caring people like Sarah Smith in my story. Following the success of similar societies in Liverpool and New York, in 1886 the National Society for the Prevention of Cruelty to Children was established by founding member the Reverend Benjamin Waugh.

In Victorian times people thought that it was wrong for the law to intervene in family life, even if the children were being harmed by their parents or carers. However, within its first five years the NSPCC managed to change this culture, and persuaded Parliament to pass the first law to protect children in abusive family situations. The 1889 Prevention of Cruelty to Children Act –

which came more than fifty years after the first law to protect animals from cruelty – became known as 'the Children's Charter'.

Since 1884 more than ten million children have benefited from the unique expertise and commitment of the NSPCC's staff and volunteers.

Today, one of the services offered by the NSPCC is ChildLine. Over the last thirty years ChildLine has helped over four million children. The service is free, confidential and available twenty-four hours a day to any child who wants to make contact because they are upset, scared or in danger. The online service provides advice, help and a space for peer support on the message boards.

When I write my books about troubled children I do my best to give them happy endings. I can't work that magic in real life. But if you're really anxious about anything, remember that ChildLine is there to help you. They will listen to you and understand. Don't be afraid to get in touch. Call 0800 1111 or visit www.childline.org.uk.

Jacqueline Wilson

ALL ABOUT THE VICTORIANS

Clover Moon's story takes place in London during the reign of Queen Victoria. Read on to find out more about this important period in history . . .

Queen Victoria ruled for sixty-three years from 1837 until her death in 1901. Born in 1819, she was only eighteen years old when she became queen!

Queen Victoria married Prince Albert, and they had nine children together. Queen Victoria's descendants are still on the British throne today – Queen Elizabeth II is Queen Victoria's great-great-granddaughter.

Like Clover Moon, many Victorians were born into extreme poverty. Children from very poor families wouldn't have gone to school; instead, they'd go to work in factories or mines, or as chimney sweeps or shoe blacks; or they might have sold items like matches or flowers on the streets. Many Victorians were so poor that they were forced into workhouses –

factories where people worked in terrible conditions
in exchange for scraps of food and a place to sleep.

In contrast, other Victorians, like the Rivers family,
were extremely rich! Boys from wealthy families were
sent to school and often to university. Wealthy girls, on
the other hand, might have been sent to a 'finishing
school' where they would learn to become a 'lady',
taking lessons in French, singing and dancing,
playing the piano – and even curtseying!

The legacy of the Victorian era is very much still
felt around the world today. It was a period of
great human ingenuity – now called the Industrial
Revolution – during which British scientists and
engineers invented key technologies that have
shaped the modern world. But it was also a time of
great hardship and suffering for many poor people
in Britain and around the world who were powerless
in the face of the might of the British Empire.

Jacqueline Wilson has written many other wonderful stories inspired by the Victorian era – have you read them all?

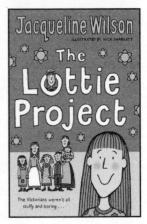